BLACKWATER

EMILY BLAKENEY

ISBNs:

979-8-9930661-0-3

979-8-9930661-1-0

979-8-9930661-2-7

Senior Editor: Andrea Lard, The Creative 5280 LLC

Editor, Interior Design: Kay Lard, The Creative 5280 LLC

Printed in the United States

This book is dedicated to ferocious women.

PROLOGUE

S hadows are expected to do as they are told. Follow along silently. Don't make a mess. All shadows follow those rules.

All, except for mine.

You see, there are times when it lingers a moment too long, or looks left when I look right. There are times when it creeps along the walls, though I remain still.

And so, like a spider, I stay hidden in dark corners and high perches. The Grays will step on me, squash me, and spill my guts, if ever I'm caught.

Even so, that is not what I fear most. Last time it got loose, there was death. With every passing day, the shadow grows stronger. It grows sharper teeth. Whatever binds us grows weaker.

And so, it must be killed.

ACT I
THE GHOST AND
THE SERPENT

I

THE GIRL IN THE CAGE

PRESENT

In this cage, they keep me chained. They think they understand who I am, what I am capable of. A sliver of doubt keeps them careful.

But a sliver is not very much, and careful is not enough.

The manacles around my wrists have burned a raw, red ring into my skin—they're charmed to mute any Weaving, but I am no Weaver, so it just burns. My magic does not fit into their neat little boxes. It will only slither back out when no one is looking. And the manacles are nothing compared to the punishment the Grays have inflicted upon me for the past two days. Punishment for evading them for so long, and making them look like the fools they are. My body is a map of their retribution.

They stroll into my cell and use their blunt weapons, their steel-toed boots, their bare hands. Nothing sharp. Not yet. They keep me drugged with a sedating drug in my water. It tastes like the anoxin that grows on the fringe of the eastern border of the woods. Years ago, I learned the hard way what it tastes like.

They've left me curled into a tight little ball. My left eye is pounded shut, and my skull throbs, but I've denied them the pleasure of a scream. I cling to that.

It could be worse. The woman in the neighboring cell is almost dead. She's of the night; I can tell from the traces of exaggerated rouge and charcoal that streak her cheeks. Her green skirt, now faded to a brownish hue, is tattered with holes and rips from overeager customers. Though her pallid skin sags, she's probably not much older than I. The past few years have taken a heavy toll on all of us, especially women. She likely has a family at home, waiting for her. Worrying for her. She made a living by the hands of men, and now she might very well die by them, too. The sight of her slow death fills me with caustic rage.

Wait, Iona. Wait.

My shadow turns its head toward the door to the cells, pulling my gaze along after it. The door creaks open to reveal another Gray. They are all unrecognizable when they wear their masked helmets, designed with spikes jutting out of the sides of their head and metal tongues lolling grotesquely out of gaping mouths.

They look like beasts unleashed upon us, when they're really thoughtless little men following the orders of their faraway king.

Regardless, it is effective.

The higher the ranking, the more horrific the mask, so this one must be important. Earlier, I heard another Gray call him a general. Metal eyes leer down at me, horns spiral and curve out and back in around where his ears would be. He strides to the middle of the room, hands clasped behind his back, keys jangling from his belt with each step.

For what feels like a very long time, we watch each other.

There is a litany of weapons at his waist: a gold-pommeled sword, a heavy spiked mace, and daggers everywhere. The mace gleams, but just a few bells ago, it was caked with blood. I watched him use it from my tiny window. Normally, the holding cells would be underground, but they have built the prison differently. Here, criminals are caged along one wall, right above the execution block, with a little window in each cell so none of the festivities below are missed. If we don't see it, we hear it.

My attention returns to the newcomer. I wonder if he is disappointed by what he sees: a gaunt little scrap of a person with hair shorn close to the scalp so that no one takes a second look, and a long, wicked scar above the left ear. A slip of a thing, huddled and shivering in the back of her cell. I must seem so small. So weak.

"I have been informed we finally caught the Ghost of Marrin." His voice has been magically distorted to sound deeper, and it violates the silence of the holding room. "But I am having the most difficult time reconciling that all this time, it was . . . you." Disdain drips from his voice, making a mess on the floor.

"Why's that?" My words are sludge from a bruised mouth.

"The Ghost of Marrin is wanted for at least four counts of capital murder, thievery of private property and assorted contraband, and let's not forget the missing children." He pauses. "I would think this person would be a bit more . . . impressive, given their crimes. That's all."

"Perhaps," I slur, exaggerating the extent of my condition, "you should look closer."

I rise to wobbly feet, but sag against the wall for support.

"You should know that the Crown has been notified. They're sending someone to deal with you. We'll see how you like The Craw. If you last that long."

The words reverberate in my mind, clear like a bell. Cutting through the fog. Time to go.

"Seven."

"Pardon?"

"Seven counts of capital murder. Not four." His whole body stiffens, and a grin spreads across my face like an infection. "You forgot the three Grays."

He goes rigid.

"Do you want to know how I did it? How I slaughtered them?"

That does it. He crosses the space between us in no time. Bending to snatch the chains connected to my manacles, he brings me stumbling to the front bars with one yank. I slam against the cold metal. Pain explodes in my face—my cheekbone.

"I *knew* those men, *you scum*," he spits from behind his mask. My face hits the bars again, again. Despite the pain, my hands work quickly. My life depends on it. "I'll kill you right here in this bloody cell. *That's* the justice you deserve—"

He doesn't finish his sentence. Dropping his key and my manacles —which have been unlocked for quite some time—to the ground, I burst through the cell door, bringing us both crashing to the floor. His heavy armor slows his reaction time, and I know exactly where to slide his own daggers: where it will hurt the most, where his armor will fail to protect him.

After all, I've done this before. Three times, to be exact. They may look like beasts, but they still bleed like men.

2

THE WRONG MARK

TWO MORNINGS BEFORE

I never intended to steal anything other than that damn book. Unfortunately, I mistook fortune smiling on me for fate baring its teeth.

I was already wandering the streets as the three suns spilled over the ocean, looking for a man with four fingers on his right hand. His name was Bart, a prolific smuggler of items I fancied. The catch was, he only appeared in the port of Marrin at specific times on specific days, so I had to be prompt. Today, he would be stationed at the docks for one bell after sunrise, and not a moment more. Bart had a schedule to keep and the law to evade.

With a tattered hood obscuring my face and a scarf over my nose and mouth to filter out the dust, I slunk through the streets, keeping my eyes downcast and my posture stooped like everyone else. It's enough to have to bear my own misery; I'd hate to have to look someone in the eyes and bear witness to theirs, too. Especially now that children have been going missing. We're up to seven. Just gone.

Here in the square, shops and parlors used to come alive with the suns. Mornings used to be a cacophony of orders, salutations, and haggling. Once, the space was filled with the yeasty smell of fresh wheat bread, the briny stench of stone fish, and riots of spindly wildflowers from the deep of the woods. Since this land hadn't seen much magic in years, the offerings were meager, but it had been a living. There used to be some good here.

Now, every stall and shop was heavily taxed by King Stefan De'Havelin and his enforcers, the Grays—so named for the dull coloring of their armor. They rendered any and all elected positions useless, redirected the majority of imported goods back to Celosia, the realm's capital, and swiftly banned any materials that would "distract workers from their toils." Like books.

The most frightening legislation, of course, was the one about Weavers. That's what we called them in the southern parts of the realm of Alvion, at least—people who are born with magic that manifests as extraordinary abilities. No one spoke of it, for Weavers were rare, but highly sought after. According to the new legislature, if a Weaver didn't promptly declare themself to the king, the punishment was extreme. And final. For why else would one hide from the king, unless their intentions were nefarious, and most importantly, *treasonous*?

There was no resistance when the Grays came. Marrin was a small port, after all, and its people had never been bold. Now, all registered citizens received a monthly ration that King De'Havelin ludicrously believed to be sustainable. He wanted us malleable. He was succeeding. Today, the square was quiet in the way things were when they had lost their souls.

Marrinians had since turned to darker ways to make a living, and, in turn, Grays became ever more suspicious and brutal, in their punishments. It's a vicious, bloody wheel that was turning, turning, turning. Hardly a day passed without someone being made an example of at the whipping post—or, on a bad day, the execution block.

However, since Marrin was still a port, it had recently become a hotbed for smuggled goods, such as weakly imbued items, weapons, potions, and bottled low-level enchantments. I'd heard whispers of other trade in the manner of *living* things, but I stayed very far away from that. If I ever came across a trafficker, I'd kill them with my bare hands.

Some things are just *foul*. But the other things could be useful. *Very* useful.

Lost in thought, I rounded the corner much too fast and collided with someone so hard the breath went out of me. In fact, I would have fallen to the cobblestoned ground if a gloved hand hadn't caught me, setting me back upright. I slapped it away, keeping my gaze downcast as I hurriedly slunk away.

"My apologies, lad," a deep voice called after me, but I didn't break my stride.

Shame, if I'd have known he was going to be polite about the whole affair, I might have thought twice about stealing the contents of his coat pockets. But I only steal from visitors, and I couldn't have drawn up a more convenient scenario to conduct a bit of thievery. I didn't dare take my bounty out of my pocket, but it felt like notes. Perhaps even a few tickets for passage. Beneath my hood, I grinned.

As I passed a series of black banners drooping against some ramshackle booths, I paused to silently pay my respects. On this day seven years ago, Queen Lorelai De'Havelin was assassinated. Her husband might be a beast, but by all accounts, the queen had been beloved.

I was almost to the piers. Gulls screamed at each other as they rode the salty updrafts, dust turned to sand, and the sound of horse hooves became bells clanging as ships came and went. No matter the time of day, this was always the busiest area of the port, which made it a spectacular place for illicit activity. With water finally in sight, I stopped in the shadow of the most popular tavern and inn, The Wit's End, to observe before I moved any closer. Picking absently at my nails, I scanned the piers.

It wasn't long before I noticed something new.

There were the usual number of ships at port. Most of the dockhands were preoccupied with rolling barrels of goods up gangplanks to make their exodus before the three suns got too high and the day too hot. With all the dust, even on what would have been a cloudless day, sunlight dribbled out through the haze. They say elsewhere the sky is blue, but all I've ever known is one of murky gray.

It was the ship at the end of the pier that I found interesting. Ships, I knew. Royal ships were made of Yarwood—a bright, golden wood imbued with the magic of the Wildwoods to the north. They're fast and sturdy. Merchant ships were usually made of a paler, less expensive wood like Spindle or Hoarwood.

But not this one. This one was black, flags and all, which could only mean one thing. Pirates.

The realization had me glancing about for unsavories, but I saw nothing out of the ordinary. Perhaps they pillaged the last town and merely wanted some ale and refuge.

Regardless, it was the largest pirate ship I'd ever seen. A shiver spider-walked down my spine at the sight. I hoped they'd leave soon; pirates were rarely welcome and often left bloody, expensive messes.

And their debauchery was left unchecked.

Rumors had been swirling for a while that King De'Havelin turned a blind eye to pirates. Some say it's because he didn't want a war on his hands, while others say it's because some, if not all, pirates were under his thumb. Why not let them carry on with their misdeeds if he shared in a piece of their profits?

Naturally, some pirates were worse than others. While most merely lived on the outskirts of the law, others had more . . . insidious reputations. Killigan Red Hands, Harran the Quick, or worst of all, Liam Blackwater, for example. Men whose names were synonymous with threats. I heard Blackwater strings the corpses of his enemies up from the masts like ghastly lanterns, the creak of their rotting bones the only warning before he strikes. And that's if there's anything left after the flaming arrows melted flesh and charred bones.

It was then that I spotted a man at the end of the pier to my right in conversation with a few weathered-looking dockhands. Right on time, as always. I stepped out into the light, anticipation singing in my veins, but stopped dead in my tracks when my shadow's head snapped to my right.

"Found you."

That voice. My breath caught, recognition jolting me. It was the same man I stole from earlier. He'd followed me.

Turning to face him, my gaze traveled slowly upwards, then up some more. He loomed over me, hands in the pockets of a long, dark overcoat. A scarf covered the majority of his face, a thicket of dark, rambunctious hair framing what little remained. Although he leaned easily against the brick, tension radiated from him in waves, tripping up my pulse. Something told me he wasn't here to tell me I'm pretty.

I took a step back, my hands flitting to the concealed daggers along my ribs. The minute my fingers found hilts, I lunged forward.

He moved with bewildering speed to shove me against the wall of the tavern, cracking the back of my head against the stones. Pain bloomed in a burst of white. I shook my head to clear it, my hood falling back, but a dull ache was already radiating outward. Pulling down my scarf with my shoulder, I spit in the man's face, teeth bared.

"Baseless," he muttered. He grabbed my throat, and I flinched, expecting a fist to connect with my jaw, but it never arrived.

That's when we got a good look at each other.

From under his mass of dark hair, sage-colored eyes glared at me. I'd never seen a shade of green like that. Soft, with flecks of silver. The rest of his features remained hidden behind his black scarf.

A sharp intake of breath stirred me from my revelation. He was just standing there, momentarily frozen.

"You're a *girl*?" he breathed. His grip on my wrists faltered as he leaned in to gawk at me.

His momentary surprise was a gift.

I surged upward, slamming my forehead into his face. Not hard enough to break his nose, unfortunately, but it served its purpose. He stumbled back, and I seized the moment to kick him in the stomach, then flick a dagger at him, for good measure. It whizzed between his legs, but the message was clear.

Without a second glance, I slipped into the tavern, running like all hell was behind me.

The Wit's End was crammed with the morning rush, and I was

uncharacteristically grateful for the hubbub. I wove through the crowd, snaking through gaps of people and ducking underneath tables, anxiously glancing over my shoulder as I went. Just as I'd skirted around a gathering of chittering women, someone snatched the back of my cloak, yanking me back and nearly off my feet. An unflattering choke escaped me.

"Give them *back*," my assailant hissed, bringing me close to his face. His glare was scalding. "You've no use for what you took."

"Notes? I don't have use for *notes*?"

His eyes widened with incredulity. "They're not—"

What a liar. "Ugly whore!" I shouted, pitching my voice as low as I could.

"What—" He didn't have time to duck before a fierce slap sent him reeling, and the women beside us descended on him, shrieking with indignation. Leaving them to it, I hurried to the stairs, taking them three at a time until I reached the top floor, then sprinted down the hallway, stopping only once I'd reached the fifth door on the left.

Panting, I jammed a lockpick into the keyhole, twisting this way and that until it clicked. I burst through, relieved that the room was empty. After locking the door behind me, I made my way to the window, shoved it open, and climbed through onto the protruding ledge below.

The town cathedral was two buildings away. If I could make it to the edge of the tavern and across the smithery without falling, I would be safe. I closed my eyes and quieted my mind. I had done this countless times. This was no different. That green-eyed stranger would not catch me today. No one would ever catch me.

You can never stop running, the voice in my head reminded me. I always listened.

Fingers gripping the indentations between bricks, I eased myself across the narrow ledge of the third-story roof, careful to avoid the areas that had crumbled away long ago. Seven windows lined the top floor, but somehow only the fifth hadn't been sealed shut by years of grime—one of many tricks I've learned from years of creeping around this forsaken place.

I'd gotten to the third window, one careful side-step at a time, when I found myself face-to-face with those eyes again. He was looking for me, room to room. Impressive. I stopped, confident there was no way he could catch me in time now. I even smiled, not having had time to readjust my scarf.

He merely tilted his head, his gaze falling to the bottom of the window. His gloved fingers slid beneath the seal and jerked upwards, to no avail. Stuck shut. I expected to watch him disappear into the next room, out of sight, but he did no such thing. Instead, he slammed his hands against the windowpane. A crack fractured the glass.

My smile dropped from my face, plummeted to the ground below, and shattered.

He punched the pane again, this time with a force that almost made me lose my balance. And again.

Shit. This one's a bit mad.

I swept past the window, knowing he'd be on my heels in mere moments. The sound of shattering glass and startled shouts from below was all the confirmation I needed.

"Fucking lunatic," I screamed.

"Fucking thief," he shouted back.

Seems I'd have to do a bit better. Once I reached the edge of the building, I leaped onto the neighboring thatched roof of the smithery, sprinted across, then finally reached the sloped roof of the cathedral. It's easily the highest point in Marrin, and possibly the structure with which I was most familiar.

Looming over everyone else, I'd spent many bells here in the shadow of gargoyles, studying contraband from Bart. It was quiet up here, and the closest thing to peace in this place without having to wander back to the gloom of the forest.

Winding between the stone beasts that lined the roof, I reached the far side and squeezed under an extended wing to crouch in front of a particularly hideous gargoyle and face the bustling crowd below. I placed a hand over my mouth and closed my eyes, concentrating on the approaching footsteps while I solidified my hasty and *very* reckless plan.

Pass me by. Please pass me by.

My eyes snapped open as a gleaming obsidian sword obliterated the gargoyle's left wing, sending bits of stone and dust exploding over the edge. Shouts of alarm drifted up from below, and I imagined the people there stopping to gawk at the scene we're making, though I didn't dare look. Although chaos was commonplace here, this was still highly inconvenient. Especially when there were Grays *everywhere*. And today, of all times.

Launching myself forward, I grabbed hold of the right wing and swung myself into thin air. The moment I let go, his sword arced down again to sever the wing from the gargoyle's back in another violent spray of pebbles. My stomach seized as I landed on my feet and slid down the slope of the roof, skidding to a halt on the second story. I'd only just stumbled into composure before I was forced backward to avoid a vicious swing.

Damn, he's fast.

A small, foolish part of me was impressed at his ruthless pursuit. He'd clearly been trained well, whereas I only had pure instinct and the advantage of a familiar setting. I'd have to focus on evasion. If he caught me, I was dead. That was clear by how hard he was swinging that fucking sword.

So, for a few moments, that was how I managed: winding through and around the gargoyles scattered around the roof while he gave brutal chase. He was nimble, to be certain, but knowing the statues' pattern like the back of my hand gave me enough of an advantage to keep him from splitting me open.

He straightened abruptly. "You didn't take what you think you did." He's not remotely out of breath.

I smiled despite myself. "Even better."

What could be more valuable than notes? I'd like to find out.

"Give them back. Be a good lass."

Poor thing. He has no idea.

Ssshhhhhing.

My head turned sharply to the left, my jaw grinding against the sudden sting in my cheek. I touched my fingers to the skin just below my eye and swallowed a gasp when they came away red. I glared at the stranger, my lips curling.

"You're toying with me."

"I want my things back."

"If they're so precious, you should have protected them better."

Something sparked in his eyes, and before I could blink, another gash opened on my other cheek. Then the sword came for my throat. If I hadn't twisted sideways at that exact moment, I'd have watched my lifeblood gush onto the floor. Incentivized with fresh urgency, I sprang to the side, but I was quickly running out of ledge, and he knew it.

I moved erratically, but he wasn't bothering to swing at me anymore. No, he was chasing me until I ran out of ground. Placing my feet very carefully, I backed up a few more paces, my eyes pinned on the advancing figure. And it's for that very reason that my boot landed on loose tile and rolled out from under me, sending me sprawling to the ground.

It was all over.

Without a word, the stranger strode straight for me, raised his sword, and plummeted straight through the ceiling. I saw his eyes flare in shock right before he disappeared into a cloud of dust.

I crawled to the hole to peer inside, disappointed that nothing was visible through the dust. I imagined debris littering the floors and flummoxed priests scampering around like ants in an anthill. I'd spent many a night up here loosening the flooring as a contingency plan long ago, but never had to use it until now. There were many little traps like this scattered across Marrin. Obscured knives, hidey holes, booby traps, and the like. Some, like this, were deadly. Others, deterrents.

In this case, he fell straight into the chapel, where the ceiling was highest, and therefore the farthest to fall. Unless he miraculously caught himself on something, it would be a while, if ever, before he got up. I sent him off with a little wave.

Crossing my legs, I decided to take out the notes I'd taken from him and see what all the fuss was about. I slid them out of my deep vest pockets and spread them out before me. There were a few notes, yes, but nothing worth all this trouble. He wasn't worried about those.

He was worried about the important-looking parchment, folded carefully in half. Two of them, in fact. I picked one of them up and unfolded it.

Words scrawled on the page before my very eyes, disappearing after I'd read them. The script was written in neat, precise handwriting, the ink a dark, goldish glimmer. The message was as concise as it was mysterious.

The Crown awaits the pleasure of thy company, but only the worthy will attend this year's Court. Details will arrive for those who are willing to play.

At the bottom, the unmistakable symbol of the king's seal appeared: a stag with towering, branched antlers, the ink animated to portray it shaking its head, swaying side to side. I stared at the image, astounded at the rarity of actual magic in my hands—

Sonuvabitch.

I yowled, dropping the paper when a sharp pain lanced through my thumb. But the parchment never drifted to the ground. Instead, it folded itself neatly into the shape of a cream-colored bird, its beak spattered with crimson where it had *pecked me.* Its wings crinkled as they unfurled. It hopped around a few times, then made for the edge of the roof to take flight.

Oh, no. Not with my blood, you don't. Blood, in the wrong hands, can spell disaster.

I dove after it, grazing the edge of a wing, only to earn a nasty paper cut on my left pointer finger. Scrambling to my feet, I leaped to swat it out of the air . . .

. . . and missed.

And now, it was too high to reach. Leaning over the balcony, I watched the paper bird until it was no more than a paper speck on the dusty horizon. My gaze fell to my thumb, and the single drop of blood beading there. I see now why that may have been important to him. But what was some bastard like him doing with something like *that?*

3

THE STRANGER

By the time I made it back to the piers, I was panting in earnest. I'd all but sprinted the entire way back, and though I'd lost the stranger, I couldn't outrun his phantom hands on my shoulder, or the musky smell of salt and suns I'd scented when he'd been so close.

It's alright. He's gone.

After this, I'd need to stay out of town for a while. The forest was calling to me. I yearned for the solitude of the trees, however bare they'd become over the years. Every moment I spent in this cesspool of clamor and noise had me longing for the serenity and peace I could only find far, far away from here.

Almost done.

A cursory glance found Bart two piers over on his ship, seemingly doing some routine maintenance to his sails.

"Hello, old friend," I called once I was close enough.

He didn't turn around. "I am timeless, ageless, shapeless. I reside inside everyone, but I am no organ. I am what is left behind but never seen nor touched. What am I?"

I pursed my lips, thinking. The answer brought a grin to my face. "A story."

The old man swiveled to face me, shielding his wrinkled, suns-weathered face. He smiled, but it seemed to take a great deal of effort. Strange; Bart could usually spare one of those. "Iona. I thought you'd come skulking around."

"You've got something for me, I hear."

He grunted, motioning for me to follow down below. He looked more tired than when I'd last seen him, a fact that saddened me a little. I'd known Bart for a few years, and though our relationship had never been anything but professional, I hated to see the weight in his eyes and a limp betraying a worsening left leg. He was too old to be carting around illegal paraphernalia like this. A dangerous trade. He'd be executed immediately for his crimes, without trial.

Below decks, Bart left me leaning against a wall while he disappeared into another room. He never revealed where he kept his merchandise. After a few moments, he emerged, and I couldn't help but hold my breath when I saw what he held.

A monstrous tome with pages yellowed and worn from a legion of hands and the passage of time.

Binding Spells, Potions, and Curses by Marguerite Thorne

For a few moments, all I could do was stare in awe, a familiar hunger stirring within me. The same hunger I always felt when Bart brought me a forbidden book, as if at long last, I had found the thing that would save me. But this one really might.

I had never seen or heard of another with a shadow like mine. One that didn't heed. It needed to be dealt with, and it was my most sincere hope that this book would finally give me a way to do that. Finally free me from that thing.

Normally, Bart joined me in my reverie, but this time, when I glanced at him, his brows were knit together, his eyes fixed on the floor.

"Bart?"

He flinched at the sound of my voice, then shook his head, sighing. "My apologies. I've been . . . jumpy lately."

"Why?"

He stopped pacing to stand up straight and peer at me with narrowed eyes. "Why? Almost every port I travel to is crawling with Grays now. There's less magic in the land with each passing day. And . . ." His voice descended two flights of stairs. "The children."

The air in the room pressed against my skin, suddenly heavy. My scalp prickled. "I heard another went missing," I said.

His mouth pressed together as he took a step toward me, drawing himself up to his full height. I'd never seen him act this way before. Distrustful. Squirrelly.

"Did you, now?"

"It's all people are talking about these days." I said warily.

He swallowed, licked his lips, and watched me for a moment, choosing his next words carefully. My pulse picked up.

"Not all. I heard of a Ghost, too. The Ghost of Marrin. A warrant for whoever it is."

You can never stop running.

"Wouldn't know about that." It was difficult to keep my voice even, when I felt as if the floor had opened up and swallowed me whole.

He grew a bit bolder. "I think, perhaps, you do." He said each word slowly, like he was trying not to spook a rabbit.

But I saw his eyes flick upwards, and I was not a rabbit.

"Bart," I whispered, dread running a finger down my spine, "is this what you truly think of me?"

He at least had the decency to look guilty as he mouthed the words "I'm sorry," but I was already clambering up the steps, my heart punching through my chest. The book was left discarded on the floor. I barely heard anything above the buzzing in my ears, felt anything besides the hot knife of betrayal twisting in my gut.

He sold me out.

He thought I had something to do with the missing children.

Traitor.

The bite of disappointment churned within me as I lurched up the stairs. As I ran, I dug a lockpick out of my pocket and shoved it into my mouth, where my gum met my cheek. I burst from the dingy ship, coiled to flee, but there they were. A whole squadron of Grays waiting for me. My teeth ground together, fists clenched, as I cast about desperately for another way, but I was trapped—a rabbit, after all.

Unless.

I moved to hurl myself off the boat altogether, more willing to either teach myself to swim or die trying, but an arm slung around my waist and jerked me backward and down the gangplank to where chains awaited me. Bart. How much did he get for selling me out?

He deposited me in front of the Grays like a sack of dirt, and though I couldn't say for sure, they seemed . . . disappointed. One turned to Bart behind me, his head angled.

Their helmets only covered half their faces—lesser Grays, then — so I had a full view of their sneers.

"Her?"

"That—that's her," the traitor confirmed. My chest ached. This was my fault. I should have known better. I never should have trusted him. I pushed the hurt down, down, lest my shadow get involved. Fear tended to invoke its wrath.

You can never stop running, the voice in my head chided. This was what I got for forgetting that. And the worst part was, there were people all around, but I knew that if I screamed for help, if I screamed at all, no one would come. Although my fingers itched for the knives sheathed at my ribs, I stilled them. Oh, I would use them, but not now. I breathed in slowly, soothing the hurt and the vitriol writhing within.

"Oy, girl."

I glanced up only for blinding light to crack across my vision and send me sprawling to the ground. Someone laughed, presumably the Gray who'd just kicked me in the mouth. Distantly, I heard the clink of coins as they exchanged hands.

"Doesn't feel like a ghost to me." Snickers.

"Anyone else want to try?" Their steel boots moved in closer, kicking dirt into my face, until suddenly, they stopped.

"If I might interrupt."

My eyes latched onto my shadow on the ground, silently pointing. To him. The stranger. He'd found me again, that unrelenting fiend. He'd miraculously caught himself on something after all. I was fucked.

"Who the hell are you?" Barked the same Gray that kicked me, marching up to the stranger. If it were another time, I might have laughed at the height difference.

"A victim of circumstance. And . . ." he pauses, ". . . her." With some effort, I sat up so I could throw him a vicious grin. His eyes hardened, clearly annoyed. "She stole something from me. Something important. I need it ba—"

"Get in line," another Gray growled, cutting him off. "You'll get your shit back once we take her in and shake her down. Anything we retrieve will be available to the public when we're through."

The stranger's eyes went glassy, his imposing figure suddenly still. It was like watching a viper before it struck, savoring its last few moments with its prey. Sensing a sudden shift in the atmosphere, the first Gray puffed his chest out, taking what he thought was an intimidating step toward the stranger, and pulled out his sword.

That was a mistake.

Several of the Grays beside me called out warnings, but they went unheeded. The stranger looked down at the sword, then back to the Gray. "Brave of you. Stupid, but brave."

"Fuck off," the soldier retorted, holding the sword out stiffly.

I winced, but couldn't look away.

The stranger tilted his head, then moved so fast my head spun. In one smooth movement, he'd drawn his sword and disarmed the guard with a flick of his wrist, then rammed it down the Gray's open mouth and out the back of his head. He waited a moment, then pulled it out. Blood spurted, painting the docks glistening red, as his body crumpled. The shocked silence of the moment was broken only by the soft splash of the dearly departed's sword hitting the water.

Undaunted, the stranger strode toward us, kicking the body of the Gray off the pier on the way. That, too, made a sad little splash.

My laughter, sudden and deranged, burst from me like a flock of birds. I laughed and laughed until a hand grabbed my neck to shove me back to the ground. Still, I couldn't stop myself.

This man might just kill us all.

"Give her to me," the stranger said calmly, ignoring me, "and we won't have any more incidents. I'll deal with her, and you'll never see either of us again."

A thick Gray to my right stepped up bravely, choosing wisely to keep his sword sheathed this time. He said something in hushed tones to the rest of his men, who glanced to the stranger, then backed away a few steps.

"Please, mate. In the name of the Crown, peace. We don't want this to get any nastier than it already is, eh? Chalk it up to a misunderstanding?"

The stranger's eyes narrowed on the man, his words sharp as his sword. "I've been quite clear, mate."

"She's property of the Crown. They're—they're sending someone, alright? A commander. This is bigger than theft. Please," he pleaded. He pleaded.

The stranger said nothing, the menace rolling off of him answer enough.

"Look, I know who you are. Let us take her, and you'll get all your things back once she's been dealt with. You've the Crown's word."

By this time, more Grays had arrived, completely surrounding us. At least twenty.

"You think I don't have friends, too?" The quiet of the stranger's voice was an eerie paradox to the horrific violence he'd displayed moments before.

"I know you have . . . friends," the Gray assured him, desperately trying to defuse the situation. "But the king will be quite displeased. Come now. Peace?"

Who was this man, that he could murder a Gray in cold blood, in the light of day, and not only were they letting him go, but begging for peace?

For a moment, I was convinced it didn't work, that his black blade would take more lives. But then, the stranger surprised me. Taking a step back to sheathe his sword, he slid his hands into his pockets. "I'll be waiting."

Uneasy silence was the only response. Even the gulls had fled the scene.

And yet, I couldn't tear my gaze from his face. He glanced back, and this time, when our gazes locked, I knew it for what it was: a promise that I would not get away again.

I spit a bloody glob in his direction.

The tension shattered when rough, gloved hands clapped me into chains and yanked me by my hood to my feet. Off the pier, a crowd had formed at news of an altercation. An arrest. And not just any arrest, but the Ghost, who was suspected of theft, murder, and any other crime for which an offender hadn't been publicly apprehended. In fact, there was nary a crime I hadn't committed, according to the Grays. I was their favorite scapegoat, and the citizens of Marrin didn't ask questions. Especially now that children have started going missing. And while I would never call myself a paradigm of morality, I had no interest in something as despicable as that.

Every crime I've ever committed was a matter of survival—well, and perhaps sometimes petty theft. But even then, I'd always been careful to only steal from visitors. It almost made it worse—how long I'd evaded capture, for with every passing day, more and more crimes had been blamed on me. Or rather, The Ghost.

And look at the trouble I found myself in now. Damn my wandering fingers.

Rocks pelted my arms, some called me appalling names, others jeered and spat. There's nothing unhappy people love more than something else to despise. And yet, I found myself to be most preoccupied with what I was leaving behind. But every time I glanced over my shoulder, someone was in the way. In the end, I was only able to catch a glimpse of the pier once before we turned the corner.

Alas. The man in the black coat had already gone.

4

ALMOST

I f I cannot escape this place, I'll make sure they kill me long before I'm hauled off to The Craw. But if I am to die here, I'm not greeting the Proctor alone.

The manacles had been unlocked for quite some time, thanks to the lockpick I shoved in my mouth before capture. I only had to bide my time until I could lure someone with keys close enough to snatch them.

I stand slowly, wiping bloody hands on my bloody shirt. He got me good with his blade; I've now got a nasty gash down my sternum. I do what I can to cover it with my leather vest, but it's bleeding badly. Soon, it won't matter anyway. I turn to let the woman beside me out… and stop. My fingers, tacky from dried blood, wrap around the bars to her cell, and for a moment, just a moment, I lean my forehead against them, squeezing my eyes shut, blocking out the sight of the still body in the cage.

I hope she found peace at the end. I hope she didn't die afraid.

My only regret is that I'm not strong enough to kill them all for what they've done to her. The anoxin still has me in its throes, blurring my vision and dulling my senses. My reaction time is slowed. Once the adrenaline wears off, it's going to be very difficult to fight.

No time to waste.

Bending carefully, I pick up the Gray's mace from a pool of blood. It's heavy, but it will serve my purposes here. Stealth no longer matters after the mess I've made, so all that's left for me is the element of surprise. Unlocking the door, I slink downstairs.

"General?" A voice calls. Another Gray downstairs. There shouldn't be very many of them this early.

I clench the mace in my sticky hands and almost sprint down the stairs. "Wore out, are you?" The guard calls again.

Only a few more steps. My shadow precedes me, except it doesn't look like me. It's taken the shape of the Gray I just killed. I hiss through my teeth against the inevitable flare in my shoulder blades when it behaves badly.

Boots scuff the floor, coming to meet me. "Didn't put up too much of a fight, did she?"

I round the corner, and we come face-to-face. "She did."

The mace smashes into where his neck meets his shoulder. One blow has him careening to the side. For a moment, I'm doused in panic when the mace won't let go of his armor; the spikes stuck in his flesh. I heave with waning strength once, twice, and the mace jerks out just in time to collide with his head and send him sprawling to the floor. The third and final blow sees him dead, his mask crunching beneath the weight of the weapon. I hunch over, panting, as I wait out the scorch of my shoulder blades and the fatigue that ensues when my shadow plays.

There's a poison in me. As long as I can remember, I've been plagued with these little episodes. Dark spots, I call them. Moments of emotional duress when my shadow stretches its legs and bares its teeth. I've had them ever since I can remember. Sometimes, my shadow is helpful.

Usually, our goals and intentions align. But not always. Sometimes, it lashes out, and anyone who gets in the way is out of luck.

That is what frightens me most. The uncertainty.

I stand over the Gray, panting, hot blood spattered over my face and arms. Dropping the mace to the floor, I pitch to the side and almost empty my guts. Head spinning, I straighten, only stumbling a little.

I peer out the nearest barred window to find that the edges of night are starting to lighten. Dawn will be arriving soon, and with it, the next shift of Grays. I won't last for much longer.

Lurching for the front door, hands outstretched, it's all so clear. I can feel the dust on my face, see the suns as they rise, smell the must and heat of the port.

I'm going to make it. I've done it. I've evaded them again.

My hand closes around the latch as pain explodes in the back of my head, and the last thing I register before the void calls me back is laughter.

5

THE DEAL

Time passes in painful, blurry spurts after that. I wake in another cell, chained to the wall. When I am conscious, all is pain: my face, my head, my body. I can scarcely lift my head. At first, I refuse the putrid water and stale seed bread they toss into my cell, hoping that I'll die of dehydration before they can claim the satisfaction of killing me themselves. Unfortunately, they catch on and force it down my throat instead.

When I try to simply heave it back up, the subsequent beating is enough of a lesson not to try that again.

During brief blips of wakefulness, I do hear things—snippets of talk from the other side of the cell.

"Posted bond at fifty golds—"

"Fifty golds? This entire port couldn't cobble that together." Grating laughter. "She's got two more days, then it's the block for her—"

"Might as well sharpen your sword, then."

"Hurts worse when I don't."

It's hard to keep track of my remaining time when I can't seem to stay awake. Darkness claws me under, tucking me in tight. I dream of the stranger from a few days ago standing outside of my cell, peering down at me. I can't muster the strength to lift my head anymore, nor do I wish to, for the pain. Even in my dreams, it hurts.

"This is how you keep your prisoners?" The stranger asks, his voice slicing through the cavernous dark.

A Gray appears at his side. "Act like an animal, and we'll treat you as such. She killed two of us, mind you."

"I wouldn't run around telling people that." His accent is so refined compared to the harsh talk of the Grays.

The dream goes hazy, and for a few moments, their words bleed together. "You said the bond was fifty golds?"

"Aye," the Gray rumbles, then kicks at the cell door. "What a joke. She en't worth a bucket of piss."

"Perhaps not to you." Coins clink. "Here you are then."

My dream stutters over itself, for quite a while passes before anyone says anything. "Yer serious?"

"And ten on top of that, for your discretion."

Another Gray wanders over, attracted by the first Gray's sounds of astonishment. "Wot's this then?"

The stranger sighs under his scarf, and I try to blink through the smog between us, but it's no use. My head throbs. "I'm taking her off your hands, gentlemen."

The Grays share a look. "Yer paying sixty golds for that? Wot's yer angle? Wait one more day, and she won't bother no one ever again."

"I don't see how that's any of your concern," the stranger replies.

A pause, then the second Gray speaks. "You know wot? Bond's gone up to one hundred golds. Then you can have the little shit, mate."

The edges of my dream shimmer when the stranger retorts, "Sixty golds, and I keep your little secret. How's that for a bargain, boys?"

The first Gray scoffs loudly. "Wot secret are you meaning?"

The stranger takes a step closer to the Gray, towering above him. "Five days is a long time to haunt this place, and affords a man all sorts of opportunities to overhear rumors. Tell me, when you lot host your little gambling den down here, exactly whose money are you playing with? Perhaps the king would like to know why he never sees any of the bond money reflected in the ledgers."

When he's finished speaking, both men stand a little straighter, practically tripping over themselves to speak.

"We'll take the sixty golds, man. No need for any of that."

"Take her, then. Go on."

I'd laugh if I could. I might be changing hands, but I'll die all the same.

The cell door rattles open, and one of the Grays trudges into my cell. When he lifts me by my armpits, the pain in my ribs is spectacular, and I mean to scream, but it dribbles out of me instead as a pained whimper.

"Get up," the Gray hisses, jerking me to a standing position. He pulls me forward, but the moment I try to walk on my own, my head swims, the pain is too much, someone is shouting, and when my head cracks against the cold ground, the dream blinks out.

The next thing I know, gone is the weight of the chains, and I am floating. My hands and feet dangle. I lean my head against something hard and drift away, all too gladly.

I dream of flocks of paper birds taking wing to a blood-red sky.

6

HELLO, THIEF

My eyes open to an unfamiliar room.

My body feels wadded up and kicked around like a child's ratty old ball. Gingerly, I curl my fingers. Then toes. Good. Usable. I hear a strange sort of roaring sound. Is there a crowd outside? An angry mob? I touch my face carefully, wincing at a sharp pain in my ribs when I move. No new blood on my fingers. But there is old blood everywhere. Crusted on my hands, my shirt, and my face and neck. It flakes off when I move. I can't tell if it's mine or someone else's. What scares me is that I can't remember.

A brief inspection of my pockets tells me whatever I had in there before all this mess is now gone. My knives are missing, too. I raise my head a fraction of an inch.

Pain flares behind my eyes, and I groan. No to that, then.

My chest hurts too, and my mind feels sluggish, as if it's been filled with mud. I am not in the best of forms today.

I glance around to find that I'm in a small but tidy room. It undulates gently, and the motion sends my stomach into an unpleasant roll. I lay on a small cot, simple but far more comfortable than I am used to. There's a small window in the corner above a small set of drawers. Judging by the amount of sunlight brightening the room, it must still be early in the day.

Whatever day that is.

The last thing I remember clearly is being dragged to the Marrin prison. Once the beatings start, my mind slips. Perhaps it is for the best.

But reach as I might, I can find no record of what happened next. This is clearly not the Marrin prison.

So, where the hell am I, then?

Bracing myself, I sit up, one vertebrae at a time. By the time I've reached a sitting position, I'm covered in sweat and panting, not to mention the room is now fully spinning. I press my palms into my eyes, willing the nausea to subside.

Once the worst of it ebbs, I take the plunge and push myself to stand. My legs shake as if I'm a newborn foal, and twice I almost fall. The floor seems to outright push me into the wall, though I'm sure it was just my unsteadiness.

Sucking in a breath through gritted teeth, I try the door. It opens without protest. Beyond it lies a windowless hallway lined with doors, and at the end . . . stairs.

The hallway seems to be deserted, though faint voices come from above. And I can hear seagulls trading squawks. That must be the way I leave, then.

I take a few unsteady steps through the doorway, shivering when I pass through a ward. By the time I make it to the stairs, my head is swimming, and cold sweat slicks my back, but I've come this far. I finally reach the top after what feels like an eternity.

Blood roars in my ears; my heart pounds.

I open the door and step into blinding sunlight. It's never this bright in Marrin.

My hands fly to cover my face as I wince, shutting my eyes against a lance of pain in my head. Above me, seagulls scream to each other. There's also laughter. The harsh voices of men shouting, cursing, grunting. Other noises, too. A strange snapping noise and a roaring sound. The ground beneath my feet rolls, and I almost fall again.

My eyes snap open, and when I behold what is before me, I realize the execution block would have been kinder. Quicker.

Men of all sizes, some short and husky, others tall and brawny, tarry about. Too many to count. Some stop what they're doing to stare at me, while others don't pay me more than a passing glance before resuming whatever they were doing before. Enormous poles jut up from black wooden flooring to seemingly pierce the sky. I crane my neck back as best I can, and when I do, a sinking dread engulfs me.

The snapping noises I heard were massive black flags blowing in the wind.

The rolling I feel is not due to my condition at all, but the expanse of blue on all sides of me.

I am on the deck of a ship, and we are very far from any land. Not just any ship, either, for black flags can only mean one thing. This is a pirate ship.

I almost sink to my knees, but a harsh voice grabs my attention. "Oy, what do we have 'ere? Ello, little lass. Wot's your name?"

I blink, finding myself face-to-face with an enormous pirate with a gap between his two front teeth. He leers at me, and I stumble backward.

"I—"

"I didn't know we were picking up strays." He grins much too widely. Greasy hair hangs in his eyes. "Want some company?"

I don't want to go anywhere with this wretch. I shake my head, eliciting a stabbing pain.

"Oh, come now, don't hurt my feelings."

He makes to grab my arm, but I shrink away to plunge into the mayhem of the ship. Light and sounds smear around me, but I can't pick much of it apart. I almost collide with a different moving body several times, and eventually crash into something so hard my eyes burn with unshed tears. Assorted cries and curses follow me until someone grabs my forearm, wrenching me around.

I find myself staring into two dark, upturned eyes in a lean, boyish face. "Moons above, how did you get out of your room? What are you doing out here?"

I stare dumbly at the boy, the dull throb in my head pulsing with every heartbeat. Finally, my legs give out, and we both sink to the floor, he much more gracefully than I. Slumping backward, I find something hard behind me on which I can lean—a mast.

His eyes flick over me, widening with every discovery. "How are you walking right now? You're supposed to be healing." He's got some sort of refined, haughty accent I can't place.

My lips move, but nothing comes out. I'm so thirsty, so hungry, and so tired. I try again. "Where am I?"

He tilts his head, and a look of pity crosses his face. "Very far from home, unfortunately. You don't remember, do you?"

I shake my head very slowly. "My head . . ."

He seems to genuinely feel sorry for me. "I know. They cracked your skull. You very well could have died." He considers me briefly. "Still might."

But something occurs to me. If this is a pirate ship, there is a leader. A captain. Surely this is a mistake, and he can take me back.

"Are you the captain of this ship?"

The corner of his mouth twitches, but I'm not privy to the joke. "Not I."

That's when I get the distinct notion that someone—or something —is coming.

Silence descends on the ship like sunsdown as heads bow and hands clasp behind backs. A chill slithers down my spine despite the day's heat.

"Hello, thief," says a voice.

The crowd parts reverently in a fearful wake, and there he stands. A black scourge on a sunny day. His long black coat billows in the breeze, whipping against shiny black boots.

"You," I breathe.

"Me," he grins.

The sight of his face triggers something, and all of a sudden, the memories come flooding back—the chase, the betrayal, the imprisonment, the transaction, and my very imminent demise.

7

WELCOME TO THE WRAITH, DARLING

My black-wearing adversary, true to his word. Last I'd seen him, his scarf had covered half his face. But now, it's been discarded, and I can finally look upon my assailant fully.

He is nothing like the brute I thought he'd be. While there is cruelty in the snide slant of his mouth, there is an unexpected elegance to the high planes of his face and the straight-backed grace with which he moves. He's younger than I would have thought, given his skill with a sword. Perhaps only a little older than me. Twenty-something. And though he's not the largest man on board, nor the most broad, there's reverence in their eyes as he passes by.

His strides are long and purposeful. In one heartbeat, he crouches before me. His forearms rest easily on his knees while his gaze combs over me, taking in the blood, bruises, and broken skin. The more he looks, the more he scowls. Taking my chin between thumb and pointer finger, he guides my face from side to side, and I grunt with pain.

"You're supposed to be near-dead, not frolicking about my ship." He clicks his tongue and casts the boy beside him a pointed look. "Lu, I thought you set wards to keep this from happening?"

"I did," comes the boy's puzzled response. A breeze ruffles his flaxen hair.

Both their gazes return to me, and the stranger asks, "You were asking for me, sweetheart?"

"Take me home. I'll give you the fucking paper." My hand fishes around my pockets for the blasted invitation, only to find nothing there. That's right. They're empty. I have no knives, nothing. He took everything.

"You have no need of me anymore," I say, praying it's true. But the memory of the paper bird pricking my finger looms over me like a specter.

His smile falters. "Oh, if only it were that easy."

My stomach drops.

"You see, it's not just a matter of the invitations. I bought you from those imbeciles in Marrin, so the way I see it, until I am finished with you, this is where you stay."

Black bugs begin to crawl along the edges of my vision. My lips part, then close again as my pulse flutters. I thought it was a dream. A horrible dream where he came to collect and barter over me like livestock.

No. It was real.

The realization feels like a slap. "You should have let me die."

His laugh has thorns. "Oh, that's not off the table."

He leans in closer, his eyes gleaming. It's the last thing I see before I am lost to the black. "Welcome to The Wraith, darling."

8

THE STRANGEST DREAM

*C*elosia is beautiful at any time of year, but there is something *particularly intoxicating about it during estiva, when the trees and flowers are at their peak.*

Oh, and the castle.

Curious ivy crawls up its ivory stone walls, creating a tapestry of gold on all sides. Spurts of fuchsia and lilac tulips populate the gardens, and at night, fireflies meander across the lawns. I cannot bear to close my windows against the warm wafts of jasmine and honeysuckle in the air. Every morning, I walk out onto my balcony overlooking the lawns, and still cannot believe my eyes. Even after a year, this place is surely but a dream from which one day I shall wake.

This morning, I am making Vesper's bed when I catch sight of myself in her ornate mirror. My heavy, drab skirts do nothing for my fair coloring and dark features. Proctor's teeth, I am as washed out and pale as the moons in the skies. I often feel a weariness that far exceeds my sixteen years, and it's beginning to show.

No wonder he does not look my way. And why would he? I am a handmaiden. A ward's handmaiden, at that.

But it doesn't stop me from looking at him. My surroundings fade as I conjure the image of Holland De'Havelin to mind. The pristine wave of his glossy hair, those rich blue eyes that catch everything—

Everything but me.

Voices I immediately recognize drift up to the balcony, and I stride to the veranda. Peering down, I spy the top of two heads bobbing through the lawns almost directly below me: one dark, and one very nearly white. They head toward the forest, trading conspiratorial glances as Vesper's long hair whips around her face. Silas slinks after her, his pale waistcoat gleaming in the sunslight. They dress that poor boy as if he's already thirty years old. He's eleven.

They're certainly two sides of the same coin, Holland and Silas De'Havelin. Both blond-haired and blue-eyed, courtesy of their father, King Stefan, though Silas tends to favor a pale, silver palette. His severe, sharp little face doesn't help, either. But Holland is honey and suns, with the build of a warrior but the smile of an aristocrat. His warmth comes from his mother, Queen Lorelai. There's no doubt about that.

I recall, as I often do, how morose a boy Silas was when Vesper and I first arrived as wards from Savastane a year ago. So stiff and sullen, I thought if he ever did smile, his face would crack, and I'd have another mess to clean. But a few weeks later, I caught Silas and Vesper exchanging a devious grin when Holland went to drink his glass of wine, and found it to be mostly salt. Oh, they both suffered for it.

But that wasn't the point, and it certainly wasn't the last of their mischief. Now, Vesper and Prince Silas are almost never apart, though Vesper is two years behind the younger De'Havelin boy.

My fingers brush against the gold-veined marble of Vesper's balcony as my eyes track their progress all the way to the edge of the woods. On the way, Silas leaps onto the decorative border of a pond, wielding his sword. Naturally, Vesper draws her own—much to my chagrin. She's too spirited for her own good. They parry and thrust as their laughter peals across the grounds. I watch their movements closely, as I always try to do. Sometimes, when I'm certain I'm alone, I even practice the motions myself in a mirror.

It's only a bit of fun.

Suddenly, my eyes are drawn upwards when Vesper and Silas still at the sight of a new figure striding toward them.

My pulse thrums. Prince Holland.

I'm too far away to hear what he's saying, and Vesper and Silas's backs are to me. They converse for a few moments before Vesper throws Silas a look and promptly pushes Holland backward into the pond.

My hand flies to my mouth in complete and utter shock.

The De'Havelin family has been most generous in welcoming us into their home after the alliance was struck between them and our home of Savastane, and this is how she acts? She knows better than this. After all, Vesper is representing House Osias as their ward! If King Stefan hears of this . . . My mind doesn't stop spinning the entire way down the staircase, nor as I sprint into the sunlight, my skirts swishing. By the time I reach Holland, Vesper and Silas have fled into the forest, leaving just me to extend a hand as he awkwardly climbs out of the pond.

"Your Highness," I exclaim a little breathlessly, though whether that's from the running or the way his clothes cling to his skin is a debate for another time.

"Oh, Artemisia. You . . . saw that."

Our eyes meet, and I don't know whose cheeks are burning hotter. I didn't know he knew my name.

"I don't know what got into her," I sputter, backing up to give him space. "She was raised better than that. I—I assure you it won't happen again. I'll speak with her tonight."

But he's shaking his head, his teeth flashing in the sunlight. His good humor astonishes me.

"No, no. I interrupted their game, that's all. No harm done. It's—" he squints up into the sky, shrugging. "—it's hot out here, anyway. And besides," He levels a devastating grin at me. "Now I can prank them back."

I can't bring myself to return his smile. I can scarcely look at him. Lord Osias would be furious. "Please. I am so sorry."

"No apology needed. And please, you've been here for quite some time now. Call me Holland." The warmth in his voice seeps into me, and I soak it up like syrup. His touch lands on my arm, and now, now I'm smiling, too.

"Only if you call me Artie."

9

I'D SAY IT WAS A PLEASURE, BUT YOU'RE A HORROR

I twitch a finger, then another, opening my eyes. I grasp for the remnants of the dream I was having about a wondrous castle in Celosia, but they've already drifted beyond my reach.

I'm back in the same room I awoke in earlier, only now, pale moonslight puddles beneath the sole window. On the opposite wall, an orblight glows weakly, but it can only do so much to banish the shadows adorning the corners of the room. I'm scarcely afforded the chance to mull over recent events before I detect movement across from me. I sit up abruptly, despite a painful protest from my ribs, and hide my wince as best I can.

There's no telling how long he's been sitting there with his ankles crossed and arms folded. He's shed his coat to reveal a black vest embroidered meticulously with gold thread, leaving sculpted arms and most of his chest exposed, all of which is covered in harsh black ink. Buried so deeply in shadow, I can't make out the patterns.

So many questions come to mind, I can't choose right away. The captain ever so kindly deigns to answer one of them before it can leave my lips.

"You were in prison for five days. You've been here for two. Last we spoke was yesterday afternoon."

I must blanch, for he continues, "I didn't think you were going to make it. What they did to you in there . . ." He shakes his head slowly. "Vile. Even by my standards."

"Awful lot of trouble just for me," I rasp.

A glint of teeth in the dark. "It served my purpose." My pulse quickens.

A groan bursts out of me suddenly, and I slump as far as the pain in my ribs will allow. I catch movement from my left—the captain leaping to his feet—and seize the moment of confusion. Slipping two fingers into the lining of my boots, I extricate the dagger hidden there and fling it at his head.

He catches it.

I hear a whistling by my ear right before the same knife thunks into the wall behind me.

"Is that how you repay me for extricating you from certain execution?" He asks, his words laced with incredulity.

What a joke. Death clings to me like flies on a corpse.

Scrambling to my feet, I bolt from the cot toward the closed door, but he grabs hold of my shirt and hauls me backward hard enough to send me hurtling into the opposite wall. I scarcely have time to blink before he's trapped me in place with a fistful of fabric. I grimace through a wave of vertigo as he lowers his face to mine.

"What the hell are you doing? You can't just leave, you odious little goblin. You're on a ship."

"What do you want from me?" I demand, though I'm afraid of the answer. There's only one reason I can think of, and it's worse than death. I recall the memory of the poor woman, dead in her cell. All used up.

He must see the accusation in my eyes, for his own widen momentarily, although he swiftly recovers. His nose wrinkles in distaste as he replies, "While I am capable of many evils, rest assured that is not one of them." Each word a blade, sharp and curt. As if to punctuate his point, his grip on the front of my shirt slackens. "If I release you, will you behave?"

My lip curls. "Feeling brave?"

We stare at each other for a few more terse moments before he finally releases me to take a few steps back.

"Feeling much better, I see," he mutters under his breath.

Unsure what to do with myself, I skulk back to the cot, regretting my earlier burst of activity now that the slice on my chest has begun to throb again. I bring my knees up and hook an arm around them, summoning my best glare.

The captain makes no secret of his dispassionate scrutiny of me. "To answer your question," he finally says, "you have cost me more than almost a week's delay at that skidmark of a place."

He pauses, I assume, for dramatic effect. "You read the invitation."

I don't answer, but the words come to mind anyway, in gold, elegant script.

The Crown awaits the pleasure of thy company, but only the worthy will attend this year's Court. Details will arrive for those who are willing to play.

After a moment, he chuckles mirthlessly and strides toward me. "It's the only reason you're still alive. Otherwise, I would have tossed your body overboard for the mermaids to squabble over. They love human teeth for some reason." He comes to rest in front of my cot, squatting down so that we're eye level.

Faster than I can react, he grabs my hand and pushes my pointer finger straight with his thumb so that the pad is exposed. Where a small smear of dried blood is still evident from when the paper bird pecked me. He holds up the pointer finger of his own right hand to reveal a similar smear of blood. My heart sinks.

"You're here, sweetheart, because we're blood-bonded together, and until this whole ordeal is over, I can't get what I want unless you stay alive. Understand?"

"No. There has to be another way." I loathe the tremor in my voice.

"Trust me, I'd love nothing more. But alas, there's not. And now, he's expecting you." The sentiment sends chills crawling down my spine. Alarms peal in my mind.

He. As in King Stefan De'Havelin.

"I'd rather go back to prison than spend another moment with you, pirate. Once you're finished with me, what, are you going to sell me to the highest bidder? Trade me to the Pits like the others who have gone missing?"

While the exact location has remained hidden, they say there is a place called the Pits, where Weavers are taken, mostly against their will, to fight to the death. Live or die, no one returns from the place. It's one of many reasons Weavers don't speak of their abilities. No matter who finds out, they won't be seeing their families again. Either they're drafted into servitude for the king, or stolen away to a miserable life of combat for other people's profit.

His eyes narrow. "What would you know about that?"

"Enough."

One doesn't have to be a Weaver to be sold off. But it certainly makes the fights more entertaining.

He smiles. "The Pits are far preferable to imprisonment in The Craw. I can promise you that."

"I won't help you."

He takes a step forward. "You'll do what I say."

"Is she awake?" A voice comes from the door.

We both turn to find the other boy, the one from earlier with the light hair, standing in the doorway holding various vials, bandages, and cups full of something.

"Not now," the captain mutters, scrubbing a hand roughly over his mouth. "Can you come back later?"

The boy raises his eyebrows. "Me? You swore on your breakfast you'd wait until I cleared her, as I recall. She's one more fainting spell away from permanent brain damage, and you're not what I'd call a calming presence."

"I'm in the middle of—"

The other boy makes a frustrated sound in his throat, cutting him off. "You saw what they did, for moons-sake. She needs more time."

"I—" I try to say.

"Oh trust me, she is very lucid," the captain talks right over me. "If she's well enough to be throwing daggers—she threw a dagger at me, Lu—she's well enough for a little talk."

The boy glances at the knife still embedded in the wall, nodding to himself. "Was wondering about that." With that being said, he goes about setting his vials and things beside me, tossing the knives onto the bed to make room. The captain has moved several paces back to lean against a wall, arms and legs crossed. He's practically simmering. It's delightful.

"I'm not finished with her," the captain grumbles.

The boy pauses his fiddling with a bandage to glance up. And though his tone is mild, the look in his eyes is fierce. "She very nearly died. You should know, you're the one who carried her in here."

My face goes up in flames. I cannot, for the life of me, imagine anything more mortifying. I'd rather the teeth ordeal with the mermaids.

A look passes between them, and I gather that they must have these sorts of conversations fairly frequently. They're quibbling not as enemies, but more like brothers, though they don't share a likeness besides their lithe builds and height.

"I don't have ti—" But the captain stops himself, and takes a resigned breath through his nose. "Alright. We will speak later, then." He's almost to the door when he stops and turns back to me, shoving his hands into his pants pockets.

"Oh, how rude of me. You are . . . ?"

I level him with my saltiest of scowls. "Pissed."

"Odd name."

The boy beside me snorts.

I consider the merits of giving the captain a false name, or no name at all, but I decide it makes no difference in the end. So, I tell him the truth. "Iona Strider."

"Iona Strider." He grins, as if the taste of my name agrees with him.

"You?"

He inclines his head. "Liam Blackwater, Captain of The Wraith. I'd say it was a pleasure, but you're a horror."

The name clangs through me to finally crash to the bottom of my stomach like a boulder. Liam Blackwater. The worst of the pirates.

Legend has it that his ship leaves a trail of frothy red wherever it goes. They say he's a better swordsman than Holland De'Havelin. That his ship is the fastest to sail the Silver Seas.

But they never said he's young. Or so irksome.

"I'd say it was a pleasure," I reply, "but you're a despicable criminal."

"Well, now. That makes two of us, doesn't it?"

"That's enough, both of you," the boy interjects, then looks expectantly at Blackwater. "May I?"

With one last scowl, the captain turns on his heel. He's gone the moment he sweeps through the door; gobbled up by the darkness lurking outside of the room.

10

THE FIRST MATE

He leaves the room feeling much larger than when he was in it. I let out a breath I hadn't known I was holding, feeling exhausted even though I've been, apparently, sleeping all day. Beside me, the strange boy unspools a bandage and sets out some tins of various sizes. Without a word, he hands me a cup of something, and I peer down to find that it's—

"Water. Just water," he says.

I glance at him hesitantly, and he meets my gaze with a flat look. "There's no poison in there, if that's what that look is for. If I'd wished you dead, I wouldn't have had to work very hard."

He doesn't have to tell me twice. Taking small sips at a time so I don't spew it back up, I slowly drink all of it, almost teary with relief. And it's clean.

When's the last time I've had clean water? Or food? I'd planned on buying some dried meat with the stolen notes, but that didn't happen, now did it?

I fix him with my full attention. "You can help me?" I gesture to my arms, my face.

"Aye. You'll find that between the healing tinctures, my skills, and the magic aboard, you'll heal fairly quickly."

Silence lapses between us until I can no longer stand it. "Was I really that bad?"

He looks up, his face void of any pity. "They beat the ever-loving shit out of you. But I don't have to tell you that. And you were bleeding. Badly."

Perhaps another person might feel immense gratitude, or relief, or disbelief that they'd come so close to taking the Good Walk with the Proctor, but not I. I don't feel much at all. The woman in the cell next to me most likely had a family, yet it was me who left that place alive.

Me.

I fight and claw and scrabble all in the name of survival just to feel like I've overstayed my welcome. I am not as much living as I am lingering.

He sets about changing the bandages covering the multitude of cuts along my arms, and I watch his every move. At one point, he attempts to inspect my right wrist, and I flinch, snatching it out of his reach. He makes a "tsk" -ing sound. "Fractured wrist, hmm? Weren't they thorough."

He grabs for it again, but this time not as hard. "Be still."

I stare hard into his dark eyes, but give it over. His thumb brushes over the protruding wrist bone, eliciting a sharp pain. But before I can yelp for him to stop, the pain recedes, then dissipates almost entirely, leaving only a whisper. I rotate it carefully, eyes wide.

"Bone Weaver," I breathe, astonished.

"Close. Luhan. Lu, for short."

I try out the strange name, foreign on my tongue. "Luhan."

"Very good," he says dryly. "First mate, mind you."

The familiarity he seemed to share with Blackwater makes sense now. I nod.

I'd heard of healing Weavers, though they're a rarity, at least in this part of the realm. "The marks on your shoulder blades. Do you know what they say?"

I shrink away from him, my lips peeled back in a snarl. "How do you know about that?"

He gives an unconcerned shrug. "I had to start on your ribs, obviously. I have to be touching as close to the injury as possible for more intricate breaks."

He's telling the truth. My ribs no longer hurt nearly as badly, just the slice across them. I had no inkling they were broken. It was hard to pick through the pain when it was everywhere.

"I don't know what they mean. Trust me, I've tried to understand." I say.

Unfortunately, that's the truth. And though I may not know what they say, I think I know what they are. Curse marks. And I think I know what they did to me, too.

"Is that so?"

I stare into his face, searching for any hint that he may know more than he's letting on, but he seems more amused by watching me squirm than anything else. "Why?"

He merely gives a disinterested hum. "I've never seen anything like it. How did you come by them?"

Again, the truth. "I don't know. I have no memory of it."

I have no memories of a lot of things. Which I was hoping that book would remedy. Fucking Bart. But I've no intention of telling Luhan any of this. My reception has been brutal enough. They don't need to know I've got unidentifiable curse markings that impart a wayward shadow, too.

He gives me a strange look. "You must have been quite young not to remember something like that."

"Must have been," I echo.

"How . . . peculiar."

Quite.

Sensing my reluctance, he changes subjects. "Your cheekbone, wrist, and ribs are almost there. Still, be mindful. Don't go gallivanting off to pick fights until they're fully healed. The rest of you," he waves in my general direction, "will heal eventually. I can only do so much in that regard."

"Shall I thank you for your generosity?" I intone, examining the blood caked beneath my fingernails.

He laughs coldly. "Certainly not. Do not misinterpret my following orders for any kindness. Now here, put this on your cuts."

We sit for several minutes in silence, both of us just following orders. "Are you hungry, Iona?"

I'd been staring at the wall while my mind tripped over itself trying to come up with a way out, around, or betwixt this. So far, it has failed.

I blink at him. "Hungry?"

His eyes narrow. "For food? Fresh out of bugs, though. Or . . . the soul of your enemies." He squints at me. "You do look like you've eaten a bug at least once."

I blink, stunned, and then laughter, loud and boisterous, bubbles out of me. It surprises both of us. His lips twitch at his own joke as I slap my hand over my mouth to stifle the giggles still fighting for release. I'm losing my mind.

He hums thoughtfully and sits back on his haunches. "We had stew tonight. Does that sound good?" The hard edge from his voice has softened. "I can bring you some. Let you rest a little while more."

I scour his face closely for any hints of cruelty. There's something about him I'm wary of, and the more I look at him, the more I realize it's his eyes. Dark, ancient pits in an otherwise youthful face. In fact, he reminds me of those immortal woodland sprites from stories of old: delicate features that are more pretty than handsome. Slender as a willow tree and just as graceful. And yet, the strength of his grip tells me he is anything but delicate, and the shrewdness in his gaze is anything but childlike.

In the end, my pit of a stomach decides for me. I nod, eyes averted.

This time, when he smiles, there's nothing wry or demeaning about it, although I still wouldn't call it kind. He straightens, his gaze combing over me to assess his work.

"Alright. Good. Do you wish to accompany me?"

I consider the offer, but in the end, I need some time alone to mull things over, so I decline.

He doesn't seem surprised. "Stay here then while I fetch a bowl and more water for you," he orders, gathering up his supplies as he talks. "I'll return shortly. Rest."

He glances behind his shoulder once before he leaves the room, and then he, too, disappears into the thick darkness on the other side of the door.

So that's that. I'm left in a room, so silent I can hear my own heartbeat. I cast around for something, anything, and settle on cleaning my mouth out with some herbal paste Luhan left me. I run my tongue along my teeth, satisfied when I feel a tingling sensation along my gums. I start to pace, turning over the events of the day, examining each bit of information for anything that might shed some light on my current predicament.

The Crown is waiting for me. What does that mean? Are they holding some sort of event that I've accidentally sworn to attend? It mentioned a game; will there be a tournament I have to compete in?

I shudder at the thought.

The captain might as well kill me now if that's the case. I can run and I can hide, but I'm no fighter. Instinct drives me in combat, and normally, it tells me to flee. Unless—

I shake my head, perturbed at the macabre memories flooding my mind. What I did to the Grays. What I did to—

I banish the thoughts, bile rising in my gullet. I did what I had to. I'm only what they made me.

I pace some more. Pirates. I know next to nothing about pirates, except that typically, I would want to offer a wide berth. Especially the ones who make names for themselves.

So much for that.

I stop at the small window to peer outside. The moons are hidden from view, but the pearly light they cast glimmers off the black, undulating sea. I can't tell when the sea ends and the sky begins from here, and once again, I find myself feeling so very small. So very helpless. Panic, unbidden, starts to climb up my throat. My breaths stutter. No, no, no.

Don't panic. It gets stronger when I'm afraid.

But my body won't listen, and something in the room shifts. My whole body goes taut, and fear's cold fingers brush the back of my neck. Slowly, ever so slowly, I turn as the orblight starts to flicker, and the darkness, like water, ripples. The skin around my shoulder blades starts to burn.

This is how it always starts. Another dark spot flares to life. "Nonononono," I whimper. Not here. Not now.

A gnarled, clawed hand reaches from the deepest part of the shadow and unfurls its fingers one by one. Then, they curl in on each other, the nails clicking.

Once.

Twice.

Fear seizes me by the throat and shakes me hard, rendering me staked to the spot.

A tidal wave of helplessness engulfs me, an overwhelming despondence that no matter where I go, this thing that is my shadow but not my shadow will always follow. A single tear slides down my face as I break into a cold sweat.

If I had a poisoned, ruined limb, I would cut it off and be done with it. But I do not know how to sever my own shadow. Oh, how I have tried.

I cannot be trapped in here like this.

With a sputter, the orb goes out. Completely.

My body jolts into action, and I sprint across the room, scrabbling for the door. I throw it wide open and flee.

II

NEVER-ENDING NOWHERE

I shudder as I pass through the doorway, shaking off a ward that was placed there, most likely by Luhan when he left just now, to either keep me inside or others from entering. It's enough to make me pause and consider my surroundings one more time. Wards are lesser magic; anyone can learn them, although Weavers are better and able to craft more complex ones depending on their affinities. Wards are mostly physical, like barring entry, briefly changing the texture of an object, preserving or protecting something, and things of that nature. Wards have never had much of an effect on me, like entry wards; they roll off me the same way water rolls off a seagull's wing.

I've tried finding possible explanations for this, but books are hard to come by these days, and books on magic are even more scarce. I was hoping I'd find something useful in the book Bart was supposed to give me, but—my blood goes cold at the memory.

Fucking traitor.

Thankfully, most of the hurt I'd felt from the betrayal has sizzled into hatred by now. Too bad I was otherwise detained. But now's not the time for dreams of revenge.

I thought it would be easy to follow Luhan to the mess hall, but I can't find any trace of the strange boy. It's as if he simply walked into one of the spots of darkness between the orbs lining the hallway and vanished. The image becomes more unsettling the more I think about it, so I pick up my pace and plunge forward to the end of the hallway, only to find—

Another hallway. Two more, actually. One branching to the left, and one to the right.

I do a double-take, blinking. The orbs cast such a dim, watery light that I can only see up to about the fourth one down the hall before the light is swallowed completely—but the hallways look identical. Skinny passageways lined with equidistant, unmarked wooden doors. I want to assume they're where the pirates sleep, like the room I woke in, but where is the mess hall?

With a mounting sense of dread, I arbitrarily choose the hallway to my left, counting the orbs as I pass. When I reach the darkness between them, it devours me so completely I find myself picking up speed just to reach the next light. That sort of darkness is unnatural.

There is a conniving spell in place here. This ship is playing with me.

I count twenty-one orbs, and still the passage stretches before me. Dread turns to terror, cold in my belly. This is either some sort of trick or very effective magical manipulation. I stop, pressing a hand to my chest, my panicked gasps so loud it's a wonder I haven't woken every pirate aboard this ship. What if I'm stuck here, in this hallway, forever? What if I've lost my mind for good, and this is my eternity?

Suddenly, I can't breathe.

I don't care about being quiet anymore. I turn around, and I run.

My boots thud heavily against the scuffed wooden flooring, but it's as if the endless gloom swallows the noise. I have this sinking feeling that if I screamed, the dark would eat that, too. That's when I realize I've passed twenty-seven orbs, which is six more than I should have, given I haven't seen another hallway. I skid to a stop below the thin light of an orb, my skin slick with cold sweat. My half-healed ribs protest every breath, every punch of my heart. No matter where I look, all I see is an esophageal darkness. I don't know how to get back to my original room, let alone the mess hall.

Somehow, I've gotten myself trapped in some never-ending nowhere.

I try the closest door to me, but it's locked. Then another, and another. They're all locked, rattling uselessly. I'm on my ninth door and hurl myself against it, anger and panic making a madwoman of me. My fingers scrabble uselessly against the wood, against the doorknob, and panic gives way to despair.

I sniff and wipe my eyes with the palms of my hands, putting my back to the door. "Please," I whisper in a shaky voice to no one as I slide to the floor. "Please."

The pool of light around me seems to shrink, and I wonder if I will be stuck here forever, in this dark, serpentine hallway of doors. A gasp bubbles out of my chest.

"Please. I don't want to be trapped anymore."

Something clicks, the door swings wide open, and I fall right through to the other side.

12

YOUR LIFE IS MY WHIM

I land hard on my ass, cursing viciously when I bite my tongue. The fall, so sudden and unexpected, knocked the wind out of me. I take a moment to catch my breath and quell the ringing in my ears. I run my hands over my arms in a weak attempt to banish the chill that has settled over me, but it seems it penetrated a bit deeper than skin, and I tremble violently.

Lifting my eyes, I find that I fell through the door—the previously locked door—onto—

But that's impossible.

Tilting my head back, I behold stars spattered over an inky, vast expanse of sky. A cool, salted breeze brushes my cheek, confirming what I see not to be an illusion, but real sky. Somehow, that door led to the deck. I gaze up at it, befuddled. On the other side of the frame are stairs that I most certainly didn't use leading down to the bowels of the ship.

None of this makes sense.

Blessedly, my shadow has gone still. My shoulders—the markings —aren't burning anymore, either. The dark spot is over, though it's left me almost too shaky to stand.

I stare ahead, unseeing, as the implications of this encounter fully sink in.

My control over my very own shadow is slipping. Once, I'd thought that as I got older, it would get easier to control, but no, it's only gotten stronger. The shadow is patient, skulking in the darkest corners, always waiting. This is the fifth time I've seen it do that—become its own beast. The first time I can remember, years ago, three Grays died, and . . . and . . .

The thought turns my stomach, sending ice trickling down the back of my neck. If only I'd gotten hold of that book. I inhale, closing my eyes, expunging the frustration and fear when I exhale. Or at least, I try.

An infinite swirl of stars stud the sky. The more I look, the more stars seem to blink into existence. My gaze wanders over to the three moons, and they're more beautiful than any textbook would have led me to believe.

Alamene, the largest middle moon that beckons the tides. Yskara, the second largest, who determines the four seasons—estiva, autumna, hiberna, and verna, and lastly, Eri. The smallest, but most curious moon. She's a bit of a debate as to what exactly she contributes, according to books I've scrounged together. Some claim she lights the way for the dead, while others postulate she serves as a source of magic for more sinister creatures, like the witches skulking along The Spine in Celosia. The moons' visibility, it is theorized, influences that night's magic. For example, on nights when only Eri is illuminated, it is best to stay inside, for certain witches become more powerful. And when they all go dark once a year on Dead Moon night, the first night of autumna, the dead lose their way and walk among us.

Tonight, two of the three are waning crescent, hanging serenely in their ethereal cluster. However ominous their effect on our realm may be, they've always brought me peace, though I could never see them this clearly. I knew they were there. That was enough.

It is by their light, and the orbs lining the undersides of the rails, that I stand and fully grasp the scale of the ship. It's enormous. Large enough for me to run to the other end and back and be out of breath.

Too many sails to count tower over me, obscuring the skies in patches of black. The crow's nest is high enough to pierce the clouds. There is a part of the stern, behind the helm, that is raised. Two double doors lead inside, and it occurs to me that it is most likely the captain's quarters.

I creep to the edge of the ship to peer overboard. The water below seems impossibly far away, and my stomach quails at the prospect of falling, or most likely, being thrown. Above all other fates, drowning is what I fear most. What a terrible way to die.

I make my way aimlessly to the front of the ship—the bow?—and stop, gazing in awe at the figurehead at the forefront. The great skeletal maw of some enormous beast yawns open with fangs as large as a full-grown man. I shudder to imagine how ferocious the creature must have been if the remains of its mouth are this malevolent. I wonder what it would be like to see the shape of this ship heralded by these enormous teeth approaching. I'm certain it's not a predicament anyone hopes for.

"A leviathan."

I whip around to find the dark speaking to me. "Don't tell me you're surprised," it purrs.

"Dismayed, more like."

The darkness laughs coldly, and out strolls Blackwater. He's found his coat again.

He stops next to me, peering down at the beast's great orifice too. "It used to be a leviathan. A rather small one, if you can believe it."

My lips part. If that's true, I can't fathom how gigantic a full-grown one would be. "And you killed it?"

"It's a long story, but yes. Usually, I gain no satisfaction from killing things that otherwise would have left me alone, but this was an unfortunate exception." His eyes slide to mine meaningfully.

"How noble of you," I say.

"Indeed."

We both stare straight ahead into nothing as the night breeze rakes its hands over my face and through his hair. Crossing my arms, I try not to shiver. My thin clothes, now stiff with dried blood, are no match for the wind's teeth. I never needed more than this, in the dry heat of

Marrin. I catch his eyes still stuck on me, practically glittering in the moonlight.

"What?" I growl.

"Did someone tell you to take the invitations from me?"

The question catches me off guard. "I—what? No."

He waits.

"I didn't know who you were until I ended up on this damn ship," I say, gesturing to the vessel around me.

"No one put you up to it?"

The corner of my mouth twitches. "No one puts me up to anything."

"What did the letter say?"

"Wouldn't you like to know."

"Yes, I would."

And because I'm feeling difficult, I look him straight in the eyes, wait a few moments, then shrug and turn on my heel to head toward the door I entered from.

He steps in front of me. "There's no reason we can't be amicable about this."

I look him dead in the eye. "Can't read." I try to step around him, but he blocks my path again.

"Liar," he snarls.

"How would you know?"

"Because you were trying to get a book from that man who sold you out. Didn't look like a picture book to me."

My eyes widen. "How do you know about that?"

His smile turns feline. "Oh, I found him afterwards. Bart, wasn't that it? Wouldn't tell me a thing about you, other than that you're a menace and a danger to us all, among other things. Anyway, I relieved him of any interesting contraband he had, as well as his other fingers."

There's a hidden, depraved part of me that grins very, very widely at that disclosure, but unfortunately, I cannot revel for long.

"Where is it? The book?" I can't suppress the urgency I feel. I need that book. I need it.

Blackwater leans in close, pauses, then shrugs. "Wouldn't you like to know."

"It's my book," I snap.

"Shall I remind you who owns what, darling?"

"Give it to me." My words sound breathy with desperation.

He leans down and tilts his head. "If you're good, perhaps I will."

My wrath swallows me whole.

I reel back and punch Blackwater in his jaw, hard, before I know what I'm doing. His head snaps to the side with the force of it. Sharp pain lances through my wrist—the one Luhan just healed—and I gasp, cradling it to my chest.

I back up several steps, bracing myself for a painful retaliation. That was foolish. That was so incredibly foolish.

But I'd do it again.

As for Blackwater, he makes no move to give chase. He doesn't even draw his sword. Slowly, his head turns back to face me, his eyes green chips of ice. He might kill me, right here. Perhaps that's what I want.

Instead, he bares his teeth in a bloody grin. I've never seen a man look more deranged. He wipes a bit of crimson off his lips with the back of his hand, as if he's more worried about the mess than anything else, and then he chuckles to himself. Gooseflesh breaks out on my arms as I take another step back.

I see now. I see why they're afraid of him.

Behind me, a door slams open, and I almost jump out of my skin.

"There you are, I—" Luhan's mouth snaps shut at the sight of us: me frozen in fear, Blackwater looking like some sort of hellspawn.

He approaches us carefully. When he catches sight of Blackwater's face, he pales as his eyes dart curiously between us with new understanding. "Liam, did you deserve that?"

"Don't I always?" Blackwater drawls, straightening.

"Usually," Luhan replies. He turns to me, noticing the wrist I'm clutching to my chest. "Iona. I just fixed that."

But I'm still watching Blackwater, afraid the moment I look away is the moment he strikes back. In a macabre sense, he's quite beautiful with those light eyes and that crooked red slash of a mouth. As if he can hear my thoughts, he meets my gaze for one blistering moment before I look away, flustered.

Sighing, Luhan gestures for me to follow. "I've got your dinner, Iona. Come on, then. The open sea isn't wide enough for you two, apparently."

I don't dare look behind me as we head toward the stairs, even when the night croons from behind me, "You'll do well to remember, darling, that your life is my whim."

13

SUPPER

The way back is distinctly different from the way I came, despite Luhan's declaration that there is only one way to reach the deck from my room. It appears his company has the ship on her best behavior; even the pools of darkness aren't as thick and pervasive. Still, I can't help the furtive glances over my shoulder to make certain nothing follows. I'm sure my skittish behavior doesn't go unnoticed.

"How did you get up there?" he finally asks, cutting his eyes at me.

"Got restless," I lie, then add truthfully, "I'm not used to being cooped up like this."

"I placed double wards that time."

I snort. "Wards don't stop me."

Luhan purses his lips. "Does that have anything to do with the markings on your back?"

We come to a halt. Luhan stands directly under an orb, and it casts a warm sheen on his hair. He might be narrow, but there's something about him that's quite imposing. Perhaps in the way he doesn't fidget, or how he always looks me straight in the eye. Usually, people are very eager to find reasons to look away. But not him.

"I don't know."

"I'll find out if you're lying."

"I'm not. But I suspect you may be right."

He squints at me. "You really don't know what they are, do you?"

I cross my arms, feeling much too exposed under his scrutiny. "If I did, things would be much easier for me, I assure you."

After studying me a moment more, he resumes his clipped pace, and I flank him, frowning.

"Where was the rest of the crew, just now on the deck?"

"Sleeping. You'll find that this isn't a typical ship, though we still need a sizeable crew for upkeep and various acts of brutalism and debauchery. Sometimes, Liam likes to take night duty by himself."

I think about that for a moment.

"The ship . . . did something to me. I got lost trying to find you." I leave out the bit about my shadow slipping its harness.

"Ah! Lost in an endless hallway, were you?" His eyes glitter deviously in the dull light.

"It's not funny," I snap, crossing my arms and wincing at a flare of pain from my wrist. "Does that happen often?"

"To people she doesn't trust, yes. You know, come to think of it, we once were boarded by some rogues looking for gold. We found one of them, eventually. But he said there were two others with him. Never found them, though. How horrible." His flat tone is anything but sympathetic.

The thought of wandering in the gloom forever makes my skin crawl, and I grimace. The ship didn't do this the first time I'd left my room. Perhaps she didn't care for the shadow. If that's the case, I can hardly blame her. "How do I get her to trust me?"

Luhan only shrugs, and we finally stop at a door—my door. "She let you out eventually, didn't she?"

We step inside.

I smell it before I see it. Two bowls of steaming stew crammed with bits of brown meat and root vegetables, each accompanied by a decent-sized chunk of crusty bread.

One for Luhan, and one for . . . for me.

Sauntering in ahead of me, Luhan crosses his legs and makes

himself comfortable, picking up one of the bowls and digging in. After a few moments, he looks up at me again, still rooted to the spot.

"What? Shall we bless the food?"

I take a few wary steps, then stop. "What do you want in return?"

I see the makings of a sharp retort on his lips, but then something like pity flashes across his face. "Eat the food. You won't be of any use at all if you waste away. And careful—if you eat too much too fast, it'll end up all over the floor."

Tentatively, I grab the other bowl on the tray and sit across from him, marveling at it for a moment before my stomach protests and I'm spooning it in my mouth, closing my eyes in utter bliss. The broth alone is sublime. Rich, salty, and delicious.

"The meat is from Ceroh. It won't last for long, even with their preservation spells, so we're using it up first. It's consistent quality, though, and good marbling. The vegetables should last us a while yet. I traded some good millet and bulgur for those yellow carrots, so you'd better like them."

I hold my spoon up, brows raised in question . . .

"Mmm! That is a purple yam. These are called Midnight Anneliese; I got them in Haem. They're practically paying people to take them; they have such an abundance during estiva."

I stop chewing momentarily, and it's enough for Luhan to catch on. "Oh, right. Marrin hasn't had seasons for a while, has it? Damn. No wonder it was so barren and strange. What made you want to live there, anyway?"

I shrug. It wasn't that I wanted to stay, but rather the fear of leaving that kept me there.

You can never stop running.

Well, I have nowhere to run now, do I?

"No wonder the king took so long to occupy Marrin," Luhan was musing. "Such a hopeless, stagnant place."

We both tend to our stew, sopping up the remains with our bread. It has halved green olives in it, little bursts of briny flavor. Tears well behind my eyes, and I find myself wishing I had hair to hide behind. I settle for ducking my head instead.

Once I've eaten half, I set it down, leaning back against a wall. I can't remember the last time I had access to this much food. I'd gotten used to the constant gnaw of hunger over the years, but now that it's gone for once, it's as if I've severed a rotting limb. Despite my full belly, I feel lighter than I can remember. Euphoric, almost.

"Good?" Luhan asks.

Something like a smile twitches the corners of my mouth at how scantily that word covers the emotion, and the smugness on Luhan's face tells me he knows it.

"Not as good as some of the bugs I've had," I say. "But not bad."

This time, Luhan's snort rips out of him before he can haul it back, and he shakes his head. "That is disgusting, Iona."

"I'm joking," I mutter. "I hate bugs." I look down forlornly at the half-eaten bowl. "I'm afraid to eat more."

He nods in understanding. "I'll leave it here for you to nibble on. The bowls are charmed to keep the food warm as long as something's in them. You'll be happy to know we eat three times daily: breakfast, lunch, and supper. I won't be bringing it to your room again, though. You'll have to come to the mess hall. I'll show you around tomorrow."

"I—" Now I'm the one gawking. My thoughts tumble over themselves at the implications of this information. "I'm not a prisoner?"

Luhan bursts out laughing, a pretty, melodic sound. "You thought we were holding you captive? No, no. You'll pull your weight, like everyone else. For all intents and purposes, you're our newest crew member. My most sincere congratulations."

"But—the other pirates—"

Luhan shakes his head. "They won't touch you if Liam decrees it. It all depends on what you two work out. It seems like you'll have to try again, judging from what little I witnessed tonight."

Blackwater's glistening red mouth comes to mind, his white teeth streaked with blood. "He might decide to pitch me overboard."

"He might," Luhan agrees solemnly. "Well, if you're going to be taking the Good Walk soon, would you like to bathe? At this rate, the Proctor will turn you away just to preserve a certain standard up there."

14

A DREADFUL COLLECTION OF POINTY LITTLE BONES

I t's a short and quiet journey to the bathing room. Inside, it's rather large with several drains dotting the floor and corresponding spouts in the ceiling separated by stalls. To my left is a little table below a mirror large enough to catch a glimpse of one's face. For shaving, I imagine. Next to me, by the door, a towel and a pile of clothes sit neatly on a stool.

"I was hoping you'd agree, so I planned ahead. You'll find I'm good at that," Luhan says by way of explanation when I glance over to him in question. "I'll be right outside if you need me." After giving me a pat of soap from his pocket, he departs, closing the door behind him.

On the way here, I made him swear over and over to remain outside while I bathe. Still, old habits kick in, and I waste no time. After shedding my clothes, I step delicately into the very back stall and turn the lever. Luhan had warned me the water would be cold at first, but if I keep turning the lever, it'll warm as the enchantment they placed on it takes effect. Nevertheless, I hiss when the freezing water meets my skin. Shivers rack my body, setting my teeth to chattering.

Remembering the bandages on my arms, I glance down to find droplets rolling off them.

But then, just as Luhan said, the water warms, and I relax a bit, savoring how lovely it feels. I could stay here all night.

The soap Luhan gave me burns a little, but I revel in the erasure of the day's horrors from my skin. I scrub until my whole body stings, and then some more, until my skin is pink where it isn't purple or black. The water at my feet swirls rust.

Once I'm finished, I towel off, making sure I'm careful around my ribs and face, where I'm still tender. While I'm doing that, I catch sight of myself in the mirror.

Golden eyes, large and accusatory, leer at me from a face mottled with a mosaic of stark bruises. They're worse beneath my eyes and around my jaw, contrasting harshly with my pallid complexion. I run my hands over some tufts of hair along my scalp. It's almost time to shear it again. Especially now.

I don't suppose I'd be what others consider pretty, even if circumstances were different. Certainly never lovely or fair. My features are too sharp for delicacy, too strange to be beautiful. I am but a dreadful collection of pointy little bones. No one likes to look at me for long, I know that. I don't think they like the hunted look in my eyes. It makes them nervous. Makes them feel like maybe they should be looking over their shoulders, too.

They should.

I turn my back to the mirror to catch a glimpse of the markings that cover my shoulder blades. They've been there for as long as I can remember. Ragged, dark grooves in my skin. They almost look like two different languages on top of each other; the first, long, jagged lines. The second, intricate whorls and complex, wispy shapes. As if someone took a fine-tipped stencil dipped in black ink and carved into me.

I despise these marks on my back more than anything else in the entire realm of Alvion, and I'd do anything to understand what they've done to me.

And how to undo it.

Hastily, I get dressed in the clothing Luhan provided, which turns out to be dark pants and a soft, matching top. Somehow, both items fit like a second skin, and for once, I'm not drowning in excess fabric. I ponder their origin while kneeling to tie my boots and, once finished, open the door to find Luhan exactly where he'd promised he'd be: sitting across the hallway twirling an obsidian dagger in his hand.

The look on his face as I close the door behind me is strange, as if I managed to offend him. But I've done what he asked, so I couldn't be sure how.

"Do give those clothes back to me once you acquire some of your own," he orders.

I frown, peering down at myself. "These can't be yours. You're too tall."

"It matters not," he says, a little too crisply. "Just do as you're told."

He seems to get a hold of himself, suddenly. His features banish the stormy expression, like clouds parting for clear skies. "Apologies. I'm tired. Anyway, you cleaned up well enough." Did he—apologize? To me? "Who knew there was a girl lurking under all that filth, all this time?"

"Your captain had the pleasure of the same revelation when he met me."

"Oh, I heard all about it."

We share a secret smile, and together, make our way back to my room. Once we're back, he enters briefly to take the tray of bowls and spoons. "It's late. Try and get some sleep. Tomorrow I'll show you which chores you'll be—"

"Chores?"

He levels me with a look, a skill he's quite adept at. "Yes, chores. I already told you, you're our newest crew member. Which means you work for room and meals."

My expression sours at the thought, but Luhan chooses to ignore it.

He goes to leave, then stops, eyebrows raised. "One last thing. Don't try to leave your room again until I come fetch you at sunrise. The Wraith may not be as kind as last time, and who knows who you'll find wandering these halls. Sleep well, Iona Strider."

And with that, he closes the door behind him, leaving me with much to contemplate, and too much night left to pace away until the mercy of dawn.

15

LOVELY TO MEET YOU

Naturally, the soft knock on my door comes as the sky starts to lighten, which is right around the time I would normally drift off to sleep after the long night. Due to various shadow-shaped reasons, I have been nocturnal for years.

The more I thought about things last night, the more caged I felt. I might be able to move around as I please, but I'm still trapped on this ship, surrounded by hostile pirates. The only person stopping them from gutting me like a fish is a man I made an enemy of the day I met him. The moment I let my guard down around any of these men is the moment I become a cold corpse, and I can't bring myself to give that son of a bitch the satisfaction.

"Moons, did you sleep?" Luhan exclaims when I open the door. He's holding a burlap bag full of something.

My heart leaps when I realize what it must be. "My blades?"

He smirks as he hands the bag to me without bothering to confirm. "You may as well have them back. Taking away an animal's claws only makes it more aggressive."

I ignore the comparison. I have my blades back.

Moving swiftly, I turn, sliding my knives into the underside loops of my vest, which I kept. Six should do: three on each side. And I already have my boots on.

Luhan's leaning in the doorway, arms crossed. "Couldn't sleep?" The circles under my eyes must speak volumes.

"I sleep during the day, usually."

He cocks his head to the side. "Why?"

"It's safer."

"For who?"

The last blade slides into place. "Everyone."

My first lesson of the day is that, contrary to popular belief, pirates do not eat children or the hearts of their enemies for breakfast; they eat oatmeal. Sometimes salted fish.

Today, oatmeal. It's easy to make and keeps a while without any additional enchantments, according to Luhan. And then he threatens me with oatmeal quality inspection duty, which consists of scouring each individual oat for potential pests or defection, if I misbehave.

When I ask him what exactly constitutes misbehavior, I find myself immediately regretting the question as he lists out every remotely nefarious action verb he can think of, all while staring pointedly at the daggers strapped snugly by my ribs.

While we eat, I notice that I am the source of many curious stares. I don't return them and do my best to keep my head down. It feels unwise of me to pick a fight before any of us have finished our breakfast.

Meandering about the ship, Luhan informs me of the various rotations of the crew, such as fishing, cleaning, maintenance, food preparation, and weapon care, among others. Each pirate is delegated to two shifts daily, switching at midday. I doubt I'll be allowed to do anything weapons-related anytime soon. Pity.

We emerge onto the deck after a while, my nerves frayed from being so constantly on alert. Although it's still early morning, the sky a swirl of soft oranges and reds, I can tell it's going to be a bright, sunny day. The ship is already abuzz with activity.

Luhan leads me to a mess of netting and rope, catastrophically entangled, near the stern of the ship. "You'll be starting on this," he instructs, pointing. Seeing the alarm on my face at being so out in the open, he adds, "I've told you. They're under orders not to bother you until Liam decides what to do with you."

Depending on his decision, then, I might become very bothered in the near future.

I squint at the jumble of supplies, unable to figure out where I should begin. "You didn't mention untangling duty earlier."

He gives me a saccharine smile. "It's special. Just for you."

I look down at it, resigned. "And my second shift?"

"Oh, you'll be delighted. I have ten buckets of potatoes that need peeling. I'll come back for you in, oh, six bells? Do me a favor and don't need me until then. Aye?"

He doesn't wait for a response before sauntering away to correct the way a pirate with a large, white beard is scrubbing the deck. Circular motions, not back and forth, Luhan instructs.

Sighing through my nose, I sit cross-legged on the floor and grab some slimy, mold-speckled netting and set to work, blinking sleep out of my eyes as the suns climb higher and higher.

By the time I make it to supper, exhaustion is tugging so hard on my eyelids, I almost fall asleep face-down in my stew. But suddenly, I become wide awake when a certain captain strides past me, his knee-high boots gleaming like they'd just been polished. For a pirate, he always seems so . . . clean.

I stare a hole in the back of his head as he claps a man on the shoulder. From the moment he entered the room, it wasn't only my head that turned. It's as if he's true north for every person in this room. And not just because they fear him. No, they seem genuinely devoted to their captain and happy to see him. And as I observe his interactions with various crew around the mess hall, I can see why. He can be quite charismatic when he wants to be. It's strange to witness this charming side of him while knowing firsthand how scathing he can be when the pendulum swings the other way. I have the distinct feeling of being in a suns-soaked room, just to be sitting in the only slice of shade.

Aimlessly, my gaze roves around the hall, bored but on edge at the same time.

Everyone seems tired, yes, but content. Everyone, but—Oh.

There, in the corner of the mess hall, three men slouch over their meals, their faces half-obscured by shadow. They sit apart from the rest of the crew, barely speaking. One of them, the gap-toothed man I had the displeasure of meeting the other day, meets my curious gaze with a baleful glare. I avert my eyes quickly, cursing myself for not being more discreet.

Sighing, I stare down at my bowl of smoked cod and potato stew. Or at least, what used to be smoked cod and potato stew. My stomach can handle an entire bowl now, though it's always gone much too quickly.

To add to my black mood, someone a few tables in front of me is staring. At me. "Who's the kid?" I ask Luhan, who sat with me again, most likely because he was ordered to.

His eyes flick across the room. "Oh, him? His name's Matteo. He's fairly new."

"Why's he staring?"

Luhan opens his mouth to answer, but before he can, his eyes dart in front of us. "Oh, no." I turn to follow his gaze only to find myself face-to-face with . . . a kid. The kid.

Matteo. He must have taken my notice of him as an invitation, and I watch in horror as he takes a seat on the bench across from me. He looks much too chatty for my liking. It's been enough getting used to Luhan already.

"Hello," he says awkwardly.

He's young. I'm guessing somewhere around nineteen or so. Handsome in a coltish way, with his russet hair and warm amber eyes. But his innocence is glaring. Now that he's closer, it's obvious from the quality of the clothes he's wearing and the sheen of his hair that he, at one point, lived a very easy life. And while I can say the same of Luhan, the two are very different. There is a hardness to Luhan, a sharp edge behind every clipped word, that makes it evident that Luhan would not hesitate to open someone's throat. This boy is a lamb in comparison. There's a naivety to him that at once elicits a wave of both jealousy and derision from me.

"Erm, Luhan," he says, lacing his fingers together. "I have . . . news. From . . ." His eyes dart to me, lingering questioningly on my face, then back to Luhan. ". . . My source."

"Go ahead, then," Luhan says lazily. "Iona won't tell. Right?"

I shoot him the dirtiest look I can muster. He knows I could discover the location of the Pits, and I'd have no one to tell. I feign disinterest and look away, my chin in my hand.

"She saw an unmarked ship heading for The Sorrows. Thought it was strange, considering it's a poisonous wasteland now. Couldn't follow it in, of course. And she heard of another disappearance. In Haem."

My ears prick, and a sinking sensation develops in my stomach. Another disappearance. Why is this happening? How? It's a struggle to keep my expression somewhat calm. In my lap, my hands clench.

Luhan sighs heavily.

"I'll tell Liam. Thank you, Eames."

My head jerks up. "Eames?"

They both turn to me, surprised, and I might see the beginnings of dread on Matteo's boyish face. It's all the confirmation I need.

"As in . . . Baron Eames? Of Koska?"

His expression turns wary, and I feel the heat of Luhan's warning stare as it drills into my cheek. "My father, yes," Matteo says warily.

Scorn burns a hole in my belly. Some Koskish citizens were able to escape to Marrin after what the baron did. They told anyone who would listen what happened. How one day, Grays showed up and took whomever they pleased. Broke families apart. Left chaos in their wake. He, their ruler and protector, invited them in.

"I heard about him."

"Don't," Luhan cautions, but I ignore him. My blood is too hot. The faces of the Koskish people swim in my vision—they came to Marrin bedraggled, grieving, and betrayed by the very man who was supposed to protect them. Displaced from the only home they'd ever known. The worst part was: they were the lucky ones. The Koskish that hadn't been able to escape had been taken. Sold by their own baron into servitude.

"I know some of your people," is all I say, but the words are laced with acid. "Some made it to Marrin."

Some.

"He—they gave him no choice," Matteo protests, and I notice his hands are shaking. "My father was a good man. He . . . he had no choice."

"Is that so?" I say, unmoved by the desperation in his eyes. It boggles my mind that a ruler would sell his own people out like that. To oust them from their homes. My anger becomes scorching. "Did they pay him? Is that what it was?'

"No," the boy almost shouts, his eyes glassy. He takes a shaky breath, but it doesn't do any good. "I don't know what happened, only that the alternative was worse. He never told me. And now he's—he's gone."

My eyebrows raise, and Luhan scratches his cheek, looking as if he'd rather be inside the belly of a leviathan than here.

Matteo levels an accusing glare. "Does that make you feel better? He's dead. Drowned in a shipwreck. He paid for his sins, and my own uncle cast me out of Koska when he took over. I had nowhere else to go, so now I'm pissing my days away on a pirate ship, where I'm the bane of everyone's existence. Maybe now that you're here, they'll forget about me." He smiles bitterly, and it looks so unbecoming on him.

"Probably so," I mutter. Though I'd like to feel sorry for him, I feel sorrier for his ousted and betrayed people. How can he be much different than the Baron, the man who raised him? I know better than to be hopeful, when I've seen so much cruelty.

"Yes, well. Lovely to meet you." He pushes himself up from the table and strides out of the room. Carefully, I avoid Luhan's glare, but when he wants to be noticed, he won't be deterred.

"You go foraging for things to be sore at, don't you? You think he's responsible for the sins of his father?"

"His father was a worm for what he did," I hiss. "How can his son be much different?"

"He is a boy," Luhan retorts. "Why don't you direct your rage toward someone who deserves it? There are plenty."

I look away, jaw still set. Perhaps I was too quick to blame him. Perhaps my anger was misplaced. Too bad. It makes no difference. I'm not exactly here to make friends, especially with someone so quick to defend a man who allowed his own people to be spirited away from their own homes.

Even so, a pervasive sense of guilt spoils the rest of dinner.

16

MY IRE AND MY BLADES

Some time later, when the ship is quiet and the moons reign, I'm lying on my cot tossing a knife back and forth when I hear it.

At first, it sounds like a gentle rustling. Like someone next door is speaking quietly and moving around. I strain to make out any words, the knife stilling in my hand. Several tense moments pass before I understand what I am hearing, and when I do, a stricken gasp escapes me.

"Why—why did you—why did you kill me, Iona?"

I sit up, my heart rammed into my throat, punching hard. That didn't come from next door. It came from right beside me.

They're here.

They've surrounded me. All seven of them.

Three Grays, four children, all of them dead. Their eyes have long rotted in their skulls, and still, they stare at me. A little girl, her mouth nothing but a gaping hole with cracked brown teeth, asks again, "Why did you kill me, Iona?"

And I open my mouth to answer her, because she deserves an answer. They all do.

I have so much I want to say, the words gathering on the tip of my tongue, shoving and bickering as they wait impatiently for me to finally release them. I want to tell them I'm sorry, I'm so sorry, I didn't mean to, I was trying to help, I just wanted to help.

But like always, all that comes out is a jaw-cracking, guttural scream before their cold little hands start pulling on my skin, the Grays looking on grimly like harbingers of death. This is their justice. Even if I dared to run, they'd stop me; they are here to oversee my punishment.

I scrabble and flail, tears tracking down my cheeks as they hold me down, but suddenly their hands are larger and their voices deeper and—

Someone grabs both sides of my face. My eyes fly open and roll around while I gasp for air like a fish. The orblight is but a dying glow, lending just enough light to make out the shape of things.

Things like the creature crouching above me, its eyes glittering. I try to launch myself at it, but it shoves me down hard, grunting and growling and shouting my name, but it's tricks, it's all tricks, and I can't get away from it though I'm kicking and scratching and biting. My vision is blurred with tears, and someone is screaming. It hurts my head.

"Stop fighting me, dammit," the thing growls. "Strider. Strider, stop —that—" I kick my feet viciously, desperate to squirm out of its grasp—

Hands clamp around my jaw, forcing me to stare into the eyes of a madman. Eyes I know. Blackwater.

The lingering haze of the dream dissipates in an instant as my heartbeat flutters and flaps around like a bird caught in a cage. I can't catch my breath. Behind him, something shifts in the darkness. His hand claps down on my mouth, cutting off my screams.

"Hush," he commands, keeping his voice low. "You'll wake the dead if you're not careful."

Fool. The dead are already here. And they won't stop until I'm— I'm—

"Breathe," he commands, planting both his hands on either side of my head. "Through your nose—right, that's it."

Just a dream. I must have dozed off at some point during the night, unable to fight the exhaustion any longer. I don't remember lying down. But I don't want to close my eyes, either. It's when I close my eyes that something bad happens. And it's always worse at night.

Always.

So, I keep my eyes trained on Blackwater instead, allowing myself to get a little lost in his soft jade gaze as his voice rumbles through the dark.

"Breathe out. Wait. Breathe in. Hold it. Through the nose, that's it."

Mindlessly, I comply. There's comfort in his authority, and this one time, I don't want to fight. I want him to be right; I want it to have only been a dream, though I know better. I lose count of how much time goes by as we continue the exercise until my breaths are no longer gasps and the shadows, blessedly, have gone still.

Once the episode has truly passed, a wayward tear streaks down my cheek.

Blackwater smudges it away with the pad of his thumb before it can fall onto my pillow. His callous scrapes along my skin, and I shiver.

"You . . . heard me?" I rasp, afraid of the answer. My voice is raw.

Blackwater snorts as if I've said something funny, his teeth sharp in the slash of light from the window. He eases back onto his haunches. "I thought one of my men had beaten me to killing you."

The frivolity of his threat snaps me out of my daze as if I'd been struck.

He almost had me. I forgot, in my moment of weakness, that he's a manipulative, conniving, treacherous wretch of a person who will use this against me. And I am the same in his eyes. I'd be an idiot to believe any act of kindness didn't have an ulterior motive, especially if we are to be playing a game in which the rules aren't set yet.

Another tear spills over, but this time I obliterate it myself with a furious swipe as I sit up. "Don't touch me. Ever."

He flinches. Something flickers across his expression, gone before I can parse it. "You were screaming."

"Get out. You shouldn't have come here."

"I thought someone—"

"Well, you were wrong. It was just a bad dream."

He scoffs. "A hell of a bad dream, then."

"Leave."

The pirate's eyebrows arch up incredulously as he gets to his feet. "You don't give me orders."

"I just did, asshole."

His eyes narrow in derision. "Whatever terrors exist in your mind seem to be well deserved."

I bark a hollow, ugly laugh. "They are."

Silence floods the room.

"As you wish." He backs away, his mouth twisting into a cruel sneer. It's not until he reaches the door that he speaks, his eyes cold as he takes me in one last time. He makes a disgusted sound in his throat. "You know, you're right. It's better this way."

If we hate each other.

That's what he means to say, but doesn't have to.

I expect him to slam the door, but he slips out as quietly as he arrived, leaving me to tend to the rest of the long night. My face falls into my hands, and I let out a shaky breath. For a moment, it was nice. Not to be alone. Now, without my contraband books, I've nothing but my ire and my blades to keep me company.

And I do know, at some point, if I continue to burn like this all the time, there will be nothing left of me.

17

THE SERPENT AND THE GHOST

The next two days drag on without incident. A muscular, dark-skinned man, as sour as I am, has joined me in the kitchen. He's a bit worse for wear, this one—completely eaten up with scars and just the one eyeball. Together, we peel potatoes, descale cod, boil vegetables, and then scour the pots and pans so we can boil something else. He hasn't bothered to tell me his name, but I haven't bothered to tell him mine, either. I don't mind his company much, the burly mountain. He doesn't talk circles around me like Luhan, or set my teeth on edge like Blackwater. We spend many long hours in dedicated silence.

At this point, I'm in somewhat of a routine. Breakfast at dawn, then whatever rotation I'm on until lunch, which is normally something light like smoked fish, vegetables, and a hunk of bread. After that, chores until supper, then night descends. I learn that some of the crew take turns helping to man the ship at night, but I am not one of the chosen few. No, instead, I've resigned myself to feeble attempts at sleeping through the night. I say feeble because every night I've woken to the sound of my own screams, surrounded by atrocities I wish would stay buried.

Once I wake from my nightmares, I can never go back to sleep, but the breathing exercises do help. Not that I would ever tell Blackwater that.

It hasn't been all bad, though.

My bruises are better. Except for a few lingering discolored spots along my jaw, they've healed. Ribs and wrist, too. All that remains of the slash on my chest is a thin, puckered scar. The cuts on my face have resolved entirely. Expedited healing, indeed.

And in the days I've been here, the routine meals are already making a difference. I have a steady supply of energy and clarity, and my every thought is no longer driven by the mad desire to seek out my next meal. The half days in the suns have blistered my pale skin and lips, and that's just from the mornings. Once my shift changes to spending my time on the deck in the afternoon, I'll need to steal someone's hat.

There is comfort in the monotony of routine. But this, I know, cannot last.

On the fourth night, I'm finishing my supper when Luhan glances over to me. "Your bones are healing nicely, if you care."

I look up, surprised but also intrigued. "How do you know?"

"I can feel them when we're close like this. Healing breaks require touch most of the time because it's so intricate, but I can assess progress and status from farther away."

I mull this over. "How did you know?"

"Know what?"

"Know you were a . . . Weaver?"

His lips quirk to the side as he considers the question. "Same way someone discovers they're good at something. Half by happenstance, and half because I felt drawn to it. Is that what Marrinians call it? Weaving?"

I shrug. "It makes sense to me. Most people use magic like a tool, others are born with it. They Weave it."

He seems to be amused by that. "I like that, actually. In Iridisia, we call people like me Blessed. It is revered and celebrated there."

"Must be wonderful, not to have to hide like they do in Alvion," I say. "Why would you ever leave and come here?"

He looks away. "I had my reasons."

Hm. I change the subject. "And the rest of the crew? I'm assuming they know what you can do."

"Of course. I've had to heal almost every member of this crew at some point, the idiots."

I lean forward, enthralled. "And you're not worried about word getting out? What's stopping someone from leaking the information?"

He looks at me strangely. "I don't think you quite understand how this works. For one, I am not the only Weaver on this ship. There are many. And besides, even if it's not Weaving in particular, everyone here has secrets. How common do you think Weaving is, Iona?"

My mouth opens, then closes. "It is incredibly rare, is it not?"

He smiles like a cat that stumbled upon a limping mouse. "Wrong. Perhaps twenty years ago, yes. But now? Not so much."

"How do you know?"

"I have been more than one place in my life. And wherever we go, I listen."

My mind reels at the implications of that. There are no books on Weaving. All the information I have on the phenomenon is from covert whisperings and overheard rumors trickling down from Celosia, the kingdom's capital. In Celosia, so the rumors go, Weavers are free. However, they are also, I realize, more easily monitored by the king. The king, who snatches up any and every Weaver in farther away lands the moment he gets wind of one. So, then, it is possible that the information we have about Weaving is misinformation directly from Celosia to create . . . isolation. Disconnect.

"He wants Weavers to feel alone, so they don't band together?"

Luhan simply nods. "It is possible."

My brows knit together. "But why is it different in Iridisia? Why are Weavers free, and here, they are not? King De'Havelin has proven himself time and again to be a powerful ruler. Surely, he isn't afraid."

The king draws his own magic from the Celosian crown. It is imbued with a magic so old and so formidable, it is unthinkable to challenge the might of the king. Or anyone that wields one of the five First Sovereign's crowns, for that matter.

"That is the question, isn't it?" Luhan muses, resting his chin on the back of his hand. "The Iridisian king and queen have no reason to fear their own people. De'Havelin thinks he does. I would too, if my wife had been assassinated in my own home."

He's talking about the queen's assassination seven years ago. What made it worse was, Celosia and the neighboring territory from which the assassin came—I can't recall the name of it—were in the middle of alliance negotiations. In retaliation, the king gathered up his army and massacred the entire territory. There were no survivors; the excision was thorough and precise. To this day, it is a barren land. The Sorrows, it's called now. They say a poisoned gas pervades the land, deterring anything from living there for the rest of time. The Sorrows, indeed.

King De'Havelin never remarried, leaving his two sons, Silas and Holland, motherless to this day.

"Whoever assassinated the queen wasn't Celosian," I say.

Luhan shrugs. "No, but seven years ago is about when he started paying closer attention to Weavers. Is it not?"

I think back, but it's hard to separate the dusty years, and my memory isn't as intact as I'd like. But he seems to have a point. I'm quiet for a little while. "Is Blackwater a Weaver?"

I half expect Luhan to evade the question, but to my surprise, he answers immediately. "Sometimes I wonder, what with the way he wields a sword. But no, he is not. He's insufferable without additional help."

"Who does he work for?"

Luhan, who had just taken a sip of water, almost spits it back out. "What?"

I tilt my head. "Even pirates all work for someone, don't they?"

Luhan barks a sharp, loud laugh. "That may be true of most pirates, but not the Sea Serpent. Liam would rather die than defer to another person." His smile widens. "Now tell me. Does that make you feel better, or worse?"

"I'm not sure," I mutter.

"Speaking of, Liam wants to see you after dinner, oh curious one."

My head jerks up, my heartbeat ratcheting.

Inwardly, I sigh. Outwardly, I set my jaw. "And if I say no?"

His eyes widen with delight as he leans in conspiratorially. "I dare you."

I think better of taking him up on it, the little sadist.

Shortly afterwards, I make my way above the guts of the ship. I'm alone on the deck, the rest of the crew still eating. It's become apparent that The Wraith doesn't need to be manned all the time—magic guides her to her destination.

I've made my way to Blackwater's cabin when I register voices leaking from the closed doors.

"—some sort of witch, I'm tellin' ya. There's somethin' not right about that lass, and keepin' her alive puts all o' us in danger—"

That voice cuts off abruptly, but the other voice is too low for me to hear. "Captain, dearest respect, but she's a threat to us all. I swear to the skies, I saw her eyes a-glowing last night—"

This time, the other voice is loud and clear. "I am aware, Garrith, but unfortunately, I require her for my use."

"I can get you any ol' wench, if it's services yer after—"

My heart stops.

"It's not."

My heart starts again.

"What if I scare her a little, aye? Put a bit o' fear in her, so she don't try nothin'?"

"Are you afraid of a lass who is one-third your size, Garrith?"

"Hell no," the pirate roars. "Just don't trust her, is all."

Rich, coming from a pirate.

Another lengthy, cold lapse of conversation. Then, "Be gone. And if you insist on questioning my judgment, you're welcome to challenge me to a duel at any time."

Stony silence.

"No? How disappointing. Dismissed." I flinch at the acid in Blackwater's tone, even from out here.

I leap aside as the doors to the cabin burst open, and the very same man who discovered me on the ship, with the gap-toothed grin, emerges. But he's not grinning anymore. His eyes widen momentarily at the sight of me, then narrow to slits.

I dip the lower eyelid of my right eye and stick out my tongue, a realm-wide offensive gesture, but he doesn't rise to the bait. His face twists into a scathing glare before he departs, and I watch him closely until he's disappeared through the door leading beneath the deck.

"Strider. Come inside." Blackwater's voice spears through the peace of the sunset.

I glance up to the darkening sky, taking in a big breath of salty air, when I notice my shadow still watching where Garrith exited through the doors.

"Do not go after him," I whisper to it. I'm in over my head enough already. It looks to me with an air of petulance, then relents and follows me inside.

Blackwater's quarters, much like the rest of the innards of The Wraith, are much larger than they should be. The first observation that comes to me is how tidy it's kept. That is, except for the enormous desk behind which Blackwater himself sits. Maps, more maps than I've ever conceived, spill over the top. Some lay rolled up in piles, while others lay flat, still curling up at the edges. Maps in buckets, maps pinned to the wall, maps everywhere. The one nearest me depicts the entire realm of Alvion: Marrin, nothing but a speck to the south, with the monstrous mass of Celosia far north. Almost half of the continent, the Grimwood, remains unexplored. It's simply too dangerous. The witches make sure of that.

Turning away from the maps, the next thing I notice is the abundance of little treasures. Peculiar trinkets ranging from ornate to downright macabre punctuate the quarters with a dreary sense of splendor: a map on the desk is weighed down by an oddly large bird skull, a suns-stone necklace strung through its eyeholes. A skeletal hand sticks out of an ale mug, each finger bearing rings with twinkling jewels. I almost laugh at the absurdity of it as I stroll by it all.

Pirates can't resist something shiny, it seems. That, at least, we share.

Nearby, a tall bookshelf teems with books, stuffed so full I don't know how he gets them out when he actually wants to read something. An entire shelf seems to be dedicated to cures for rare diseases, illnesses, and other ailments, while another is composed of geography, herbology, and, surprisingly, mythology and folklore.

And in the corner, an actual bed, made up quite neatly. It smells like him in here. Crisp and clean, punctuated with the scent of salt and suns. With a cream-colored tallow candle quietly sputtering in a cavendish on the map-littered surface of his desk, the room might've been quaint if it wasn't for the pirate inhabiting it. I take my time perusing, and while I am being nosy, I am also desperately scooping my thoughts into some sort of coherence. For some reason, when Blackwater comes around, all sense tends to escape me. And after our last interaction, I don't know what to expect.

We did not end on good terms. Quite abysmal, actually.

"Strider," he greets me, his gleaming boots crossed one over the other on his desk. I turn to face him.

"What do you want, Blackwater?"

"Wealth and women."

I make a face.

He sighs, motioning to the chairs across from him. "Please. Your hovering like that gives me indigestion."

Begrudgingly, I do it, though I take my time. This close to the pirate, my body feels like it's buzzing, overly aware of every minuscule move he makes. I school my breaths, forcing my mind to calm.

Breathe in, hold it, expel it, wait. "I wanted to try again," he says. I cross my arms.

"I want us to understand each other, Strider."

"I have no interest in understanding you, Blackwater. Just enduring you."

"Neither of us will endure what is to come if we can do nothing but bicker and snipe like children."

"Grow up, then."

His eyes flare in warning. "Stop testing me."

"Then get to the point."

In response, he pulls out a knife and stabs it into the table. Right over a map of Alvion. Our eyes lock, and his brows raise.

How's that for a point? His expression challenges.

"I'll get right to it, then. Every year, King De'Havelin hosts an extravagant ball for his most powerful subjects. Deals are struck at these parties, power exchanged, secrets whispered. It is at these balls that wars are started, or the seeds of kingdoms planted. The most revered and feared in all of Alvion attend. The trouble is, the location changes each time. This year, I have reason to believe it will be held in the kingdom's splendid capital, Celosia, if that piques your interest."

Celosia.

My breath catches. The most powerful Curse Speakers live there. One of them could read the markings on my back and tell me what they mean. They could free me from this hell and help me find my memories. But they wouldn't do it for free.

Our gazes meet, his smirk a dead giveaway for what he's doing. He saw what I was willing to risk for that book. He knows that and much more will be available to me in Celosia.

"It's hard enough just to earn an invitation to attend," he continues. "One must either be too powerful to be slighted, weak enough for the king to slip into his pocket, or someone who intrigues him. He does so love to be entertained. And there are no second chances. Lose an invitation, or have it . . . otherwise taken from you?" His eyes skewer me, his nose crinkled. "That's shit luck."

"So now what?"

"Because we have both responded, we are locked in by blood. No going back now. To not make every attempt to attend after we've sworn otherwise is considered an offense to the Crown. The punishment is a year in the Mines. However, the invitations are just the beginning. Guests still have to earn their entry."

Details will arrive for those who are willing to play.

"There's some sort of game," I guess, understanding blooming slowly. Understanding, and a little bit of dread.

"Aye. Now tell me if you'd be so kind. What did your invitation say?"

I scowl and try a bluff. "Hang on. Why is this so important to you? I have no stakes here. I couldn't give less than a fried fuck about any of this. This is your problem."

His eyebrow quirks up. "Oh, you want to talk about problems? You killed Grays, Strider. Plural. You think they'll forget about that? I may have bought you off, but they know you now. They'll kill you on sight. And I'm sure the blackmail I resorted to doesn't help, either." He chuckles darkly to himself. "I saved you from that place, like it or not."

"Spare me the favor horseshit. You would happily slit my throat in an instant if there were a way around whatever this is."

"It would be convenient," he says almost wistfully. "Alas, you seem not to have a choice in this matter."

A serrated laugh escapes me as I cross my arms, mirroring his stance as I lean back into the chair. "I may not have a choice about some parts of this, but I can certainly choose whether I make your life a living hell or not." I let that statement sink its claws into him fully before I continue. Though he regards me with a flat glare, I can tell I have his attention at last. "We have to complete some sort of game? Or we won't get to go? You need my collaboration. What's in it for me?"

Of all things, he rolls his eyes. "I don't need your help. I just need your body at the end of this. I'll prop you up with sticks if I have to.

And you seem to be forgetting that I saved your scrawny hide from certain execution. A little thanks wouldn't hurt."

I lean forward in my seat. "I owe you nothing."

He leans forward, too. "You owe me everything."

"No. You don't understand. I will make both our lives a living, breathing hellscape if you do not provide what I want in return. I will do everything I can to sabotage your every effort. No matter what it takes, I will ensure you never get what you want, and even if you did, you'd hate it so much for what you had to go through to get it, you wouldn't want it anymore. You won't be able to stand the sight of it. This, I promise you."

After a lengthy pause, there is an austere frost to his tone. "Name your terms, you vexing she-demon."

I sit up, lacing my fingers together on the desk. "First, I have questions." He starts massaging his temples, but nods. "Why do you need this so badly?"

"Assume I have very good reasons," he drawls.

I rephrase my question. "What do you need so badly?"

"Better. But still can't answer that, love."

I scowl. "I won't be part of any trafficking, if that's what you're doing."

"It's not."

"Then what were you doing in Marrin in the first place?"

Scoffing, he swipes his hand across his stubbled chin. There's a gold ring on each of his three middle fingers. "I was investigating something. Out with your terms, Strider. I tire of this."

I raise my hand, ticking off each one on a finger. "One, you protect me. Your men will do me no harm, nor anyone else in your purview. And you most certainly won't sell me out to the Grays when we're through."

"Aye, alright. Go on."

"Two, I want my book back. And I want those too." I gesture to his overflowing collection of books. "All of them. Whenever I want."

For some reason, he seems to find that funny, but he refrains from commenting.

"And three, I want. To. Get. Paid." He snorts, but I continue on. "You're a pirate. Steal treasure or something. But I want one hundred golds in my pockets once this is through. Half up front."

He frowns. "A quarter up front."

"Half."

Our eyes lock, and for a moment, the heat from our glares is enough to sizzle the skin from my bones. But, surprisingly, he relents first.

"You will get half now. And I'll sweeten the deal, Strider, because your cooperation is that imperative to me. I'll double what you asked for. Two hundred golds. All for you. If you'll just behave."

His eyes flick over me in warning as he says the word *behave*, and I fidget in my seat. This ordeal can't be over fast enough.

"What's stopping you from killing me when this is all done?"

He laughs as if I've said something absurd. "I assure you, once this is finished, I couldn't be bothered to spit in your direction."

"Save your spit, pirate. I'll be long gone the moment the clock strikes twelve bells."

"Is that a promise? The way I see it, Strider, we have every reason to cooperate with each other. We both get what we want, and then we part ways forever. Amicably, of course."

"This is insanity," I mutter, awed into a bit of a stupor. It's so much, and this conversation is sapping my energy.

"Likely so, but I am also vowing to house you, feed you, protect you from wayward threats along the way, and then pay you an outrageous sum of coin at the end of all of this, if you'll play along for a while."

"And how exactly can you guarantee that your men won't come after me? It's no secret that some of them aren't fond of me."

"They have no choice in the matter. All crew members are Marked by me, and once an order is issued, they are obligated to comply, lest they experience a very special little hell."

"That sounds rather close to tyranny."

He merely shrugs. "It is the way of pirates. They chose to be here, all of them. And I am not an unkind leader."

Long moments pass as I soak in the details of the conversation, poring over aspects I may have missed, or ways he can exploit me. But the truth of it is, I'm already in a bad spot. It's a miracle that he agreed to any of it at all.

We shake on the terms, and the deal is done.

18

KINDNESS

"Yes, well, that brings me to my next order of business. Come with me." Blackwater rises and strides to the double doors leading to the deck, opening one of them and gesturing for me to follow.

I make no move to do such a thing. "Where are we going?"

He tsk's at me. "I am a man of my word when it suits me, darling."

"I said I'd cooperate with you. Not that I'd trust you."

"You can't have one without the other if you wish to accomplish anything. Come along now. I recall you asking for a certain book."

That gets me moving. I push my chair back and practically leap to my feet, but as I pass in front of him, he snatches my wrist to his chest. I swallow a gasp at how quickly he moved.

"Strider," he says slowly. Calmly. "Did you take something that isn't yours?"

I meet his eyes defiantly. "That's a matter of perspective."

His tone brooks no discussion. "Give it to me."

I spit the pearl earrings I'd been hiding in my mouth right into his face, but he catches them midair with his other hand, trapping them in a fist.

"Must you?" He eyes his hand with disgust.

"They'd look so good on me," I reply, "And you weren't using them anyway."

"Some of these aren't just for decoration," he chastises. "Some of these have been imbued with powerful magic. You can't run around putting them . . . in your mouth."

I don't bother looking ashamed, and he doesn't bother lecturing me any further.

"Anything else you want to return?" He eyes me warily as if he already knows the answer.

"No." I grin.

We both know I'm full of shit.

Blackwater leads me back onto the deck, past a few pirates sorting through some barrels, then below, into the web of hallways. At first, the walls echo with the raucous sounds of the crew still at supper, but as we progress, the noise fades to a pervasive silence.

"The insides of the ship don't match the outside. It's enormous in here," I muse out loud. "How?"

Blackwater only pauses to shoot me a pitying glance from over his shoulder. "I forget how destitute of magic Marrin is. In most places, magic is ubiquitous, and almost anyone can use it to perform low-level magic. This particular spell is for internal spatial expansion. It's very common with ships and buildings. Especially royal ships made in Celosia."

"I've heard of using that for smaller items, like a pocket or cellar. Never for something as massive as a ship."

"Imbued items help bolster spells, too. The more imbued objects or magical entities around, the more powerful the spell. Magic is a self-feeding system, after all."

"So, an imbued item is a magnet for more magic, then."

"Correct," he replies. I think of all the trinkets in his quarters. All the magic he must have accrued over the years.

I have limited experience with magic besides what I have read about in contraband books, so this is all new to me. It's always been a concept. A story. Never something I could reach out and touch.

"Can you imbue a person?"

Blackwater stops and turns to face me. "Certainly, although that'd be a curse. No one but Weavers should have magic in their veins, and they're born with it. Made for it. Magic is dangerous; put it in a soft, pliable human body that isn't suited for it? It'll corrode. Slowly but surely."

We turn into a new hallway.

"Why do they call you the Sea Serpent?"

He chuckles, and there's something demeaning about it. "Aren't you a curious little thing?" I shoot him a scathing glare. Don't answer then, *you tit*.

But he does.

"I imagine it has something to do with my Mark and the figurehead of my ship. The leviathan. Great, snake-like creatures that dwell in the deepest, coldest part of the sea. They keep to themselves, you see. It's exceedingly rare to find one, and if you do, well, most don't live to tell that tale."

"But you did."

"I don't take pleasure in it, but it's how I acquired The Wraith, so I also don't regret it." He shrugs. "Leviathans are loyal to no one and nothing but themselves. I've always admired that. I modeled my Captain's Mark after them, and I suppose my reputation has become a beast of its own. Many have asked for my pledge of loyalty, and many have been denied. I work for no one and nothing but my own fancies."

I don't bother hiding my eyeroll.

His eyes narrow, and he tilts his head. "What about you, Little Ghost? How did you acquire a name like that?"

I'm silent for a moment as I consider whether I wish to answer. But, I suppose, it's only fair.

"A long time ago, something happened. Something—" out of the corner of my eye, I catch a wisp of movement, but when I turn to check, there's nothing there. ". . . bad. They never caught me, but ever since then, the Grays blamed me for everything. Things they did, things other people did but never got caught for, whatever they liked. A bakery was broken into? It must have been the Ghost. The blacksmith wound up missing some high-end knives? The Ghost struck again." A bitter smile. "The funny thing is, I don't think they actually thought I was real."

I think of that Gray's reaction in the Marrin prison, when I actually knew details of the slaughtering years ago. Seven deaths, not four. The complete disbelief in his voice, and then the fury that his make-believe creature was just a gaunt, angry little girl.

There's a coy smile on Blackwater's face. "It seems like a favor, doesn't it?"

I give him a skeptical look. "How could any of this be considered a favor?"

"Simple. They made us myths. And myths live forever." He stops. "We're here."

We're standing at a door, but not just another wood-paneled one like all the rest. No, this one is a bit different. The top is rounded, and it's been stained a soft green color. A shiny brass knob juts out, and I reach out to turn it, but Blackwater grabs my wrist, stopping me.

"I wouldn't." He jerks his chin meaningfully toward the door.

"More magic?" I ask. In fact, this close to the wood, I can feel a slight difference in the air. As if it's thicker around the door. And upon closer inspection, the wood seems to *shimmer*. "The wood. It's imbued, isn't it?"

A slow sort of grin spreads across his face, as if I've pleased him. "Aye, very good. It's made using Witherwood from deep in the Grimwood."

My eyes widen. The Grimwood? Anything that survives in that place, even the trees, is bound to be a bit strange. No wonder this ship seems malevolent.

"Well, what now?" I ask.

Blackwater's grin broadens as he turns to face the door, as if greeting an old friend. "Now we enter. But it's bewitched. You must give a little of yourself for it to open."

I turn on my heel.

He laughs as he grabs my shirt and hauls me back. "No, no. I don't mean an appendage. It wants something much more valuable. A secret. It likes the taste of the unspoken. Like this." He turns to face the door and, to my great dismay, whatever Blackwater divulges is said in such a covert whisper; I do not hear it.

Whatever he said, it worked. He twists the doorknob, and the door swings open. "What did you tell it?" I ask.

"I told it I dislike it very much when ornery, sticky-fingered girls steal my things."

I scoff. "I'm not ornery."

"Take note, mind you," he continues. "Next time you come here by yourself, you will have to do the same. For now, you get in for free. My gift to you."

"It doesn't seem that difficult," I remark, following him through the doorway.

"I never said it was difficult. I said it was valuable," comes the response. Perhaps he said something else, but I stopped hearing him the moment I stepped around him to take in the room. I might have stopped breathing altogether.

We stand in a spacious room littered with worn but comfortable-looking chairs and settees, each with assorted quilts draped over their backs. Sconces and orbs cast warm, flickering light on dark floorboards, creating shadows that dance and waver. One wall is nothing but glass, allowing a view into an ominous, void-black sea. During the day, I imagine it's beautiful.

Hell, it's a strange kind of beautiful now.

I turn my attention to the rest of the walls in the room, my hands clasped tightly in front of me. I'm looking at shelves and shelves of books. More books than I've ever fathomed. Shelves so high I'd need a ladder to reach. I pace the length, entirely overwhelmed. Endless sections of encyclopedias, histories, linguistics, spells and incantations, poisons, anatomy and physiologies of any and every creature ever conceived, and . . . stories. Walls of adventures and misadventures, ghost stories and poetry. An abundance of words. I could live in this room and never tire of it.

Even the tables scattered throughout the room are stacked with leaning piles of books, as if someone couldn't choose, so they didn't.

I lovingly touch the spine of a grimoire, already yearning for whatever lies between its yellowed pages. Books are scarce for the wealthy, almost nonexistent for everyone else. Our history is almost exclusively obtained through royal decree and rumors. But to have a collection such as this?

I turn to face Blackwater with a new understanding. This much information alone could make a man exceedingly dangerous.

"The king would have your head if he knew about this." My voice comes out breathy with awe.

Blackwater, who'd meandered to a chair and stretched out like a cat, gives a careless shrug. "He can try to take it from me. We'll see how that fares for him."

I allow myself a small smile. "It's wondrous."

"Yes, it is," Blackwater agrees. "It's taken me years to cultivate the collection. Now, Strider, if you pilfer—"

"I won't," I interrupt, shaking my head vigorously. "I swear it."

His green gaze relents. "Alright, then. That being said, you may come and go as you please. If there is any particular book you're needing, just say it. The Wraith has a knack for finding what you're looking for. And she's always listening, the busybody."

For a few moments, I'm lost in the overwhelming feeling that I have just attained something I've wanted for a very long time, and now that I've got it, I'm not certain what to do. There are so many stories, and only one of me. I've never wished for a long life; in fact, at times, quite the opposite. But now, in this room, I find myself pining for more time.

I've come to stand behind a cerulean chair, my hands clamped around the high headrest. "What's in it for you?"

The pirate leans forward to brace his elbows on his knees, watching me intently. "Would you believe me if I called it a kindness?"

I study his face, taking in the shrewdness of his gaze, a challenge in the curl of his lips. His beauty is a trick. I can never let my guard down with him, even when he seems benevolent. In the end, everything he does, in some way, is self-serving. How could he have reached this level of notoriety otherwise?

I look away, resigned. "A lack of cruelty is not kindness."

Something like approval flits across his features. "Indeed. Now. I doubt you had much to work with in that wasteland, and it will benefit me for you to develop a wider understanding of magic and our history. After all, you're not in Marrin anymore, and the realm of Alvion, you'll find, is complicated. You're no help to me ignorant." His eyes flick up and down my person on the word *ignorant*, but I choose to ignore the jab. He's only needling me. And he's right. There's very much I don't know.

"I can come at any time I want?"

"Aye."

"And all I have to do is tell the door a secret?"

He scoffs, shaking his head. "It's no trivial thing, Strider. And the more you feed it, the hungrier it gets. Start small. Anything you've never spoken will do."

"Who else comes here?"

He moves to stand, brushing nonexistent dust from his pristine black trousers. "Myself and sometimes Luhan. That's all. I hope we can occupy the same space from time to time peacefully." He gives me a pointed look.

"No promises," I say, already losing interest in the conversation and gaining it elsewhere among the shelves, so I didn't particularly notice or care when he selected a book from the pile in front of him until he placed it in my hands.

Binding Spells, Potions, and Curses by Marguerite Thorne

I'd been so surprised by the library, I'd forgotten why I came here in the first place. I can only stare, the words I want to say eluding me.

"Not sure why you were so eager for this book. I was quite bored with it, although you do seem quite interested in curses, Strider."

"I am interested in a lot of subjects," I reply. Hugging the gigantic book close to my chest like a child would a doll, I prowl over to a particular section of interest: poison. It's my sincere hope that Blackwater gets the hint and leaves, but instead, I hear quiet footsteps coming near. Every hair on my arm raises, my heartbeat ratcheting. My spine goes ramrod straight, and my fingers yearn for a blade, but I don't turn around.

"Before I go," he croons, his voice so close to my ear I can feel his breath on my neck. "There's one last thing."

While his left hand grips the sensitive juncture between my neck and shoulder, his right hand, starting from the ridge of my hip, meanders up my side to my ribs. I watch, my breath measured though my insides writhe, as his hand slips smoothly into my hidden internal vest pockets and pulls out the slender gold band I nicked earlier from his quarters.

I run my tongue over my teeth, disappointment sour in my belly. I genuinely liked that one. And then Blackwater surprises me again.

I feel the cold bite of something on my skin and look down with alarm to see him clamping it there, at the top of my bicep. The gold glitters in the soft orblight, the color bringing a bit of warmth to my ivory skin. I try to face him, but he stops me by grabbing the back of my neck, effectively pinning me in place, facing the shelves. The pad of his thumb presses hard against my spine. A warning.

"I told you not to touch me," I murmur.

"I told you not to steal from me again," he replies.

His grip tightens around the back of my neck, then releases. I whirl on him, glaring, but he merely leans against the shelving, his head angled to the side. "You're not in Marrin anymore, Little Ghost. There are rules now. My rules. But for now, keep this as a down payment. Gold suits you."

Of all the things I expected him to say, it wasn't that. I frown down at the band, studying it. "You're serious?"

He smiles wolfishly. "It matches your eyes."

Shrugging him off, I cross the room to claim a green velvet chair. It's large, soft, and accommodates me easily as I pull my feet underneath me. Blackwater watches me as I do so, hands shoved in his pockets, a smug expression on his face.

"Anything else?" I snap.

He rocks back on his heels. "It's so wonderful to see you appeased."

"So generous of you."

He clicks his tongue. "I'll leave you to it, then. Learn about the world, Strider. After all, you live in it now."

Become useful to me, is what he means to say.

He delivers a small, sharp smile before turning on his heel and slipping from the room, leaving me with too many words and never enough time.

19

PIRATES AND THEIR OPINIONS

The next few days are measured in chapters. And secrets.

Blackwater was right: every day, the door is hungrier for a bigger secret. I started small by telling inconsequential things I'd never told anyone, like my intense dislike of insects of any sort. The fact that I've never experienced a thunderstorm. I'd never learned to swim.

Today, I've never been kissed. It's always seemed so trivial. I never cared. It always seemed far more intimate than . . . other things. *Other things*, I have done.

And yet, when I whisper the words, my cheeks blaze.

"And if I catch you uttering a word of this to anyone, I'll hack you up into splinters," I add hurriedly after it creaks open.

Proctor above. I'm threatening inanimate objects. I walk a few steps, stop, then shuffle backward.

"I won't hack you into splinters. But I will deny it. Keep that in mind."

Yes. Feeling better about that one.

Binding Spells, Potions, and Curses has been a disappointment so far, at least for my purposes. While I have learned some curses, it has not helped me determine what is etched across my shoulder blades, how to undo it, or whether I want to undo it. I don't want to just break the bond. I want to kill it.

From what I've been able to cobble together over the past several years, curses are contingent on the act of imbuing either the person directly or an object that, ideally, is always close to the victim. What sets curses apart from simple spells or charms, though, is the fact that they leave a mark. And so, it would make sense that if the curse caster wanted to be discreet about it, cursing an object, rather than a person, is the superior approach. I gather that when it came to me, the caster couldn't have given a fuck about subtlety. And what makes understanding my curse difficult is that every individual speaks to and uses magic in their own way.

While curses themselves are universal, the language used to cast them depends on the curse caster. And if it was a Curse Speaker, who did it—a Weaver who can cast and read curses innately—then the curse will be all the more difficult to parse, and harder still to negate. So, while I can learn the mechanics behind curses all I want, it doesn't shed much light on the darkness trailing me, or what I can possibly do to dispel it.

My shadow acts of its own volition, usually when my emotions are running high, and every time it acts out, it seems stronger than the time before. I am on a countdown to find a way to stop it before something else happens.

I cannot let what happened all those years ago repeat.

And so, I devour every book that might be remotely useful to me. And while I learn a lot about other things, I learn nothing of my predicament.

A long time ago, I thought I must be a Weaver. But as I've

gradually pieced together stories and accounts of how Weaving works, and especially after my conversation with Luhan, I've discarded that idea. Weavers are born with their own unique magic coursing through their veins. It has nothing to do with symbols or markings. Conversely, whatever it is that plagues me has everything to do with what is written on my back. I don't know why else they would burn as they do whenever my shadow comes to life. If I could just understand how or what it means, I could free myself. I could save myself.

Ten nights have passed since the deal was struck, and so far, I have spent each one in the solitude of the library. The days pass quickly now that I can mull over the information I'm able to glean here. Sometimes, my eyes snag on the band on my arm, but I don't take it off, although half the time, I come close.

There are a few times each night that I doze off, always unintentionally, but I haven't woken up screaming. I do dream, though. However, the intensity of the nightmares has lessened for the time being, somehow quelled by the gentle rustle of pages and undulating candle flame. It has helped to have a shred of something familiar when everything else I've ever known has been ripped away.

More pirates have joined Luhan and me at supper. Basi is the name of the pirate I have kitchen duty with, although that is all the information I have gleaned about him. I think he's started to sit with us because neither of us tries to talk to him. We ignore him, but in a kind and respectful way.

Tonight, Basi has joined us along with three others: twins, by the look of them, which is to say, the same exact look, named Arjun and Ishaan. Though they share a long, straight nose and inquisitive eyes, Arjun wears round spectacles, and his dark hair sprouts up in manic tufts.

In contrast, Ishaan is rather neat. It comes to my attention quickly that Ishaan either can't speak or chooses not to, for his hands are always making rapid gestures that only his brother understands. Arjun seems more than happy to interpret, although he has more than enough to say all by himself.

A hard-looking man named Jon sits on the other side of Luhan. The top three buttons of his shirt are undone, and I notice a menacing tattoo of some snake-like sea creature over his heart. It must be the Mark that Blackwater mentioned—what binds the crew to him.

"You two finally reach an agreement?" Luhan asks me quietly, interrupting my reverie.

"If you want to call it that," I respond between chews. "I assumed he'd have told you already."

Luhan bobs his head from side to side. "He did. Although he was quite short about it all. I was hoping to get a better story from you."

"You seem rather entertained by all this."

His smile is nothing short of ebullient. "Liam is flummoxed by you. I'm enjoying it immensely."

"Hmm," I hum idly as I take a bite of a potato. "He's generously given me permission to visit the library."

"Brave of him. What have you been reading about?"

"Curses."

The smile falters. "Wonderful."

Another voice asks, "And what interest do you have in curses, Iona?"

I look up sharply to see Arjun watching me keenly, and a defensive flush creeps up the back of my neck.

"I like knowing how things work."

He nods, sharing a knowing glance with his brother. "It's all so interesting, isn't it? Shame, how little magic is left in Marrin. One doesn't realize how much of an influence magic has on everyday occurrences until one visits a place like that. No change of seasons— very little variation in the weather at all, scarcity of crops, weaker spells, charms, and enchantments . . . just grim."

I don't have much to add to that, which doesn't matter anyway, for he opens his mouth to say more but stops when Ishaan signs something to him, then glances toward me.

"Ishaan wants to know how long you lived there," He translates.

I look to Ishaan as I say, "As long as I can remember."

A look I don't understand passes between them—approval? But that doesn't make sense. They clearly pity anyone who lives without magic. And perhaps I would feel the same if I'd known different circumstances. But I didn't, and I don't want their pity. And if they know so much, they may as well be of use.

"There were these blackberry bushes in the forest, once. But they're all gone now. All fruit-producing bushes and trees in Marrin died a few years ago. Why?"

"Lack of magic," Arjun answers immediately. "Magic comes from the land, you know. It's been that way since the First Sovereigns ruled. The crowns they wore, the ones that the five rulers still wear today? The land bore them all for the First Sovereigns to wear. And so, when magic gets scarce, land is the first to suffer. Especially the further away it is from one of the crowns. Marrin is very far south of Celosia, and so . . ." He lets me connect the dots and shrugs. "It can't be helped. There isn't as much magic as there used to be."

"Why has it changed?"

I notice the whole table is listening now, including the ever-aloof Basi.

Arjun glances over to Ishaan, who signs rapidly, then looks to me, his expression shrewd. "Tell me this. How many Talents in Marrin?"

I blink. "Talents?"

"Erm," Arjun hesitates, but Luhan interjects.

"He means Weavers, Iona."

My mouth opens, then closes, then opens again. "I have no idea. No one talks about it, or they get taken."

They get taken anyway.

"If you had to guess," Arjun prods, leaning forward.

I glance at Luhan, remembering our last conversation about Weavers. "If I had to guess, quite a bit."

A corner of Arjun's mouth lifts, and this time, I know he's amused. "And why is that, Miss Iona Strider?"

"Because I can't think of another reason De'Havelin would send a squadron full of Grays to completely take over the place. They arrived one day years ago and never left. They said it was to take over control of imported goods, but I never quite believed it. They watched us so closely. Why do you ask about Weavers?"

Arjun goes to answer, but Ishaan stops him with a hand to his chest. He shakes his head, gesturing to me. In sync, they both turn to me. "Ishaan says you know the answer."

I stare at them both blankly, and down the table, Jon barks out a laugh. "Don't be demeaning, you two. Tell the girl what she wants to know."

But they ignore him, tilting their heads, and I mull over the information until the answer blooms like a flower. I lick my lips, frowning. I had asked where the magic is going, if it isn't in the land anymore. And he brought up Weavers . . .

It clicks.

"You're implying the magic has . . . left the land and seeped into people instead? That's why Weavers are being born?"

Ishaan's expression is triumphant, while Arjun's borders on sly. But I only have more questions. "You said magic was originally from the land. Why does proximity to a crown matter, then?"

Arjun's smile becomes slick. "That's it. You're asking some dangerous questions, you know." He leans in. "Story has it the land made the First Sovereigns their crowns. Magic was so abundant, the land so plentiful, that magic rewarded them for their rule by forging itself into crowns, so that as long as they ruled in harmony, there shall be prosperity and balance. But the First Sovereigns couldn't live forever, although they did live for centuries. A gift from the crowns, you see. That is why there used to be ubiquitous magic. But over the years, wars and alliances, deaths and betrayals drove their successors apart, and now, they all govern their realms alone. There are no more alliances, only distrust and greed. And that affected the magic. Now, it varies widely. Dangerously abundant in some places, while all too thin in others. Things have changed."

I don't have much to say to that. I knew the story of the First Sovereigns, but I'd never thought to connect the loss of access to other realms to the loss of consistent magic here.

"And what about you? Do you know about Weaving, Miss Iona?"

I meet Arjun's gaze fiercely. "No. I don't. Stop asking me that."

The brothers share a glance again, and I notice Arjun give an almost imperceptible nod as if I passed some sort of test. My scowl deepens.

"Do I meet your standards?" I ask, and beside me, Luhan looks away, snorting. To my surprise, I catch stoic-as-a-statue Basi trying and failing to stifle a small smile.

"No standards, only curiosity," Arjun replies, palms up. "You don't strike us as a common pickpocket. You don't talk like one, either."

"Pleased to surpass your expectations," I intone. "I'll use words with fewer syllables next time to make myself more digestible for you."

This time, Luhan can't stop his delighted laughter. "Arjun, you're more of a snob than I am. Shut the hell up." That gets a chuckle out of Jon, too.

Ishaan grins widely while Arjun's eyes widen in mock alarm. "Not possible, Luhan. If your nose were any higher in the air, you'd have a crick in your neck." Then he turns to me, dark eyes glinting with mischief. "I like you, Miss Iona. I meant no offense."

"What about you two, then?" I point my fork at them, and it comes perilously close to Arjun's nose. "Do you do anything special?"

It still feels strange to ask the question aloud, but they talk of it so casually here, I'm going to have to get used to it.

They blink at the same time, and I repress a shudder. Twins.

Arjun looks to Ishaan, mulls over whatever it is that his brother signed, then looks back to me, his eyes dark and thoughtful. "Well, Ishaan is what we call back home, an Escalator. Emotions are his specialty. And as for me, well." He smiles widely, displaying white, straight teeth. "I deal in truths and lies, Miss Strider. I taste them on my tongue, sweet and sour."

He must see the surprise widening my eyes, for he chuckles. "Why the fear? You are sweet as blackberries. Or did I not ask the right questions?"

My smile feels tight on my lips. So, it was a test. I should have known. I'm sure Blackwater put him up to it. "I suppose you'll just have to see."

His eyes flicker with challenge, but he seems to decide against it. "I harbor no ill will. I am merely ensuring the safety of my ship." He looks about covertly for a few moments, then leans in close, whispering under his breath. Ishaan observes with a knowing expression.

"The wisest thing you can do is ask questions, Miss Strider. Remember that."

It's late, very late, when someone knocks on the door of the library.

Three knocks in such quick, harried succession immediately set me on edge. I wait, hoping that perhaps it was a mistake, but then a voice calls urgently from the other side, "Iona? Iona, are you in there?" Whoever it is sounds out of breath, as if they ran all the way here.

I rise and pull two blades from my ribs, but make no move toward the door. "Who wants to know?"

The voice is familiar, but I can't place it. "Come at once. Captain's orders."

I step a bit closer, clutching my blades in both hands. "Why?"

There's a note of exasperation in his voice now. "Look, we don't have much time. You must come now. It's Luhan."

Luhan?

Bounding across the library, I fling open the door to find Jon, the pirate from tonight's supper. "What happened?" I ask, my heart kicking hard against my ribs.

Jon offers me a bland smile. In his hand, he's holding a vial of dark, viscous liquid. "Drink this." Three strange things happen then, all at once.

The first being two other men step into frame, both of whom I recognize. One of them is Garrith, the gap-toothed man who was calling for my removal from the ship. The other is the man with long, stringy hair. Ulric, I believe. I've seen him skulking around with Garrith.

Second, Jon's shirt is still unbuttoned, but the Mark over his heart no longer depicts a writhing sea serpent, but a skull with a gaping mouth that gives the impression it's screaming.

And third, I do it. Like a puppet on strings, I lift the vial to my lips. And I would have drunk it, spurred by some sort of compulsion I can't understand, if my shadow hadn't intervened.

20

A LITTLE TWIST

One moment, I'm lifting the vial to my mouth, the next, my shadow rips it away and flings the liquid into Jon's face. The burning in my shoulders threatens to bowl me over, and I stumble back, reeling.

It's been years since the shadow has done something like this.

Jon's agonized shrieks ring in my ears as he shoves me away to claw at his ruined eyes. Blood streaks down his cheeks, staining his hands dark. Garrith lunges to run me through with his sword, but I miss it by a moment, kicking it aside, and ram a blade to the hilt through his right forearm. He jerks back, howling, as Ulric swipes at me with some sort of curved blade. A scimitar?

"Kill her, Ulric," Garrith bellows.

I spring away, but not before Ulric opens a gash on my hip. With a banshee scream, I flick a blade, and then another. The first finds a home in his left shoulder, the second in his right. It surprises him enough to buy me a few seconds to run for the door.

I've only managed a few steps before Ulric charges me, swiping his sword low in an undercut intended to slash my shins clean in half. I manage to get off the ground in a sloppy leap, but a fist finds my gut mid-air and knocks the wind out of me. I land sprawled on the ground, and a vicious kick sends me skittering across the floor and into the wall, wheezing.

I see the shadow before I see the man.

Rough fingers wrap around my neck and hoist me up, up, until my feet are kicking helplessly in the air. Pitiless, bloodshot eyes glare at me as I start to choke.

Nearby, Garrith has finally jerked the knife from his arm and watches from a few paces away with cold amusement. Somewhere in the room, Jon is still screaming about his fucking eyes. Desperately, I cast about for anything, anything at all to use, but there's nothing nearby except for—

A stool.

Instead of kicking out, I muster all my strength and kick hard behind me, against the wall. Ulric takes a step back to catch us, but trips over the stool, sending us both toppling to the floor. This time, I'm ready. By the time we hit the ground, I've plunged a blade into his chest and given it a little twist.

But I'm not finished. I jerk it out, then shove it in again, and again, and again, until his chest is more holes than flesh, and my hands are coated up to my elbows in gore.

As I slowly rise, I catch sight of Garrith standing there, gawking. Mouth gaping like a fish. I doubt he imagined that it would be difficult to kill me, or that he'd watch one of his companions die tonight.

Well. They should have left me be.

I draw another dagger so that I'm holding one in each hand, and point the one in my left toward Garrith's chest.

Beneath me, my shadow spreads like a pool of blood until, one by one, the gentle lights of the library sputter and die. The darkness that envelops us is complete. I'd never beat a man like this in a fair match. But they set the rules themselves when they tried to poison me, so I feel no guilt playing a few tricks of my own. The marks on my back flare to life, and I grimace through the scorch of them. In this instance, I welcome the pain. Though I may burn, I become powerful.

And in this darkness of my own making, I can see perfectly fine.

With gritted teeth, I rush the pirate, hacking at all that exposed, soft flesh. I can't stay put long enough to deal a death blow, so instead I prance around the giant, delivering slice after slice to his arms, back, torso, until his entire body is covered in gashes weeping red tears. Death by a thousand cuts. And the bitch of it all is, this man could be covered in slices and bruises, and these hands would never tire of dealing more. The gouges between my shoulder blades blaze hotter, and with it, my fury. I am a pyre that burns and burns and burns.

"What devilry is this?" Garrith screams, his face mottled with rage as he lunges, his sword arcing wildly. "What are you?"

He swipes wildly, but I've already sprung away. I duck beneath a frantic slash, lunging with my own blade and smiling with satisfaction when it opens another gash on his forearm.

I'm forced to duck, wincing as the tip of his sword slices into my shoulder, then pivot sharply to avoid another relentless blow. He's getting faster, not slowing down.

Perhaps I am not the only one fueled by fury. If that is the case, this must end. I glance down at my blades, to the shake of fatigue in my hands that signals the beginning of the finale.

Sucking down a deep breath, I scuff my boot against the floor. The pirate stiffens, then rushes for me. I meet his charge, but at the last moment, I turn sharply, slide under his outstretched blade, and haul myself onto his back, intending to slit his throat and finish it. With my legs squeezing his sides and my blades so close to gifting him a ruby necklace, I can almost believe I'm going to survive. But when a hand twists around, grabs me by the neck, and hurls me across the room, that fragile hope gutters out like a candle.

Fortune has never favored little spiders.

When I open my eyes, the walls are pulsing in and out, wavering. I realize, too slowly, he hurled me all the way out of the library and into the hallway.

He's upon me before I can stand. He kicks me hard—once in the chest, once in my stomach. Curling in on myself, I reach for a dagger —my last one—but he kicks it out of my hand, sending it skittering across the floor. When I lunge for it, the heel of his boot comes crashing down on my knuckles.

I have the span of a heartbeat to steel myself for the pain before he grinds the bones of my right hand into sharp little pieces.

My vision crackles, and my ragged scream rends a hole in my chest.

"That was for Ulric." He twists his heel, and unbearable agony lances up my arm. "That was for Jon. And this—" he bends down to press cold steel against my throat. A trickle of blood runs down my sternum. "—is for The Vice, who ordered you dead the moment we told him about you."

My eyes close.

But the sword never completes its path. It shudders against my skin as Garreth makes a strange, gurgling noise. Blood spurts onto my face and neck, and my eyes snap open to behold the glistening point of a black sword jutting out from his gut. But before I can make sense of it, it's gone, and I wonder if I'm already dead and this is hell. But then a horrible, sluicing sound echoes through the hallway, and Garrith's body slumps to one side, while his head rolls to the other.

Behind him, Liam Blackwater sheaths his blade as he glares at the corpse with scorching contempt. His eyes practically glow through the gloom, his face pale with wrath. He kicks the body aside, lip curling, and then his eyes latch onto mine.

He kneels before me and grips my chin, but I jerk away from his touch. He told me they'd heed him. He lied. And if he lied about this, he has lied about more. All anyone ever does is lie, betray, and hurt, and I can never forget it. I'll never forget it.

"What happened?" His voice is low and urgent, his eyes poring over me, taking in my mangled hand, the blood that is both mine and not mine. The bouquet of bruises and fresh, weeping cuts.

"Your dogs. They got loose."

Blackwater narrows his eyes, first at me, then toward the library, once again alight as if nothing is amiss. As if there aren't one and a half corpses in there, bleeding on the furniture. Without a word, he leans down to slide one arm beneath my knees, another beneath my arms, and lifts me. I cradle my hand to my chest as bitter tears slide down my face. It hurts.

Footsteps rapidly approach, and Luhan emerges from the shadows, looking harried, like he'd run the entire way. His hair, normally perfectly in place, is as disheveled as I've ever seen it. The color drains from his face as he takes in my current state and the decapitated corpse on the floor. He peers inside the library, drawn by Jon's agonized whimpers, and shudders at what he beholds.

"Moons above, Liam."

"Take her to my quarters. I'll be up shortly."

Luhan hesitates. "Not her room?"

"No," Blackwater snaps. "Do what I say. Go."

Blackwater, with more gentleness than I'd have expected, transfers me to a stricken Luhan before unsheathing his sword, striding into the library, and slamming the door shut behind him. And though Luhan wastes no time rushing toward the deck, no pain would be great enough to stop my satisfied smile when fresh, agonized screams start leaking from the library.

21

TENDERNESS

For a few moments, I go elsewhere. My senses recede, my thoughts scatter, and while I'm aware of the bobbing sensation of being carried down the hallway, I don't really process it. I am vaguely aware of the soft hum of Luhan's voice, but it's as if I'm underwater, and I can't seem to make out any actual words. At some point, my gaze sinks down to my blood-sticky hands, and suddenly they are all around me.

The dead.

I don't look up, but I feel it when one of them comes close enough to whisper in my ear. I squeeze my eyes tight, but her rough, long-dead skin scrapes over mine, eliciting a violent shudder.

"You can't help it, can you, Iona?" She asks.

That's how I come back to myself. Screaming.

I wriggle and flail out of Luhan's hold, half catch myself when I fall, then scuttle away to plaster myself against the wall. I wish more than anything that the shadows would take me away. Far, far away from this place. I slide down to the floor, cradling my hand.

"Iona—"

"Go away," I shriek, my vision blurry. "Take me back to my room. Just take me back."

I squint at Luhan's approaching shadow, wavering in the dim light, and look up to find that he's got his hands up, palms facing me. He looks sad, though his voice is steady as always.

"Easy." He takes another step toward me, and my whole body tenses to bolt. "You're hurt. I need to ge—"

"Fuck. Off."

He sinks to a crouch. "You need healing, Iona. Now."

With my good hand, I clutch the front of his shirt and bring him close. My arm is shaking, and I can't seem to catch my breath. "How can I trust you? How can I trust any of you?"

I look down at my broken hand, my fingers like little snapped twigs, and suddenly my chin starts to tremble, and my eyes burn.

"My hand," I sob, a great, heaving thing.

Arms wrap around me, and I press my face into Luhan's shirt, grateful to hide my tears. It does nothing to help the shaking, though.

"Don't worry. I'll fix your hand. I'll fix all of it." His embrace tightens, and he makes slow, reassuring circles between my shoulder blades. I clutch him to me, tears soaking through his clean shirt, and time passes as my breath slows. But I can't stop thinking about how I just . . . did what Jon told me to. Renewed horror at my bizarre obedience almost drowns me.

"Jon had poison. He told me to drink it and I . . . I almost did," I say in a stunned whisper. I hear—and feel—Luhan sigh. "Without a second thought, even though I knew—"

"Jon could compel people."

It takes me a moment to understand.

"It wasn't your fault. He was a Weaver, as you call it."

Oh.

It's less a word and more a release of breath and pure emotion. I don't know what I thought had happened—it was too quick. I suppose deep, deep down, I knew he had forced me to do it, but a man with the power to force anyone to comply with his whims with just a word? That's . . . I can't comprehend that right now.

I should be dead.

"How are you still alive if he told you to drink the poison?"

I decide to lie. I hardly understand the shadow myself, and I wouldn't know how to begin to explain it to someone else. I've seen it do that before—affect corporeal things, although it itself is just a shadow. If I have an object in my possession, it can be affected by the shadow as well, though it rarely happens. It can affect others, too, if it touches their shadows. If I am holding a knife, and my shadow can reach someone else's shadow, it can stab them with it. I've seen it.

"My hand shook, and it splashed the poison in his eyes first."

I hear him inhale sharply. "Thank the moons. But I'm so sorry, Iona."

I don't want an apology. I want a few hours alone with Jon and my blades. "He said it was for The Vice." His grip tightens.

"Luhan," I pull away and look hard into his eyes. "Who is The Vice, and why does he want me dead?"

A sigh escapes him as he pushes his hair back. "Let's get your hand dealt with, and then we'll talk."

I don't budge, though my hand is screaming. "Please."

He slides a hand along my shoulder blades, helping me to my feet, but when he moves to pick me up, I recoil. "They didn't fucking hobble me." Squeezing my eyes shut, I try again. Softer this time. "I can walk."

Luhan raises his hands in surrender, but his hand hovers around my arm and back in case I decide to crumple to the ground. As we climb the stairs, he responds, "You are owed answers, yes, but the man to give them to you is a bit busy at the moment. He'll be along shortly, and then you can ask him all you want."

The moment we enter Blackwater's quarters, Luhan ushers me to the bed. I balk, making a face. "Not there," I protest, digging my heels in when I see where he's leading me.

He sighs. "What I'm about to do is going to hurt. Trust me, you're going to want to be somewhere comfortable."

Fear clogs my throat. "Am I going to lose consciousness?"

His mouth flattens into a grim line. "Most likely. The small bones hurt the worst. Hurry, now. We wasted enough time as it is."

Sucking in a deep, shaky breath, I climb onto the right side of the bed as Luhan pulls up a stool. His face is wan, his eyes drawn and tight.

Very lightly, his fingers brush against my bad hand, which is rapidly taking on a purple-bluish hue and swelling. More tears leak from my eyes at the mere sight of it. I turn away, so he can't see how hard I have to grit my teeth to keep from whimpering.

"I have to touch it to feel the breaks and guide the bones back together properly. I'm sorry, Iona. This is going to hurt like hell."

I squeeze my eyes shut. "Do it."

Thankfully, I lose consciousness fairly quickly, although not before experiencing the sensation of someone pulverizing my hand. Bone by broken bone, by the very same candlelight that illuminated the conversation in which Blackwater promised his men could not harm me.

I waver in and out of wakefulness, and it becomes hard to tell between hallucinations and reality.

At some point, death sits beside me, a steadfast companion. His voice is velvet and low as he murmurs to me, only me, while his eyes burn feverishly bright through the haze. They are not red or black, but the lush green of life itself. His hands hover over me, as if uncertain, and then finally settle on cleaning the dried blood from my neck, my face, my arms with a damp cloth.

Death is tender to those he has been waiting for.

His eyes flick up to something I cannot see, and his mouth sets.

"It's my fault," he whispers. His head falls into his hands. "I'm so sorry." Agony spurts up my arm, and then I am lost in another dream.

22

POISONOUS DREAMS

I am going to get into so much trouble.

I cannot believe I allowed these numbskulls to talk me into this.

Vesper glances behind her, her dark eyes honeyed by the afternoon suns. The shadows of the Grimwood caress us as we delve deeper into the forest. Trees whisper and shiver as birds trill, leaping among the branches above our heads. Tiny, unseen creatures rustle inside piles of leaves, and a frog makes a high-pitched chirp as we pass by a stream. Magic, like a cool breeze, brushes against my skin, an ever-present reminder that we are no longer in Savastane, and haven't been for four years now.

Time flies when one is doing things they shouldn't. I wish Holland could have come, but his maid said he wasn't feeling well today.

"V, you said it wasn't far," I chide, skin prickling as we delve deeper and deeper into the forest. It's not strictly forbidden, per se. There is no line of demarcation beyond which one cannot pass. But the Grimwood is like the ocean. Best to keep by the shoreline, where it is shallow. Swim out too far, and one runs the risk of drowning. Or getting eaten by a lurking beastie.

And there are many beasties in the Grimwood.

"I thought it was right here," Silas mutters, his silver-blond hair almost blinding me as it catches a patch of sunlight. He walks in a circle, hands on his narrow hips, frowning deeply as his eyes scour the immediate area.

"I did too," Vesper echoes from behind a tree. Underbrush crunches beneath her boots as she tromps around. "Artie, we swear. There was this tree, and it definitely had a Witch Mark on it."

I whirl to face her, eyes wide with disbelief. "A Witch Mark? And you brought me? You should have told King De'Havelin immediately."

"Well, but Artie," Vesper says slowly, making pointed eye contact with her partner-in-idiocy.

"We could tell it was old. And witches aren't harming anyone out here. We merely thought it was intriguing."

I let loose an exasperated sigh. "Right. How could you tell it was old?"

They share a blank look. "The bark," Silas retorts with all the confidence of a young prince. "It was clearly very old."

I can see the regret in their faces clear as day, and though we're seven years apart, I feel decades older than Vesper at this moment. I open my mouth to order them to turn back to the castle when Silas lets out a victorious whoop, and he and Vesper take off. Huffing an annoyed breath, I give chase through the thick foliage, ducking underneath branches and dodging thorns.

"Here it is! I knew it was close," Silas calls.

"I knew it was farther east," Vesper replies.

"I don't recall that being voiced, *ward*."

"You just didn't hear me, *Your Highness*."

"I don't remember these berries being here."

"You don't remember anything, Silas."

"Hm. These look delicious."

I follow their voices to finally emerge into a little clearing. Vesper and Silas stand triumphantly beneath a wide brim of branches bearing yellow leaves. And though I'd love to stare at the pretty canopy above us, it's the trunk my eyes seek. Gnarled, wizened bark coats the tree, and just there, true to their words, are strange, harsh symbols carved by what could very well have been nails. Actually, there are two sets of markings.

Wait.

I step closer.

The second set of symbols can't be Witch Markings. Because if they were, I wouldn't be able to read it. But I can read these very well.

Someone has cursed this place. With poison.

"DON'T EAT ANYTHING," I screech, turning in time to see Silas swallow, then freeze. Two dark purple berries fall from his hand and roll away. His eyes widen, and Vesper goes white as a ghost.

"Silas?" Terror has both hands wrapped around her throat, strangling her words.

"I'm alright," he says in a shaky voice. "I don't feel anything. I—"

His eyes roll up in his head, and he drops to the ground, jerking. Vesper's scream tears through the air as she drops beside him, her hands hovering over the poor boy's body.

"What do we do? Artie, what do we do?" She shrieks.

I cast about wildly for a solution, my hands clamped over my mouth. Every curse has a way to break it. It's the balance. There has to be a balance . . .

"Vesper, I need you to think," I say, coming to kneel beside her. "Those berries, they weren't here yesterday?"

Her chin trembles. "I don't remember them, but I—"

I shake my head sharply. "Listen. And yesterday, how many sets of markings on the tree?"

Her head whips to the right, and I can see her mind scrambling to work through the panic. "There was only the first. I know it. The second set is new." She looks at me with fear in her eyes. "Someone came after we left and cursed it, didn't they?"

I nod gravely, but don't have time to explain more. The whites of Silas's eyes are a gruesome sight, and his face is starting to turn purple. We have but moments before it will look very much like we murdered the prince.

"Fast, V," I pant, standing. "Is there anything around us you didn't notice yesterday? Any flowers, leaves, anything?"

She mirrors my movement, her eyes darting here and there as she clenches and unclenches her hands. I've no doubt she understands how dire this is, and how bad it will look if Silas dies alone in a forest with two Savastanian girls.

In jerky, halting movements, she totters around, examining various bushes and plants. On the ground, Silas is silent.

And still.

They're going to execute us.

If we can't save him, we are to die.

"This," Vesper shouts, ripping some orange flowers from the ground and scattering my secret thoughts. "This wasn't here."

Without a moment to spare, she places them in my hand, and I shove them in Silas's mouth, praying to any god that will listen that we aren't too late. Vesper collapses beside me, finally letting herself cry.

Silas does nothing. He's stopped breathing. Proctor, don't take this boy. Don't take him.

Vesper takes him in her arms, rocking him back and forth. "Please," she beseeches no one in particular. "Please."

My face falls into my hands. We've ruined the alliance Vesper's parents worked so hard to make. It's all ruined.

A wet, ragged cough has me jerking my head up to find Silas lurching forward.

On all fours, he violently vomits up a stream of dark purple gook as Vesper tearfully pats him on the back. Our eyes meet, and I could faint from relief.

"What happened?" Silas asks in a hoarse voice, once it seems he's expelled not only the poison, but also everything he's eaten in his entire lifetime.

"You almost died," Vesper sobs, covering her face in her hands. "Someone poisoned the berries by cursing the tree, and you almost died."

Silas glares at the tree, the outrage clear on his face. "How do you know it's cursed?" To that, Vesper says nothing.

"How do you know?" He repeats in the tone of someone not used to repeating themself. His eyes narrow on her accusingly, and I cannot stand it.

Unreported Weaving is a punishable offense. And I've been hiding it right under their noses. But I couldn't bear to leave Vesper. What if the king were to send me elsewhere because of it? I can't leave Vesper alone. I can't.

And so, I never told a soul besides Vesper what I can do. Not until now. "It's not her," I say softly. "It's me, Your Highness. I'm a Curse Speaker."

His shrewd gaze comes to settle on me, and I suddenly resent the impassivity they ingrain in royalty. He is most likely calling to mind what it means, exactly, to be a Curse Speaker. While anyone can cast a curse, they are usually small things. Simple things. Bad luck. Nightmares. Even something like this, poison, isn't too terribly complex a curse to cast. I doubt it was someone like me who did it. But it's the same logic as Weavers.

Someone casting a curse from a book cannot compare to a Curse Speaker, who can interpret any cursed language and craft curses of their own. Curses that linger, fester, and are far harder to break. Yes, a curse that comes from a tainted soul is far more fearsome than one that comes from a book. For this reason, people like me keep their talents a secret.

I have no wish for anyone to fear me. I've never cast a curse in my life and never intend to.

Long moments pass, and I feel I may wilt under Silas's scrutiny, when finally, he rises, sinks to one knee, and throws his arms around me.

"Your secret is safe with me," he says in my ear. "You saved my life. I cannot thank you enough."

My eyes burn, and beyond him, Vesper starts to cry all over again, her face splotchy and red.

Silas releases me to stand on wobbly legs, and Vesper rises to support him. "Explain to me what happened," he commands, always the haughty prince, even after a near-death experience. But there's a slight tremor in his words, and his lips are pale.

I approach the tree, hesitant to touch it. "There are two sets of symbols here, you see. One of them I cannot read. This," I point to what must be the Witch Marks, "is what you two saw yesterday?"

They nod, both faces drawn.

"And this is new?" I point to the second. More nods.

"The second set is a curse," I say. "It means poison. I just . . . didn't see until you'd already . . ."

My eyes fall to the ground, but Silas makes a noise in his throat that draws them back up. "No matter. You sorted it out when it mattered, didn't you? Please continue."

Beside him, Vesper beams at me with red, watery eyes.

"Well, curses, as with magic, only work in balance. If someone casts a curse, a way to undo it must also be nearby. So, in your case, if there is poison, there is also an antidote."

His silvery brows etch deep lines in his young face. For only a boy, he frowns like he's suffered one hundred years. And he's always possessed a cleverness beyond his youth. "Always?"

"Always."

He studies me a moment, as if he's seeing me for the first time. "What does casting a curse exact, Artemisia?"

He's referring to the symmetry again. To cast a curse, one has to give something up in exchange. Or suffer an affliction of equal measure. And curses are much more punishing than mundane spells. It's an astute question for a child. He's going to make a fearsome ruler one day.

"It depends on the curse. Whoever cast this one, for example, may have gotten violently sick afterwards. There is always a push and a pull, a rhyme for a reason, and so forth."

For a moment, his careful mask slips, and for some reason, the young prince Silas looks on the verge of tears. But the moment passes, and his carefully cultivated demeanor slips back into place.

"You're not asking the right questions, Silas," Vesper interjects.

He turns to face her, his silvery eyes gleaming. "Oh? And what is that, then?"

"Someone tried to kill you and frame me," she snaps. "Don't you see what this looks like? Someone followed us and knew we'd return."

His expression goes slack as his eyes flit back and forth between us, and I hold my breath until finally, he reaches a decision.

"No one will speak of this. Ever. Understand?" Vesper nods immediately, but I hesitate.

"Your father should know—" I start, but Silas cuts me off.

"He can never know," he argues emphatically. "No one in my family. Not a soul. Swear to it."

His eyes bore into mine, an unrelenting barrage of silver ice. "Yes, Your Highness," I whisper. "I swear."

I keep my word, but I don't quite understand.

23

PICKING A FIGHT WITH THE WIND ITSELF

M y eyelids flutter open to find Luhan still sitting beside me, staring at my hand. It's been bandaged, and when one of my fingers inadvertently twitches, it sends a shooting pain up my arm that elicits a nasty curse.

"Welcome back, princess," Luhan murmurs, taking a deep, tired breath. He sits slouched on the stool, his long legs propped beneath him at various angles.

My eyes roll slowly around the room, and I find I am still in the captain's quarters, in Blackwater's bed.

"How long was I out?"

"Mmmm, we are closer to dawn than farther away. How do you feel?"

"Like I was dragged behind a carriage for a week through the Spine." Gingerly, I drag myself to a sitting position against the headboard. "Were you able to . . ." I gesture down to my hand. "Salvage it?"

A proud smile spreads across his face, and I sag with relief. "Of course I was. You doubt me?"

I shake my head.

"It will take a week to fully heal, though. We'll need to change the bandages often, and if I catch you trying to use it before I say you can, I'll toss you overboard. I'll need to assess the progress twice a day to ensure the smaller, more delicate bones are setting correctly. They can be pesky."

Now that the adrenaline has worn off, I'm left feeling like a husk of a person with a cartload of soreness from the throttling. While I was sleeping, it appears that Luhan took the liberty of applying healing antibacterial paste to my shoulder and stitched up my hip, too. I'm glad I wasn't present for that.

Anticipating my needs, Luhan places a mug of water in my good hand, and I drink deeply. I'm setting the mug down when the double doors swing open and Liam Blackwater stalks through. His eyes are bright with the frenzy of bloodlust. His black, usually spotless clothes are soaked in blood, and his hair is a tumult.

The moment we lock eyes, all the fury, all the blame come hurdling back in an instant, and I vault off the bed and onto my feet despite Luhan's dismayed protests to *lie the hell back down.* My body protests the sudden movement, but the pain is only a flicker compared to the blaze of my wrath.

He's made it across the room in only a few steps. "Strider, I'm—"

"Don't," I rasp, shoving him square in the chest with my left hand.

"Just listen—"

"Listen? To you?" I'm incredulous. I could scream. "That was my first mistake."

I shove him again and again, my rage an insatiable beast. And though I may as well be punching a wall for how much damage I'm actually doing, he accepts the barrage stoically. I distantly register Luhan's shouts, but I pay no heed.

"You lied," I snarl, pushing Blackwater into a wall, right beside one of his overflowing bookcases. My hand, still on his chest, claws into his vest. "You told me you'd protect me. You gave your *word.*"

He says nothing, his expression betrays nothing, and it infuriates me.

"I'm a fool for believing you. You're nothing but a scheming, wretched liar. You failed me." That does it.

He flinches as if struck. I recoil, stunned by his reaction. I scrutinize him, picking apart the sudden weariness in his eyes, the defensive hunch of his shoulders. Though his gaze remains steady, he doesn't try to hide it, either. I've uncovered some sort of old pain.

This is what I deserve. To see him raw like this. Hurting from some lingering wound. I'm disappointed by how little satisfaction I draw from it.

"You're right," he rasps, his voice hoarse as if it's been run over coals. "Go on."

My lips part, then close. I want to rage, I want to spit in his face and knock down the walls, but the urge to fight is gone, and I have no interest in pushing someone who clearly isn't going to push back.

His hands slide up my wrist, as if he intends to take my hand in his, but then he freezes. "You're bleeding."

I follow his gaze downwards, to where the waist of my pants was rolled down so Luhan could stitch up the gash on my hip. The stitches that I must have torn in my haste to reach Blackwater. Blood trickles down the jut of my hip bone.

"Goddammit, Iona," Luhan mutters from behind us.

When I lift my gaze to Blackwater's face, there's a split second before his eyes leave my hip, and I catch a glimpse of something that looks like horror. I watch his gaze get stuck on every bruise, every slice. By the time he gets back to my face, he looks downright wretched. He swallows before he speaks.

"I did fail you, but I didn't lie. At least, not knowingly."

"I don't want your excuses, Blackwater."

His voice lowers. "I can explain."

Curiosity wins out. "Talk, then."

His fingers brush my elbow, startling me. "I'm sorry," he mouths.

Now it's my turn to flinch. I don't know what to do if he's not punching back.

With our faces this close, I realize I'm still holding on to his vest. With a breathy gasp, I let go, then turn for his chair. Only once I've sunk down and propped up my right hand do I lift my gaze to his again, noting he's followed me across the room but opted to stand instead of sit, resting his hands on the back of the chair opposite me. Reluctantly, Luhan rises and follows suit, perching solemnly beside his captain.

Blackwater is the first to speak again. "Tell me what happened, if you can. Spare nothing."

And so, I do, recounting every violent, red detail. Well, except for my little shadow trick, of course.

His face remains blank as the events unfold, though there are a few times his jaw twitches, and his nostrils flare once, when I mention the poison. When I am finished, he takes his time, mulling it all over carefully.

"What I told you about the Mark is true," he says after a while. "Once you're Marked by a pirate captain and thus belong to their crew, you cannot disobey a direct order." Here, he looks at his first mate. "Those three were Marked. By me, and by someone else. A man whose thrall is, it seems, more powerful than mine."

Luhan's expression darkens, and I get the impression he can already anticipate where this is going. It's nowhere good.

Blackwater returns his attention to me. "My Mark, as you know, is a leviathan. A writhing sea serpent."

I click my tongue. "I noticed that his looked different when he . . . he—" Bile crawls up my throat at the thought, but I swallow the acrid taste down. "There was a skull on his chest. Not your leviathan."

Blackwater nods as he rotates the chair to straddle it backward, propping his forearms on the backrest. He and Luhan share a pointed look before he continues, but the time for withholding information from me is well behind us now.

"Treacherous knaves," he mutters, shaking his head. "They must have somehow covered the original Mark up, and when they made their vows to me, it was mine that became visible, though my orders meant nothing. A highly skilled illusionist could have hidden the original, I suppose."

"But why was your Mark no longer visible when they attacked me?"

It's Luhan who answers. "If I had to guess, it's because they were following the original bestower's orders. The Mark of a captain is a powerful magic, mind you. It's no easy task to disguise or hide one. Even an illusion spell can only do so much when the Mark's magic is actively working."

I lean forward, unable to prolong asking the question that has been burning a hole through my tongue this whole night long.

"You said 'his'. You mean The Vice?"

Blackwater breathes deep as he runs a hand over his mouth. Luhan looks equally grim as he crosses his arms and fixes his gaze on the ceiling.

Blackwater says, "He . . . ah, damn it to hell. He's the one bastard you don't want looking your way. He's king of the pirates, Strider. And somehow, he's taken notice of you." There's a reverent hush in his voice, and even the candle between us seems to mind its crackling. The night breeze has died down outside, shrouding us in dreadful, foreboding silence. When Blackwater meets my eyes again, there's a hunted look in them I recognize all too well; it's the same expression I have worn every day of my life.

"Me?" I sit back in my chair, dumbfounded.

I'm no one. I'm a common thief, a shadow on the wall, nothing but a meddling ghost. Surely, there is a mistake.

"Who exactly is The Vice?" I'm equally horrified and intrigued.

The captain smirks. "That's just it. No one has ever seen him and lived to tell the tale. He's a faceless phantom. An invisible king. He's deathless."

"No one is deathless," I scoff, but there's not as much conviction as I'd like.

Luhan's lips thin as Blackwater leans toward me, eyes glittering. "Careful now. He is every man, and none of them. You may as well be picking a fight with the wind itself, for all the good it will do. And mind your tongue. You never know who's listening."

A chill runs cold fingers down my spine. "But you said he's king of the pirates. Does that mean you serve him, too?"

His laugh is mirthless. "Oh, he's sent many men my way, hoping to sway me. But I reject him every damn time." His lips curl enough to show teeth as he stands to his full height. Behind him, his wavering shadow slices the room in half. "If he wants you, for whatever reason, he'll have to go through me first. And then we'll see whose sword is sharpest."

Luhan flashes his captain a warning glance, but Blackwater pays no mind.

I fold my arms as best I can, despite the bulky bandage. "I don't know what he could possibly want with me. That's the truth. I'm of no consequence. I'm no one."

"I beg to differ. You are a walking consequence."

"And I've only just begun," I retort.

Blackwater looks at me hard, as if he can see through my skin, to the very fabric of my soul. And then he merely looks away, exasperated. "It makes no difference what he wants with you, or why he wants you dead. You're mine until the end of our deal. And so, my darling, you'll need to learn how to properly defend yourself."

My features slacken in surprise. "You want to teach me to swordfight?"

"I haven't a care what weapon you choose. But you can't be a frail, defenseless, damsel . . . " Here, he ducks and catches the heavy paperweight I hurl at his head while trying in vain to hide his smirk, " . . . anymore. This world, my world, is riddled with men like that, and while I will protect you as promised to the best of my abilities, you deserve a fighting chance." As he speaks, he prowls around the desk until he's made it in front of me, the corner of his mouth lifted into a devious grin as he grips the arms of my chair. "Besides, I'm rather impressed with what you did back there. I shudder to think of the little beast you could become with a little guidance."

I straighten my spine and lift my chin as I say, "I shudder to think that I, a frail, defenseless damsel, was able to do that to your trained men."

He cocks his head to the side. "Not mine at all, it seems. We picked them up in Marrin, actually, and I remember hoping Jon's Weaving would be useful. I was wrong."

Horribly.

He releases the chair, straightening, and starts to pace once more. I get the impression he does this quite frequently, and glance over at Luhan. He's staring at the floor, lost in thought.

Suddenly, he leans forward to ask, "And what of Jon? Does he live?"

Blackwater's gaze becomes arctic. "It became clear he was under some sort of enchantment preventing him from divulging any information about The Vice, his orders, his motives, or anything remotely useful. Once I realized that I was wasting my time, he was dealt with."

Luhan leans back, clearly disappointed. "Not surprising."

"No," Blackwater agrees somewhat distantly. "It's not." His gaze darts to me again. "I inspected your room and reinforced the wards, preventing anyone but me, Luhan, and you from entering or leaving. If you'd like, you can stay here tonight or be escorted back to your room. Either way, you should rest. Heal. I'll also exempt you from your daily tasks. But once you are ready, I want you to start training. I'll arrange for an instructor."

"When will I be expected to train?"

His brows furrow as if it's a stupid question. "Dawn. So it won't interfere with your chores."

I glower at his tone. "Is that all, then?"

His eyes narrow to slits. "I am trying to help you. They could have easily killed you tonight."

"I'm not the one with twelve holes in my chest."

He stops pacing to stare at me, his posture rigid. "Must you fight me about everything?"

"You're the one putting a sword in my hand."

"Yes, to point at someone else, for devils-sakes," he snaps. We glower at each other in taut silence as he scrapes a hand through already wild hair, but neither of us is willing to be the first to relent.

"I am trying to give you a fighting chance," he finally hisses through gritted teeth, jabbing a finger at me. "Take it. Just . . . take it. The devil knows you don't have any problem taking anything else."

I kick my chair back as my gaze slides to a wide-eyed Luhan. "Get me out of here."

We step onto the deck beneath a blanket of constellations just as a sea breeze caresses my cheek, and suddenly, I feel I'm taking my first real breath since the incident. My shoulders drop, my hands, fisted at my sides, release.

But as we make our way across the deck, I stop. There's a creaking —a slow, rhythmic creaking—that doesn't belong. My eyes flit left and right but find nothing out of place. And then I notice the pools of blood on the floor.

Ever so slowly, my eyes turn toward the heavens and find only hell.

I'd have thought Blackwater had simply dumped the bodies overboard after he was done, but I was wrong. No, that would have been too discreet.

Damn. It was a lovely night before the bodies.

Three dead men swing gently in the breeze, secured by ropes with giant hooks on the ends that have been shoved brutally through their guts. Poor Garrith is missing his head. Ulric has so many holes in his chest, the stars peek through them.

And the last, Jon, is missing all of his fingers and both ears. I see now why Blackwater took so long to meet us in his quarters; it must have been tedious work to flay him like that. I only know it's him because of his eyes. Well, the lack thereof.

Luhan places a gentle hand on my back, seemingly unmoved by the horror swaying above us. "You don't have to look."

But I do. I do have to look.

"There might be more here. More men working for him, I mean."

I catch Luhan nodding in my peripheral vision. "We will pick through the crew one by one tonight."

"But how can you tell? Blackwater said they couldn't divulge information even if they wanted to. And they could lie."

But as I say it, I remember my conversation over dinner with a certain eccentric pirate who can taste the truth.

"Arjun," I breathe, turning in wonder to look at Luhan.

His tight smile confirms it. "And while they may not be able to elaborate on The Vice's plans, they also can't lie about who they serve without getting caught. I've never known a magic powerful enough to get past Arjun in that regard. We'll find them." His voice softens. "We've never had a reason to doubt the Mark before."

My eyes cut to his. "I don't have a Mark."

Shrugging, he replies with a cheeky grin, "Keep mouthing off to the captain and perhaps he'll give you one."

But I don't respond or move to follow Luhan when he starts toward the stairs. In the distance, the night's edges are starting to lighten with the arrival of dawn, but the world is still quiet, still asleep. That is, except for the little bird hopping around cheerfully on the ledge of The Wraith.

And at first, it isn't anything out of the ordinary, this bird, until I realize it's made entirely out of paper.

Cupping my hand, I initially approach it the same as I would a frightened animal, although, come to think about it, it's neither an animal nor frightened of me. I straighten, suddenly feeling quite foolish. It hops right into my trembling hand and promptly unfolds to reveal creamy parchment and a message written in wispy, elegant letters.

"What is that?" Luhan asks, peering over my shoulder.

"Get Blackwater," I breathe, my pulse ratcheting. "Tell him it's started."

24

MESSAGE IN A BIRD

earest revelers,

The Crown eagerly awaits the pleasure of thy company at Court. But first, as always, a little game. Please collect the following by Dead Moons Night:

A piece of the sky

A beast unkillable

A foe's precious possession

Accomplish these three tasks, esteemed friends of the Crown, and thou will be welcomed into an opulent night of splendor.

Fantastically,
    The Crown

ACT II
THE GIRL AND HER SHADOW

25

A THOROUGH ASS-HANDING

Twelve days after the attack, Luhan clears me to begin training. The sparring room, much like the rest of the ship, is impossible.

It's much larger than it has any right to be, for one, with a roped-off ring in the center for training. It is also where the pirates keep their weapons. And there are *multitudes*. All sorts of gleaming swords, scimitars, knives, and rapiers hang on one wall, polished within an inch of their lives.

Every one of them gleams black as pitch.

I'm so engrossed in them I don't hear him come in until he's right behind me. I startle, and then startle again when I realize who it is that will be guiding me in the noble art of killing.

Basi, my silent kitchen duty partner.

With his wiry build, I never would have picked him for a warrior, but I might have said the same about Blackwater once. And I would have been killed for a lapse in judgment like that.

Although, with his vast collection of scars, it is no stretch of the imagination that Basi has seen his fair share of combat.

With a grunt, he motions for me to follow him to the center of the room, where he turns to face me with one dark, shrewd eye.

There's no warning.

One moment, we're facing each other, on opposite sides of the ring; the next, he's drawn his sword, lunged for me, and nearly sliced me in half. I hurl myself out of its way with a horrified shriek and manage to catch myself in a sloppy roll.

"What—"

I scramble backward, my heart in my throat, and snatch a low-hanging sword off the wall. I bring it up in front of me to block a brutal attack that would have cracked my head right down the middle. My arms burn with the effort of staving him off, sweat trickling down the back of my neck.

The problem is, I've never been very strong.

All too quickly, he heaves, and the blade crashes down as my arms give out. My mind goes blank with panic, but my body reacts.

I twist to the side, then take a series of quick side steps. My sword swings around me in a clumsy arc and somehow ends up pointed at his neck. It would have been impressive if he hadn't seen it coming. With an almost bored expression, he grabs my wrist with his left hand, wrenching it aside and squeezing so hard I have no choice but to release the weapon. It clatters to the ground at the same moment he hooks his leg around my ankle, jerks hard, and sends me sprawling.

I hit the ground with enough force to leave me breathless. Though whether it's the impact or the shock of what my body just did, I can't be certain. What the hell were those moves?

When I regain enough breath to sit up, I find the point of a sword dangerously close to my chest. Basi crouches next to me, glaring.

"You claim you never left Marrin. You lie." His accent is harsh and halting, his voice rusty from disuse.

"What do you mean?" I gasp between pants.

"That was a Celosian sequence," he hisses, leaning closer. "How did you know it?"

Astonishment courses through me. "What are you talking about? I just . . . twisted a little bit."

"No. Very distinctive. The footwork, the grip of the sword. I've seen it many times."

I shake my head emphatically as my heart starts racing. "I've never been to Celosia. I must have seen one of the Grays do it. They . . . they used to practice in the courtyard all the time, and sometimes I'd watch. I never thought I actually learned anything, though."

He eyes me with deep skepticism. "No one is that observant."

"Get Arjun in here, then," I protest. "I'm not lying."

And I did not expect to be handed my ass this early in the day. "Who taught you?" He asks.

I laugh darkly. "No one."

He doesn't have to know about the times my shadow gets involved. But this . . . this was new. It felt like muscle memory . . . but that can't be right.

Or perhaps I simply don't remember.

"You have instincts you shouldn't have, and skills you haven't earned."

"Then teach me. Properly." There's a sudden desperation in my voice. "Please."

A few tense moments pass, in which he bores a hole in my head with his stare, deciding whether or not to trust me. Whether he wants to impart his precious violent wisdom to someone he doesn't know.

"What do you want from this?" He finally asks. Good question.

In fact, it is the question I've been asking myself since Blackwater told me I'd be coming here. All my life, I've only known how to run away. Always the prey, never the predator. I quite like the idea, for once, of being able to stand still without the fear of something bigger coming to get me. To stand a chance. To stand at all, instead of slithering about in the shadows.

"I—" I scrape an exasperated hand over my face. There are so many things I could say. I could threaten. I could beg. But in the end, with a long-suffering sigh, I settle on the ugly truth. "In this realm, if violence is inevitable, you might as well teach me to fight back properly. Otherwise, I'm going to leave a hell of a mess. I . . . lose control when I get angry. It never ends well. And someone is always sticking a blade in my face."

"Anger can be a useful tool," he says. The point of the blade wavers, then lowers.

"Then you're going to love me."

He motions for me to stand, and I do. "This will be difficult. You will condition your body first. Then, strength training, sparring, and only once you can win a fight without a weapon at all, will I teach you to wield one."

"Done," I say, a little too eagerly.

I cross the room to where the sword lies on the floor, pick it up, and hang it back on the wall with the other gleaming weapons. I allow myself one last, longing look before turning my back on them, for who knows how long. Not forever, though. I'll make certain of that. I turn to find Basi watching me warily.

"I'm ready."

He shakes his head. "No, you're not."

Dawn is just beginning to lighten the sky when I emerge from the belly of the ship, slicked with sweat and trembling. After stretching for what felt like an eternity, then following him in a series of, what seemed at the time, simple exercises, I now must somehow confront the rest of the day knowing the same sordid fate awaits me tomorrow, and the following day, and the day after that. Each session will focus on a different set of muscle groups: legs, core, and arms.

This morning, Basi walked me through a bit of all of them to preview what is to come, and now I can barely will my wobbly legs to carry me across the deck. If, at some point, I sit down, I may never stand back up.

I hang my head and lean against the wall for a moment, catching my breath. A cool sea breeze brushes against my skin, and I close my eyes, relishing the fresh air as I gulp it down. The briny tinge to the air is finally starting to grow on me. How strange it is that only a little while ago, I had to wear a scarf around my face to filter out the dirt. And now, here, the air is so clean and crisp that I can see for what feels like forever; the horizon a clash of blues in the distance.

This early, there are a few men already milling about, but by the time the suns have risen, the deck will be teeming with activity. Across the way, Blackwater catches my eye from where he's chatting with a burly pirate. He acknowledges me with a curt nod.

Now, I'll not thank a man for giving me the tools to defend myself from a circumstance partially of his own making, but I can admit he's done more than most would have. I can't very well bite the hand that, instead of taking my daggers away, gave me more.

I nod in return, my eyes lingering on the muscles of his shoulders as they bunch and stretch as he helps to relocate a few barrels. Tattoos, a kind of black that eats the light, snake their way up his arms and across his shoulders in delicate whorls I can't help but admire. I picture a much younger Blackwater, a whirlwind of ambition and fearlessness, getting them inked to commemorate a successful ship sinking or stolen treasure. He must have been intolerable.

Only when he turns toward me again do I tear my eyes away, my face burning at my strange lapse in discretion. I cannot afford to lose focus for a moment, least of all because of him.

Not when there's a game at hand.

26

UNKILLABLE

The rest of the week passes in a manic haze. I attack every chore with a feverish intensity I feel compelled to maintain, lest I collapse. I don't utter a single word during supper, so intent am I on keeping my eyelids open and not drowning in my soup. Sitting down, then subsequently getting up from the bench, is its own special little hellcape that I prefer not to dwell on.

And to make matters worse, when I whisper a secret to the library door and enter, I find that I am not alone tonight. In one fluid movement, I pivot, my hand outstretched for the door, when Blackwater purrs, "Strider. Please join me."

My shadow pulls on me, straining toward Blackwater's voice. *Traitor.* Cursing quietly, I turn to face him. "Oh, I'd hate to interrupt."

Only his eyes move, flicking up from the book propped in his lap. By the time he looks at me, my shadow has gone still. "It's never bothered you before."

Warily, I make my way to my usual chair, albeit much slower than normal. My thighs ache from the squats and strength exercises Basi had me doing earlier, and I have to press my lips shut to cage a groan when I finally ease myself down.

"Poor darling. That bad?"

I scoff, reaching for the book I've been reading the last few nights.

"Basi overestimated my muscle tone," I mutter. "Even my eyeballs are tired."

Blackwater flashes a sympathetic grin as he crosses a boot over the opposite knee. "It will get easier with time."

I nod, although I can't help but feel incredibly impatient for the day I can walk normally again. Lift my arms. Sit. "You say this as if you have firsthand experience."

"I do. That's why I thought him best for this particular . . . assignment. I know his ways, and while it may seem tedious and, on some days, downright impossible, he's a master in his own right."

I cock my head expectantly, and with a soft sigh, he closes his book on a finger to save his place.

"Basi is a good man. I've known him almost as long as I've been captain of The Wraith, and I trust him. But make no mistake, he's one of the most deadly men you'll ever encounter."

"I believe you."

He nods. "Listen to what he says. I've learned a thing or two from him myself, the wily bastard."

"Such as?"

His lips quirk. "I've always been decent with a blade, but it was Basi who taught me how to be worth a shit without one."

"That seems to be important to him," I reply, pulling my legs under me with more than a little effort as my gaze wanders around the room, taking inventory of the same worn furniture bathed in the same soft flicker of the candles. If I close my eyes, I can still see the blood spatters on the floor. It never stopped me from returning, of course, what happened here. But I also haven't forgotten. The slice on my hip left a thin scar.

Blackwater, who is much too observant for his own good, says in a softer voice, "You are safe here."

"For now," I reply distantly, my eyes restlessly roaming over the nearest book spines. Not only did Blackwater and Luhan comb through the remainder of his crew one by one, but the library was spotless the following day. If I hadn't had the proof on my own person, I'd have thought the whole ordeal a horrible dream. I truly believe Luhan would rather throw himself into the sea than suffer a modicum of disorderliness aboard this ship. And I don't know how he removed the bloodstains from the floorboards.

"You're not going to like what I have to say," Blackwater begins.

"It's never bothered you before," I mimic, but I accidentally crack a smile as I say it, and he actually chuckles.

"I've been thinking about the tasks."

"So have I." To say the least.

A piece of the sky, a beast unkillable, a foe's precious possession.

The tasks aren't anything like I'd imagined. Not at all. I have no idea where to begin, and yet I can't stop turning the phrases over and over in my mind like coins. They feel like riddles, almost—riddles with many possible answers.

We can go anywhere in theory. However, the clock is ticking. We have a little over two months. The thought is as exhilarating as it is daunting.

"I believe I have a place to start," Blackwater continues, leaning forward to lace his long fingers together. "Unless you have any suggestions?"

"I'll let you take this one."

He smirks. "How kind. Now then. Roarke is a small territory about a fortnight from here. Beautiful gardens and excellent wines. Heard of it?"

"I've seen it on a map." The map in his quarters, actually.

"It's a scenic place, though fairly unremarkable. As of late, when we dock, I keep hearing things. Remarkable things. At first, I dismissed the rumblings as nothing but rumors. But the rumors have persisted, and now, I'm starting to think they might be true." He sighs, crossing his arms. "It seems Roarke has a bit of a problem."

I raise my eyebrows, and when Blackwater's mouth curls into a sly grin, my stomach somersaults. What was that? "There are few things more unkillable than a fire-breathing, furious dragon. Wouldn't you agree, Strider?"

An incredulous cackle bursts out of my throat. "HAH. You want to kill a dragon?"

"I want us to kill a dragon." The smile sharpens.

"I can barely hold a sword," I protest, but my heart is racing. "And dragons are enormous."

"Never stopped you before. How did you manage to inflict that many gashes, Strider, in a man twice your size?"

"He underestimated me."

"And when you broke out of your cell and murdered those Grays? What about that?" Everything about him—his languid tone, his relaxed posture—indicates a man entirely at ease, almost bored, except for his eyes. They always give him away, like a cat's tail. They glitter like this when he's setting a trap.

"I had nothing left to lose."

He sighs, clicking his tongue. "Don't tell me you're afraid of a little old dragon. Where's the fearless girl I met in Marrin?"

"The word you're looking for is reckless." For I fear plenty.

"How about meddling?" He asks.

"I prefer clever."

"Irritating."

"Rambunctious."

He snorts. "Obnoxious, but potentially useful?"

"Mm, if you're lucky, Captain."

His smile broadens. "I love it when you call me Captain."

I make a face. "I'll roll around in your blackened bones after the dragon roasts you alive, Captain."

"Oh, stop exciting me," he sighs dramatically, stretching his arms out to either side and laying his head back, leaving me with a view of the golden column of his neck and sharp jut of his stubbled chin.

Right. That's enough of that.

"Roarke," I repeat, clearing my throat. "What about Grays? They'll know my face by now."

"That they will. But Roarke is a sovereign territory ruled by a duke. So, no Grays."

Well, well, well. "You must consider yourself very clever."

"Always have," he replies, fixing his eyes on mine as he raises his head. "Wouldn't be a bad idea to get some clothes of your own at the market while we're there, though. I'm sure you're probably sick of hand-me-downs from Luhan."

He has a point there. Some clothes of my own would be lovely. And my hair . . . I'd shorn it off again five nights ago. But perhaps it's time I let it grow out, now that the Grays have seen me, and the rather distinctive scar above my ear.

"I'll take you up on that, actually."

His grin turns slick. "Might I recommend a few particular items of clothing?"

"No. You shan't. Do we know why this dragon has chosen to terrorize Roarke, then?"

"Does it make a difference?"

"Dragons are intelligent. It might."

"It might," he echoes, watching me with a curious look on his face.

Another question occurs to me. "And if we succeed? Is there some sort of reward or treasure?"

He leans forward, eyes glinting. "I might have overheard whisperings of a reward for whoever slays the beast. You'd get a cut, of course. In addition to what was already promised."

I cross my arms, sitting back in silence as my thoughts ricochet around my mind. Typical pirate, risking both our lives for the mere possibility of treasure. The risk seems to far outweigh the benefits, but I don't have a better idea at the moment.

And the clock is ticking.

"You said a fortnight from now?" I finally ask.

"Correct."

"And how do we kill a dragon, Captain?"

He shrugs, flashing me a charming smile that I'm sure has won him his way many, many times. "Oh, I'm certain we can puzzle it out. Never met a creature I couldn't kill."

I have.

The next morning, we focus on my core in training. The day after that, arms. Then balance.

All too soon, we're back to legs.

It never seems to get any easier, until one day, I find that it's not as difficult as it used to be. I can hold a plank for longer, squat deeper. Complete ten more push-ups than the week prior.

Time is slippery like that. I hold it in my hands and stare at it, daring it to move, and it never does. But the moment I blink, it's gone.

27

GHOSTS IN THE GARDEN

The morning we arrive in Roarke, the sky is an unblemished, brilliant blue. The kind that promises a good day.

In fact, I'm staring up at it again, lost in thought and enamored with the color, when the shout that we've spotted land rings out, kicking my heartbeat into a frenzy. Cheers and shouts of excitement drift through the air. Abandoning my current chore of buffing out unsightly scratches from the deck, I step onto the nearest railing and lean over the water precariously to see for myself, holding on to a bit of rope as I do so.

And there it is. The tiniest speck of green amidst the sparkling, silver sea. I smile as my stomach flutters at the sight.

Roarke.

Our first adventure.

It doesn't seem so bad.

It's been three hours since we docked. Two hours since the crew officially departed from The Wraith, and one hour that I've been wandering around Roarke's central market, completely overwhelmed.

This place is crawling with life. I don't mean in the way that Marrin was, with families and houses squashed on top of each other, the place a constant clamor of desperate people clawing their way to the top just so they can breathe.

No, not like that at all.

I've never seen such colors. Silver ivy spills down from iron wrought balconies overlooking the city, cascading so low to the ground I could touch the leaves. Every so often, spurts of yellow and orange trumpet-shaped flowers adorn the stone entrance to a tavern or food stall. The shops here are not only larger and less smelly, but painted vibrant colors of lilac, turquoise, rich blue, and more. Clean cobblestones gleam beneath my boots, and pale barked trees provide a canopy of shade from the relentless heat of the suns.

The views are only half the allure.

Shops hang enormous bushels of aromatic herbs like lavender and mint from their doors, and aromas of spiced wines and roasting meats waft through the air. It's the first thing I buy with my down payment: a skewer of slow-roasted waterfowl coated in honey and cherry vinegar. I follow it with a bowl of fresh plums drowning in cream and a cup of spiced wine.

Once my stomach is content and I'm no longer a slave to the smells of cooking food, I move on to finding a wardrobe of my own.

Although the majority of the crew headed straight to the tavern, The Bawdy Baron, I spot a few out and about at the market, perusing like me. I note Basi browsing some handmade rapiers, and catch Arjun and Ishaan bartering with a vendor over what appears to be a deck of cards. As I draw closer, I realize they're not haggling at all, but arguing passionately about their place of origin and what they were traditionally used for (according to Arjun, these are Iridisian cards used to foretell the future at marriage ceremonies).

I chuckle to myself and slip past.

Further into the market, the stalls become a little more specific and much more expensive. One woman advertises potions: one to revisit your favorite memory every night in a dream, another claiming to invoke the feeling of falling in love, but it wears off if it rains. One man, sitting among various baubles and doodads, asserts that they are bespelled tokens to bring the bearer safety, luck, or charm.

A young woman sells minor enchantments to enhance one's appearance: a pair of earrings to thin the nose, an eyebrow piercing to fill out the lips, a lavender colored tonic to expedite hair growth. There's a longer line for her.

I bump into a wealthy-looking woman leaving her stall, mutter my apologies, then hurry along my way.

After a few more stalls, I finally find what I'm looking for. Beneath a massive, emerald and cream-colored tent lie tables and tables of clothes. And above the tables, more clothes hang by wires. Patrons mill about, picking up items and then putting them down, and in the back, heavy cloth drapes hang over a few poles to provide interested buyers little alcoves where they can try things on.

The clothing ranges from downright gaudy, fraught with frills and beads, to simple and practical. It doesn't take me long to find what I want.

Once I've assembled it all, I take them to the back, ensure they fit, and make my way to the front to pay. My old clothes are spirited back to the ship by some house-owned low magic that cost me just two coppers.

The woman accepting payment, graying at her temples, looks me up and down, lips pursed, when it's finally my turn. From the conversations I overheard as I waited, it's clear she owns the place.

"Ye'll want to get some enchantments with that," she says matter-of-factly.

I frown. I've been allotted quite a bit of coin, more than I know what to do with, and my instinct is to squirrel away every bit of it unless absolutely necessary.

"Climate control, for one. Keep th' suns from boiling ye alive in those leathers, keep ye from freezing yer ass off when the wind gets to bitin' ye. Mayhaps some reinforcin' for those arm guards, too."

My eyes narrow. "How much?"

"Five golds will do for the clothes. Seven, including the enchantments."

I scoff. "I could craft these spells myself if I had a mind. Five and one silver."

Her thin lips crack into a challenging smile. "Seven."

"Three if you keep trying me."

"Five golds is a bargain, Kira," purrs a voice from behind me. "And she'll take the enchantments, too. By chance, do you still have that spell to oil leathers?"

I whirl around, brows furrowed in a deep scowl, to find Blackwater leaning against a pole, hands buried in the pockets of his overcoat.

"Get away," I hiss, flicking my fingers at him. But he ignores me and instead saunters over to lean on the counter next to me.

I turn back to find Kira's entire demeanor has changed, her hard eyes softened by a warm grin. "The 'andsome Captain Blackwater," she coos. "To what do I owe th' pleasure?"

"The pleasure is all mine, believe me," Blackwater replies, snatching the coins out of my hands and handing them over to her. "You look well, Kira. It seems you've met my—" He pauses, "—scullion wench, Iona Strider."

I extend my hand. "Lovely to meet you. He hired me to help with his stomach spasms. They've become violent."

Blackwater takes a deep, steadying breath and clears his throat. "Kira, I was hoping I could speak with you for a moment about something."

"Anythin'," she replies, gladly shifting all her attention back to him.

"I've been hearing things about Roarke. Rumors, if you will," he says.

Her smile falters. "That so?"

Blackwater lowers his voice. "You got a dragon that needs killing?"

Her face pales. "No," she whispers. "Liam, don't. Not ye too."

Blackwater leans forward. "Why don't you tell me what you mean?"

She peers around, but for the moment, the shop has cleared, and I wonder if that has anything to do with Blackwater's entrance.

"Alright. It . . . it takes every three years. Harry saw the thing flyin' away once. The duke keeps us all safe, mind ye. He struck a deal with it. As long as it can have what it was promised, it don't hurt no one. It's never come for the town. But on the next Dead Moons, it'll be time again. Time for it to take another."

"Another what?" Blackwater asks a little too sharply.

Kira swallows, looks down at her hands. "The dragon takes one o' the duke's daughters every three years in exchange for the safety of the town."

Blackwater says nothing, but his eyes are a green pyre.

"How many has it taken?" This time, it's me who asks the question. Blackwater shoots me a warning glance, but I pointedly ignore him. Kira's voice has become so soft, I have to lean over the counter to hear. My shoulders brush against Blackwater's, but I pay no mind.

"Four," the woman shudders, covering her mouth with a calloused hand. "So kind and so young, all of them . . . Oh, the girls. He's only got one more. Little Rosie. And then the deal will be done, and the dragon will leave us forever."

Horror trickles like ice down my spine. I spare a look at Blackwater, but he's got all his attention on the woman.

"Kira," he whispers. "What if that's not the end of it? What about Farrow and Yris?"

Her eyes shine like glass, but she looks away, her mouth a hard, trembling line. "We can't afford passage," she whispers tersely.

I can feel the anger spreading, like a drop of blood in water, throughout my chest.

I open my mouth to say something, but Blackwater cuts me off with a hand around my bicep. "We'll pay him a visit," he says. "And Kira?"

He reaches into his coat and, pulling out a generous handful of golds, places them into her hands.

Though refusal is plain on her face, the look in his eyes brooks no argument. "If we don't come back, take your family and leave this place. As soon as you can. See that man over there?" He points through the tent flaps, across the way. "His name is Basi. He will escort you safely, and this will be more than enough to start fresh."

She looks up at him then, with disbelieving eyes and parted lips. "I don't care what they say about ye. Yer a good man, Liam Blackwater."

A corner of his mouth lifts. "Thank you, but I hope not."

We left the tent shortly after that, once the clothing was laced with all the enchantments Kira thought necessary. When she discreetly handed the gold back to me, I balked, but she insisted that it was her gift to a friend of the captain's. I informed her that under no circumstances are we friends, but she heard none of it and sent us on our way.

Outside the shop, I can feel Blackwater's eyes on me, taking inventory of my new wardrobe. I purchased a black, high-necked, sleeveless shirt that displays a lovely asymmetrical slice of skin, starting from below my left collarbone to just above the one on my right. Dark, form-fitting pants hug my lower half, adorned with three new sheaths: one hangs low on my hips, while the other two band around each of my thighs. All three are already outfitted with blades. In addition, I found some sturdy black boots that end below my calves, and selected some leather arm guards, too. I figured some fireproof gloves weren't a bad idea either, although whether they hold up against dragonfire remains to be seen.

But my favorite purchase is the coat.

Right now, it's thigh-length and sharply tapered at my waist and shoulders. The fabric is a lovely indigo crushed velvet, but it's the thick, silver-embroidered leaves that make it stunning. They crawl along the cuffs of my sleeves and upturned collar in intricate swirls, branching out from the middle, too, where the buttons are.

Kira warned me it tends to have a mind of its own, this coat, changing its appearance as it deems fit. But for now, it suits my purposes well enough. I'd bought some other clothes too, but they're being delivered to The Wraith later.

I come to an abrupt halt. "Stop."

"Stop what?"

I turn to the pirate in a huff. "Stop looking."

His eyebrows shoot up. "I can't look at you?"

"No."

He snorts. "You picked well, that's all. Silver and gold." He's talking about my eyes.

I wrinkle my nose. "Don't."

He shoves his hands into his pockets, procures a bright red apple, and polishes it on his lapel. "Don't what?"

"Say things like that."

He takes a bite, chews thoughtfully, and swallows. "Things like what?"

Instead of answering, I pluck the apple from his hand, inspect it, and take a bite out of the opposite side.

He'll not be getting this back.

He sighs with great resignation. "I was afraid of this." He roots around in his pocket and brings out an identical apple. "This way to the dragon, then. Mind the fruit."

The duke's manor sits in a valley hedged by pale blue mountains, set apart from the bustle of the town amidst a sprawling garden. It was easy to find. Once we left town, all we had to do was follow a tree-lined path. Led us straight here. We enter through tall iron gates, and immediately, we're greeted with the sweet perfume of fruit trees and flowers in bloom. Fountains spout sparkling water, and marble statues in the shape of frolicking young women smile blankly at us as we pass.

There are many servants in the gardens, all immaculately dressed and well fed, but too preoccupied to do much more than nod or give a tight-lipped acknowledgement before they bustle away. Not a single person smiles at us.

"The duke knows we're coming," I mutter to Blackwater under my breath as we brush up against some lilacs.

"Of course he does," Blackwater replies. "I made our presence no secret. And he's got spies everywhere, no doubt. He'll be waiting for us."

"This place is lovely," I say, then hesitate.

"But?" The pirate's gaze flicks down to me.

"But no one is talking. They're not even looking at each other. They seem . . . like ghosts."

Despondent is the word.

He takes a while to respond, his eyes tirelessly scanning the gardens. "They've seen too much death."

We are received at the door by an elderly butler with a shock of white hair and blue, watery eyes, wearing a green coat that's been starched within an inch of its life.

"Captain Blackwater," he greets us. "And who might your guest be?"

This time, I answer before Blackwater can. "Iona Strider."

His mouth curves into what one may have been a smile, but it looks more like an unfortunate spasm. "Pleasure. You may call me Harris. This way, please."

We follow him into the manor, where we are greeted with a splendid view of a spiral staircase and several other butlers standing at attention.

I do my best not to gawk in wonder as we follow the butler toward the back of the house, past a room devoted solely to musical instruments, and another with an entire wall made of glass, looking out over the gardens. I realize that almost every window is curtain-less, to allow as much light to stream in and flood every nook and corner as possible, as if they're doing everything they can to banish any hint of darkness.

It's as we're passing from one room to the next that Blackwater leans down and brushes the small of my back with a hand.

"Do not steal a thing."

The deep timbre of his voice stirs me. I keep my eyes straight ahead but allow a devilish grin to peek through. And I make no promises.

Let him be a little nervous.

Suddenly, we find ourselves in an opulent sitting room, characterized by gold crenelations and furniture to match—the kind that is far grander than it is comfortable.

The duke is, in fact, waiting for us.

He lounges on a chaise, reading a book. A spritely-looking man of average build, he's blandly handsome, and perhaps in his forties. Upon our arrival, he sets the book down and rises to his feet with a generous smile.

"Captain Blackwater of The Wraith," he cries, throwing his arms wide, as if they're old friends. "What an honor. What an honor indeed."

"You flatter me," Blackwater drawls, coming to a halt. "You have a grand home."

The other man looks around with widened eyes, as if he's seeing it for the first time himself. "I do, don't I?" Then bursts into booming laughter. "Come, come, sit, sit. I don't have all this furniture so we can stand around. Harris? Bring us some tea. Mademoiselle, what tea do you like? Oh, Harris, just bring all of it." The butler promptly leaves to bring us all the tea in existence.

The duke sits back down on the chaise, and Blackwater and I select two different plush chairs across from him. Once we've settled, I find the duke's eyes have fallen on me, and I do my best not to fidget. Or snap my teeth at him.

"What striking features you have, my dear," he says, leaning forward. "Those cheekbones of yours could slice a man's heart out. And those eyes. My, my!"

The best I can offer is a sickly smile.

"Where are you from, my dear?"

"Marrin."

His mouth pops open with exaggerated surprise. "Oh, you poor thing! What a dreadful place. Had you been there long?"

"As long as I can remember."

He shakes his head. "Well, you're away now. And you and the captain are . . .?" He glances between us, and we both seem to lurch a bit out of our seats when understanding hits.

"Barely making it," I respond tonelessly.

"Professional acquaintances," Blackwater says at the same time.

A tense silence ensues in which the pirate and I glare daggers at each other, but it's broken by the arrival of the tea. I've never had such a thing. It tastes like the flowers outside, but also dirt. I add several spoonfuls of honey, which does wonders to improve the taste.

"Your Grace, I fear I must address why we have come," Blackwater says once the clinking of spoons against cups has subsided. He, I notice, chose black tea and added nothing to it. How awful.

"Oh, don't bother. I know why you're here," the duke interrupts hastily, waving a hand. "The dragon. You want to kill the dragon."

Blackwater smirks as he leans back in the chair as if he owns the place. "Are we so late to the party?"

"Quite," the duke responds primly. "Many have come to slay the dragon, and many have failed. You'll not return, Captain Blackwater, if you seek out the dragon of Roarke."

"And what is it, exactly, that makes this dragon so impossible to kill?"

The duke merely shrugs. "She's a dragon."

"Tell me. Why did it come here in the first place? Dragons are typically quite solitary. To seek out a highly populated area like Roarke is peculiar."

My eyebrows raise in approval at the insightful question.

The duke frowns and sets his tea down. "How should I know?" Blackwater fixes the duke with that eerie green stare and waits.

The duke, it seems, isn't accustomed to silence. It's not long before he rises to his feet and begins to pace around the room. He's squirming.

"I did the best I could. When it came to Roarke, all those years ago,

I did everything I could. But this dragon is the fire-breathing type, you know, and it could demolish the entire town if it took a notion to it! I couldn't allow that. So, we . . . well, we reached an agreement. And we have had peace ever since. It has never attacked the town, thanks to what I did. Not once."

"And all you have to do is send one of your daughters to their death every three years," Blackwater intones with an accusatory glare.

The duke slams his hand down onto the low table between us, his face red. Blackwater doesn't so much as blink. "I have sacrificed more than you could ever imagine for my people. My family has ruled Roarke for many generations. You saw how abundant this land is with prosperity. These people need me. You can't possibly understand. And how could you? You're a—well, you're a deviant."

"A deviant that is about to kill a dragon for you."

"Yes, well, that remains to be seen—"

"Papa? Is everything well?"

All three of our heads swivel toward the stairs and the sweet voice. At the top of the landing stands a girl. Can't be older than eighteen, with a heart-shaped face and pale, pink-gold hair that falls to her waist in soft waves. She wears a cream dress that flares at her hips, embellished with blush-colored floral patterns at the bottom of the skirts. She's beautiful. She's young. And if we fail, she's to die.

"Rosie, my sweet," the duke scrambles to regain his composure. "Don't mind us. This is the good—well, the esteemed Captain Blackwater, and his associate. Erm, Iona Strider."

Rosie offers us each a warm smile as she floats down the stairs. "It's a pleasure to meet you. To what do we owe the kindness of this visit?"

The duke's face darkens. "They want to try their hand at . . . well—"

"You're here to attempt to slay the dragon," Rosie finishes for him evenly, peering into each of our faces.

"My lady," Blackwater says with a charming smile. "There's no 'attempt' about it."

She smiles right back, but there's a hardness now beyond her years to her pale blue eyes. "Forgive my cynicism, but I've heard that before, Captain."

Her gaze falls to me. "Let's leave the men to their talk of dragons. I tire of the word. Would you care to walk with me?"

"Yes, my lady." I set my honey water on the table, only for it to be immediately swept up by Harris.

"No need for formalities. They feel so cold," she says as we leave the room side by side. "Rosie will do."

I smile at her. "Please. Call me Iona, then."

We stroll through the gardens, stopping now and then so she can point out the species of flowers, bushes, or fruit trees. It turns out, Rosie and her sisters are—were—quite involved with the gardens. They'd spend hours planting, weeding, and pruning.

"Those were my favorite days," she says as we stop to sit a moment under a trellis dripping with tiny, yellow buds. A servant hands me a cold glass of fresh-squeezed orange juice, complete with a sprig of mint. "The five of us. And now, every time I pick up a spade, I feel like retching. They'd be so disappointed in me."

I haven't spoken much while we've been strolling, and I have no idea what I can possibly say now to remedy the profound losses this young woman has suffered. "The statues. They're your sisters, aren't they?"

"All but one." She points to one statue, set apart, of a man with his arms spread wide, whom I now recognize to be the duke. "That was the first of them. The others, my sisters, were my idea. It gives me a small bit of comfort to look out and know that even in death, they're still among the flowers."

And then I understand. They're not just statues; they're grave markers.

"We never can recover the bodies," Rosie whispers, her voice brittle and cracking. "But there's always something left of them—a bit of clothing, a piece of jewelry. I always find something to bring back, so their souls can rest at home. I suppose I will see them again soon."

"Were they all so resigned to their fate?" We start back on our stroll, the early afternoon suns dappling through tall trees that shade our path.

She gives me a sharp look. "Perhaps not. But Calla, the eldest of my sisters, died when I was six, so I've had all my life to prepare. I've never known another fate."

She's quiet for a time, and then, she says softly, "I do have bad days, though. Days when I think to myself, 'I could run away. And be free of it.' On those days, I take a walk through the town. I see my people, and the lives they've built, the families they've made, and by the time I return from my walk, I no longer wish to flee." She fixes me with her pale blue eyes, then, and there's steel there. "I will do what I must for my people. If my life is the last price to be paid, then so be it. My sisters felt the same. I do not expect others to understand."

"Oh, fuck off with the martyrdom. There must be another way," I retort, forgetting myself. A few servants stiffen, and one backs up a few paces.

She rounds on me. "There is not. Do you know how many have come here, as you did today, claiming to put an end to this . . . horror? Hundreds. Hundreds of heroes, much stronger than you, have come to this place, and not a single one of them has ever returned. So, forgive me, Iona, if I've grown tired of it all."

"But why is it that your lives are the ones that are forfeit, instead of your father's?"

Her face pales. "Bite your tongue. My father begged the dragon to take him instead. It did not want him. The dragon is the evil here, Iona. And my father has been a magnificent ruler. Roarke is prospering. Don't you see that?"

My heart breaks at the conviction in her voice. I cannot hope to change her mind.

Before I can stop myself, I reach out for her hand. I can't put my finger on it, but something about her calls to me. I feel a strange sense of protectiveness over her. Perhaps it's her innocence, or her unwavering conviction. "I'm sorry. You see, I am neither strong nor a hero. But I would like to help you. The realm could use more people like you. And more gardens."

Her eyes dip down, and I can tell she's thinking hard about something. Finally, she says, "I'd like to show you something."

She brings me back inside, to a corridor lined with four paintings of four dead girls.

The eldest appears to be a bit older than I, and the youngest is a little older than Rosie. All four have kind eyes and spirited smiles, their heart-shaped faces and light hair making it obvious they're of the same kin. They all have eyes the color of the edges of a frozen lake, except for the sister next to Rosie, the second youngest. Hers were lavender, irises ringed with silver.

Rosie glides down the corridor, touching the paintings as she passes them. "Calla, Amaryllis, Marigold, and Aster." She stands apart, contemplating them, although I get the impression she frequents this room all the time.

"Calla was the first. The eldest. She was twenty-eight when she died. I was six. And every three years after that, I've watched another of my sisters leave and never return. Three years ago, I lost Aster."

The girl with the lavender eyes. "What of your mother?"

"She did not survive my birth."

Everything about this place is tragic. I take a deep breath. "Tell me how it happens."

"They go alone. That's how it must be. There's an orchard about half a day's walk from here, and that's where—" She swallows. "That's where it happens. I go the next day to bring back what's left. I don't—I don't know who will bring back what's left of me. My father can never bear it."

We look at each other, and for a while, there's nothing to be said. Finally, I ask, "Is there a way to kill it?"

She sighs. "A few years ago, a contender brought a sword that he claimed was imbued with magic that could kill anything. Cut through dragon scales, even. But he never returned. I gather that, if his claims were true, he never got the chance to use it. I imagine that sword must still be out there, somewhere. If you can survive long enough to find it."

My eyes return to the painting of the last sister, Aster, and my gut twists painfully. On the way back to the receiving room, I find myself stuck on something. If Rosie's eldest sister was a older than me, let's say around thirty, and she was the first of four to start the three-year cycle, then that would have been twelve years ago, so she would have been born at least forty-something years ago. That would mean the duke is at least sixty, but . . . that can't be. He doesn't look a day over forty.

"Your father," I say hesitantly before we reach the room where he and Blackwater reside. "He looks so young."

"Yes, I suppose so," Rosie replies in the tired cadence of someone who's said this many times before. "He likes to tell us that it's because the land, and therefore, the magic, is happy with his rule, so it's extending his stay. It was the same with the First Sovereigns, all those centuries ago. The magic here is old. Strange. You'll see."

28

FRUIT OF THE ORCHARD

I don't think either of us expected to be so disturbed by the circumstances here when we set out earlier this morning. And now, suddenly, everything feels a little bit sinister. Outside of the manor, the wind I thought smelled like flowers this morning is tinged with rot, and all the colors feel obscene in light of so much tragedy.

It's a while before either of us speaks as we exit the property. Once we're a healthy distance away, we rehash our separate conversations, mine with Rosie, and Blackwater's with the duke. My experience, it turns out, was a bit more fruitful than his.

While the duke also told Blackwater about the orchard and how to get there, he neglected to inform him of the sword.

"Interesting omission," I comment as we plunge into the thick of the woods. "You'd think he'd want us to know about a sword that can cut through dragonscale."

"Perhaps he doubted it would make a difference," Blackwater muses, but he sounds unconvinced. "Or Rosie lied, and it doesn't exist."

I glance up at him, shoving a branch out of the way as I do so. "But why would she lie?"

"I don't know," he replies, ducking under another branch. "But something isn't adding up somewhere."

The images of the sisters' serene paintings float to the surface of my mind, twisting my stomach. "How does your sword fare against dragonscale?"

Blackwater shrugs. "Most blades can cut through dragonscale, although not very well. But that doesn't seem like the real issue. It seems this isn't a typical dragon if it's been so difficult to kill."

I glance over to him, and he elaborates, "But yes, if there is a sword out here that will make quicker work of killing this thing, we will need to make it a priority. That's all."

I frown. "If it's not a normal dragon, why didn't they warn us?"

We share a look, and despite the suns' warmth, I fend off a chill. Already, problems are mounting.

"I don't like this."

"Don't worry, Strider. I've seen worse."

I throw him a skeptical look, and we lapse into troubled silence.

It's not so bad, the journey. Birds call sweetly to each other, and leaves flutter and rustle as small creatures startle at our passing. The woods are dense, but not to the point where we're having to fight our way through them. There's a path we can follow, presumptively from those before us. Go north through the woods, the duke had told Blackwater, then follow the river downstream until you find the orchard. It'll find you after that.

The suns are high in the sky when we emerge from the woods to find a roaring river beyond some tall, reedy grass.

Blackwater jerks his chin to the right. "Shall we?"

Swallowing, I nod.

"Did you leave anyone behind in Marrin?"

It takes me a moment to process the question, as I was lost in my thoughts. We've been walking for ages along this damn river with nary an orchard to be seen. "What?"

"Did you leave anyone behind in Marrin? Parents? Friends? Perhaps, a young lad who had eyes for only you?"

I don't respond right away. Sifting through my memories is like leafing through a book, only to find chunks of the story missing. It can make it hard to tell the truth sometimes. "The only people who gave a damn about my departure are the Grays."

Blackwater regards me carefully, and when it becomes clear he's waiting for more, I add, "I never knew my parents, alright? They just weren't around. And I never—ah, got close to anyone. Is that not obvious?"

I point to my shorn hair. The unsightly scar above my left ear. He blinks. "Huh."

My gaze retreats to the sunslight glinting off the river. "I preferred to stay unseen."

"Like a ghost, one could say."

My chuckle is little more than a breath, but he surprises me by continuing to say, "It doesn't work, though."

"What doesn't work?"

He gestures to his own hair. "You can cut your hair off all you like, but the problem is your face."

My walking slows. "What about my face, Blackwater?"

He stares at me blankly, shaking his head as a breeze stirs the long grass around our legs and runs its fingers through his unruly hair.

"Do you recall, Strider, when I found you at the tavern, and I pushed you up against the wall? Your hood fell."

The side of my mouth lifts at the memory. "Yes, and when you saw I was a girl, it sent you into such a stupor I walloped you and got away."

I almost walk right into his arm, which has gone straight out in front of me like a bar, stopping me where I stand. I glance up at the pirate, only to find that he's peering down at me with a look of complete stupefaction.

"Firstly, I recall no such walloping. Secondly, that's why you think I reacted that way?"

"Is it not?"

He studies me, a peculiar sense of amusement having overcome him. "No," he says. "It's not."

And then he turns to leave, his coat flapping behind him as he flicks his wrist. "Come along, now."

I stand there, frowning after him, until he glances over his shoulder and calls after me again. Not knowing what else to do, I jog to catch up.

"I wasn't always alone," I amend when we're side by side again. "I was far from the only orphan in Marrin. There was a whole pack of us, once. I learned to pickpocket from the older kids when I was younger."

Some of my first clear memories. About seven years ago, by my count. "What happened? Did you grow apart?"

Guilt threatens to swallow me whole. "Something like that. I learned—" I swallow. "I learned that it's easier for Grays to hunt a flock, as opposed to individuals. Seems obvious as an adult, but . . ."

"It gets lonely," Blackwater finishes for me.

"It gets lonely," I echo quietly, nodding.

"Where would you sleep?" He asks.

"It varied. Sometimes abandoned homes when people left . . . or died. Sometimes the woods. It would depend. Never the same place twice."

"And you'd only sleep during the day."

"It was easier to scavenge for food at night. Less competition," I lie. The truth is, between my nightmares and my shadow seeming to be stronger at night, it became clear to me that sacrificing a good night's sleep was far better than the alternative. "What's with all the questions?"

His eyes slide to mine. "You're answering."

"Well, erm, what about you, then?"

"Oh, I sleep at night. Like you're supposed to."

I scoff. "No, you don't."

His smile is almost sheepish. "I quite like the night sky, that's all. It's always been a comfort to me when I'm feeling lost."

For a moment, I'm struck by how lovely his face is when he forgets that he's supposed to be a brute. "Where does the great captain of The Wraith hail from?"

His smile falters. "There are people who would kill for that information."

I shade my eyes from the suns as I look up at him. "I'll kill you without that information."

That elicits a good chuckle. "Well met. Ah . . . I grew up in a place called Talis. Heard of it?"

"No."

"Good. It's more village than city, about a month's voyage east of here. I've been all over, Strider, and it's still the most beautiful place I've ever seen."

"More so than here?" I find it hard to believe that anywhere is more beautiful than this place. I've never seen such colors: the lush green of the trees, the vibrancy of the blooms, the gentle pastels of the shops populating the city market.

"This? This place is nothing like Talis," Blackwater scoffs, shaking his head adamantly. "It's too showy. Take away all the flowers and paint, and it's nothing special."

"But Talis is?"

He shrugs. "I always thought so."

In the same moment, I am both happy for him and very sad for myself. "But," I muse, kicking a rock out of the way, "you left."

He tilts his head back to the skies, looking like a man completely at ease with himself. "The realm is too big to stand still, Strider. And I've always felt most like myself when I'm adrift. When I can go anywhere and be anyone."

"Perhaps one day I can see Talis."

He smiles at me, and for a moment, he's not a pirate captain. He's a young man thinking of home. And though I've never known what it feels like to have a safe place, a home, to retreat to, I wonder if I can one day make one for myself.

Abruptly, Blackwater stops, shattering the warmth of the moment. I follow suit. To our right, the forest stretches on ahead of us, but we've reached the crest of a hill. I hurry to the top, where Blackwater stands overlooking the valley. Once I can see below, I understand what brought him pause.

The trees. They change.

This must be the place. And as we continue to move closer, apprehension sinks its claws into my skin.

The moment we cross the threshold into the orchard, I register a slight popping sensation, almost like a change in pressure. That's the first of the oddities.

The tree trunks have become shortened, withered, and gnarled, their bark slick like the gray scales of a snake. Black, oily leaves sprout from the branches, instead of green. Grass doesn't grow here. Or at least, if it did, it was all scorched away.

The worst of it all lay scattered about, creaking hollowly in the wind.

If this hellish place is to be called an orchard, the bones must be the fruit. Skeletons, blackened from dragon fire, litter the area. Some have remained whole, propped against a tree, their mandibles unhinged in a silent scream, while others have been dismantled entirely. We both have to watch our step, lest we trip over someone's femur or tibia.

Well, they're not using them anymore.

We've not made it far before suddenly my blood goes cold, and I halt where I stand. I grab the arm of Blackwater's coat, pulling him to a halt beside me. "Do you hear that?"

He stills, his eyes darting this way and that. Very slowly, he draws his sword. I draw two blades sheathed at my thighs.

"I don't hear anything," he murmurs.

"Exactly," I mouth. "The birds. They stopped."

Our eyes meet.

I see Blackwater's attention swerve to the sky, behind me. Before I can react, he throws us both to the ground, so hard my teeth rattle, but it doesn't matter because the sky has split apart, and I can't even hear my own scream as the realm goes up in flames.

29

THE BEAST OF THE SKIES

I open my eyes to a world devoured by flames.

My ears are still ringing, and for a moment, I panic that I'll never recover my hearing at all. Surely, there is nothing left after a sound like that.

Blackwater pants above me, having thrown us to the ground a moment before the dragon unleashed a belly full of fire, swooping so low to the ground its claws raked deep grooves in the dirt.

"Now what?" I demand, reaching to pick up the blades I'd dropped when Blackwater shoved me aside, only to hiss and snatch my hand back. They burned me.

A welt is already forming on my palm from where I grabbed the glowing hilt, still steaming from the dragon's fire. Abandoning them, I scramble to my feet and draw two new blades from my hip. "We haven't found the sword."

"I'm still unconvinced it exists," he grunts, glaring at the clouds.

"But what if it does?"

If Rosie lied, we might very well be damned. But if Rosie told the truth . . .

"Then by all means, Strider." He gestures about us. "Let's find it."

We take off at a sprint, following the river to our left. Rosie said it was near here, but I see nothing of the sort. Sweat trickles down my back as my head swivels this way and that, but all I see are rows and rows of strange, dead trees. With each gasping breath, I start to wonder if Rosie did lie to me. What if it's a red herring? We might have to kill this thing with our hands.

And the suns just disappeared.

No, they're still there. Something's blocking them.

We look up to find the dragon plummeting toward us, wings tucked tight against its enormous, scaled body. Instinct bellows at me to pivot, and we both duck into the trees as the beast spreads its wings wide at the last moment before it lands. The sound it makes when it collides with the ground is deafening, and we're thrown to the ground by the impact.

Groaning, I stumble to my feet as fast as I can, twisting around to face this thing. It is as beautiful as it is fearsome.

Black scales cover the lithe beast from its long neck to its barbed, swishing tail.

Dark claws churn the dirt as it prowls toward us, its maw gleaming with fangs that could rend me into pieces. While it's definitely not yet a full-grown dragon, it's still the size of three grown men put together —big enough to slaughter both of us. Easily. I find it surprising how relatively small it is, but I don't have time to dwell on it.

Fuck.

It crashes toward us, snapping dead trees in half as if they were twigs.

I roll out of the way, but Blackwater meets it head-on, swinging his ebony sword straight for its chest. The blade skitters off the beast's scales, but he has that shrewd look in his eyes. Quick as an adder, he jabs his sword forward again, but this time he angles his thrust upwards, beneath the scales.

The wound isn't fatal, but it's enough to make the dragon scream.

I cover my ears, cringing away from the horrific sound. It's heartbreaking. It sounds like a soul getting ripped in half.

Enraged, the dragon swings its head like a gigantic pendulum, releasing a bone-shaking bellow as it attacks. Every time I think it's got him, Blackwater leaps back just enough to keep his appendages and his life.

But he's rapidly approaching the river, and soon, he'll be out of ground. "Fuck," I mutter, taking a running start as the dragon charges Blackwater, snapping at him with a vice-like force no man could survive. Baring his teeth, Blackwater rears back, and I know he's going to try to sever the creature's tongue, but it won't work. He won't be getting that side of his body back.

It's my turn.

With a barbaric screech, I drive both my daggers deep into the flesh of the creature's hind legs, mimicking Blackwater by digging them down and underneath its scales. But I'm not finished. I yank the one in my right hand out, blue blood spurting all over me in the process, then drive it in again into a higher spot on its flank. I do the same with my other hand, grinning with satisfaction when the beast screams again, lurching into motion.

The trouble is, I don't let go of the knives when the beast launches into the air. It's too late, I've stabbed a path all the way onto its back. Grasping the ridge of spikes along its spine, I ease my way toward its head, teeth gritted as I hold on for dear life as it bucks and thrashes in the air.

From the ground, I hear Blackwater shouting something, but between the deafening booms of the dragon's beating wings and my own heartbeat, I've no idea what he's saying.

I've made it to its shoulders when it decides to do a barrel roll. For a second, I manage to hang on, but my grip could never have been strong enough to withstand being completely upside down. With a blood-curdling scream, my fingers slide off the spikes, and I hurdle through nothing but air.

I land not with a sickening crunch, but a painful splash. While I had planned for my breath to be stolen away, I didn't anticipate the cold.

And I never learned to swim.

My limbs flail uselessly. I'm at the river's mercy. I tumble through the cold current, never breaking the surface. Even if I could swim, I don't know which direction is up, and I'm out of air. My body cracks against a rock, and when I open my mouth to cry out, water surges down my throat. My chest has just started to burn when I'm hauled upwards by the collar of my jacket, and suddenly I'm out of the water, coughing, sputtering, and gagging.

I'm dragged onto the muddy bank of the river, where I take a moment to heave up the watery contents of my stomach on shaking hands and knees. Once it's all out, I sit back on my heels, wiping my mouth with the back of my hand.

"All better?" Blackwater asks, peering at me from behind a curtain of dripping hair.

"I might have one more go in a few moments," I rasp between heaving breaths, glaring at the sparkling river that just tried to kill me.

"Take your time."

I glance at him, making a concerted effort to ignore the way his clothes are clinging to his body. "This is turning out to be a real bitch."

A thin trail of watery blood trickles down the side of his face as his lips flatten. "Quite."

My eyes widen. "It got you."

Seeming quite unruffled, he taps a finger to the blood and brings it in front of his face. "Only a scratch, darling. Although if you'd like to kiss it better, I'll not decline."

In the face of certain peril, his ego persists.

He rises, offering a hand, but I slap it away and stand on my own, glancing around as I do so. Aside from the roaring river, it's so still here. The orchard is far behind us now, a sick-looking blight amidst the green. Here, the land rolls gently into hills, interrupted here and there by small, errant trees or a bit of scrub. From the riverbed, it's easy to spot the pond.

"Liam," I breathe, pointing. "Look."

The closer we get, the faster my heart rate becomes until it's thrumming behind my ears. An almost perfect circle of clear, blue water, as if a giant poked their finger straight into the ground. And at the bottom lies a glittering sword.

The water is so still, it doesn't even ripple with the breeze.

Sighing, the pirate kneels at the water's edge and places his palm flat against the water's surface. It's frozen solid. Someone or something did not want us getting this fucking sword.

30

DEPTHLESS, INDOMITABLE EVIL OF MAN

"Of course," I say, crossing my arms. "Of fucking course."

Frowning, Blackwater draws his sword and drives it straight into the ice. It barely makes a dent, and the tip skitters off.

"Damn," he mutters.

"What are the odds you think we can trick the dragon into melting the ice with its fire?" I ask, wincing as a dark serpentine shape rises above the orchard into the sky. Even from here, I can hear the slap of its wings in the air.

He shakes his head, his attention fully on the approaching dragon. "Try again."

I glare at the ice. There has to be a way. I clench my fist, only to curse at the searing pain from the blister I incurred when I tried to grab my daggers earlier.

Oh.

Perhaps we can use the dragonfire after all.

I reach into the pocket of my jacket and slip on the heat-resistant gloves I'd bought earlier today, praying that they're strong enough to resist what I'm about to put them through.

"Blackwater, how fast can you run?"

Though every muscle in his body is coiled for attack, and the promise of death gleams bright behind his eyes, the pirate still manages to grin. "Depends. Am I running away from a certain death or toward a beautiful woman?"

I look around. "Hazard a guess."

He sighs. "Pretty damn fast."

We have only moments to formulate a plan before the dragon hurdles out of the sky with a deafening screech. Blackwater meets its claws with his sword, deflecting them with no small amount of effort. The beast swoops upwards in a wide arc, flips onto its back, then careens toward us again, but he's already running.

Which was wise, because the dragon's mouth opens wide, a dastardly glow forming in the back of its throat.

"GO NOW," I scream, fists clenched and heart racing from where I crouch behind a scrubby bush. I may as well have saved my breath, for that's the very moment the heavens open and spew forth fire. I have to throw an arm over my face and turn away from the blistering heat. I might not have eyebrows after this.

I allow myself one breath, two, before I dart from my hiding place and snatch up the daggers I littered in Blackwater's path. The daggers that are now scorching hot with dragon fire.

Praying to whatever entity listening that the pirate hadn't been incinerated, I sprint to the middle of the ice and kneel, baring my teeth against the heat of the blades even through the gloves.

Heat-resistant, my ass.

And then, summoning up all my rage, all my fear, all I have left, I hack.

The blades hiss when they meet ice, hot steam billowing into my face as I stab again and again and again with both hands. At first, I don't accomplish much of anything besides a series of angry little dents. I keep going, though, grunting and snarling with the effort. Sweat trickles into my eyes and down my back.

It occurs to me that if it wasn't for my endurance training with Basi the past several weeks, I'm not certain I would have been able to sustain this for as long as I have.

Finally, my work is rewarded.

I strike, and a hairline fracture spreads. Another, and five more zig-zag along the ice. One more, and the ice splinters with a groan and a crack, and my hands plunge straight into the water. Gritting my teeth against the frigid temperature, so cold it's white-hot, my fingers wrap around the hilt of the sword, and with the last of my strength, I pull it.

Steel rings through the air as the sword slips from the water. I stare at it, praying it'll be enough. The weapon is surprisingly heavy; its hilt is composed of what seem to be white scales crusted with greenish-blue jewels. It doesn't look remarkable. It looks like a sword. And other than a lingering cold at my fingertips, I don't feel any great magic.

Proctor above, please lend a hand.

Gripping the sword tightly, I take off running.

I arrive to find Blackwater in the valley of a hill, swinging furiously at the raging beast, but it's clear that he's grown tired. He's still able to fend off the dragon's relentless attacks, one after another, but at some point, he's going to run out of energy. The dragon, on the other hand, shows no sign of tiring, even with its injuries. A lash from its tail strikes out, and I watch with dread as it catches the pirate square in the chest. Though he lands somewhat gracefully in a roll, I can tell he's running out of stamina, and the attacks are getting harder to avoid. His chest heaves, teeth bared with exertion.

This must end now.

"Look what I found," I holler from atop a hill.

The dragon stills, its massive head swiveling my way. Its glittering eyes register me first, then the sword in my hand.

The pirate is instantly forgotten.

It rampages toward me, its jaws opening wide to swallow me whole. I raise the blade, take a running start, and leap off the hillside, aiming for the dragon's exposed neck.

I collide instead with the dragon's barbed tail, and the blade flies out of my hand. When I hit the ground, I roll a few times, finally coming to a painful halt on my back. I'm too stunned to get up. My vision swims. When I come to, the sky is purple. I blink, squeeze my eyes shut, then open them again. It's not the sky, I realize. It's the dragon's eyes.

Lavender ringed with silver.

It's got me pinned beneath its claws, and its snout is so close, I can feel the hot smoke of its breath on my face, smell the sulfur. Death is a heartbeat away.

But I've seen purple eyes like that before.

Exactly like that.

And when the duke was recounting his experience with the dragon . . . he had called it a she. How would he have known that?

Oh no. I've gone and lost my mind. But what if I'm right? Those eyes.

"Aster?" I choke out, tears streaming down my face from the smoke. I can scarcely breathe from the heat. "Are you . . . Aster?"

The dragon freezes, then rears back, its pupils no more than pinpricks. "Aster?" I say again, disbelief and shock shaking my voice.

Its—her—grip on me slackens, then releases entirely.

No, no, no. We've had it all wrong.

Suddenly, the dragon whirls around, teeth bared, wings flaring wide, but Blackwater's too fast. The white sword is a blur of motion as it arcs downward to deliver the killing blow.

"STOP," I shriek, vaulting to my feet.

It's not going to work. He's going to kill her. He has every reason to slay this dragon. I could be wrong. I could be completely misguided and doom us both. And yet—

"LIAM. DON'T."

The blade continues down its path. My scream tears through the air as the sword meets the dragon's scales, my hand flying to my mouth—

And then it stops.

A strangled sob of relief claws out of my throat, but it's short-lived. The dragon's tail whips around and knocks Blackwater off his feet, sending him sprawling.

"NO," I scream. Moving faster than I ever have in all my life, I somehow reach him and throw myself on top of him the moment before the dragon rears back to incinerate us both.

"Please, Aster," I plead, staring into her glowing maw. I can see the column of fire in the back of her throat. I can feel its heat on my face and smell the acrid sulfur. Blackwater struggles to throw me off of him, but I elbow him in the face. "We didn't know. PLEASE. STOP. FOR ROSIE."

The heat intensifies, and my eyes close. I hope I don't feel it. I hope—

And then the heat dissipates, and all I feel is wind on my face.

My eyes crack open in disbelief, and beside me, I feel Blackwater exhale sharply. The dragon, Aster, backs away from us, watching warily. A low growl rumbles in her throat.

"Ffffffckkkkkkk," Liam says, laying on his back to rub where I'd jabbed his face. I reach behind me to pat him on the leg. But I can't take my eyes off Aster. I can't believe it.

"The sisters were never killed by a dragon," I breathe. "They—" I gesture helplessly to the beast a few paces away from us. "—they become them."

Blackwater's lips part as he sits up, his wide-eyed gaze darting up to Aster. Trying to find a trace of humanity in the enormous creature. For a moment, no one makes a sound. Even the dragon remains stoic as she silently regards us.

"Aster . . . the sister who sacrificed herself three years ago?"

I open my mouth to answer, but when I look at Blackwater, I realize he isn't asking me, but her. I also notice that he's burned. A red, angry-looking blister covers his neck.

Aster lowers her great head, closing her eyes. A lump forms in my throat. She looks like she's . . . ashamed.

He turns to me. "How . . .? How."

"Rosie showed me their paintings. I recognized her eyes."

That would explain why there's never anything left of them but clothing. They never died. They changed.

But why? How?

Understanding unfurls slowly, then all at once. I also, at this moment, realize I'm practically sitting in Blackwater's lap, and hastily remove myself to my own little patch of burned grass.

"We were lied to. Just . . . differently than we'd thought." I lean back onto my arms, trying to wrangle my thoughts into coherent words. "This whole thing is a fucking curse. That's why the trees look like that back there. It's where the curse takes place. And curses are caustic magic. They debride, and they rot things over time."

Look at the gouges on my back. They will never heal. Am I rotting from the inside out, too?

"And it makes sense that it occurs every three years, in a defined space. Curses are specific like that."

Blackwater stares at me, and I can tell his mind is sprinting to catch up to my line of thought. "I saw no curse marks on the trees back there."

I nod my head in agreement. For every curse leaves a mark. A scar. "The actual cursed object or person must be somewhere else." I study Aster. "It's not the daughters themselves, or surely they would have known. It must be around here somewhere, though."

"But. Every curse must have a way to break it. It's part of the balance," he continues. After all, he read the book too. "You think if we find the origin of the curse, we can break it?"

"No curse is unbreakable," I say, repeating what I'd read verbatim.

Blackwater scowls fiercely at the sword. "That means someone thought this sword posed a threat. They sealed it away in ice to prevent anyone from using it. There's no other plausible explanation as to why it was like that."

"It seems that whoever sealed it away never wished for the dragons to be slain at all."

"Why curse the girls at all, then? They're giving up their lives one way or another."

And then it clicks. The duke's young face, seemingly frozen in time. He'd told his daughters it was because the magic blessed him with slower aging, and perhaps that was true, but it's never enough. People in power always want more. There is always a justification for others to suffer, anyone but themselves.

We share a glance.

A great weariness comes over his face, then, and I'm certain he can see the same in mine. It's a particular fatigue I feel only when I'm reminded of the depthless, indomitable evil of man.

The girls were never the curse. They were the price the caster of the curse paid.

Carefully, I get to my feet, wincing. I make my way as non-threateningly as I can to Aster, who does not seem to care much for my nearness. She huffs a fiery breath and lunges, sending my heart straight into my throat.

"I'm not going to hurt you," I murmur, hands up. "I . . . I'm sorry. I'm so sorry, Aster."

She stills long enough for our eyes to meet, and then her massive head swings away, dismissing me. I wouldn't have much interest in apologies from a stranger either, come to think of it. I'd be much too furious.

"Aster," Blackwater says, coming to stand beside me. "What about your sisters?" That gets her attention.

"We're going to break the curse," I promise her. "But we will need some help. All the help we can get."

That's all the information Aster seems to need. Chuffing, she gathers herself to her full and terrible height, flares her wings, and launches into the sky. We watch her go until she's little more than a black speck in an orange sunset.

After picking up all our dropped weapons, we head back to the orchard.

31

HEAT

Daylight has all but leached from the sky by the time we reach those cursed trees. There's barely enough light to see by for me to lift the blade of the white sword and drive it deep into the trunk of a tree, twisting for spite.

The effect is immediate.

One by one, starting with the tree I stabbed, they begin to die. Really die. The branches curl in on themselves like spindly hands closing into fists, black leaves withering to ash that dwindles to nothing before it ever reaches the ground.

We're left standing in a wide, flat field of scorched dirt.

"Half done," Blackwater murmurs, glancing around with his arms crossed.

He's right. If this is where the sisters became dragons—where the curse was intended to take place—killing the trees will only prevent the transformation going forward, not end the curse. This place was only the conduit, after all. Not the origin. If the curse caster knew what we'd done, all they'd have to do is designate another area.

We have to find the curse's origin before that can happen. But I have a fairly sound theory on where to begin the search.

What's done is done, though. The girls will never be humans again.

Sighing, I sheathe the white sword at my hip, doing my best to hide the weariness I feel from the day's events. And I can't stop shivering, although the jacket is doing well enough at hiding it for now. It started with my hands, a bone-deep chill, as if I never removed them from the icy pond at all. And now, it's spread to my wrists.

I'm starting to wonder if the spell that encased the sword in ice had a more lingering bite than I initially thought. I hardly had time to ponder the ramifications of sticking my hands in it at the time. Neither of us did. I wrap myself tighter in my coat and shove my hands as deeply into my pockets as they'll go. It's not so bad, now that my fingers are numb.

"When we arrived earlier," I say as we set off at a trudging pace along the river shoulder to shoulder. "Did you feel a . . . I don't know. A popping sensation?"

"Come to think of it, yes. I meant to comment on it, but the dragon seemed more important at the time. What are you thinking, Strider?"

I take care to arrange my thoughts in order before I propose my theory. "If I were Aster, and my life was taken away from me like this, I would be furious. And I'd want revenge. But we know that she hasn't gotten it. None of them torched the town for letting this happen. None of them exacted revenge on the manor."

"Well," he counters, "They can't exactly burn the manor to the ground. Their sisters still lived there. Do you think . . . hmm. You're proposing that the orchard acted as a barrier of some sort. The dragons couldn't move past it even if they wanted to. Otherwise, they could have potentially spirited the remaining sisters away." He chuckles darkly, shaking his head. "Roarke has never been in any danger. It's been about perpetuating the curse this entire time."

"Well, I felt no such sensation when we left the orchard. They're free to fly wherever they wish now."

"The poor darlings," Blackwater observes, but absent is the usual note of flippancy.

My lip curls in the dark. "It makes me sick."

I'm about to go on about my many ill feelings I harbor about today's events when I spot a patch of scraggly, tube-like kinderweed on the bank of the river. Straying to the side, I snag some out of the ground and shove it in my mouth, grimacing against the sharp bitterness.

Blackwater, darting a look over his shoulder, does a double-take, his mouth tightening. "Strider, if you were hungry, you could have said so. I brought food."

Ignoring him, I chew until the flavor disappears entirely, then spit it out into both hands. Before he can react, I stand on tiptoe and slap one hand onto his neck, right on top of the burn.

"Ow! What the fuck—"

"Hold still," I command, tightening my grip, and within a few moments, I can visibly see the tension leave his body as the burn starts to heal. He stares at me in wonder as his pain dulls, then vanishes entirely. I know from experience how quickly it exerts its effects.

"How did you do that?"

"Kinderweed." I say, lacing my fingers together and mashing the mess between my palms to take care of the welts there. Instantly, a cooling sensation takes place, followed by a pleasant numbing as the irritation and inflammation are leached away. "You have to chew it to activate the healing properties. It's bitter at first, but once that goes away, it's good to use."

"Let me guess. You read about it."

I shrug. "It was prudent to know which plants are edible, which can kill you, and all the wonders in between. Sometimes, they were all I had for food."

I throw the chewed-up mass into the river, wiping my hands on my pants now that my hands are cured of one ailment, at least. When I turn back to Blackwater, he's looking at me with an inscrutable expression.

Before I can address him, a tiny burst of light lands on my arm, and I shriek, batting it away.

"What are you doing?" he snaps, grabbing my arm as I swat another tiny light away. They're surrounding me.

"What do you mean, what am I doing? We're being ATTACKED."

"If you hurt a single firefly, I'll kill you myself."

I hesitate, arm suspended in mid-air. "A . . . what?"

He gives a long-suffering sigh before he answers. "You didn't have fireflies in Marrin? Actually, I believe that. Strider. Please don't hurt them."

Chastised, I lower my arm. "Why are they here?"

They're everywhere. In the last few moments before the suns disappeared for good, they suddenly appeared, lighting up the dark with their tiny, fragile bodies, like our own little constellations.

"I've heard it said that they appear only to people who are lost, to help light their way home," Liam says.

"Well, no time to spare, then."

"We'll put them to use another time."

I come to an abrupt halt. "What are you on about?"

He scoffs. "You're fighting a losing battle against your eyelids, Strider. And if you think we're finding our way back through those woods in the dead of night with only firefly glow and moonslight to guide our way, you're delusional. We'll sleep here, then finish this in the morning."

"I could find the way back with my eyes closed," I mutter under my breath. Louder, I argue, "Out in the open? Here? You're deranged."

"Whatever creatures roam these lands are used to a dragon prowling around. We have nothing to fear tonight. And if it's any consolation, I'll keep watch."

He does have a point about that, although I'd never admit it. And, after today's events, I am feeling drained.

We stroll on a little further through the sparkling night, but once we find a soft patch of grass beneath a sprawling oak, it's clear I've reached my limit. I sink to my knees with a heaviness I feel in my marrow and make a small fire. Although night brought a cooler breeze, it's still plenty warm out here.

So, I have no good excuse for why my teeth have begun to chatter. The cold has made it up to my elbows now.

After a small dinner of dried meat strips we'd brought along, I curl into a tight ball on my side, hoping my jacket can still hide the worst of the shivers. I just have to get through tonight, and I've endured worse. This is nothing.

Except, I might be freezing from the inside out.

"Strider?" I hear Blackwater lower himself in front of me.

I open my eyes to frown up at a sliver of jaw, the glimmer of green. "I was asleep."

"The fuck you were. You're shaking like a leaf."

"It's nothing," I insist.

Warm, calloused fingers wrap around my hands, and I sit up, snatching them back. He sucks in a startled breath through his teeth. "Your skin is ice," he accuses, searching my face. "What happened?"

"I'm guessing the ice the sword was stuck in wasn't just an obstacle after all," I mumble, shoving my hands into my armpits. Now I have very cold armpits. "It's as if it's spelled to punish me for outsmarting it."

I don't know which is colder, my hands or the ice in Blackwater's voice. "Why did you hide this from me?"

"I can handle it."

He groans, tilting his head back toward the sky. When he lowers it, his sigh is audible. "It's spreading, isn't it?"

My sullen silence is answer enough. He takes a moment to contemplate. "You won't be able to keep yourself warm for much longer once it's spread beyond your arms. Does circulation help?"

I can see where he's going with this, and I cannot allow it. Rolling over to face away from him, I mutter, "Nothing helps. Keep watch, Blackwater, and wake me when it's my turn."

I hear him take a seat behind me, close to my back. "As you say, Strider."

And though sleep comes swiftly, it doesn't stay.

I wake sometime during the night, my entire body trembling. My hands and arms are ice, and no matter how I rub them, I remain freezing. If anything, it only makes it worse. My teeth are chattering so loudly, I'm shocked that nearby woodland creatures haven't stopped by to see what all the racket is about. I can stand to suffer through it only for a few moments more before I swallow my pride and open my eyes.

Beside me, Blackwater is lying on his back, his face illuminated by the three moons as he watches the stars. There's an awed reverence on his face that rewinds time and transforms him once more into a boy. A boy who yearned to find the very seams of the realms and sail on past. My eyes flick up, and for a moment, I marvel too.

Constellations sparkle as if someone tossed a handful of glitter too high, and it all got stuck. Fireflies still swirl around us here and there, lending a surreal, dreamy feel to the deep night. But then, a shiver courses through my body, and the spell is broken.

I reach out a trembling hand and tug on the sleeve of his coat. He turns his head, and our eyes meet. A look of understanding passes between us, and without a word, he sits up and shrugs off his overcoat. Once he's finished, he scoots closer to me, and I sit up too, so he can wrap it around my shoulders. It takes me a moment to pry my arms apart, so tightly did I have them crossed over my chest. But his coat is warm, and it smells like him. The sea, and suns-soaked leather.

The thing absolutely swallows me.

Once he's satisfied I'm wrapped up tight as can be, he guides me back down, facing away from him. The encounter, so far, is surprisingly bereft of 'I-told-you-so's.' The realization knocks something loose deep within my chest.

"Easy now," he says in a rumbling baritone, and I startle when he settles in behind me, close enough that I can feel his breath on my neck. His body is shockingly warm, and I press myself flush against him, desperate for relief against the cold. His arms snake around my waist, and his hands brush the length of my arms until they find my fingers.

His callouses scrape, not unkindly, against my skin. Gently, he rubs each finger of my hand, my palms, my knuckles, using deliberate, circular motions. Now and then, he rubs the length of my arms, but mostly, it's my hands that he focuses on.

"What would you do, little thief, without your clever fingers?"

I respond with a soft, tremulous laugh.

"Does it hurt?"

It did at first, millions of little pinpricks at the tips of my fingers, but . . . no one has ever touched me like this. I've never wished for it before.

I shake my head. "D-d-don't stop."

"I won't."

I watch him methodically massage my hands through slitted eyes. The gentle repetition in the glow-flecked night is hypnotizing. All my life, I've been a creature of solitude. I eat alone, skulk alone, and most importantly of all, sleep alone. I've never broken that rule. Not until tonight.

"Close your eyes." His voice wraps around the very core of me like a blanket, warm and heavy. Sleep tugs impatiently at my eyelids, and between the soft leather of his coat and the furnace of his body, I'm fighting a losing battle.

"Wake me to take watch," I murmur. He shushes me.

I close my eyes, fully intending on waking up in a few hours to relieve him, but exhaustion crashes over me like a storm and pulls me under for the rest of the night.

32

WINGS, FIRE, AND TEETH

I sit up, blinking blearily in the morning light, still wrapped tightly in a pirate's coat. A strip of dried meat lands in my lap. "Good morning, darling."

Blackwater reclines propped on his elbows a few paces in front of me, chewing on his own breakfast, sunning himself.

"Hmmph," I croak, gnawing on the leathery strip.

"How do you feel?"

Last night's events flash before my eyes, but I refuse to let any mortification show on my face. Instead, I pull his coat sleeves back to reveal my hands, trembling, but still functional. My fingernails, I note, are a sickly blue, and I can't feel much, but blue is better than the black flesh-death of frostbite. The chill has spread to my shoulders now, though. I roll them, wincing.

"It's spreading, but I can manage."

"Let's finish this. Quickly. Are you ready?" Our eyes meet, and I give a sharp nod.

Before I can protest, he reaches down to help me up, and I don't miss the look of alarm that sweeps across his face when he touches my icy fingers.

"It'll be alright." Whether it's him or me I'm trying to convince is anyone's guess. "They might have frozen entirely if it weren't for you."

He gives my hand a little squeeze. "Anytime."

I get to my feet, but when he turns, I pull on his hand. "You trusted me yesterday when I told you not to kill Aster. Why?"

Confusion draws his brows together. "Why would you lie?"

I scoff. "To free myself if you'd been killed? And besides, what if I'd been wrong?"

He ticks his answers off on the fingers of his other hand. "One, you're not getting away from me that easily. And two, one of us has to take the plunge first. I suppose it'll just have to be me."

"The plunge?"

"To trust each other. Like how you trusted me last night to warm you right up." He grins, then jerks his chin. "Come on. It's time to finish this."

We look down and seem to realize together that our hands are still clasped. Without a word, we pull apart and begin our trek back to the manor.

But the entire way back, Liam's words replay in my mind, and I can't help but wonder if I, too, have taken some sort of plunge.

The moment we set foot into the manor gardens, a scream rends the air. We both draw our swords—his black, mine white—when Rosie erupts from the house, flinging the doors wide. She races down the stairs, skirts in hand, and doesn't stop until she's thrown herself around my neck, weeping.

"I kept watch all night for you," she sobs into my shoulder, squeezing me so hard my ribs grind. "When you didn't come back, I . . . I thought—"

"We were tired," Blackwater supplies, only for Rosie to set upon him next, yanking him down so she can wrap her arms around his neck.

"Did you do it?" She disentangles herself, beaming at both of us. "Did you slay the dragon?"

My nose scrunches. "Not . . . quite."

She falters, lips parting, but whatever she intended to say is cut off as her father appears at the head of the stairs next. "By the crown, you've done it!"

By now, every servant on the property has emerged from the manor to gape at us. Lovely. An audience.

We stand very still as the duke hurries to meet us and grasp our hands in thanks.

Neither of us says a word as he chatters on about honor, sacrifice, and so on. Finally, he calms down a bit. "How did you do it? How did you slay that ulcerous monster?"

"We didn't."

The man turns to Blackwater, puzzled. "Come again?"

"We haven't killed the ulcerous monster. But we will."

The duke's smile twitches as he takes the smallest step back. Rosie, for her part, has lapsed into watchful silence.

"I'm not certain what you mean," the duke says slowly. Carefully.

"We met the dragon, alright," I snarl. "It was strange, she had lovely lavender eyes. Just as Aster did."

Rosie's face pales. As for her father, he freezes in place.

"What a disturbing thing to say," he recovers, unlined face contorted in sudden rage. "How dare you mock our loss. How despicable."

"You sacrificed your own daughters to a curse," I spit, pointing the white blade at his chest. I may not have the dexterity I usually would, what with my affliction, but I can still hold a damn sword. "That's why there's never anything left of them. That's why they always go alone. They might not be sacrificing themselves to a dragon, but you're sacrificing their lives nonetheless. And then, when a true threat to your little system showed up, you sealed it away in ice."

Now that I'm looking at him, it's so obvious what's happening.

His youth despite his older age. He'd claimed that Roarke's magic was rewarding him, preserving him, for his benevolent rule, but that wasn't it. No, he was getting it from the curse. Immortality, for the lives of his daughters. Forever is a long time to justify the sacrifices made to attain it.

"You're feeding off them. Your daughters. You never tried to stop it. You're the one who started it in the first place."

Now it's Rosie's turn to back away, her eyes wide and shiny.

"Lies," the duke shouts, looking to his remaining daughter. "I would never. I could never. I loved you girls. You know that."

She turns to us, livid. "My father could never be capable of such a thing. Guards!"

Out of nowhere, at least thirty guards rush for us, the air ringing with the kiss of steel as sword points surround us.

"There I was, hoping she'd take our word for it," Blackwater mutters to me.

"Guards, take them away," the duke commands, spittle flying. "Find the darkest, coldest cell in Roarke and leave them there to—"

A flesh-splitting roar threatens to shatter the very foundation we stand upon, and everyone claps their hands over their ears, wincing. Everyone but Blackwater and me.

I've never heard a more beautiful sound in my life. Lifting my eyes to the skies, I smile.

Aster, in all her mighty glory, descends from the clouds and slams to the ground in an explosion of dust and pebbles. I notice that she took care to land outside the gardens, so as not to destroy her and her sisters' pride and joy, and if there was any lingering doubt that it was in fact Aster, it is now banished entirely.

Aster is not alone, either.

More blood-curdling bellows send the duke's soldiers fleeing for their lives as three other dragons appear in the sky, heading straight for us: one slick silver, one mossy green, one sapphire blue.

The sisters have come.

They land as one, giant maws lined with fangs, tails swishing. But they make no move to attack. In fact, all four of their massive heads lower as a figure cuts purposefully through the lawn, her skirts billowing furiously behind her from the turbulence of the dragons' wings.

She stops before them, no larger than their forearms, and peers into their eyes. Eyes, I can now see, the color of pale blue sky, except for one.

And for a while, no one speaks, no one moves. I don't think I breathe. And then Rosie speaks.

"Aster." She points to the black dragon. "Amaryllis." The green. "Calla." The silver. "Marigold." The sapphire.

As each of their names is called, they lower their heads to meet her outstretched hands, and at the last one, Rosie bursts into tears.

Of course, she needs no further proof than to look into their eyes. They're her sisters.

For whatever reason, I turn away. Let them have their moment. It's been twelve years since they've been here, together, in this place where they once were happy.

Unfortunately, there's still the matter of the duke.

"Rosie, Rosie," he stumbles toward her, his voice saccharine with pleas, "You must understand. I did it for Roarke. Roarke needs me, Rosie. And now you see that they never died, anyway—"

She rounds on him, her delicate face contorted with wrath, and behind her, the sisters rise to their full and terrible height. Steam hisses from their jowls.

To me, she extends her hand. I know exactly what she wants. I heft the white sword to her, and she catches it easily, never taking her eyes from her father. Her father, who traded his daughters for youth. His daughters, who loved him, and their flowers, and each other.

Rosie strides over to her cowering father and lifts the sword.

"The contender, all those years ago, claimed this sword can kill anything. What do you think, Papa?"

He's wailing now. Sniveling. "No, please. Please. You can't be left on your own. You won't know what to do."

She laughs bitterly. "If I'm old enough to die for my people, I am old enough to rule."

"You don't know how to be alone. You'll get taken advantage of, lied to, abused!" Her eyes narrow to blue slits. "Never again."

And with that, she strolls past him to the statue she'd pointed out to me yesterday—the one the duke had placed in the garden. His eyes widen, and he lurches to his feet, his arms flailing as he screams.

"YOU UNGRATEFUL GIRL. Look around you. I have provided for you all this time, and this is what I get? This garden, this house—"

"I'll provide for myself."

"Look at what your sacrifice will provide! Look around you at all the beauty, all the peace! Please, Rosie. Think of your people. They need me."

But his words don't seem to reach her. "My sisters started dying when this statue appeared, now that I recall. Figures. I always hated this one."

And with both hands, she lifts the sword and severs the statue's head. Black, acrid smoke spills out of the top, as if trapped inside for centuries, and a putrid smell fills the gardens. I lurch as the frost leaves my body in an almost painful rush, and Blackwater grips my elbow to steady me. I throw him a grateful glance.

The statue's head hits the ground, shattering into thousands of fractals that skitter all over the garden. I bend down and pick two pieces up gingerly. Strange symbols have been etched into their surface, so faint I couldn't see them earlier.

Familiar symbols.

I slip them into my pocket for later.

In front of us, the duke has fallen to the ground, writhing. Before my eyes, his skin begins to shrivel, his dark hair growing white, then sloughing off entirely. He's aging like the trees in the orchard.

But before he manages to die, the sisters surround him, rear their heads back, and release a torrent of flames. When they're finished, there's nothing left of the duke. Not his clothes, not his skeleton, not his ash. Just a black mark on the dirt.

All those extra years, and not even his corpse remains.

By midday, I'm standing on the pier beside The Wraith. Blackwater has already rounded up the crew and boarded, leaving Rosie and me to say our goodbyes.

She hugs me again, which I find delightfully informal now that she's the duchess of Roarke.

"Don't be a stranger, Iona," she warns, her eyes glassy despite the wide smile on her face. "If you ever need a friend, you've got one. In all of us."

She gestures upwards, where Calla, Aster, Amaryllis, and Marigold make lazy loops in the sky. I imagine, as a citizen, it will take some getting used to. Of course, after she took some time to collect herself, she held a town meeting. It was evident from the gasps and cries that the people of Roarke were quite shocked to hear what happened. If Rosie hadn't built up such goodwill and trust already with her people, I doubt they would have been as accepting of the news.

Rosie will be a good ruler, and I don't imagine it will take too long for Roarkians to get used to the change. The image of the suns glinting off the sisters' wings is one I'll take with me for the rest of my life. I think of the faces from the paintings. The sisters are as beautiful as before. Only different now.

"And here. Before I forget."

She moves to hand me the white sword, but I stop her.

"No. I couldn't. That's yours." It goes unsaid that she's already paid us the reward. Turns out Roarke is very wealthy from wine exports. The duke wasn't exaggerating, at least in that regard.

But she shakes her head. "I insist. Swords belong to heroes, do they not?"

I snort. "If that's true, I'm the last person that should have it."

She tilts her head. "Hero doesn't mean what you think it does."

Guilt twists in my stomach as I remind myself why we came here in the first place. For a stupid task. "Maybe the next time I see you, I'll have a better grasp on it."

Her eyes twinkle as she says, "I took the liberty of naming her, by the way. Cursekiller." Her eyebrows bob as she says it. "She's yours."

I take the heavy thing from her and can't help but feel a small seed of accomplishment. I did help someone. Even if we came here for entirely selfish reasons, does that negate what we did?

I'm not sure.

But . . .

"Are you certain you don't need it here?"

"Oh, Iona," Rosie sighs. "We have all that we need. I have my voice, my title, and my mind. And my sisters have their wings, fire, and teeth." She squeezes my hand, and we tilt our faces to the sky. "Save your concern. No one will ever hurt us again."

33
WHEN THE KINGDOM ISN'T LOOKING

That night, I walk to supper alone. I was late finishing up my chores for the day and was the last to leave the deck. I don't mind it, though. I've spent the day in a bit of a daze, which I attribute to exhaustion and perhaps a bit of shock.

But not all of it was bad.

Earlier, I took Cursekiller to hang on the wall in the sparring room, with the rest of the weapons. I am in no way ready to wield that heavy thing, but it will serve as very invigorating inspiration in the meantime. She looked so lovely, a vision of white among the ebony weapons.

I fling open the double doors to the mess hall and prowl inside toward the kitchen. But as I do, a feeling of unease begins to creep over me. It's strangely quiet in here.

And the pirates. They're staring.

Gazes dart my way, but when I meet them head-on, they're quickly averted. And worst of all, they're smiling at me.

I'm stopped by a hand on my arm by one pirate, Flint, who simply whispers, "Atta girl."

Someone else hoots, "Good on ya, lass."

I quickly change tactics and refuse to look anywhere but the floor until I find my seat next to Luhan, who promptly slings an arm around my neck and wrenches me downward, crowing, "And here she is, the hero of legends."

"What are you on about?" I squawk, slapping him in the chest, and he finally releases me. "I didn't kill anything. And how does everyone know what happened?"

Luhan laughs delightedly. "You're still in one piece, so clearly you did something right. And that lovely white sword that was hanging on your hip isn't exactly subtle."

Instead of the few stragglers that usually share our bench, almost the entire crew has started to crowd around, and though they're mostly chatting among themselves and eating, the frequent looks in my direction are obvious. I glance at Luhan, worried.

"What do they want?" I whisper.

"A story," another voice responds, and I whirl to find Liam straddling the bench beside me. "What good is an adventure, if no story comes of it?"

"Oy, you gonna tell us about the dragons or not?" Someone calls.

"Get on wi' it, then. I've got night duty," someone else says.

Liam and I share a look, and I gesture to him with my chin.

Needing no further encouragement to hear himself speak, Liam begins. I have to admit, he's a compelling storyteller. He has the voice for it, too. The pirates are enthusiastic listeners, cheering when Rosie is introduced and shouting when we fight Aster. When the duke is reduced to ashes, they raise their mugs of ale, their approval echoing off the walls.

Once the story has been told and supper is coming to an end, I jolt when someone whispers in my ear. "Aye, good on ya. It's easy to swing a sword. Harder to know when to put it down." And then a hand gruffly pats the back of my head, but before I can respond, the old man has already shuffled across the room and taken his seat. He tips his mug to me, and I return the gesture. I sit up a little taller after that.

Later, I learn his name is Teller.

After dinner, Liam and I stand together on the deck of The Wraith, just as the suns are beginning to slip away. I fish around in my coat pocket and produce one of the broken pieces of cursed marble I took from the garden.

Not to steal, but to prove we completed our first task. Perhaps it didn't end as we thought, but a curse is pretty damn unkillable, although if you ask me, the real victory was the death of an immortal man's ego. Either way, seems like it's a task accomplished.

"How do we do this?"

The moment the question leaves my lips, movement catches our attention. Our heads swivel to the railing, where a little paper bird awaits, hopping around anxiously.

Liam arches a brow and makes an "after you" gesture toward the paper creature. Closing the distance between us, I hold out the shard of marble, cupped in my hands, and almost squeal when the bird hops onto them.

I'm even more surprised when its claws latch around the marble, which should have been impossible for the tiny thing to lift, and with a few flaps of its wings, the creature takes off into the evening.

Arms clasped behind his back, Liam watches the little bird disappear into the orangey-blue swirl of twilight.

"One down, two to go," he remarks.

My stomach drops at the thought. If the other two tasks are going to be as harrowing as this one was, I don't know how to prepare for that. I thought that once the excitement of it all wore off, I might feel prouder of what we did, but right now, all I feel is sorrow and disgust at what happened to those girls. The curse went on for twelve years.

"What is it, Strider?"

I emerge from my dark thoughts to find Liam watching me pensively. I shake my head, muttering an excuse, and turn to leave.

He steps in front of me, blocking my path, and I glance up. "Not now."

"Strider."

I make a low noise in my throat, try to sidestep, and find him in my way again. "Liam, I don't know what to say."

He grabs my wrist, but not unkindly. "Something bothering you?"

"Is something not bothering you?" Frustration heats the back of my neck. What would someone like him know of feeling powerless, the way those girls must have felt? The way I have felt, all my life? I need to be alone to process what we saw. For in the world I'd known, it had always been easy to blame the evils I saw on Marrin's lack of magic, and the strife it created. The desperation. But Roarke had an abundance of magic, and it made no difference.

"I don't like what we saw any more than you did," he says.

I find his calm grating, and guilt wells up inside of me, cooling quickly into the sharp point of blame. "How much did she pay us for heroically ending the curse that her own father used to sacrifice four of his own daughters?"

He stares evenly at me. "The reward was fifty thousand gold coins." An absolutely egregious amount.

"How lucrative," I mutter, twisting to leave. It's not fair of me to hurl my anger onto Liam, but I don't know where else to put it. I need to be alone. I've almost made it to the door when the sound of his voice brings me pause.

"It would have been, I suppose."

I turn around to face him. "You didn't take it?"

His hands are in his pockets, his expression thoughtful. "Don't be fooled. It's not that I couldn't bring myself to accept payment for a service rendered, no matter how ghastly. It's that I can steal or bargain my way into more wealth whenever I wish, and she could offer something I felt was much more valuable."

I take an involuntary step forward, arms crossed. "And what was that?"

He, in turn, takes one toward me. "A favor. The most valuable currency in all the realms. Is that more palatable for you, Strider?"

I expel a breath. "None of that was palatable, Liam."

He laughs. "Don't tell me you're deciding to have a crisis of conscience now?" I shrug, arms out wide, but he continues. "Don't forget. You got paid for what we did in Roarke. By me. So the way I see it, if you want to say I'm a scoundrel, you're right here with me."

"Trust me, I haven't forgotten."

I turn on my heel to leave, but he stops me with a hand on my shoulder. His rings flash in the waning sunlight.

"Or, you could look at it another way." His voice is a whole register lower. Conspiratorial. "There is much to be done when the kingdom isn't looking. And who's worried about one little pickpocket, and a greedy, self-serving pirate? Then again," he clicks his tongue, "I'd have thought you'd already know that."

I hold his stare, but when heat climbs up my neck at the memory of his body molded over mine all night long, I recoil as if burned, berating myself all the way to my room. Roarke entailed much more than I anticipated, and my mind has never been such a mess.

34

SOMETHING BAD, AND
SOMETHING GOOD

Luhan meets me on the dock the following evening. I'm surprised he actually shows up, given the noncommittal response he gave me when I asked. The way I judge it, we've got a couple of hours before the suns go down. Should be plenty of time.

"What is it, Iona? I'm missing a Bishops tournament." He joins me by the railing, the silver surface smooth below. He's referring to an apparently beloved card game that the pirates love to play. Their hollers echo all the way to the library sometimes, and though at first it annoyed the hell out of me, now it's become another ambient sound of The Wraith.

Apparently, the ship docks overnight once a month, allowing them to hold their tournament. I thought I'd take advantage of that.

I stare at the gentle waves, bracing myself for what comes next. He's sure to mock me for this, but if I'm to function properly in this environment, it must be done.

"I need your help."

"With what?" Intrigue curls the edges of his voice, like burning paper.

I drag my eyes from the water to his face, then pointedly back to the water.

It takes only a few moments before his eyes flare in understanding. "Oh. You want to . . . go for a swim? Now?"

I nod. I even hauled some rope over so we had a way of climbing back out.

Realization gleams in his eyes as he crosses his arms. "And is swimming something you did a lot in Marrin?"

" . . . No."

"Hmm."

Too late, I register the wicked edge of his smile. Too late do I realize that Luhan is the worst person I could have asked to help. "Well, in you go then."

With both hands, he shoves me into the sea.

"*You cu—*" The cold hits me like a wall. I plunge underwater, arms and legs flailing about.

Accomplishing nothing.

A second splash signals Luhan's arrival, and soon after, I'm yanked above the surface, gasping for breath.

The instant air enters my lungs is the instant I start shouting.

"I could—have—drowned—by myself!" I have to pause every so often to accommodate for when my head slips below the surface, my appendages pushing wildly to keep myself afloat.

Somehow, I manage to fight my way over to him and push him underwater, only for him to shove me off and back beneath the gentle rolling waves, cackling the entire time.

"But it's much more fun this way," he chortles gleefully.

"You're supposed to be teaching me," I gasp, spitting out mouthfuls of salty seawater.

"I am," Luhan insists, splashing me. "My methods are just unorthodox. Stop paddling like that. Do this." He flips over to float lazily on his back. "You don't have to fight everything all the time, you know. Let the water hold you up, or you'll tire yourself out."

After a few more minutes of desperate flailing, I finally give up and mimic Luhan, letting my body float to the surface. Above us, the sky has become a saccharine pinkish-purple dotted with a few early stars. Voices drift on a sea breeze from the ship, and I realize with a pang of fear how far we've floated from it. But glancing over to Luhan, I can see that he doesn't seem concerned in the least. In fact, his eyes are shut, and he looks more peaceful than I've ever seen him.

He'd stripped off his shirt before jumping in, and water runs in rivulets down his wiry, muscled frame. Despite the many hours he's spent in the sunlight, his skin has remained unblemished and pale, as if preserved by a spell. He truly is beautiful, like an intricately carved sculpture from another place, another time. From the moment I met him, I thought his mannerisms and design seemed better suited for a castle than a ship.

"Oh, stop with the staring," he cracks open an eye, and in the soft dusk, it's the color of burned honey. "Actually, don't. I live for the attention."

"It's strange to see you like this," I say, turning back toward the sky. "Peaceful."

"I'd be like this all the time," he retorts, "if it wasn't for you people needing constant direction."

"Please. You like being occupied."

I expect a response, but when he's silent, I flip over onto my belly, paying attention to the way I push my hands and feet through the water. Not panicked, but controlled, like he's doing.

Except Luhan's looking beneath us, eyes wide. Slowly, I look down too.

Where the water was silver, it's now become dark, dark blue, as if something—

Something is rising toward the surface. Something absurdly massive. We don't have time to get out of the way before it's too late. The strangest part is: Luhan's laughing.

He's laughing as something hard and slightly rounded rises above the water, taking us with it. Water streams off the edges, sparkling in the dying light, and I fight to regain my balance on hands and knees. Beneath us, the surface is smooth and grayish-green, covered in bits of anemone and coral.

And then everything is still, and finally, I dare to raise my head. Beside me, Luhan is still hooting with laughter.

"Lu? What is this?"

In response, he points behind us, and, following the gesture, I can see something sticking out of the water, something scaled with humongous yellow eyes looking right at me.

Now, it's my turn to laugh, my hand flying to my forehead in awe. "It's a sea turtle." We're on its shell.

"They like to surface at this time of day, when the predators dive to deeper waters for the night," Luhan says, finally having laughed himself into a slap-happy exhaustion. "This one, I must admit, is rather large. And it's a female, by the way. You can tell by the color of the shell. The males are much darker."

"She's not . . . afraid of us?"

Luhan shrugs. "No reason to be. We'd never hurt them."

I move next to him and flop onto my back. Almost lazily, he flicks me in my ribs, and I flick him back.

"Tell me something bad and something good," he says after a while.

I turn only my head to him, my cheek against the slick shell, a question on my face.

"It's something I used to do with my sister," he explains softly. When his eyes meet mine, I get the impression he's allowing me a rare glimpse into the life he led before The Wraith. A life he seems to guard quite carefully.

"Was she younger or older?"

"Older. Her name was Gwyneira. Gwyn, for short. You remind me of her, sometimes."

"How so?"

His eyes go distant. "She could be difficult to read at times. Closed off and distrustful. Growing up, we had to be . . . mindful of things. But if she decided to trust you, it was like watching a flower bloom that only you could see. The best feeling in the world."

I feel the edges of my lips curving. "Something bad . . ." A strange feeling comes over me as I lie there. I have the sudden sensation that this moment is a frosted pane of glass. On one side, the way I feel right now. Blissful and warm. And on the other side, sorrow that it has to end, and that if I'd had my way, none of this would have ever happened at all.

I didn't know I could feel such different emotions twined together, but I do. Deeply. "My something bad is I'm afraid you're not a very good swimming teacher, Lu."

He gasps, his head whipping toward me. "You're alive, aren't you?"

"No thanks to you."

"Ungrateful. See if I ever help you again."

"Actually, I was going to ask you to help me cut my hair. I've started using a growth tonic. I'm afraid it's going to come in looking dreadful."

He squints at me. "I'll consider. What's your good thing?"

I have an answer immediately. "I never imagined, ever, that I'd see a sea turtle."

"It's not often they surface so close to the ship," Luhan comments.

"And, Luhan?"

"I'm still right here?"

"I never thanked you for all the times you healed me."

To my astonishment, he pats my head, but his small grin reveals how touched he actually is. A real grin, not the one he wears when he knows he just landed a veiled insult. "You never asked to be hurt, Iona."

"I know it tires you to do it."

He shrugs as if it's nothing, when I know it's not. "I'm resilient."

"What about you? It's your turn," I say.

He considers me for a moment, his eyes dark again in the waning light. He seems to be warring with something I can't see, and for a moment, I think he's going to shirk his response, but he surprises me.

"I lost someone. Someone I loved so very much. It's been years, but some days, like today, it feels like a bone that never set right, so I never regained proper function." He pauses, takes some time to frown at the darkening sky. "I'm sorry, Iona. I didn't—erm, forget that."

"No," I grab his arm. "Don't be sorry. Not about that. I . . . I know what you mean." My voice softens, and I hesitate. "Can I change my answers?"

"If you must." But his eyes are soft, his smile encouraging. Luhan is like me. He'd rather get his teeth pulled than say something earnest. Perhaps that's why we've always seemed to understand each other. The jibes and the bickering might be what we say, but what we mean is something else entirely. Luhan likes to pretend he's either perturbed, bored, or in control of everything so no one catches sight of his loneliness. I do that, too.

I've never talked about this, and now that the words are lined up on my tongue, I'm afraid they're going to come out ugly and pathetic. Perhaps they are. Although something tells me that even if they did, Luhan wouldn't mind.

"There is much of my life I don't remember. I imagine it must have something to do with this," I gesture to the scar above my ear, "though obviously, I can't actually know. All my memories are of Marrin, though. I have no recollection of my mother, father, or anyone who raised me. It's always been . . . me. It's sort of funny. Being alone isn't hard until you realize you're not supposed to be alone. But then I start wondering about them, my parents, and I wonder what they looked like, and whether they—" My voice breaks, and I clear my throat. "I don't know how to miss them. I don't know which parts of me are theirs, and which are my own. And sometimes I wonder if it's easier, that I don't remember . . ."

Our gazes meet.

". . . so you don't have to experience the slow but inevitable forgetting of them," he finishes quietly. I sit up to cross my arms over my chest, hunching over my crossed legs, and he sits up too. He scoots next to me until our shoulders touch, his arms wrapped around his bent legs. "There is no proper way to grieve, Iona. But it must be done. There will be times you wish to stop swimming and let the current take you. And that's alright. As long as you float."

I swallow around the stone in my throat. "Luhan? What happened?"

But he shakes his head. "Another night. I promise."

I nod. "Then tell me something good."

His head whips to me. "That was my something good."

It is less a laugh and more a guffaw that pierces the dusk. My shoulder knocks into his, and he sighs as he looks up at the faint stars. "Mmm, something good. Do you know what Iridisians believe about death?"

I shake my head gently. Inside my chest, a fist squeezes my heart to the point of pain. "There is no death. Well, our bodies die. But our souls stay here, where we felt love. Why would they leave and go someplace they have never known? No, they go to the Eto trees. You'll see one, one day. White bark, silver leaves. Other places might call them shrines, but for us, when we wish to speak to the ones we miss, that is where we go. That is how they wait for us, for the trees keep their souls. And so, no one is ever gone. Just elsewhere."

I rest my temple on his shoulder. "That's really beautiful."

He hums his agreement. "You know, I haven't seen my family in a long time. I miss them terribly. We didn't part on the best of terms." He sighs. "But perhaps once you and Liam are through with your nonsense, we can take a little trip to Iridisia and you can meet them. See an Eto tree."

"I'd love that," I breathe. Iridisia, with its sparkling glaciers and snow. "But . . . how? King De'Havelin sealed all entrances to other realms years ago."

"Once a door exists, it can never be destroyed. Only hidden. Trust me. There are still ways to get through for those who know where to look." He jostles his shoulder, and I look up at him. "What is your new something good, Iona?"

"I'm happy I'm here with you, Lu."

He smiles at me. "Me too."

35

LIRAEL AND MATTEO

The next few weeks pass on a downward slope.

After no small amount of sweat, pain, and practice, Basi deems me worthy to move on to actual sparring. Not simply going through the motions, but actual fist-to-skin contact. No more drills, laps, or push-ups, though I still do those beforehand, and sometimes, during the night, if I can't sleep. Finally, I'm learning to fucking fight.

I love it.

I may leave each lesson bruised and panting, but I've never felt this accomplished in my entire life.

One night, I catch sight of myself in the small mirror in the bathing room and pause.

Consistent, full meals have banished the hollows beneath my cheeks. Long days toiling beneath the suns have warmed my skin from its former corpse-colored complexion and even bestowed a freckle here and there. I am no longer skin and bone, but strong and capable. My hair, expedited by the tonic I stole in Rourke, now reaches my neck. Luhan has indeed been helping me manage it. I run my fingers through the dark and unruly waves that frame my face and hang in my eyes. All the nutrients from the fish we eat have imparted a healthy sheen, and it's softer than I expected. The scar above my ear is hidden for once.

I'm strong enough now to hold the girl I used to be in my arms, and there's so much I wish I could tell her.

Not everyone is either a mark or an enemy. You can't hate a world in which you never took part. You're not alone. Someone else is looking at the night skies, too.

The following evening, during supper, I catch sight of a lone figure sneaking from the mess hall. This is of interest to me for three reasons: One, this is not the first time I've noticed this behavior, but in fact, the fourth. Two, last time I disregarded peculiar behavior, I was almost killed for it. And three, I don't trust that self-righteous little brat Matteo anyway. He's up to something, and I intend to find out.

I don't bother excusing myself as I rise from the table and slip out after him.

Silently, I track the movements of his shadow on the walls. It leads me upstairs to the deck, but I make sure to wait a little while before I emerge after him. Once I'm satisfied I've waited long enough, I ease open the door and creep down the steps onto the decks. At first, he's nowhere to be seen. I scan the masts, but he's not up there. He's not at the helm or in the crow's nest. That leaves . . . the figurehead.

Silently, I snake up the nearest rope and shimmy up to one of the beams presiding over the deck. The closer I crawl toward the front of the ship, my suspicions are confirmed. I hear voices. One is unmistakably Matteo's, hushed as it is, but the other is . . .

A female.

There is no other female on The Wraith.

Matteo comes into view, having climbed down the sea serpent's orifice and perched on its lower jaw between its fangs, almost at the water's surface. And in the water, right in the middle of some animated story, is a mermaid.

My mouth pops open in complete shock.

We aren't in sanctioned mermaid territory, not anymore. And she shouldn't be able to speak above water, anyway. No mermaid can, since the Peace Accords were put into place twenty-some years ago. Before those took effect, mermaids and sirens used to rule the seas, and consequently, dragged innumerable ships to a watery grave. Their voices alone could entrance any man and send him into a euphoric stupor, so that by the time they set upon them with their needle-like teeth and flesh-rending claws, they didn't even know they were dying. Legend has it, their skeletons are still smiling at the bottom of the ocean, where their souls remain trapped for mermaids to feast upon.

And so, mermaids and sirens became the focus of an oceanic massacre. For years, they were hunted and killed. To this day, they say that's why the seas are silver and not blue—because of all the pearl-colored merblood that was spilled. Sirens, which were rare to begin with, were rendered extinct entirely. Finally, the Peace Accords were struck, and it was agreed upon by King De'Havelin and the mermaid Queen Adrias that mermaids would remain in the cold waters of the north and give up their voices above the water's surface. In return, men would no longer hunt their kind and vowed to stay out of mermaid territory altogether.

Interaction between the species is entirely forbidden, as the only peace that could be found was one of severance.

But I'm sure as hell looking at one now, and she's nowhere near as savage as the stories would lead me to believe. She just looks like a girl. Round, innocent eyes, the sparkling color of shallow seawater, and pale, opalescent hair floating in swirls around her small shoulders. In the moonslight, it glimmers with subtle shades of pink, blue, and purple. Her sapphire tail shimmers with a ghostly luminescence beneath the water as it sways lazily back and forth.

They're so engrossed in their conversation, neither notices me at first. Judging from the easy familiarity of their body language, they seem to be . . . friends? I shake my head, incredulous. Breaking an

Accord like this is no small matter. If something were to happen on either side, the repercussions could mean retaliation. They could mean war.

Finally, the mermaid sees me and gasps. Matteo swivels to face me, guilt flooding his expression.

"Iona," he breathes. "Please. Don't be alarmed."

"Oh, I'm past that, don't worry." I jump down from my perch to lean over the rail. "What are you doing?"

He looks at the mermaid, whose pale face has gone even paler, then back to me. "Talking to my friend."

"I see that."

He sets his jaw defiantly. "I've known Lirael all my life."

I don't miss the look of great affection that passes through Lirael's features when he says that, and it's all the confirmation I need to know it's the truth. They look to be about the same age.

"This is why you sneak out of supper early?"

He nods, looking chastised. "I didn't think anyone saw me. Or cared. It's the only time I know someone isn't out here." He tilts his head, then. "Do you want to come down here? And meet her?"

I take a deep breath, smoothing my forehead with the palms of my hands. This is stupid.

Stupid and reckless. And yet, I find myself swinging my legs over the ledge anyway, carefully climbing down the leviathan to perch next to Matteo.

"Lirael, this is Iona," Matteo says quietly. "Iona, meet my best friend."

"You're far from home," I say by way of greeting.

"Not really. I'll be back before sunrise." Her voice has a musicality to it that I've never heard before.

"How are you—"

"Able to speak above water?" She smiles faintly. "I've always been able to. Iona, are you going to tell on us?"

Beside me, Matteo shifts uncomfortably, and I scowl at them. "I should. This is—"

"She saved my life," Matteo blurts. "When the shipwreck

happened, I should have died with everyone else. With my father. But she saved me and brought me to land, where someone found me. Does that sound evil to you?"

"Of course it doesn't," I snap. "It's not about that. It's—" I sigh heavily. "Swear to me you two idiots will be more careful. This could start a war, and that's the last thing we need."

"We know," he says hurriedly as a wide smile breaks out across his face. A pleased, conspiratorial look passes between the two of them.

Their innocence is heartbreaking. My hand claws around Matteo's shoulder. "Be careful. I mean it."

He returns my solemnity in an instant, and suddenly, he's years beyond his age. "I won't let anything happen to her. Ever. I swear."

And although I don't feel good about it, I also have no intention of inserting myself into yet another problem. I have enough of those. And now my guilt for being a horror to Matteo is assuaged. So, with a parting grunt, I haul myself back up the leviathan's mouth and leave them to it.

36

POWER

It's been about two months since I joined the crew of The Wraith. Most days are fairly routine: training with Basi in the mornings, chores during the day, and nights spent lost in whatever book I'm reading at the time. Recently, Liam has been making some appearances, although most of the time, he doesn't stay. He arrives in a swirl of coat, strides across the room, straight to the book he wanted, then leaves me to it. He might make a stray comment or two, but other than that, he seems fairly set on creating space between us.

Which is most certainly best.

But the last few nights, there's been an uptick in nervous energy to him. More pacing, more scrubbing his hands through his hair, and along his jaw. He's stewing. And tonight, when the pacing starts again, I decide to say something about it.

"What's the matter with you?" I snap my book shut in my lap.

His eyes dart to mine, as if startled to see I'm here, and an apologetic smile blooms on his face. "I'm sorry. I get lost in my thoughts sometimes."

"Mmm. You must have dozens of them."

He chuckles airily as he sits on the couch directly opposite me, stretching his long legs out in front of him. "It's the tasks. If we're to have it all finished by the end of estiva, that gives us about a month left. And nothing is coming to mind."

"You'll think of something," I yawn into the back of my hand.

He sighs and leans his head back. "All I've been doing is thinking. And while we have no shortage of enemies, the question is, who brings the least amount of trouble? Or, conversely, which would result in the largest benefit, if I were to pick a fight with them?"

He's speaking of the third task, a foe's precious possession. I've been thinking about it too. The difficult aspect is that, between Liam and me, our enemies are never a single entity. They're all part of a larger being that would incite more trouble than it's worth if we were to attack.

"Remind me what happens if the Vice is killed," I say.

"The Vice is never killed, only the man using the name. But to your point, the man who did the killing becomes the new Vice, and on and on it goes, an endless cycle of killing."

But my mind is already spinning. "And how do others know that a new Vice has risen?"

"Do you remember the marks on the traitor's chests? The skull?"

"How could I forget. It was almost the last thing I ever saw."

"Those Marks will change depending on who the new Vice is. If it were to become me, for example, those who have sworn fealty to the Vice would develop a sea serpent Mark, and therefore obey me, until I died."

"Could you step down?"

He shakes his head solemnly. "Not how it works." He pauses, frowning. "In a way, to be the Vice is to be cursed. You're the most powerful man to sail the seas, yes, but death will be peering over your shoulder for the rest of your life."

"It sounds like another form of prison."

"Yes, well, ask one hundred men what power is to them, and you'll get one hundred different answers."

"Well, what about you?" I ask, drawing my knees to my chest and setting my chin on one. "What is power to Captain Liam Blackwater?"

He hesitates. "That's a complicated answer, Strider."

"I'll try and keep up."

One corner of his mouth lifts. "If you'd asked me when I was a lad, I'd have told you that beating my stepfather just once in a sword fight was power. To this day, I see him in every opponent I face. If you'd asked me when I'd finally managed to leave in search of my own purpose, I'd have said power was a ship. And when I was starting to make a name for myself, I would have told you that stories are power, because legends are unkillable. But, power is a fluid, elusive thing. The moment it's caught, it slithers away and becomes something else."

"And now?"

He blinks, coming back to himself. "What is it for you now?" I ask again.

His gaze drifts to the massive windows depicting the black void of ocean in the night around us. "When I'm out there, and it's just me and the constellations and the seas, that is power." His eyes lift to mine. "And you?"

I unfurl myself, one leg at a time. "Control."

He studies my face. "What a peculiar answer."

"Not to me."

He crooks his thumb and forefinger into an L shape and rests his head there. "Well, the obvious question is, control over what?"

Control over my shadow, over the nightmares that plague my sleep, the memories I have, and the ones that seem to have been misplaced— and the markings on my back that burn. And most recently, control over the infuriating way my blood stirs when you walk into the room. Control over the bad habit of fixating on your cruel mouth when you speak.

My lips quirk. "Everything. You've never felt . . . on the cusp of something you don't fully understand?"

A smile lurks in his eyes as he watches me carefully. "Can't say that I have."

Well, now, I'm curious. I slip off my seat to saunter over to where Liam lounges on his couch. His eyes follow me the entire way, though he doesn't move a muscle. I perch on the very edge of one of his armrests, careful not to let his fingers skim my hip, while bracing myself with a hand on the headrest.

"What of your body?"

"What of it, Strider?"

"It's never wanted for something, against your better judgment?"

A grin tugs at one corner of his lips. "Historically, both entities are united in their goals."

My gaze, which had been following along the path of his clavicles, snaps back to his.

"*Historically*?"

To that, he says nothing.

Rising, I stroll past him until I reach the bookshelf. I reshelve the book I was reading and reach for another when suddenly, I feel his presence behind me. I didn't hear him get up. I turn to face him, my pulse thrumming. With one hand planted on the shelf, the other in his pocket, he very nearly has me caged in between him, the shelves, and the couch he'd occupied only moments ago. He couldn't resist.

"I'm still not grasping your meaning. Enlighten me." His voice is smoke.

I laugh softly, leaning my shoulders against the shelves as I arch my back. He merely tilts his head expectantly.

More often than I'd like to admit, I think about that night in Roarke, though we've never spoken of it. I wonder if it would feel the same if he touched me again, or if it was nothing more than spells, exhaustion, and years of loneliness. Sometimes, I have this bizarre urge to test myself against him again and see how much control I really possess. I've wondered about him, too. Whether he'd felt it. In the beginning, I'd thought the urge to put my hands on him came from animosity. But now that time has passed . . . Well.

I might be close to getting my answer.

I throw the book to a nearby chair, then slowly lift my eyes up to his as I hum a low note in my throat. "Have you ever felt on the verge of losing your grip? That all it took was one little misstep, and you'd do something . . ." I take the lapels of his coat between two fingers, rubbing gently, ". . . catastrophic?"

Without breaking eye contact, his hands fold over mine to lift them from his coat and place them in the small of my back, where he pins my body over them with his own. "I've always prided myself on being a man of careful restraint. However, now that you mention it, ever since a certain wild-haired, smart-mouthed girl barged into my life, I have felt on the verge of disaster quite often."

To punctuate his words, the fingers of his right hand wind their way through my hair and pull, ever so slightly, so I have no choice but to look at him. Not that it's ever been a chore. Especially now, when his skin is bathed in the soft flickering light of a nearby candle, sharpening the cut of his cheekbones, the elegant columns of his neck. The silver specks in his eyes glow like dying coals.

"You like my hair?"

He gives a funny little chuckle as his left hand comes to rest on my hip. His thumb digs into my hip bone, hard enough to elicit a sharp inhale from me.

"It suits you," he murmurs, taking a step closer until everything is leather and salt and *him*. He's intoxicating.

"And my mouth?"

His eyes dip to my lips before lowering his head a breath away from mine. His knee wedges my legs apart. "A dastardly mouth."

A slow, vicious grin spreads across my face.

Yes. This, too, is power.

The moment before my eyes flutter closed, though, something moves across the floor behind us. It's our shadows, a hopeless tangle.

But while Liam's mirrors him perfectly, mine sways strangely back and forth. But before I can make any sense of it, my shadow lurches upwards in a grotesque arch and opens its mouth to devour Liam's shadow whole.

Horror douses me like cold water, and I inadvertently gasp at the gruesome sight.

You can never stop running, the voice in my head shrieks. The voice that has always been there, warning me to stay away, never to get too close to anyone. I have always heeded the voice, except for once, and they *died*.

I never considered that he could be hurt by me, too. Like *they* were. I cannot allow that to happen. This can never happen. *Ever again.*

My horrified gasp breaks the spell, and Liam jerks back. He clutches my shoulders as he registers the fear in my face and tries to find the source of my sudden change of heart.

Shit. I'm so stupid.

"Strider?"

Shoving him backward into the couch, I scramble out from under him, face burning as I back away.

"You can have my help," I cut him off. Scrambling for an excuse, I say the first thing that comes to mind, even if it's vile. I *am* despicable. "But I'm not offering anything else for your use."

A look somewhere between bewilderment and disgust passes over his face. "I have no intention of *using* you, Strider."

Guilt is an oil slick in my belly, but there's a spark of anger within me, too. Resentment that I can't be touched without an overwhelming sense of dread negating any pleasure I might ever feel.

Frustration for being in this situation with him in the first place, for not anticipating something bad. And anger at him for looking at me like that. Touching me like that. I wish he still hated me. Hate has always been so much easier to understand. The spark turns into a blaze roaring inside of me.

"You're using me *right now* to get what you want. Don't pretend. But I have a limit, and it ends with the game. You're not entitled to me."

He's composed himself by now, but something in his eyes still looks a little stricken. "Entitled? I expect nothing—"

"Good. Keep it that way."

Turning on my heel, I make for the door, but before I've made it two steps, Liam stops me by grabbing my bicep. I whirl indignantly to face him, only to find that his surprise quickly gave way to outrage. It's evident in the hard line of his mouth, the set of his jaw, the ice of his eyes.

"A simple *no* will suffice." His voice sounds distant and cold, a far cry from the silk it was mere moments ago. "I'm not in the mood to suffer the pretense that your change of heart has *anything* to do with me, or 'expectations' I have of you. I have no interest in anything you're not willing to give, and to insinuate otherwise is insulting."

Suddenly, he leans down to take hold of my chin, his eyes probing my face. His voice comes out strained. "Strider, what is *hurting* you?"

I flinch as hot tears sting my eyes. I can't look at him. Wrenching away, I leave without a second glance and don't stop until I've made it to the sparring room. I slide down one of the walls, my face in my hands.

Breathe in, hold. Breathe out, hold. It is quite some time before my breaths steady, and my hands stop shaking. My thoughts, like dandelion fluff, scatter about. Try as I might to catch one, they somehow manage to drift just out of reach on a phantom wind. But I do know this.

When Liam enters the room, I am pulled to him like a dip in the floor. When he glares at me, I can't breathe, but when he smiles, I am a pyre. I will bully, push, shove, and instigate fights with him, so starved am I for his touch. I *hunger*.

I could devour him.

I shake my head violently, jumping to my feet. After a delayed moment, my shadow follows. It's rippling gently, like waves in a pond, pulling toward where I imagine the general direction of the library to be. Where Liam must have remained. Its hands are outstretched, fingers splayed, as if reaching for him. My shoulder blades *burn*.

And I incinerate.

"STOP," I scream into the silence, kicking savagely at my shadow on the wall. It's not nearly enough.

"FUCKING. GO. AWAY."

Ripping a knife from its sheath, I stab it into the wall, right into my shadow's chest. Another into its head. Its guts. I don't stop until every knife I own is stuck in my shadow, and I'm panting, and tears blaze trails down my cheeks. It's not enough. I stalk over to the gleaming wall of weapons, jerk Cursekiller from the wall, and watch my shadow waver. It shakes its head at me.

"I hate you," I tell it. "I always have and always will."

And then I ram the sword right into my shadow's bowels on the wall. Wood splinters around the gouges with every jab. But when I stand, my shadow does too, mirroring my movements perfectly. Cursekiller accomplished nothing.

My exhale is a slow, disappointed hiss as I smudge the tears from my face.

Because of this thing, I am never alone.

Because of this thing, I will always be alone.

37

REDS

The following morning, the suns beat down on my back as I scrub barnacles from the hull of The Wraith. The rope I've fashioned into a looped seat digs into my thighs, though I've mastered the balancing act by now. I pause to swipe at the sweat on my brow with my forearm, expelling a breath. I've become the favorite for barnacle duty since I'm by far the lightest crew member, even after gaining some muscle. After all, someone has to be in charge of hoisting me around, and back up when I'm finished. I don't mind it all that much, though, and it's easy work.

With one abrupt jerk of my blade, I send a spiny purple barnacle plopping into the sea beneath my dangling boots. When a series of angry waves slaps against the hull, my gaze plummets to the water. It's been peaceful all morning. What's this?

I twist in my makeshift seat, frowning toward the skies. Not a cloud to be seen. A series of shouts rises up from the deck above me, and a thread of alarm spikes. I look wildly about, seeing nothing, and my confusion grows. And then I realize my mistake.

I was looking above the waters when the threat was coming from *below*. At first, all I register is a massive, dark shape rising from the deep at incomprehensible speed. It can't be a leviathan—it's too bulky.

No creature I can fathom is this huge. I gawk as it breaks the surface in a spray of seawater with a deafening roar.

It's a ship. Golden panels sparkle in the sunslight, dripping with water. Pristine white sails crack in the breeze, and I can even see its inhabitants milling about on its deck.

Inhabitants wearing . . . red. All of them. The moment I realize exactly what has emerged from the sea, I slam my hands on the hull in rapid succession.

"Up!"

No response. I pound louder, harder. Arjun seems to have abandoned his post.

"Do you hear me? Up!"

Nothing.

"BRING"—*pound*—"ME"—*pound*—"UP!" I shout, panic seeping into my voice. "OR SO HELP ME."

Suddenly, I'm yanked up so forcefully, I almost topple over. It wouldn't be the first time.

The moment I reach the railing, I scrabble over it, looking over my shoulder with dread at the gilded ship now cutting toward us. Someone jerks me upright, and my gaze snaps forward, only to find that it's Liam who pulled me up. Everything about him is tense—the set of his jaw, the vice-like grip he has on my shoulders, the way his eyes are fixed on the horizon as he absorbs the revelation that there is an entire ship of–

"Fucking Reds," Liam sneers, shoving me behind him as he stares at the looming threat. Quickly, he turns to Luhan and says something in his ear. Lu promptly strides off, disappearing below the deck.

I push his hands off, still acutely aware of what—almost—transpired between us last night. "Why is a ship of Reds coming toward us? And what do we intend to do about it?"

Reds are horseshite news.

There are three tiers to the king's enforcers: Grays are the lowest level of threat, enforcing the king's law, keeping things in order, and providing general means of upkeep. Reds are the second tier. They arrive when peace is no longer an option, and someone, or something, has made themselves difficult to vanquish. While they're not as widespread as Grays, they have deadlier weapons, access to more powerful magic, and are much harder to kill. I've never seen one before, but it doesn't take a brilliant intellect to know what's coming our way. The blood-colored armor speaks for itself.

The worst and final tier is the king's Rooks. His own curated collection of assassins; his secret weapons. No one knows exactly who they are or what they're capable of. Just that they're the most powerful Weavers in the realm, and they're the reason no one wants to pick a fight with Celosia. If you ask me, they're fucking traitors. I'd spit in their faces if only I knew where to aim.

If Grays preserve the peace, it is the Reds who make wars, and the Rooks who end them.

Liam's voice cuts through my thoughts as he calls the crew to attention. He's hopped nimbly onto a barrel, holding loosely onto a mast above him with one arm. "Well, my fellow miscreants, it seems we have some unwanted company today."

An assortment of grumbles and snickers ripple through the crew, and I study everyone's faces. No outright fear that I can see. Annoyance and uncertainty, yes, but these men don't seem to be afraid. My shoulders relax slightly. But the image of Liam's tight jaw still lingers in my mind, though all traces of it are gone now.

He continues, "They're going to board. And we, being the hospitable gentlemen that we are, are going to let them. Just like the last time they jumped our bones, they'll poke around and leave when they don't find anything of value to them. *Follow my lead.*"

He pauses, and when he speaks again, his voice has lowered to a deadly pitch. His gaze lands on each and every crewmember, and when it finds mine, it feels like a match struck against tinder. "I've no desire to pick a meaningless fight with the king's little red men. Not today. We can be cordial, right, men?"

Sardonic laughter booms all around me.

"We can oblige them in their duty, no?"

The laughter turns into snarls as the expression on Liam's face darkens to something downright sinister. "But if they step one hair out of line, we'll slit their throats and leave no evidence. Aye?"

"*Aye, Captain*," the crew roars back, their fists pounding the place on their chests where I know their Marks to be.

"Get information, you lousy knaves," Liam barks with a flick of his wrist, and it is done.

By the time he hops down from his barrel, the crew has formed surprisingly neat lines on the deck. I watch in amazement as they do so, only to be jarred from my observations when Liam finds me once again.

"To the back with you," he mutters, dragging me along with him to the very last row of pirates. He deposits me in the middle, beside Teller, the oldest pirate here. His white, bushy beard cascades all the way down his front, and his blue eyes crinkle as he flashes a reassuring smile.

"Ever met a Red?" Liam asks tersely once I'm in formation.

I shake my head, grimacing.

"They're deplorable. Do not—listen very carefully—give them any reason whatsoever to start a tussle. I've seen them burn down entire ships over nothing more than a slight."

I glance him over, my frown deepening. "You're being rather welcoming, aren't you? Just letting them come?"

"It is much easier to allow them to stomp around for a few moments, lose interest, and leave than it is to inconvenience us all because my ego demanded a pointless display of dominance. There is nothing unusual about an inspection, and they *love* to inspect me since I have no established loyalty to the king."

"Could we have outrun them?"

He seems to find that question insulting. "No ship is faster than The Wraith. But it isn't wise to try to run from Reds. They, as it turns out, can be quite the vindictive bastards. Even if I'd have seen them coming, the outcome would be the same. And they can call in reinforcements."

I swallow, looking beyond him at the approaching ship. Boarding is imminent. It's close enough that I can see the king's sigil on its flag, the golden stag with branching antlers. "You've been through this before?"

A sharp nod. "The first time was long ago, and it didn't end very well. Since then, I learned cooperation yields the best results. They're checking for forbidden imbued objects, spellbooks, and the like. They won't find them. We'll be on our way soon, as long as it isn't Balor."

A chill races through me, though I've never heard the name before. "Who?"

An unusual expression flickers across his face. Dread. "A commander I have history with. Think if crotch lice were a man."

My face scrunches. "Sounds like what someone deeply familiar with crotch lice would say."

He ignores me. "This isn't his route, though. Come to think of it, I haven't heard tales of him in years. Perhaps he slunk off and died." He glances over his shoulder and straightens.

"Listen." He frowns at me, thinking. "Stay back here, out of sight. It'll be over soon. And if the worst happens?" He tugs at one of the many blades tucked snugly along my ribs. "You have these. Use them."

"Liam," a voice calls the moment before Lu appears behind us to throw Liam something—my coat. Well, it decided it's more of a cloak today. Liam catches it and, in one movement, drapes it around my shoulders and over my head.

"Keep this on just in case. And don't make eye contact with any of them if you can help it."

I pull the hood back far enough to peer out from beneath it. "Why not? They couldn't possibly know who I am."

"No, I doubt they would," Liam agrees. "But yours is a face that's not easily dismissed, and I don't want to draw their notice."

Without further explanation, he pulls the hood back into place and weaves back to the front of the ship. I'm grateful for his departure, for my face is suddenly *blazing*. Only now that he's gone can I breathe and look around. In front of me are five straight, neat rows of men standing very still. Too still. The atmosphere thrums with heady anticipation, their hands hovering around their swords like flies on a corpse, and I realize that perhaps it's been too long since they last tasted blood. Eyes gleam with the prospect of violence. One man licks his lips like he can taste it already. I am reminded why these men are here, on this ship, and not anywhere else in the realm.

Because only here, with one foot in a grave, are they alive.

I hazard a look at Teller, the older pirate with the full white beard, and our gazes meet. "It's gen'na rain," he says in a gravelly voice.

My eyes flit to the unblemished, beautiful blue sky and then back down, searching for any signs of jest. None. So, I nod and offer an encouraging smile.

The wind picks up, snapping the sails. My eyes narrow on the massive, gold-painted ship only a few yards from us now. Its masts spear the sky, and by my guess, at least sixty men could fit there, maybe more. It's bigger than The Wraith. At its prow, a scorpion, its stinger poised to strike.

Standing motionless at the forefront, Liam watches them approach silently, but I can tell that his mind is cycling furiously through every possibility, every way in which this could end badly. Beside him, Luhan looks on, leaning against a mast, his arms crossed, lips flat in a prim display of annoyance.

Finally, their ship lumbers to a stop beside us, and the soldiers toss their anchor overboard. It takes a few moments, during which I scarcely breathe, but a wide plank crashes down onto our deck, and they board. But not before I hear Liam hiss through his teeth when he sees who exactly it is that is commandeering the ship.

"Balor."

38

ABOMINATION

Only five of them board; the rest remain observing from the deck of their gilded ship.

Motionless, like little red statues. This close, I can finally discern what they look like: their armor adheres tightly to their bodies like reptilian scales painted with blood. And then there's the masks. They're shaped in the likeness of a human face, with indentations for eye sockets, and a raised portion for a nose, but that's where the similarities end. The rest is blank. No mouth, no distinguishable features. It's as if the red material has melted into their skin, and I can't imagine how it comes off. I suffer a chill at the eerie sight.

They come to a stop a few paces in front of Liam, with the broadest of the five in the middle, and the other four flanking him, two on each side. I gather the one in the middle must be in charge, then. He's set apart by his armor, accented in gold, whereas the others are solid red.

And he's tall. Too tall. He looks like a wayward tree that grew bent at the wrong angle, yet it still manages to stand.

For the longest moments of my life, no one says anything. The leader's masked head turns this way and that, studying The Wraith, its occupants, and its cargo. Whatever he makes of it, his features are hidden. It's impossible to know what he's looking at. When his head turns toward me, the back of my neck prickles in warning, although there's no chance he can see me all the way in the back. And yet, his gaze lingers so long that my fingers start itching for a blade. There's something about him that feels wrong, sending a trickle of cold sweat down my shoulder blades. I'm a heartbeat away from flicking a dagger into my hand when he finally turns back to Liam.

I'm not alone when I let out a shaky exhale, but my eyes stay pinned on that man. No, I won't be letting that thing out of my sight.

And then he begins to speak.

"Young Liam Blackwater. What a delight. Last I saw you, you were sinking in a burning ship. How thrilling that you survived." His voice is coarse and otherworldly. And yet, it sounds as if he's speaking right into my ear. I flinch at the strange magic and fight the urge to swat at it like a bug. If he can do that, what else is he capable of?

"You forgot the 'captain' part," Liam points out.

"My apologies. Quite an impressive specimen, this ship. I practically did you a favor, it seems."

"By burning down the first ship I called my own, and killing almost my entire crew? I wouldn't call it that, no."

"We never can agree, can we, boy? Although I do see you learned your lesson. It never bodes well for those who run from me. Nothing stirs up an appetite quite like a good chase."

Fear and disgust ripple through me, but Liam remains seemingly unfazed.

"What can I do for you, Balor?" he asks, the collar of his overcoat turned up around his neck.

The commander takes an intimidating step forward, and though he speaks quietly, I can hear every horrid word. "You know the answer to that. My offer still stands. Sail for me. You squander your skills leading this life of aimless degeneracy. He could offer you more power than you've ever fathomed, and anything you've ever wished. *Anything*."

He takes another step forward, so he and Liam are face-to-face. Every instinct I have urges me to drive every knife I own into the man's flesh, to get him away from Liam, but I tamp it down.

Do not *get involved. You'll only make it worse. He can handle this.*

Liam doesn't so much as blink. "I have no wish to sell my soul to a cowardly king. Or anyone, for that matter."

A horrible, wheezing laugh escapes the commander, an old, dying sound belonging to a crypt. "You call the king a coward, but what does it make you for not picking a side?"

"Tell me, to what sides are you referring?"

"Those who serve the true king, and those who will suffer."

A wave of unease washes over me. The king already leaves little room for disobedience.

What else could he have planned? How else can he cripple his own people? Liam waves a hand. "Perform your inspection and get off my bloody ship." There goes that horrid laugh again. Like claws scraping down stone.

"Oh, how I'd love," the commander says, "to flay that impetuousness out of you."

"Say the word, and we'll see who flays whom," Liam sneers.

And for a moment, the commander appears to consider it. Every muscle tenses, bracing for violence. No one moves. No one breathes. Even the wind dies down in anticipation.

But Balor merely steps aside to turn to the Reds behind him, nods once, and they stalk off in opposite directions. Two head toward the stairs, but Liam stops them short with a knife thrown neatly between them. It embeds itself in the door with a dull *thwack*. They lurch back, twisting around in shock. One draws his sword.

"Not so fast. I'll be sending my first mate along as well. You understand."

Both of their heads turn to the commander, but he's busy assessing Luhan, as if noticing him for the first time, although I know he isn't.

"Luhan Kat'tai. The Iridisian runaway. How fares the sea for you? Has it been worth it?"

Luhan visibly stiffens but says nothing.

The commander takes a step closer, hands still behind his back. "I heard your father fell ill. Pity his healer son isn't there to nurse him back to health. Although, seems you're not as talented as you'd like to be."

A change comes over Luhan then. His eyes flare as his mouth contorts in a show of fiery emotion I've never seen him display, but before his hand reaches his sword, Liam steps in front of him to shove him behind.

"That's enough," Liam snaps, stepping so close to Balor their noses almost touch.

Too close, apparently. One of the remaining two subordinate Reds draws his sword and charges Liam, who spins around, grabs the man by his face, and brings it crunching into his bent knee. The Red's mask cracks like glass. He flops to the floor of the deck, moaning, but Liam isn't quite yet finished. He places a heavy boot on the man's throat, then glances behind his shoulder to Balor.

"Leave my ship now, and he can live."

Something tells me that if I could see Balor's face, he'd be smiling. But he doesn't say a word. So, Liam's boot presses even harder. I'm certain the man on the floor is trying to scream, but all that comes out is a strangled gurgle.

"How about now?" Liam asks.

Balor angles his head. "If you must."

It may as well be a death knell. The man's windpipe makes a wet popping noise beneath Liam's boot, and his body goes still.

"You could have saved him," Liam sighs, stepping over the corpse.

"We'll never know, will we?" With a jerk of Balor's head, the remaining three men begin their search, one above deck, the other two disappearing down below with Luhan. If they're disturbed by their leader's actions, their masks hide their reactions. That might be for the best.

"This shouldn't take long," Balor is saying conversationally, as if there isn't a corpse between them with a caved-in neck. "As long as you've been a good pirate."

"I'll save you the trouble. I haven't been. How much gold will it take for you to hastefully fuck off?"

"Don't play stupid, pirate. I've no interest in *gold*," Balor says.

When an edge creeps into Liam's voice, it makes me realize how deeply his loathing for this man runs. He may look in control, but I've been around him enough to read his body language. It's a tightness around his eyes, a hunch to his shoulders, a clawing of his fingers for the hilt of his sword. It instills a certain terror within me, to see Liam so affected by this man.

"Why are you here? This isn't your route," Liam says.

"No, it's not. I've been summoned to investigate some missing naval ships. Perhaps you've heard?"

Liam doesn't react.

Balor hums a note, a sound like a dying gasp. "Eleven of our finest ships. Vanished. Strange, no?" As he speaks, he begins a slow, meandering stroll. First, circling Liam, then he starts toward us. "So, forgive me if I must inspect a few things. It's just that my comrades are presumably dead."

A wave of fear drenches me. Beside me, Teller shifts a bit closer. In front of me, I see Arjun and Ishaan clench the hilts of their swords.

From where he stands, Liam looks on. He even flashes a sardonic grin. "Perhaps they'll turn up."

Every eye above deck follows the commander as he peruses each and every man, walking the length of the row, then starting down the next. Sometimes, he stops only to stare into someone's face for an uncomfortable length of time, for no apparent reason other than to deeply unsettle everyone on the ship. It's working. Sometimes he mutters to himself in that raspy, frayed voice of his, and with every step he takes closer to me, my dread rises.

He's made it to my row now. Each step reverberates in my chest, and inadvertently, my eyes flick to Liam, who, by all accounts, seems to be observing with the barest of interest. But where he holds his sword, his fingers are white, and I know that he's planning for the worst. If Balor is a commander, killing him could very well be an act of war.

How far will this escalate before blood is spilled?

Commander Balor comes to a stop in front of Teller, and I do my best to keep my eyes trained down. I'm thankful for the folds of my cloak to hide my trembling hands, although I wouldn't be surprised if this evil entity could somehow smell my fear, or taste it. I picture a sickly smile on his real face. I clench my daggers tighter and fantasize about ramming them through his eye sockets.

"Your name?" Balor demands.

"Teller."

"What are you doing on a pirate ship, old man? You'll catch your death out here. Such hollow, breakable bones. Such music, to imagine them snapping."

"Mebbe in time. But not today."

"What makes you so certain?"

Teller shrugs, his pale blue gaze unflinching, and when Balor takes a sudden step closer, several things happen at once.

Liam abandons his post, sword in hand, and surges toward us.

Every pirate onboard, me included, lunges toward Balor, weapons drawn. A sudden wind kicks up, one so strong that it sends a barrel flying across the deck. I don't realize it knocked my hood back until suddenly, Balor's head whips around to face me.

Time slows as we stare at each other, Balor and me. He takes an eternity to speak, and in the meantime, I feel the blood drain from my face, my belly a slimy fish flopping around. And then he says the strangest thing.

"Ah. He didn't tell me there's more of us running around."

Us?

Before I can react, his fingers wrap around my throat and squeeze, but it doesn't matter because Liam has reached us, and his sword is mere inches away from Balor's head and—

Then we're gone.

In the blink of an eye, Balor is about to be decapitated, and in the next, we're on top of the quarter deck, and I'm on my knees, fighting the urge to hurl my guts up as the realm spins and bucks. But I can't move too much, or the blade biting into my throat might sing for me. It might just be the last thing I ever hear. Every pair of eyes turns to us, every mouth ajar in awe of what Balor just did.

The disappearing trick must be new.

"Who's this, Liam? You didn't introduce us." Balor calls down below.

Liam's form slices through the swarm of people to glare up at Balor, sword still in hand.

Our gazes fasten, and I give a nearly imperceptible shake of my head, setting my jaw.

You can't win like this. He'll kill me in front of you. Right here. We have to think of something else. Don't let me die like this.

I will the words to somehow penetrate his skull as my eyes drill into him. If Balor suspects me of holding any importance to Liam whatsoever, I'm finished. He's clearly depraved. He'll do it. My heart sinks as I behold the malice glittering in Liam's eyes as he stalks toward the balcony. He's too far gone, the promise of the bloodshed of his enemy too alluring to forsake. He's going to try to fight his way out of this and lose.

Or at least, he was. Liam Blackwater, it turns out, is nothing if not adaptable.

Between one moment and the next, he molts the murderous expression in favor of a lazy smirk as he sheathes his sword and saunters the rest of the way through the crew. I'm equally horrified and mesmerized by how easily he oscillates between emotions like that. Makes me wonder if anything is ever truly real with someone like him. Someone who dons expressions like articles of clothing and discards them just as easily. It must take a toll.

"Who, Iona? What could you possibly want with her?" The detachment with which he speaks jars me, though it's exactly what must happen.

"I could ask you the same question."

Is it my face? Does he somehow sense my marks? What does Balor recognize in me?

Have I met him before?

Liam crosses his arms. "I have my . . . uses for her for the time being."

Balor glances down at me, or at least, I think he does. "Trust me, boy. You don't want any part of this *abomination*."

The word breaks skin, and I flinch, then gasp as Balor's sword digs into me. I feel a drop of blood trickle from my neck to stain the collar of my shirt. Unbidden, my eyes find Liam's, who looks on with only a distant expression of amusement.

"I bought her in Marrin," Liam explains. "Fetched a decent enough price, though I've found her enthusiasm a bit lacking. She's a good deal more trouble than she's worth, come to find out."

His eyes lance carelessly through me, and I avert my gaze so he can't see the hurt. Like all good liars, he's weaving enough truth into the lie to make it impossible to unravel. After all, I did refuse him last night. How much does he really resent me for that? How far is he willing to go before he decides it's not worth it? *I'm* not worth it?

No. *It's not real. He doesn't mean it.*

But the glance of uncertainty he throws my way, as if he's truly grappling with the idea of letting Balor win, feels too close to the truth: that I am a small price to pay to avoid inciting a battle to the death with a ship full of Reds. Balor doesn't miss it either. He makes a sympathetic hum as he tightens his grip on me, pulling me closer against the hard planes of his body. My breaths are no more than flutters lest his sword slice further into my neck.

"I wish you'd heed me," he calls to Liam. "No one likes a stray. If a dog can't be muzzled, best to put it in the dirt before it bites someone."

"And yet, you won't kill me."

"No. Not outright. Last time you refused to sail for me, I left your ship in smithereens. This time, your little beastie will do. I intend to gnaw away at everything you want, everything you hold dear, until you come crawling to me, broken and hollow. One way or another, you will choose a side."

"I will never serve the crown," Liam swears vehemently.

I feel rather than see Balor's attention swivel to me, a fingernail scraping against my spine. His voice has gone quiet as a grave. "They won't have a choice about it. No one will. But you know all about that, don't you?"

Dread creeps into my bones. "I don't know what you're talking about."

But I'd like to.

Ignoring me, Balor turns back to Liam. "Perhaps I'll cut her open and see what comes out."

Liam flicks a hand in exasperation. "There are more where she came from."

It's not real. He doesn't mean it.

The commander shakes his head, ever so slowly. "Not yet. But there will be."

Balor's blade presses in, then hovers over my throat. I close my eyes, my molars ground together, wondering what it will feel like to drown in my own blood.

Instead, we disappear.

39

A GRIMWOOD WITCH

I put up a hell of a fight, but they manage to wrangle me into yet another fucking cage. Immediately upon reappearing on the red ship, a sack was shoved over my head so I wouldn't be able to keep track of where they took me. Between that and the disorientation from Balor's magic, they were successful. I have no idea where in this ship I am. Only that I'm in a cramped, lightless room, the only decoration to speak of a dingy, abandoned mirror on the wall across from me. The only light comes from the crack beneath the door, giving me little to work with.

So, I am to be Balor's prisoner. It seems that between Liam's ambivalence and the mysterious interest he has in me, he decided to spare me after all, which may end up being worse than death depending on his proclivities. But for the moment, I'm just happy he didn't slit my throat. Proctor knows he seems to delight in Liam's misery. How many other sadists does the king employ?

They're all so vile. Every last one of them.

Groaning, I haul myself to a sitting position and prop myself against the wall. My cage is small, composed of iron bars. It's not tall enough for me to stand. They'd relieved me of my knives and lockpicks along the way, the bastards.

Well, the obvious ones at least.

I reach into the inner waistband of my pants and, very carefully, split a seam near my hip.

Two lock picks tumble out, and I grin.

Now for my second immediate problem.

My gaze lifts to the other cage in this small windowless room, adjacent to mine. Its occupant has been silently watching me, but now she slinks out of the shadows to wrap long, pale fingers around the bars of her cage. Owlish storm-colored eyes peer at me out from under a knotty nest of hair that isn't quite blonde, isn't quite red either, but some sort of soft orangey shade in between. And on her forehead, between her brows, three circles arranged in a straight line, shaded in with silver ink. The largest circle is in the middle, the two smaller ones on either side. Alamene, Yskara, and Eri. Our moons.

The marks brand her for what she is. A witch. And not just any witch, either. A *Grimwood* witch—they're known for worshipping the moons. It is rumored that Grimwood witches are born without hearts, just hollow cavities in their chests; their noxious magic comes at the cost of their souls. There are *lots* of things said about witches. But what I know to be *true* is that anything that thrives in the Grimwood is either prickly, poisonous, or extremely difficult to kill.

"What do you have there?" She rasps. My lockpicks must have garnered her interest.

"Are there guards outside of this room?" I counter in a hushed voice, ignoring her question.

She studies me curiously before answering. "Two during the day. One at night. But they leave for meals and breaks."

"Armed?"

"To the teeth."

The notion of fighting two armed Reds doesn't sit well with me. Night it is, then. I can wait. It is now late afternoon. Sitting back, I draw my knees up to my chest and glance at the wall across from me to my shadow. It mimics me, though unlike me, it is not shackled. No cage can hold it, so I might as well use it.

"Tell me when there is only one guard."

For a moment, I look mad, as my shadow merely does what I do. And then, it nods.

Satisfied, I glance over at the witch, but she's slithered back into the far side of her cage, and all I can see is the ethereal gleam of her silver marks.

For many bells, we say nothing. No one comes inside. And then, "How long have *you* been here?" I ask the dark.

"Weeks," comes an eventual reply.

"Why?"

Her eyes glint as she shifts closer. "They took something of mine."

"No," I begin to stretch. "What do they intend on *doing* with you? Why not just kill you on sight?"

That's generally how witches are received. Ever since their banishment into the Grimwood, the punishment for an infraction is death. They are despised by the kingdom. Decreed as evil heretics.

Her gaze hardens. "Witches fetch a fair price in those fighting pits of theirs. They find our magic unusual. We entertain them."

My lips part as I digest her words. "You're saying the king's own men take part in The Pits." Another realization dawns. "*They* are the ones kidnapping people? Making a profit?"

I knew the Grays turned a blind eye to it, but this . . . I taste copper and realize I've bitten my tongue. In my darkest moments, I'd harbored suspicions, but the confirmation still burns a hole through my guts. They go around checking other ships for trafficking Weavers so they can take them and be the ones to sell them off instead. This entire realm is *fucked*. Is this what Balor plans for me, too? Am I about to be sold into The Pits?

"They do as they please," the witch says.

"Not today."

"You're on a ship swarming with soldiers," she remarks. "What do you plan to do?"

"I'll think of something. I'm not about to sit and wait around." I regard her carefully. "How did they catch you, anyway? I thought Grimwood witches were supposed to be fearsome."

She tilts her head. "If I am a witch, what, pray tell, are you? I've been watching the shadows since they brought you in. They emanate from you. Cling to you. And you reek of curses."

I lurch forward, coming face-to-face with her as closely as the bars will allow. "Can you get it off? The curse?"

She shakes her head. "Not I."

The hope sputters out as quickly as it ignited. And then, my shadow lifts a slender arm and points to the door.

"Well, I hope you make it out of here one day." I set to work unlocking the gate, twisting the pick this way and that–

"But my mother could. She's a Curse Speaker."

I don't bother with a response. Her mother isn't *here*.

For a while, the only sound is the quiet tinkering of my lockpick.

Then, the witch says, "They have my Familiar."

"What's a Familiar?"

"The companion I've had since I was but a sprout. My oldest, dearest friend. I let them capture me, so I could rescue her. If my Familiar dies, part of my soul dies with it."

I pause, genuinely intrigued, but still uncertain whether I can trust her. "What's in it for me?"

"Let me out, and I'll take you with me. Off the ship."

My eyes narrow on the grime-covered witch. "How?"

"If I can find Lucy, I will have enough magic to open a portal and take us home."

"To the Grimwood?"

"Yes."

That gives me pause. I glance over at her, but I can glean nothing from her serious expression.

"Someone is coming to get me. They'll be here soon."

Her eyebrows raise. "Are you certain?"

Yes. No.

I want to be certain.

However.

Reason dictates that Liam could very well decide that it's easier this way, that it's not worth the trouble. He said it himself: to pick a fight with a red commander is to pick a fight with the king. And I saw that flicker of uncertainty cross his face. As badly as he wants to go to the ball, is it worth taking on an entire ship's worth of Reds because of *me*? I am a means to an end. There is a decent chance Liam Blackwater will sail on and simply find another way to get what he wants. I could hardly blame him for it.

And yet, I can't entirely let go of the notion that he won't. He might be a scoundrel, but he isn't heartless. And the simple truth is I'm not done with him yet. And I was hoping that he wasn't done with me.

Regardless, I know how people in cages get treated around here. This witch, if she's true to her word, is offering a way to finally get answers about my curse. It would be an unexpected shortcut to a very roundabout way of getting what I want. And though I'd be abandoning Liam, there's a chance he's already abandoned me. Either way, this is my only option at the moment.

I don't feel like waiting around. I have my own blades.

I study my fellow prisoner, my very best hope: a twig-twirling witch, whom the realm would have me believe to be a sinister flesh eater with nothing but tricks and deceit up her sleeves. But when I look at the witch in front of me now, all I see is a young woman who's been taken from her home, too. We're not so different.

With a satisfying click, my lock pings open. But instead of rushing through, though, I stay still, listening for any approaching footsteps. There's a moment where two deep voices drift by the closed door of our room, but they continue on their way to eventually disappear. Three Reds would be a hell of a lot worse than one. Only once it's been completely silent for twenty heartbeats do I push the gate open, taking care not to let it creak.

Striding over to the witch's cage, I crouch, and she stalks forward from the shadows to meet me at eye level. She moves soundlessly, as if she isn't actually touching the floor, but hovering above it.

"Are you going to let me out to play, dark one?"

"Do you swear that if I do, you'll help me get off this ship *alive*?"

Her bloodless lips twist into a smile. "So very distrustful. Yes, I will take you with me once I have found my Familiar. And what will you be doing in the meantime?"

Balor's red fucking face flashes through my mind. "I want my knives back. And," I flex my fingers. "I'd like a word with the commander."

Concern tightens her features. "But you're all alone."

I glance toward my shadow on the wall. And very slowly, it looks back at me. The witch, for her part, doesn't seem bothered by it in the least. "You have your Familiar. I have . . ." For lack of a better word, I point.

She keeps her gaze trained on my shadow. She seems quite fascinated with it. "Does she listen to you?"

"When it's convenient. It wants me to live. So that's good."

"Can she hurt others?"

I work my jaw. "From time to time."

"And when you tell her to stop?"

I give her a pointed look. "There's a reason I want to speak to your mother."

She turns back to me, aghast. "But she's your Familiar. She loves you. You cannot forsake her."

"It's not a Familiar. And that thing knows nothing of love."

Her eyes flash with emotion. "*Everything* knows something of love."

"It is not up for discussion," I hiss, and though she looks as if she has more to say, she draws away.

Irritated, I fiddle with her lock for a few moments, and then it too springs open. But she doesn't come out. Not yet.

"I've pieced together that they keep their weapons on the floor above," she tells me. "Your knives are most likely there. The soldiers' quarters lies below us. Go down there, and they'll swarm you like ants. I will find you once I've released Lucy."

We both look to the door.

But first, the guard. Poor thing.

40

HAVOC

Our plan commences with the witch's scream. Not so loud that other guards will hear, but certainly loud enough to alert ours. I step into the shadows behind the door, just before she starts to shriek.

"Someone! She's—Eri above, she's going to kill me!" Her voice is drenched in panic and fear, and I silently applaud her wiles.

The guard bursts into the room a few heartbeats later. Strangely, I didn't hear the jangle of keys, though. He turns to the witch's cage on his left, putting his back to me. Just as I'd hoped. I emerge from the shadows to plant a vicious kick in his lower back. He half stumbles, half lurches into the bars, and the witch surges to meet him, grabbing hold of his chest plate to hold him there, pinned against her cage. Her grin is sinister, and I catch a glimpse of too many sharp teeth inside that weren't there a moment ago.

Wasting no time after I kick the door shut to stifle any noise, I stroll behind him, grab hold of his skull, and smash his face against the bars. Once. Twice. After the third time, his mask cracks. After the fifth time, his skull. Blood trickles down the bars and spatters the wall in front of him.

I've given him a new red mask.

Only once I'm satisfied do I let his corpse slide to the floor, though I'm still not finished with him. Squatting next to the body, I root around in his pockets for what he used to open the door. Nothing. Sighing, I sit back on my haunches, my gaze combing over him for what it could be. And then, it snags on something shiny. A gold ring on his right hand. While the witch slinks out of her cell, I get to work prying it off his finger. Once it's off, I get to my feet and go to the door. When it closed, it locked again. But if I'm right . . .

"Open," I command, but of course it comes out in the strange language only magic understands. When I push it open, it obeys, and I feel a rush of adrenaline at the small victory. Turning to the witch, I find her wearing an exultant grin and promptly hand her the ring.

Her brows raise in question, but she accepts it nonetheless.

"Use it to find Lucy. You're the one who needs to finish quickest," I answer her silent question. "I can find another."

"What is your name? Since we are to be allies." She offers a pale, freckled hand. "I am Willa. Of the Grimwood."

I take her hand, then hesitate. "Iona . . . of . . ."

Of Marrin? No. Of The Wraith? Absurd.

From where do I hail? Ah. ". . . the dark." I finish. "Iona of the dark."

She seems to find that satisfactory. "I will find you once I have my Familiar."

I nod. "And in the meantime, I will wreak havoc."

My first priority is a weapon. Any will do, though I'd prefer to find mine.

Once I've slipped out of the room, I choose left, hoping that at the very least, the hallways all converge, and it doesn't matter if I chose the wrong way. I can already tell the inside of this ship is much larger than The Wraith, and they used a similar spell to enlarge the guts of it.

It serves as a reminder of just how many soldiers reside on this ship. However, nighttime has descended, so hopefully most of the soldiers are sleeping. Perhaps this won't be so terrible.

As I sprint, I make not a sound as I fly down the hall, but I'm forced to come to a halt as I approach a corner. Pressing myself against the wall, I take slow, deep breaths to quell the furious thudding of my heart while I listen.

Nothing.

I round the corner and find myself face-to-face with a Red, standing at silent attention outside some heavy iron doors. And beyond him: stairs. Going up. And next to them, a door that I can only assume obscures the set of stairs going down.

Everything freezes.

Basi's voice whispers in my mind: *What are your advantages? Seize them. However small.*

The one and only advantage I have is that I saw him before he saw me. I expected to fight, and he did not. And he has a very sharp, curved sword hanging at his belt that I very much desire.

Without a moment's hesitation, I jab him in the throat once, twice in his side, and launch my knee beneath his chest plate. He crumples to his knees, releasing a garbled groan. Taking advantage of our positioning, I shove him against the wall with my whole body in what might look like a lover's embrace from afar. It is anything but as I slide his scimitar from its sheath and slit his throat in one fluid motion. He makes a few wet gurgles before he hits the floor, and I take care to sidestep the expanding puddle of crimson beneath him. The scimitar comes with me, as does the ring on his finger—now on mine. That part at least was easy enough.

Although there goes any dream I had of stealth. I've gone and made a mess.

Sighing, I step over him to head for the stairs, then hesitate, my gaze flicking to the heavy doors beside which the soldier had been stationed. Willa and I had someone guarding our doors. Could there be more captives willing to help overtake the ship? I glance at the corpse. Time is of the essence, now that there's another body. So, I'll be quick.

I pull on the door handle and slip only my head inside to take a peek. To say I looked around. My eyes go wide at what I see, and I swallow a groan. I wrench myself back outside, planting my back against the door. My hands massage my temples, my eyes rolling in the back of my head, but it's too damn late. They saw me.

This couldn't get *any* worse. I fucked this up for myself, didn't I?

Groaning, I open the door again and squeeze through once more, letting myself into a room of more cages. But this time, they house children.

Well, three little ones, and two teenage-looking girls. Sisters, by the look of them. Both glare at me with forest-green eyes trimmed in gold, complemented by the lovely olive shade of their skin. Oh, but their wings.

The younger of the two's wings drag behind her, bent at strange angles. Feathers litter the cage like dandelion fluff. But the older girl has no wings at all. Just bloody, tufted stumps. I can see plainly in her face that it is fresh, what they have done. Her cheeks still glisten with tears.

They're Avian, the two girls. Legend has it that back when all five of the First Sovereigns' crowns were united, they could take to the sky as gigantic birds. Alas, their realm, Ereas, was sealed off with the rest of them years ago. I have no idea how they got here. Only that they are very far from home.

As I approach the cage, all five pairs of eyes start to widen when they realize I am no soldier. For a moment, we stare at each other, thoroughly perplexed. I've no use for children or bird people. I am already risking too much as it is. *Damn* these men for these wretched sins.

Damn them all. Well, now I know why the children have been disappearing. As if the king doesn't have enough, he's taking the littles, too. So that they can—what? Grow up in the Pits fighting all their lives?

I take a step forward, putting a finger to my lips. The children watch with panicked, round eyes. The Avian sisters scowl, simmering with distrust, and the one who still has her wings pulls the little ones close to her. The older one looks as if she can barely see straight through the pain.

"I won't hurt you," I assure the children quietly, squatting down to their eye levels. Two girls, not more than ten, and one boy, who can't be older than five. Their clothes are filthy, their eyes glassy with fear. Their little faces, which should be plump and ruddy, are gaunt. Like mine, not too long ago.

"Have they hurt you?" I ask, wrapping my fingers around the bars of the cage.

They shake their heads, and a quick glance to the younger Avian girl, the one with the broken wings, confirms it to be the truth. I feel my shoulders sag in relief.

"But they've been starving us," she whispers tersely in a strange, melodic accent. *Us* sounds like *oos*. "They want us whole so they can sell us to The Pits, but hungry, so we fight."

Unbidden, my eyes flick to her sister, and I'm instantly flooded with guilt.

"They will take mine too," she continues quietly, her voice shaking with dread. "Our wings sell for gold. A lot of it. They want to see if Aya survives it first—having them taken."

My gaze latches with the older Avian girl, and the despondence I see makes me realize I killed the guards way too quickly. There was room to make them suffer. I won't make that mistake again.

My attention goes to the children. "Are they—"

"These children have magic," she finishes. "That's why they were taken."

They're Weavers.

"What's your name?" I ask the younger Avian girl.

"I am Lark. My sister is Aya."

My fingers touch my chest. "Iona."

I cock my head, thinking.

"You." I point to the smallest girl. "What does your magic do?"

She glances uncertainly at Lark and Aya, whom it seems they've come to regard as their guardians, and with a kind nudge, Lark encourages the girl to step forward. Squeezing her eyes shut, and balling her fists, her little face tightens with concentration. At first, nothing happens. Then, she lifts off the ground, maybe a few inches, and hovers there. Her eyes open, her expression triumphant.

"Can you do that to other things?" She shakes her head.

"Hmm." Not helpful here. I look to the next one. "What about you?"

The older little girl comes forward, suddenly nervous.

"It's alright," I tell her, painfully aware that every second that passes is a second in which someone could stumble upon the corpse outside this very door. I imagine yelling won't exactly expedite things, though.

She points to the band on my arm. The gold one I stole from Liam, which feels like eons ago. "What, you want compensation?"

"Take it off," she says in a small voice, "And hold it in your hands. Where I can touch it."

Frowning, I do as she asks, unclasping it from my arm and holding the band in both hands where she can reach. She reaches out a tiny, dirty hand and touches it, and suddenly, with a surprised gasp, I'm jerked to the floor, and my forehead clashes painfully with the bars of the cage.

"*Aaaghhhk.*"

Struggle as I might, I can't pull my hands away from underneath the band. It's so heavy it's crushing my fingers. Biting back a shriek, I glare at the little girl, who, it seems, can change the weight of things. She's glancing at the other little girl and fighting a smile.

"Change it back," I grind out, wondering if I'll still have use of my fingers after this.

With a small smile, she touches it again, and I end up sprawled on my back, the stupid band clenched in my throbbing fingers. Delighted giggles greet me from inside the cage, and I am reminded once again how I'd rather face an entire army of trolls than three impish children.

Although that one was useful.

I sit up, my gaze landing lastly on the little boy as I massage my poor fingers. "Your turn."

But he's ready. He claps his little hands together, and as they part, I catch sight of what appears to be a tiny spark of lightning.

I stare at it, shocked. It's a small thing now, but if he grows up— no. *When.* This is why those in charge are so eager to leash them so young. Because one day, when this child grows up, he could very well command the skies.

I make quick work of the locks on their cages but hold my hands up when they try to make for the door to the rest of the ship. "No. You'll need to stay here. It's about to be dangerous out there. You," I point to the little girl who can manipulate weight. "Once I'm gone, make the door heavy. Too heavy for anyone else to push in. Understand?"

She nods but frowns at me. "How do I know you'll come back? What if you forget about us?"

The question, for all its innocence, is a lance through my chest. I kneel so that we're face to face as I remove the gold armband and cup it in my hands. "You see this? A friend gave me this, and I like it immensely. How about I let you hold on to this and keep it safe until I return?"

Her eyes light up with the mission, and I turn away before my ribs can squeeze any tighter around my heart. I tell them of the witch, who may or may not come to retrieve them on my behalf if I run into trouble. If we both survive long enough to get to that point.

"A *witch*?" Aya demands, her disgust allowing her a moment of lucidity.

I shrug. "Sorry. Handsome princes don't seem to be on board at the moment."

"But—where are you going?"

"To clear a path. Someone will come for you when it's safe," I promise one last time before leaving them. I get no response other than a little wave from the boy, the others merely looking on in grim determination. I understand their reluctance to hope. Why should they, when the world has given them nothing but sorrow? Far be it from me to promise them safety. I don't know if such a thing exists. But I can try to get them off this fucking ship, and whatever they determine for themselves after that is up to them.

Back in the hallway, I head for the door that leads down. Once I reach it, I crack it open and indeed hear the sounds of sleeping quarters below: the creaking of hammocks, snoring, and hushed conversation.

I take a few steps back, grip the scimitar, and look to the shadow. My shoulder blades begin to prickle as it turns to me. It never fails to unsettle me, even after all these years.

My words are simple. "Kill them all. You're good at that."

The pain from my markings flare to life, causing me to almost double over, but my shadow pays no heed as it glides along the wall to the opening and disappears into the darkness. From the one other time the shadow has done this, that *horrific* day, I know that it cannot impart physical damage and be very far from me. And so, I shut the door carefully and lean against it as a trickle of sweat slides down my neck. I cannot hide, and so, I wait. The pain is brutal, so I focus on my breathing.

In, one two three four. Hold, one two three four. Out–

And so it goes for some time, until a chill brushes my cheek and I turn to find the shadow emerging from the closed door. It droops in a way I've never seen, and confirms that this sort of exertion wears us *both* out. The first time it truly broke loose, I blacked out. At least this time, I had some control over it, instead of it acting on its own volition. The pain from the markings, blessedly, begins to die down.

"Tired?" I ask it.

It nods, leaning against the doorframe to slide down to the floor.

"How many?"

It holds up a three, and then a seven. Thirty-seven.

It's a staggering amount, and I fight to keep my composure. No wonder it's drained. "All dead?"

Though it's clearly tired, it puts its hands on its hips, as if to say, *Why don't you go see for yourself?*

I bat my hands at it, having no desire to see its handiwork down there. No one even screamed. "Very well. I'll take it from here. Rest."

If my shadow killed that many, that still leaves at least that many
Reds to go, and one commander.

41

IONA OF THE DARK

Once I've reached the top of the stairs, only after I've peered around both ways for any signs of trouble, do I proceed. A prickling sort of terror crawls along the back of my neck. The same one I felt around Balor earlier. I wonder if he's close.

I continue, ears straining, until I pass a set of doors. The moment I hear one of them creaking open, I'm already whirling around, scimitar in hand. Out walk not one but two Reds, sans their usual armor. They're not even wearing their masks, and I'm momentarily stunned to discover how young these men are. I'd barely call them men. They stop mid-conversation to register me, and that's all the time I'm willing to spare before I attack. Boys, men, it doesn't matter. I'm killing them all the same.

It conjures a memory.

"Both of you? That's hardly fair," I protest, looking between Basi and Luhan with a sinking feeling.

Twisting, I avoid a blade that very nearly would have severed my wrist.

"Prepare for unfair," Basi responds, sending a powerful strike my way. "Two against one. Use it to create chaos."

I parry a blow from Luhan, but instead of deflecting it entirely, I use my momentum to shove him backward into Basi, catching him off balance. When he rights himself, it's at the point of my blade. "Like this?"

Basi nods. "Like that."

Except this time, I drive the blade mercilessly into the Red's chest. When I yank it back out, it brings a violent spurt of blood with it, spraying my face and neck. His companion gawks as he crumples, regaining his balance quickly and charging at me. I block his sword from drawing blood once, twice, but the third time he swings at me, he carves a hefty slice out of my left shoulder. Hissing, I lunge with renewed vigor, and this time, when he arcs his blade, I meet it with a twisting blow of the scimitar that sends it flying from his grip and clattering to the floor between us. He blinks at me, as if he never could have imagined that someone like me could best him in swordplay. Our eyes meet. And I see the exact moment he decides to underestimate me.

He lunges to retrieve his sword, thinking he'll get to it first. It'll be the last mistake he ever makes. Perhaps at one point, before Basi got a hold of me, this boy would have outpaced me. But not anymore. I beat him to it, kick the sword away, and ram my own blade up through his stomach.

For a heartbeat, his shocked brown eyes meet mine, and I'm struck with a torrent of guilt. He falls to his knees, but before I turn away, I hear him mumbling something. Squatting in front of him, I keep him from falling into his own puddle of blood by collecting a fistful of his shirt and holding him up.

"What was that? I couldn't hear you over the sound of the Proctor calling."

Even on the eve of his own death, the boy manages a sneer. "You won't get away from him." Pink spittle bubbles on his lips.

"Who?"

"The commander. He'll—he'll—"

"What?"

The Red's lips twist into one final smile. "He always leaves a mark." And then he dies.

I release my grip, and he slides to the floor unceremoniously. I leave him lying face down in a slick pile of his own innards. I attempt to wipe some blood from my mouth with the back of a hand, but give up when I only succeed in smearing it around.

After trying a few doors, I finally reach the armory. It's also around that time alarmed shouts start filtering from down the hallway. I need to find my knives and that witch and get the hell out of here. I ardently wish I hadn't taken Cursekiller off to spar earlier today. It would have made everything much, much easier.

I wade through the room of gleaming weapons, sifting through all sorts of pointy devilry until finally, I find my blades tossed into a haphazard pile on the floor.

Bastards.

Quick as I can but taking care not to cut myself, I gather them up and slide them back into their sheaths, wincing at the searing pain in my shoulder. Grimacing, I cut off more fabric from my shirt and wrap it tightly around the wound. That'll need stitching.

The shouts grow louder, closer, and I'm off at a sprint back the way I came and almost collide with someone. My hands react faster than my mind, and I've almost rammed one of my blades into an eyeball, teeth bared like an animal, when I realize who it is.

"It is only me," Willa says hurriedly.

There's something different about her. Her cheeks and lips have color in them, her eyes bright where before, they'd been more gray than blue. Even her flame-colored hair seems to gently float about her, as if on a breeze.

"Did you find your Familiar?"

She opens her mouth to answer but closes it as at least eight soldiers come pouring around the corner, swords drawn. They must have heard the screams, and this time, they're ready for combat. I glance sideways at the witch; one brow arched in question.

She meets my eye and reacts instantly, slipping past me into the armory. I slam the door shut behind us and lower the heavy bar across it the moment before the Reds reach us. The door shudders beneath the pounding from the other side, but the bar holds.

"We don't have much time," the witch says, her fingers dancing over the weapons. "Pick something pointy."

"Worse places to lock yourself in," I muse, eying a short, black staff no longer than my forearm. I pick it up, turning it back and forth. On one side of it, I notice a scrawl of old language. Although I don't recall learning it, it seems familiar, and the more I squint at it, the more certain I become that I know what it says.

"If death is a reaper, this, his scythe."

I stumble backward, mouth agape, as the staff lengthens in a sudden spurt. On either end, a curved blade, one of white steel with veins of crimson, the other dark crimson, veined with black. Even the backs of the blades are lethal, heralded with sharp, bristled spikes excellent for jabbing. Gingerly, I toss the magnificent weapon from hand to hand. It's light. Agile. Malevolent. I run a finger along the crimson blade, only for it to retract with a whisper of steel, leaving me with a more traditional scythe. I touch it again, and it slides back out. The other end behaves quite the same.

I shall call this one The Twins.

My reverie is interrupted by the sound of splintering wood. The Reds are going to break through in a matter of seconds. We are out of time.

Across the room, the witch has set her sights on a long, coiled whip. She's picked it up, eyeing it with a look of loving familiarity. The whip part of it is barbed with hundreds of savage little needles, like thorns. A weapon made for flaying. It will suit our purposes nicely.

Our eyes meet.

"That one yours?" I ask her.

"Since I could walk."

Inwardly, I shudder. "Can you fight?"

"Since I could walk."

She brings her hands in front of her, and I look on in stunned silence as the tips of her fingers blacken, as if dipped in ink. The stain seeps all the way down her wrist, halfway to her elbow. Her nails, already sharp before, have become horrible, sharp talons. Her teeth, rows of needles.

"May their souls wander the realms for eternity for the hurt they have brought their own people." She touches the moons on her forehead with her three middle fingers, and her eyes flash silver.

And then the door splinters into pieces, allowing ten angry Reds to storm right on in.

Willa acts immediately. The whip cracks through the air, catching two in the face. One of their noses is ripped clean off; the other loses an eye. They both crash to the ground, almost tripping the Reds behind them.

Then I get involved.

I swing the blades with all my might at the flock of Reds, catching one in the chest. He goes down in a spray of blood, screaming as I plant a foot on his chest and jerk the blade back out.

Another comes charging for me, but I jab him right under the chin with the spikes on the backs of the blades. He reels back, choking, and I end him quickly enough when I drive the business end down onto his skull. As I kick the body aside, a Red swings at me, screaming furiously. I don't have time to move. But the second before his blade skewers me, he's jerked backward by a whip, coiled painfully around his neck. He throws a dagger at me, but I dodge it easily, though it knocks a lantern to the floor. Glass shatters as a small fire lights up the back wall.

Glancing up, I catch a Red sneaking up behind Willa, blade raised to relieve her of her head. With a flick of my wrist, he drops his sword and collapses to the floor, a dagger protruding from the center of his forehead. A single drop of blood trails from the wound, down his nose, and drips off his chin, and I silently thank Basi for insisting we refine my aim.

A furious scream snatches my attention in time to see another Red backhand Willa to the ground as he yanks the whip from her clawed hands and flings it across the room.

"Disgusting witch filth," he spits, kneeling over her sprawled form.

"We should have exterminated all of you a long time ago. Moons-loving fanatics."

I lunge for her, but a Red grabs my arm, forcing me to engage with him. I try to end him quickly, but I'm distracted, and he grazes my cheek.

That could have been your eye. Pay attention.

We dance and hack at each other for a few turns before I'm able to slash a jagged line from his right hip to his left shoulder. Guts and intestines spill onto the floor with a wet plop, and I take advantage of the slippery circumstance to throw myself at the last one before he has a chance to overpower me. But his move set is tired, and one I have been trained over and over to anticipate. With a grating spark, our blades meet between us, The Twins locked against his sword, and for a moment, our faces are so close I could kiss him. So close, he doesn't see me reach for a dagger, nor when I ram it up the under part of his jaw.

Panting, I spin to help Willa only to see she doesn't need it after all.

I watch in awed horror as the Red leans closer, perhaps to slit her throat, only for the witch to reach up with one clawed hand, grab hold of his throat, and rip it out. Blood gushes out of the ragged hole onto her face as she shoves him away, tossing the flesh in her hand aside as one would a peach pit.

That was the last of them.

We meet in the middle of the room, breathing hard. I retract The Twins but keep them in my hand at the ready.

"Can your Familiar help us?" Willa asks me.

"I told you, it's not a Familiar," I say. "And it's tired. It killed every Red asleep in the barracks."

Color drains from Willa's face. "Impossible."

"Go see for yourself. I had to. Anyway, there are more captives downstairs that need to come with us," I say between breaths, my hands on my knees. "We have to go back for them. Children. And two Avian girls—both wounded. They ripped the wings off one of them."

She flinches, then glances to the fire, the one started by the Red's wayward aim and the resulting shattered lantern. It's getting hard to see through the pervasive smoke. Between the two of us, we have no way of putting out that fire. We share a look of alarm.

"Our way out is down there. We can get them on the way," she finally says.

"Let's hurry."

We only make it a few paces before footsteps come thudding toward us, and more Reds accost us, this time wearing armor, but no masks. Now, these men will be more difficult to kill.

"Halt," one of them commands. "Lay down your weapons. The commander wants you alive. Come with us, and we'll take you to him."

"I'll find him without your help." I release The Twins, their blades coated with blood and bits of gore now. "And I'll lay down my weapons when I'm dead."

The Red in charge snorts in derision. "So be it, then."

They rush us, and I intend to charge them right back, but the witch lays a hand on my shoulder, jerking me aside at the last moment.

A beast surges past us, a mottled gray and black blur of fur. The men freeze, horror etched on their faces, right before the beast rips into them. Their swords are butter knives against a maw full of fangs and four sets of long, black claws. Arms are ripped from bodies, heads from necks. One man gets taken up into the beast's mighty jaws and spat out as nothing but pulpy mush. Between the copper tang of blood and the spreading smoke, I could retch. But I stay composed, somehow, although I'm coughing something terrible.

Once the soldiers have been dealt with, the beast turns to face us. It's the most enormous wolf I've ever seen. Its yellow eyes pierce through the haze as it trots back to where the witch stands. Feeling queasy, I avert my eyes from the bits of flesh still stuck in its teeth.

"This is Lucy," the witch says fondly, running a blackened hand through her Familiar's long, blood-spattered fur.

I incline my head to the beast and could swear it grins at me. But the moment is cut short by the thunder of footsteps heading our way. Every time, I am seized by the fear that it will be Balor.

I make a snap decision. My top priority is for the children to get off this fucking ship.

"Go," I hiss at Willa.

She shoots me a questioning look, but I press on hurriedly and tell her where the other captives are. "Start evacuating them. I'm going to let the Reds take me. If I don't come back for you soon, leave without me."

"But—"

"*Go.*"

She throws me one last look before she and Lucy disappear into the smoke, and the Reds come pouring around the corner. This time, I do not resist them, and they don't question it. I'm bloody and tired. But what they don't know is I'm also hoping their commander is willing to shed some light on my disposition before I find a way to sink this entire wretched ship.

42

A DARKNESS THAT OVERSTAYS ITS WELCOME

That first gulp of clean air almost brings a tear to my eye. But then again, I've already got tears coursing down my cheeks from the smoke. With a rough push, the Reds send me staggering out into the night, alone. I place a hand on my heaving chest, measuring my breaths. Another bout of coughing and gagging overtakes me, and my thoughts go to Willa and the children.

Please, let them make it. Whether I join them or not, please let those littles get out of here. I know the Proctor would be kind to them, but not so early. Not yet. Please, give them a chance.

"My, my. You've made quite a mess."

A familiar, hollow voice rakes nails down my skin and sets my teeth on edge. I straighten and wipe some blood from my face with my forearm. My cheek burns where I was cut, and my shoulder throbs.

It seems that while I was down below, clouds have besieged the sky and obscured the moons, leaving the rest of us in utter darkness. Beneath my feet, the great ship heaves, and ferocious waves slap the hull as the sea roars beyond us, angry and frothing. The resulting spray mists my face, but it's not enough to scrape off the scales of dried blood there. No matter what I do, I always seem to be covered in blood.

And it seems a storm is coming.

Wind whips my hair around my face as I reply, "Are you surprised?"

"Not at all."

My eyes probe the pervasive dark as I slowly prowl my way across the deck, my fist clenching The Twins so hard it's shaking. The moment I see him, I will strike. I have to, or I'll lose my nerve.

"How do you know me?" I ask.

"We are the same, you and I."

"No. You're a pawn. I would never serve such a despicable man."

His voice jumps down my throat. "*We are the same.*" Peals of brittle laughter emanate from somewhere, seeming to come from all around. It sounds like the night itself is patronizing me.

"Don't you wonder where your magic comes from, Iona?"

"What magic?" I bluff. How does he know about the shadow?

"Don't you wonder what you are, if not a Weaver?"

"Tell me," I snarl, whipping around behind me but finding nothing there.

He knows I'm not a Weaver. How?

"We are the first of many." More deranged laughter. "We are perfection."

At that exact moment, lightning flashes, and I finally get a momentary glimpse of the entire deck. Of the peril I'm in.

I am surrounded by Reds. They stand still as statues, swords drawn but resting at their sides. There must be at least forty of them—more than I'd thought, all obediently awaiting orders.

But I did not see Balor.

I come to a stop, turning in a slow circle where I stand.

"Come face me," I scream.

These men have been taking children from their families, just to make a few coins off them at the Pits? And they have the gall to call Weavers the menace, when their hands run scarlet with blood? The king has taken away everything from us. Let him see how he likes it when I take away something of his.

A finger trails down my cheek, tucking a bit of hair behind my ear. I freeze, though my body screams at me to move.

"I'm here, sweet," Commander Balor whispers from behind me, his face so close to mine I can feel his cold breath in my ear. Cold, as if he's not a man, but something else entirely.

I don't care what he is, as long as he dies if I stick him with something sharp.

Time to find out.

My curved blade lashes out where his face should have been but meets only air. Another bolt of lightning crackles between clouds, and during the brief illumination, I see that he sprang backward, sword drawn, but he's not on the defensive. I have to keep everyone's attention on me, and *not* the witch downstairs evacuating precious cargo.

"Fight me," I shriek, jabbing where he was, knowing he'll be gone by the time I get there.

"*Coward.*"

I hear the distinct hiss of a blade whistling through the air and leap out of the way in time to avoid an arm severance. If I hadn't learned to lean on my hearing all those dark, dust-hazy nights in Marrin, I'd be bleeding out right now.

"Shame," comes Balor's response. "We could have understood each other."

Lightning flashes, and this time, a sky-shattering roll of thunder drowns out the clash of our weapons finally meeting each other. Cutting winds tear at me as we come together only to fly apart, then meet again. His footwork is brutal, but I've been trained to anticipate this. I know how to fight Celosian soldiers. The problem is, he's much stronger than he looks, and he adapts with every blow I attempt to deliver.

We dance across the deck of the ship, advancing and fading, deflecting and delivering to the cadence of the approaching storm. I'm forced to rely on my own intuition between lightning strikes, whereas he seems to see me either way. At least they're coming faster now, the sky flickering with them more often than not. The rumble of thunder vibrates the floorboards, signaling a storm is but moments away. Every time our blades meet, I move in for the kill, but he always finds a way of shoving me off or twisting away. He's making me chase him, knowing I can never catch him. He's *exhausting* me.

Suddenly, we're plunged into a darkness that overstays its welcome. I falter, unable to rely on my hearing over a deafening crack of thunder, and that becomes my undoing.

A savage blow knocks The Twins out of my hand. My left hand, clenching a dagger, thrusts inward from the side, catching him beneath the ribs, but the victory is short-lived. Covering my entire face with the palm of his hand, fingers digging into my scalp like claws, he smashes me into a pole and pins me there. Pain explodes from the back of my head.

I can see nothing. Hear nothing but the furious snap of the sails, the grumble of thunder, the roar of the sea as it tumbles and clamors over itself. Someone grabs hold of my hands from behind and binds them so tightly, I lose circulation immediately. But I feel every moment when Balor slides a blade down the right side of my neck, right where it meets my shoulder. Blood seeps down my front, and though it's a fairly shallow cut, I grunt through the pain.

"Why did you take me?" I demand.

Truly, I don't expect him to respond. So, when he does, it sends shockwaves through me. "I was going to take you back to him, sweet. But unfortunately, you're not going to make it."

"Who are you talking about?" Something tells me it's not King De'Havelin. Otherwise, why refer to him as 'the *true* king'?

I almost don't hear him when he speaks, so soft and brittle is his strange voice.

"I wonder how easy it will be to kill one of us." Removing his hand from my face so I can see, he dips his left hand into the wound in his side.

His fingers come away coated *not* in blood, but something oilier and darker. Almost black. There's absolutely nothing I can do about it when he pushes them, hard, into the gash he made in my neck. The agony is spectacular. I've never felt anything like it, like my skin is being peeled off my very body. A pain so surreal, things that aren't there writhe in the dark. For a moment, I think I see the shape of a serpentine monster slithering through the night straight toward us.

"My blood won't kill you right away," Balor continues as his right hand begins to drift up my face, to cradle my cheek. "You'll slowly lose your mind from the pain, though. I hear it's agony. This is my primary gift. What is yours?"

"What do you mean?" I grind out, struggling to no avail against the bindings.

He pauses, facing me, and wipes a hand across his eyes. His mask parts like sludge, and I find myself staring into eyes of burnished gold.

Exactly like mine.

His mask clots back into place, covering his face once more. "My primary gift is poisonous blood, and my secondary is the blinking. One trait is active, the other passive. Don't you wonder why your emotions tend to exacerbate your abilities?"

He's right. The dark spots, when my shadow is most active, always happen when my emotions are heightened. As for the secondary gift, I realize with a jolt that it's the wards. It must be the way wards don't affect me.

"How do I break the curse?" I plead. "Please. Tell me."

"Curse?" His laugh is little knives digging under my ribs. "It is no curse." His fingers graze my lower lip, pulling it open to reveal my teeth. "It's a blessing. There is no tithe we must pay like Weavers. We are *elites*."

My ears ring.

All this time, I've been telling myself that somehow, the curse had bound that shadow creature to me. Where I go, it follows. Two sides of the same coin. But I was wrong. We are one and the same. I've been the monster all along. Why would Balor lie? How else could he understand my magic so well?

"Then what are the marks on my back?" I shriek in his face, desperation making me reckless. "Tell me."

He shakes his head, seeming to revel in my turmoil. "It is our eyes that mark us. Nothing else."

That's it.

I jerk my face down and bite his finger as hard as I can, and for once, it is his scream that fills the air. But I don't stop, even when he digs his fingers deep into my wound, or when he knees me in the stomach repeatedly. No, I don't stop until my mouth is full of his blood, and my teeth have bitten straight through his flesh.

With a gross meaty thud, his finger falls from my mouth to the floor between us, and I flash him a crimson sneer. "Look at that. I left a mark, too."

"You little cunt."

Something whistles through the air and collides with Balor with a jolt. Together, we both look down to find a flaming arrow protruding from his shoulder. He gasps, extinguishing the flame with his own hand as he brutally yanks it out. And while up until now, he seemed unkillable, the pained gasp he just emitted gives me sudden hope.

The rest of his men aren't as lucky.

A chorus of thuds arises around us as several bodies collapse to the floor, flaming arrows protruding from heads, necks, and spines. The rest of the Reds scatter into a chaos of shouting, heads swiveling wildly as they try to find the source of the onslaught. But Balor only laughs. A high-pitched, hysterical noise that will unnerve me for years to come. Even as his men fall around him, he laughs.

"He came after all."

Lightning flashes again, this time cutting a jagged path from the sky down all the way to the sea, illuminating a gargantuan, skeletal sea serpent with a yawning mouth of fangs bearing down on us. With a crash to rival the impending storm, a massive plank of wood hinges out of the darkness and decimates a length of railing as its hooks gouge deep holes into the floor.

And for a moment, the chaos freezes, and every face turns to the plank as realization, and probably a sizable amount of dread, settles over the Reds. Then the moment passes, and from out of the bowels of darkness, the pirates of The Wraith come screaming. More flaming arrows arc over them as they teem onto the ship, casting each furious face in a malevolent orange glow and setting their dark swords agleam.

This time, throwing knives pierce through the night too, finding their marks with wet thuds. Left and right, Reds are dying, but still, an unholy number of them remain, and now, they're livid. Balor abandons me to disappear into the swarm of moving bodies, shouting commands.

It is but an instant before both sides collide, and the clash of steel rings through the air as the bloodbath begins.

43

TRAVEL BY UNUSUAL MEANS

S laughter is an ugly affair, and, still tied to a pole, I can do nothing but watch.

The air swiftly becomes tinged with the foul smell of blood and shit, so thick and oppressive, I have to hold my breath not to gag. And the sounds—a symphony of pained grunts, screams of rage, gurgles, death rattles, and, of course, the clang of steel meeting steel. I catch a Red going in for a kill, sword raised high above his head to deliver the final blow, only for a red-haired pirate to relieve him of his head. It tumbles to the floor with a wet thunk, and, for good measure, the pirate sends it overboard with a good kick. He laughs as he does it.

I find Basi in the chaos, his skin glowing in the firelight. He moves like a maelstrom, cutting Reds down as they move into his path. Most of the time, they never see him coming, and those who do are ended quickly enough. One Red takes him on, hauling not a sword but a massive battle ax that he swings around like a toy. Basi ducks the first blow, using his forward momentum to slide on his knees on a deck now slick with blood.

The Red follows his movement, pivoting to bring the hammer crashing down on Basi's skull, but Basi *catches* it in both hands, a hair's breadth from his head. Loosing a guttural bellow, tendons bulging out of his neck with the effort, he yanks the war hammer not away from him, but *toward* him, clean out of the Red's unsuspecting grip. Flipping it around so that the business end is pointing away from him, Basi hacks deeply into the Red's chest, sending blood spurting everywhere as the blade goes all the way through.

I'm so engrossed in watching Basi in action, it comes as a shock when someone cuts me loose. I whirl around to find not a person, but a well-aimed ebony knife embedded into the pole. I scour the chaos for the source but see nothing but juddering bodies.

Into the madness I go.

Weaving through at breakneck pace, I have to lurch to the side to avoid contracting a mortal wound—well, another one. Out of the corner of my eye, I see Luhan engaged in a brutal sequence of swordplay with two gigantic Reds, and for a brief, panic-stricken moment, I consider running to his aid when they corner him against the ledge. And yet, Luhan doesn't look the slightest bit concerned. He merely raises his non-sword arm, palm up, and claws his fingers.

The Red on the right drops to his knees, keening, as his hands seize his head. His partner springs back, bewildered, at the strange behavior. Luhan's hand forms a fist. The Red's skull caves in like a wadded-up piece of paper. His body slumps to the ground, and his poor partner scarcely has time to react before Luhan runs him through with his sword.

It never occurred to me that manipulating bones had more implications than healing.

Our gazes meet, and Luhan flashes me the corner of a wry grin before vaulting off to his next victim. I'm a bit too horrified to return the pleasantry.

When I fling open the door, the hallway is hazy with smoke. I hope Willa's gotten the littles out of here. Taking a deep breath and steeling my nerves, I plunge inside.

My eyes water. My throat burns.

I have to stop a few times to breathe past the burn from the poison. At least the maze of corridors seems to be empty of Reds. But the closer I get to the belly of the ship, the worse the smoke gets. So bad, in fact, that I almost trip over something on the ground when I turn the corner on the second floor. Not something. Someone.

Aya, the older Avian, crouches close to the ground, her arms wrapped around one of the littles. I squint. The little girl—the one who has my arm band. They both look terrified as they look up at me through bloodshot eyes. Aya looks exhausted.

"It's me," I croak, pulling Aya up by her arm. "What are you *doing* here?"

"The witch came to get us, but we got separated," Aya coughs. "I can't *see*. And I have no way to defend her." She looks fiercely down at the child in her arms.

My chest twinges. "Well, I do. Come on."

Willa had said the way off the ship was back toward where we started, so that's where we head. The smoke, by now, is thick enough to blind, and tears streak down my face. I can hear the little girl coughing horribly and worry twists painfully in my gut. We're almost there when the sound of approaching footsteps pierces the haze. My hand snatches The Twins from my hip, my body already lurching into motion—

Too late, I realize the Reds are coming from *behind* us.

A scream tears from my very core as I pivot to shove Aya and the girl to the side as an arrow whooshes past my ear to thud into the floor. I rush the Reds, swinging The Twins, and find my target in one of their chests. The one *who wasn't* wielding the crossbow.

Gritting my teeth, I swing again as the crossbow releases another arrow just before a whip cuts through the haze, wraps around his face, and relieves him of the skin there. He crumples to the ground, screaming. The Twins silence him.

Willa emerges from behind him, her face wan and speckled with blood. But it's when her attention pinpoints behind me, her eyes widening with horror, that I whirl to find where the second arrow went.

The little girl stands still, her face frozen, shoved behind Aya. Aya, with an arrow shaft protruding from her neck. Our eyes meet, and her face contorts in pain as she slides down the wall, leaving a stark trail of blood above her.

Her mouth slackens, and her eyes go blank.

My hand goes to my mouth, though no sound comes out. There is no smoke. There is no battle upstairs. Only a girl named Aya, who died on the ship of an enemy in a strange realm.

There's no time to mourn her.

Lurching forward, I scoop the girl up, but at the last moment, hand her to Willa instead.

I say to the little girl. "Whatever you do, don't look."

And then I bend down and gather Aya into my arms. I will not leave her here. I left the Marrin woman in her cell, but I *will* ensure Aya gets a proper burial. She's slight, but even so, I stumble for a moment when I get to my feet. Once I stabilize, all Willa needs is a nod, and we are off.

She brings us, of all places, back to the room where we were kept. We come to a stop in front of the dusty, floor-length mirror that was stationed in front of her cage, and immediately, I realize there's something peculiar about it. Instead of reflecting the empty cell, the mirror shows a dense forest of Aspra trees, their trunks hunched over and gnarled beneath showers of rich green, fan-shaped leaves. Fireflies glow intermittently beneath the shelter of the trees, and I almost believe I can hear the ghostly hoot of an owl and the deep bellow of frogs.

Or perhaps the poison is already beckoning my brain into madness. "What is this?" I whisper, in awe of the magic on display.

"Witches can travel by unusual means. Mirrors do in a pinch, although if they're warped, Eri knows where you'll end up. The others have already gone through." She gestures to the forest, but I see no trace of them. It occurs to me that the bastards set this mirror up in front of Willa's cage to tantalize her, her home just out of reach.

"What will happen to them?"

"They clipped the Avian girl's wings. Some of my sisters are healers. She may yet fly. As for the children, they will grow wild and free with the flowers of the field, and we will raise them as our own." Her large, expressive eyes tighten sadly. "But when they come of age, they will have to forge their own paths. I wish the life of an exile on no one. Now, come."

With that, she steps into the mirror, and I am left to follow. My heart wants to hurt for them all, but I can't afford to feel anything but fury right now.

Later, I will ache for them. Already, my grief for Aya threatens to obliterate me.

I step through, swallowing my unshed tears. The mirror pools around my skin, and suddenly, I feel the brush of a fern against my elbow. Smell the musk of soil and underbrush. Hear the rustle of branches as creatures jump from tree to tree.

So, this is the Grimwood. It doesn't seem so horrible.

"Where in the Grimwood are we?" I ask Willa. Her skin has adopted a milky glow, and her hair is most definitely floating. The little girl stands holding the witch's hand with wide eyes.

"We are near the Spine. Where my harrow lives."

Harrow. That must be what Grimwood witches call their coven.

She takes Aya from me with a gentleness that forms a lump in my throat. Now that we aren't in imminent danger, I can see how unnatural the violence Willa displayed was for her. She is no natural killer. Death carves hard lines and lives in the eyes of those who inflict it, but I see no echoes of it in her. Now that we are away from that horrid ship, it's evident that whatever life she lives in the Grimwood, it is one of peace.

"I will give her a respectful rest," Willa promises, her voice thick with emotion. "The Grimwood takes care of the souls released within its woods. She will not make the Good Walk alone."

I nod, not trusting myself to speak, as Willa sets Aya in a soft bed of grass, then turns to me.

"You were right about your friends coming for you. So then, what is your decision? My magic has a limit with Eri only at half capacity. The portal will close soon."

I look around me, taking in the rustling leaves, a little bubbling creek winding nearby. I yearn to be free, and this is my chance to disappear into the forest and make a new start. Peace and quiet, at last. I take a small step forward, toward Willa.

But something pulls me back, and I curse myself for the decision I know I must make. Liam came for me, knowing this attack would mean war. He *came* for me. I can't abandon him. I made a promise to him. And I will see Willa again.

"I cannot," I say in a fragile voice.

"You're certain?"

"Yes," I grind out, setting my jaw against the sorrow I feel. "But before I go, how can I find you again?"

"The Aspra trees will show the way. Tell them I owe you a debt."

I crouch low, hug the little girl tight, and tell her to keep the armband, that my friend won't mind. Rising, I extend a bloody hand to clasp Willa's.

"Goodbye, Willa of the Grimwood. Whatever is said about witches, let it be known they do have hearts."

She smiles, and it is tired but earnest. "Farewell, Iona of the dark. I hope you find the answers you seek."

And with that, I step through the mirror. For a moment, I stand there staring at the wall. I can still hear the sounds of the forest. With a sharp inhale, I pivot to reach a hand in after Willa, but I'm stopped by a pane of dusty glass reflecting a hollow-eyed girl with a single tear tracking down her bloody cheek.

44

SOMEONE'S CUR

Back on the deck, the battle rages on. There's carnage everywhere I look. And my shoulder is becoming unbearable. Pulling my shirt to the side, I glance down to see that my veins have blackened around the wound, like scorched tree branches. A wave of nausea rocks through me. I have to get off this fucking ship.

Delving back into the butchery, I fight my way through, stopping here and there to assist where needed. Arjun and Ishaan cut in front of me, blocking my path, their hands full with three burly Reds. With a grunt, I leap onto one of their backs and slit his throat before he can shake me off. While I'm up there, I drive a blade straight down into the top of the nearest Red's skull, although he slices me good in the forearm before he goes down.

I crash to the floor along with the Red I'd leaped on, but grab hold of Ishaan's proffered hand. When Arjun sees my neck, he gapes, eyes wide.

"What is that?" He demands.

"Poison," I grimace.

"That has to come out," he sputters, leaving the remaining Red to bleed out on the floor.

"I know," I gasp, though there's no reason for me to be out of breath. "I'm going back to The Wraith."

"Go now," Arjun agrees, his hands fluttering. "*Now*. We have antidotes onboard, but they only work if it hasn't spread too far. You cannot let it get to your heart."

I spin on my heels and run, panic trickling down my spine and into my belly. I might die. I really might die. Shoving bodies out of my way, I sprint faster than I've ever run in my life.

Somehow, I make it to the plank without further incident, and move to step up on it–

But I hear that voice. That horrid, phantasmic voice. And he sounds gleeful. I turn in time to see Balor about to skewer Matteo, right through the middle. Matteo's sword lies shattered on the floor, and with the way his right arm hangs limp at his side, he's clearly injured. I look around, but no one seems able to extricate themselves to help him.

No one else is coming.

I let loose a growl of frustration but charge anyway. Somehow sensing me, Balor spins around and deflects my blow before I could cleave him in half.

"You're running out of time, sweet," he taunts, driving me back easily. I feel weak, and my stance is unsteady. My vision wavers.

"*Go*," I scream at Matteo, and I'm relieved when he actually obeys, scurrying off hopefully to safety. We exchange blows, but my limbs are filled with sand, and with a flick of his wrist, Balor disarms me. The Twins skitter out of reach. The tip of his sword pokes into my collarbone, hard enough to draw a pearl of blood.

"Do it," I snarl, my vision swimming. "Just do it."

"Oh, gladly," he replies, and rears back to end it—

"You'll not be touching her again."

Balor freezes, but the sword stays where it is.

To our right, a Red jolts as a black sword bursts abruptly through his chest, spraying blood everywhere. The sword disappears through the hole, leaving the Red to drop to the floor, and out steps Liam. That's not the only corpse in his wake. No, the more I look, the more it becomes clear that Liam has been busy carving a path of carnage, death on his heels like a faithful hound. His clothes, black as they are, are sodden with blood, his skin slicked with crimson.

"Captain Blackwater. Took you long enough."

Lightning shatters the sky, followed by a deafening crack of thunder.

Liam flexes his fingers as he prowls toward us. "Why don't you take that sword off her, and point it at *me* where it belongs?"

"Ah, but this hurts you more."

For emphasis, he pokes the sword deeper, and a trickle of blood runs down my front. It doesn't hurt, though. Not in comparison to the spreading poison. Liam, however, lurches forward, like someone jerked a string in his chest.

"Face me, Balor," Liam snarls.

The pressure eases, and I gasp in relief when the point of Balor's sword vanishes to the sound of a sigh. I drag myself to the ledge and slump against it.

"Both Blackwater boys, their skills wasted. Pity there's only one left."

"I don't expect you to understand. All you've ever been was someone's cur."

"Something's coming, Blackwater. And it won't be kind to little snakes that get in the way."

But Liam has that mad look in his eye that he gets after he's started killing, like one day, he might not stop. Like he's no longer a man to be reasoned with.

"Well then." His smile is a scythe. "Let the bloody massacre commence."

They lunge for each other, steel clashing, as another bolt streaks through the air. They move so quickly, I have difficulty tracking them as they dance across the deck. Balor is a blur of red, lashing out with precise strokes aimed not to maim, but kill. But quick as he may be, he can't catch Liam. Liam, who always seems to be two, maybe three strokes ahead. Where Balor strikes, Liam is no longer, already moving in from somewhere else. It doesn't take long before Balor shifts from offensive attacks to defensive, losing ground against Liam's merciless onslaught. That's when he starts the insults.

"Your poor brother," Balor sneers as he barely stops a blow from opening his belly. "Killed before he could make a name for himself. And your mother. If only you'd gotten the cure in time. She might still be alive."

"She died because of you," Liam hisses, meeting Balor's sword in the air with his own and slamming it down to the ground.

And then Balor pauses. "You'll see her soon."

With that, he winks out of sight.

Surprise takes over Liam's expression, but he recovers quickly, leaping backward as his eyes dart here and there. Lightning lances through the sky, and Balor appears suddenly to Liam's right, his sword cutting through the air in a deadly attack. If Liam's reaction time were any slower, he'd be dead. But he meets the blow, teeth gritted with the effort.

"Decided to kill me after all?"

Their swords clang together in a chaotic rhythm. Balor disappears into thin air twice more, only to reappear in a different spot. The second time, Liam suffers a long gash on his forearm. He doesn't seem to notice, so hellbent on death is he.

"If not by my hand, hers," Balor replies.

"Who?"

Balor looks over to me, and a chill races down my spine the instant before he winks out of sight again. But this time, Liam does something different. While his right arm clutches his sword, his left seems to probe the air, as if he's feeling for something. It's subtle, but there is no wasted movement when Liam is in combat. He makes slow, deliberate steps, first forward, then backward, then—

Liam pivots sharply on his heel, driving his sword up in a brutal thrust.

Balor appears with a crack of lightning, his sword raised to strike Liam down.

There is a moment in which both men are frozen in one last death strike, but then, Balor's sword clatters to the deck. A wet gurgle dribbles from his lips, and he sags against Liam's sword, buried to the hilt in his gut. Their faces meet, and lightning crackles.

But if Balor had more to say, death paid no heed. And besides. He's said plenty.

With a jerk, Liam removes his sword from the corpse's chest, and the commander's body crumples unceremoniously to the deck.

Liam steps to the side, panting hard. Blood trickles down the side of his face as his chest heaves with exertion. He sheathes his sword, then raises his head. And somehow, through the pandemonium, our eyes find each other. And the last of the knots in my chest finally comes loose.

He's alright. He *came* for me.

He came for me.

Without permission, my body is moving, my feet stumbling over themselves to get to him. My movements are disjointed and ungraceful, but I urge myself forward anyway, scarcely aware he was doing the same before we collide. His arms wrap around me tightly as he cups the back of my head with one hand, pressing my cheek to his chest. I have so much I need to tell him, but my voice is raw from screaming. And I am so tired.

"*Liam*—"

The last dregs of my strength drain away, and I drop. Liam clutches me tightly, and though I feel the rumble of his voice in my chest, I can't make out what he's saying. Slowly, he guides us to the ground. My pulse thrums weakly, and a downward glance reveals my veins have blackened to my shoulder, and almost to my heart. I can feel it there. Like my chest is full of tiny shards of glass.

I'm going to die.

But so will the shadow.

"Strider? What happened?" Liam's voice seems both close and very far away. I feel his hands on my face, sticky with blood. They lower to my neck, to the source of the poison. A finger grazes the gash, and I moan through my teeth, the agony too much to withstand anymore. I want to tell him everything, but the words stick like burs in my throat.

"Shit," he hisses. "Shit. Strider? Can you look at me?" He sucks in a breath. "Strider, *look at me*."

I didn't realize I'd closed my eyes. I open them, but the amount of effort it takes frightens me. He hauls in another shaky breath, brushing his thumb across my cheek. It's so unexpectedly gentle, it almost breaks my heart. He wastes that on me.

"Balor poisoned me," I croak, trying to focus on his face. His lovely, bloody face. Strands of hair stick to his forehead. I try to brush them off, but my arm won't lift. "It's spread. Too far."

For a moment, he looks stricken. Devastated. But then his features harden, his jaw sets, and his mouth twists into a snarl. "Not yet, it hasn't."

There's no warning before he slides one arm beneath my knees, the other under my shoulders, and hauls me up. There is no time for gentleness now, and the pain is blinding. But, lying my head against his chest and letting my eyelids flutter shut, I can almost convince myself I'm somewhere else. Somewhere separate from the pain. But suddenly we come to a stop, and we lower to the ground. Hurriedly, he props me up with my back to his chest, both of us in a sitting position.

He's taken me back to The Wraith, and it's quiet here, more so without all the fighting. The grumbling rolls of thunder and persistent whips of lightning don't seem so terrible anymore, now that we're home.

"Stay with me, Strider. I've got you." His voice is even, and so calm, I barely hear it over a sudden roaring. For a moment, I can't understand what it is I'm hearing, barreling toward us at incomprehensible speed.

And then the rain comes.

I gasp when the deluge hits us like a cold wall, plastering my hair and clothes to my skin. It's enough to jolt me into lucidity before I am lost to the pain.

"Liam," I manage, twisting to look up at him. "The poison has to come out. Before it reaches my heart."

"I know." He pauses, his features going taut. "You know what I have to do."

I nod, my breath coming in shallow gasps. He'll have to suck it out. We both know I may not return from the agony. Balor meant for this to happen, I realize. He *wanted* to put Liam in yet another situation where he would most likely fail.

I feel him moving behind me, but I don't know what he's doing until it's in front of my face.

"Bite this," with his left hand, he places his belt in my mouth.

I inhale deeply through my nose as he sets his right hand at the base of my throat to steady me. Unadulterated fear has me in a vice. His left hand covers mine, squeezes, and brings it to my stomach as his mouth lowers to my ear.

"I have you. Alright? I'm not letting you go."

I nod, squeezing my eyes shut as I bite down on the leather. He lowers his head further to the curve between my neck and shoulder. I feel the wet of his mouth on my skin.

And then, pain erupts from every corner of my body, and my mind shatters into white, burning oblivion.

45

SOMETHING OF LOVE

Spasms rock through me, oscillating between intolerable muscle contractions where my legs and fingers twitch wildly, and moments where my entire body falls limp and my bones droop.

Endless cycles of pain, and pain, and more pain, and it's not long before my muscles ache and quiver with exhaustion. My body is no longer mine to control, but Liam's. Every so often, he pauses to spit out black poison, and in those moments, I sag against his chest, breathing hard through my nose. I thought the pain from the poisoning was the worst I'd ever felt, but I stand corrected.

It's as if the poison has taken root within me, and it's dragging my insides along with it. My very flesh feels torn asunder by barbs being yanked out by a cruel and careless hand.

I understand what Balor meant when he said I'd lose my mind. With every passing second, it splinters into smaller and smaller pieces, and I worry that if I survive, I won't be the same. This is the sort of pain that changes someone.

Time slows to an excruciating crawl. Pain is my master now. There is no before or after, only now. Only this agony. The rain washes away the tears cascading down my face. The leather in my mouth keeps me from begging for him to stop, to let me go. And I'm glad of the storm, the thunder drowning out my guttural moans.

Unconsciousness would be a mercy, but it never comes. Yet through it all, Liam never releases my hand, and it's the one thing that keeps me from shattering.

After what feels like an eternity, the spasms slow and lessen in intensity.

Liam pauses, for most likely both of our benefits. "Just a little bit more. Stay with me."

I nod, setting my gaze on the clouds as cold rain pelts my face. Without another moment's hesitation, he starts again with a renewed vigor, and my body burns. Proctor's teeth, it hurts.

Then the pain begins to recede. Slowly, but the difference is stark. With every ebb, my breath comes back into my body, and my muscles, blessedly, slacken. And finally, Liam lifts his mouth from my skin. I spit the leather out and hiss through my teeth in relief, stunned it's actually over.

I slump into him, greeted with a level of exhaustion I've never known. Gently, Liam hoists me to the side in the crook of his elbow, leaving my knees bent over his lap as my head lolls into his shoulder. His gaze scours my face, and I can't help but press into the hand he places on my cheek.

"You did it," he breathes, a note of astonishment in his voice. "You're extraordinary, Strider."

The tenderness of his words breaches a fissure and cracks me completely open. With the last vestiges of strength I have, I fling my arms around his neck, obscuring my face there as a juddering sob overtakes me. Without hesitation, his arms wrap around me, his fingers winding through my wet hair to cradle the back of my skull. I burrow into him, succumbing to all my rage and grief and fear and hate. I grit my teeth against the onslaught, but it won't stop. I can't breathe.

"I've got you," he soothes in a low, measured voice. "I know, Strider. I know. Breathe."

We rock back and forth as I painstakingly excavate every emotion I had to suppress to survive on Balor's ship. They pelt me like stones, and I'm thankful for the slow circles he draws on my back. His soft murmurs, coaching me through breaths. He's my only rope as I lower myself into the black to confront what I did on that ship. What it makes them. What it makes me.

"We need to get you inside," he says once my breaths have slowed some. "Your wounds need attention."

I scrub my cheek with my palm and notice the blood still caked on my hands. Everywhere. "No."

"No?"

"This b-blood. I want it off."

His brows raise. "You . . . now? But your gash."

"Now." Suddenly, I need to be clean more than I need air. I need all traces of this blood, this filth, off of me. Now. There is so much of it. My breaths flutter through me as hysteria clamps down on my chest like a hungry mouth. "*Please.*"

Extricating myself from him, I try to stand, but my legs wobble so badly I fall right back down into his lap.

Stand. Up. Idiot.

Fury bubbles to the surface as I bite down against a pathetic groan, but my muscles won't comply.

I try again and I fail. I take care to turn my face away, so he can't see my shame. I can't even *stand*. And for some reason, that's what does me in. I dissolve into ugly sobs.

"Stop. Strider, stop. You've lost too much blood." He loops one arm beneath my shoulders, another beneath my knees, and hoists me up. I clutch at his shirt as if I'm drowning and stare up at him, blinking rain from my eyes.

"I'm sorry," I whisper.

He glances down at me. "Hush." He softens. "I have you now."

A tear rolls down my cheek, and I bury my face in his neck again. It's starting to feel like the safest place in all the realms.

He takes me to his quarters. Once inside, he sets me down in a chair beside his bed and opens a door I previously had thought led to a closet, but actually, leads to a small but clean bathing room. The stall inside is a dark, stone structure. He flips a lever, and a stream of water begins to fall from the ceiling, not unlike the rain outside, but hopefully a little warmer, and a little softer.

My teeth chatter as chills rock through me.

Liam steps back to look me over, his brows drawn together. I doubt he can make out much, knowing how much blood, both mine and others', still covers me. It feels like it's soaked all the way through me, staining my very bones.

"I'm alright," I murmur, my eyes trained on his boots. "The w-worst is my arm. I just want to get out of th-these clothes."

"You can wear something of mine when you're finished." For the first time I can remember, he looks a bit uncertain of himself. "Do you need help?"

"Ju-just my shirt." I grimace, thinking about the gashes on my shoulder. "Cut it off. It's ruined, anyway."

He remains rooted to the spot, and it brings a faint smile to my face.

"C-come on, Blackwater. It's not as if you've never taken a lady's sh-shirt off before."

"There's usually not this much blood," he mutters.

Reluctantly, he drags himself over to me, and I fold over my legs, exposing my entire back to him. I brace myself.

I decided on Balor's ship that if he came for me, I would tell him about the shadow. The marks. I'm too tired to keep secrets anymore. If he's willing to incur the wrath of King De'Havelin for me, the very least I can do is be honest with him. Whatever that entails. But even before tonight, it was clear I could trust Liam with my shame. I just wasn't ready for what that meant.

Gently, he gathers my filthy shirt in his hands and, using a shorter blade, slices the fabric straight down my spine, leaving nothing but my thin bandeau beneath. The shirt falls away with a wet slap, but I continue to hold the front to my chest. And then I wait for the questions, the accusations, the resentment, and the blame for not telling him what's etched into my back.

The room grows silent, except for the heavy drum of rain on the roof. I draw in a shaky breath, hold it, release it, and wait.

Yet, I only feel the calloused pad of his forefinger whisper across my shoulder blades, along the symbols there, then down my spine. My skin forms gooseflesh where his fingers trace the marks, my body yearning to arch into his touch. My lips part, a sigh barely contained within them. And then he removes his hand, and I brace myself for retribution, but all he does is crouch before me and raise my chin with a finger. When our gazes meet, there is no trace of resentment or disgust on his face. But his eyes are glittering with *something*.

"Strider." There's so much emotion in his voice.

"I know. I sh-should have told you about it sooner. At first, I didn't trust you, but then . . ." I gulp down some air. "I was afraid you'd n-never look at me the same. They're hideous. I'm *cursed*. And after all this time, I still d-don't know what to make of them. I'm sorry."

His fingers move to lightly brush my jaw, and I flinch away from his touch. I expect him to withdraw his hand, but instead, he cups both sides of my face, forcing me to meet his gaze. "It changes *nothing* between you and me. And I'll look at you however I please. But Strider, they look like they'd have *hurt*."

For some reason, a fresh batch of tears burns my nose as they streak down my face. "I wouldn't know. I don't remember much of my childhood." I draw his attention to the scar above my ear. "This most likely has something to do with it. I remember living in Marrin for the past seven or eight years, but beyond that, my memories are all smeared around."

He wipes away a tear with the pad of his thumb, and this time, I don't jerk away from his touch. "That's why you wanted that book on curses so badly. The one that started everything."

"And why I want to go to Ce-Celosia. I'm hoping a Curse Speaker there can help me decipher the curse and break it. Or tell me what would happen if I did."

The divot between his eyebrows deepens. And now, the hardest part.

I tell him of my shadow. How it acts of its own volition, how it seemingly wants to protect me and ensure my survival, but I don't know how to trust it. I tell him how afraid I am of it, and how badly my markings have been burning of late when the shadow takes its own liberties. They are somehow connected, the markings and the shadow, though how, I can't be certain. All I know is that the worse my shadow behaves, the worse the markings burn. I'd thought up until now that the markings caused the shadow, but Balor seemed to feel differently. The question is: why would he lie?

And if the shadow is an extension of myself, what does that mean about me? Has it always been part of me? And what does it mean that it's getting stronger?

"Strider," Liam pulls me from my darkest thoughts with a hand on my knee. "Balor plays games. It's how he's always been. You can't let him get to you."

"But he knew I had strange magic just by looking at me. My eyes," I ground out, shivering again. "We ha-had the same eyes."

Liam hesitates. "I knew him before he was a Red. He had blue eyes."

"Not anymore," I try to shout, though my voice is almost gone. Hardly more than a rasp. I'm starting to feel myself fray. I thought I could withstand telling him all of this, but perhaps I was wrong. "Something happened to him. The same thing that happened to me. What if I'm like him?"

He shakes his head vehemently, his eyes flaring. "You're *nothing* like him."

And that's what sets me off, like a mirror shattering. Pieces of me skitter all over the floor as I grab hold of his vest with shaking hands. "Oh? I'm not? How do you think you were able to defeat his crew so easily? You want to know how I killed a third of his m-men? I sent my —*the* shadow—in their quarters and told it to kill them while they were sleeping, while I held the blade that took their lives. So, ask yourself this, Liam. Wh-what happens if it decides it likes the color of blood, and wants to see it again? What happens if I tell it no, and it ignores me? What happens if I tell it *yes*, because I liked it, too?"

For a moment, Liam looks overcome, as if for once in his life, he has no response. He glances down at my grip on his vest, then back to me. Then, to my utter disbelief, he raises himself onto his knees and encases my face sternly in his hands, his fingers winding through the hair at my temples. His chest rises and falls with a deep breath, and when he finally speaks, he sounds so incredibly sad. "Strider, just because you can imagine the worst version of yourself, it doesn't make it true."

"He called me an *abomination*." I fling the word at him as shame surges like a swarm of hornets. "I am *wrong*."

But Liam is undeterred. "Do you remember the night you had that nightmare, and I came to your room?"

I suppress a groan. I was a menace to Liam that night. I was so distrustful, so backed into a corner: all teeth and claws. I never could have imagined he might have been genuinely trying to help.

"I had told you I heard your screams, and that was partially true. But I also saw your shadow."

I freeze; my breath suspended in my throat.

Liam continues, "I never mentioned it, because to tell the truth, I thought I was going insane. But now that I know this, I realize your shadow was just . . . wanting to help. And for some reason, she sought me out to do it."

Everything knows something of love.

Behind Liam, my shadow paces around the candlelight. Its movements are slow, as if it's still exhausted. Like me. For once, it looks away first.

I lean back in the chair, grasping for something to say, but the truth is, I'm worn thin and riddled with holes. I search Liam's face but find only a reflection of my own exhaustion.

"She likes you," I say tiredly. "Always did."

He tilts his head, one side of his mouth lifting into that crooked grin I know so well. It sets something in me at ease to see it. He leans forward on his knees to follow me back into my chair, bracing his arms on either side of my hips. "And Strider? N*othing* about you is hideous. I tried to tell you in Roarke. You're exquisite." He pauses, then amends, "I thought so from the moment I saw you."

The words linger between us like wisps of smoke, and in that moment, something shifts inside of me. I don't yet know what it means, but I feel it all the same, like the first flower blooming in a barren field, or a heart beating a little bit faster than it should.

By now, steam has begun to billow out from the bathing room, and I am once again reminded of the blood still caked onto my skin.

I swallow, taking the moment to compose myself.

Sitting up, I shirk the shirt off completely, still covered by a bandeau. But to my surprise, Liam busies himself by propping one of my boots on his knee and sets about unlacing it. There's something about watching him do it with such care that hurts my chest.

"How did you find Balor's ship?"

He glances up from his work. "Lirael."

My mouth pops open. "You know about her, too?"

He snorts. "Of course I do. She's always around, waiting for Matteo to come out," he says with a note of disapproval. "But for once, she was useful. She took us straight to you."

"She could have been seen."

"She was careful." Now the other boot.

"I never thought I'd owe a mermaid for anything."

"You more than paid the debt by saving Matteo's life earlier. Trust me."

Silence stretches between us, and I'm content to simply watch Liam's deft fingers work. My boot thuds to the floor, and Liam's gaze rises to mine, a schemer's grin on his face. "Shall I do your pants, as well?"

I shoo him with a flick of my wrist. "You've had enough excitement."

"Are you cert—"

"*Go.*"

Chuckling, he obliges me by rising and crossing to the other side of the room, pointedly keeping his back to me as I have a devil of a time taking my own pants off. By the time I've stripped to my skivvies and limped to the bathing room, I wonder if I'm going to be able to make it back out.

46

THE GIRL IN THE HIGH CASTLE

Easing myself onto the dark stone floor of the stall, I tip my head back into the warm stream, sighing with relief.

Already, red runs in rivulets down my body.

After a while, I reach for the bar of soap and roll it between my palms. The infused oils permeate the small room quickly, and I bask in the clean, rosemary scent. Running my hands through my hair, down my neck and body, I watch with great satisfaction as all the blood flakes off in droves, tinging the sudsy water pink as it drains through the cracks between stones.

But it keeps coming. I scrub first with the pads of my fingers, then my nails, raking them down my skin with increasing fervor.

There's . . . so much of it.

The lifeblood of that young boy I killed, and even then, his last words were stained with hatred. If I hadn't gotten whisked away on that ship, those children would be damned. Willa would have never gone back home. Lark would have lost her wings. Aya might have lived, only to die later in a cage. Or perhaps she'd have made it out one day. I'll never know.

There must be hundreds more ships like that. It could have been me. If they'd wanted to in Marrin, they could have wrangled me onto a ship. I could be in The Pits *right now*, torn asunder by someone—or something—with more to lose than I.

I feel no guilt for killing those men. In fact, I'd do it again. For nothing. No, what I don't understand is why I escaped the cage, while so many others, innocents, won't.

Drawing my knees up to my chest, I scrape my hands through my hair and realize that the soldier's ring is still on my finger. The one I used to unlock their doors. Some small noise of disgust grumbles in my throat. I don't want any reminders of that place on me. Not the blood, not the wounds, and not this fucking ring. I tug on it, hard, only to find it stuck fast.

A trail of blood on the wall.

My heart rate spikes.

The wet thunk of an arrow.

Get it off. Get it *off.*

If only I'd been faster. Aya died because of me. She is not the first innocent to die because of me.

Grunting, I twist and pull and yank, but the foul thing doesn't budge. Panic crests over me, and I feel my eyes start to burn, when a voice comes from outside. It's distant, like he's across the room.

"Strider?"

I pull again, to no avail, and something between a sob and a groan comes out. I might just pull my fucking finger off.

"Strider?"

"*What?*"

His voice is closer, this time. The other side of the door. "What's wrong?"

A girl named Aya died tonight. I wasn't fast enough to save her.

"Nothing."

The door flies open, and Liam barges in, holding some clothes. He looks braced for a fight. Not me, curled up on the floor, sopping wet, all out of sorts because of a goddamn *ring*.

"It won't come off," I snarl, still twisting and yanking fruitlessly.

His eyes drop to my hands. "What is that?"

"A soldier's ring." My voice breaks. "I can't get. It. Off."

His lips flatten in confusion, but he recovers himself quickly and, setting the clothes down on the counter, drops to his knees. Without warning, he ducks into the shower to sit beside me, our backs to the wall of stone.

"What are you *doing*?" I balk.

Blinking water out of his eyes, he slicks his hair off his forehead, and for a moment, I am utterly struck by him. Those soft, verdant eyes paired with that straight, inky thicket of hair. His is a face beyond my wildest imaginings.

Keeping his eyes very intentionally trained on mine, his hand trails down my bare arm, all the way to my right hand. He raises it, pushing his thumb beneath my middle finger to extend it, and brings it to his mouth.

"May I?" The timbre of his voice conjures a shiver down my spine.

It is a fight to keep my voice even. "If you must."

And for the second time tonight, Liam Blackwater finds a very good reason to put his mouth on me. My finger slides into his lips, and I feel his tongue, hot and wet, gliding across my skin. Enthralled, my lips part, and my breaths come in little shards as he works. Before I can catch them, my eyes begin to wander.

He must have been in the process of taking off his bloody shirt when he heard me, for at the moment, he wears none. It's hard not to gawk at the lean panels of muscle that line his stomach, and the exhilarating sculpt of his arms and shoulders. Between the two of us, there is more skin on display than not, although neither of us seems to mind all that much. It's just skin.

So then, why am I staring?

I feel the moment his teeth latch onto the ring, and as if I were breakable, he ever so carefully slides my finger out of his mouth, keeping the ring between his teeth. He spits it out into his hand, frowning as he examines it.

"I killed him for it," I explain quietly. "It's what they used to unlock their doors. And I wanted my knives back."

His eyes slide to mine. I know what he's thinking. We can use the ring for the third task, *a foe's precious possession*.

But what he says is, "Whatever hell you gave them was deserved."

I lean my head against the stone. "I know."

I'm quiet awhile, closing my eyes as the water runs down my face, my back. Then my eyes open. "What about the crew?"

"I left Luhan in charge. They'll be celebrating all night long, I imagine. Between the gold undoubtedly on that ship and the weapons, we've acquired a massive haul. They'll leave the rest to burn."

"I didn't think it'd be that easy to sink a ship full of Reds."

"It helped that they didn't see us coming and weren't prepared," he admits. "And we've had practice."

Practice? I make a mental note of that little comment.

"Strider." He pockets the ring, then lifts his knees so he can rest his forearms on them as he turns to face me. As he does so, my eyes track a drop of water as it trails down the long line of his nose. "Do you want to talk about it?"

No.

My immediate response is no. But.

I have to get it out. If I don't tell him what happened now, I'll lose my nerve, and the story will grow ivy and thorns, and I won't be able to touch it without pricking a finger. And I'm starting to realize that if I keep building castles out of all my fear and distrust, one day, my towers will be too high to climb.

Besides, Liam came searching for me tonight. Not only that, he risked his entire crew and ship for me. For *me*. And now, with his warm body pressed against mine, with the intimacy of what he did tonight to save my life still dawdling between us, I am running out of reasons to pull away from him.

So, I start at the beginning. I tell him about Willa and her quest to find Lucy and then stumbling upon the captives. The three littles and the Avian sisters. I explain the helpless rage I felt, and how I set my shadow loose on the sleeping soldiers.

I don't spare any details of the violence or the killings, not to boast, but because I know he will understand the weight it has put on me. Death begets death, and even when it's necessary, it is still a heavy load to carry all on my own. When I reach the part about Aya, he places a heavy hand on the back of my neck. I am not used to verbalizing something that hurts so much.

I will see her, slumped against that wall, for the rest of my life.

Only once I'm well and truly finished does Liam finally speak. "I thought for certain he'd have killed you by the time I got there."

"He certainly tried."

He averts his gaze, contrition pulling his features tight. "It's because of me."

"No. It wasn't. He was bringing me to someone. I never found out who. I don't think it was King De'Havelin."

"Me neither."

The dead hold all the cards.

Liam's gaze goes far away as he murmurs, "He spoke of impending war."

"What does he know that we don't?"

His eyes flash. "I don't know. But I plan to find out."

Reaching up, he shuts the water off.

47

PEACE

He leaves me to change into the clothing he brought, which turns out to be one of his shirts—a dark, long-sleeved, billowy silk thing that reaches mid-thigh on me, some pants that are much too long, and soft undershorts. I manage to get the shirt on, wincing, and make the decision to forego the pants, but keep the shorts. His shirt is practically a dress on me, anyway. And it smells of him, of salt and suns and rosemary soap.

I towel-dry my sopping-wet hair for a little while, but soon my muscles start to fatigue, and I give up, leaving my hair in a damp, dark mass. At least it's no longer dripping.

Silently, I push open the door to find him sitting on the edge of his bed, facing me, wearing only a pair of dark pants. His fingers are laced together, his elbows resting on his knees. My eyes can't help but dip momentarily down his chest, skimming along the defined ridges of his stomach, all the way to the low V that disappears beneath his waistband. The elegant whorls of his tattoos serve only to accentuate the lean muscles of his arms and chest, and I find myself wishing I could spend a day studying them, unraveling each intricate pattern and shape. I can make out some of them, at least. The sea serpent on his chest, over his heart, for one. His Mark as captain. Its scaled body winds and curls all the way down his arm to the top of his hand. That one alone must have taken days to complete.

Reluctantly, I raise my eyes to his face, but whatever he's thinking, he's keeping carefully hidden. With two fingers, he beckons me.

A shiver jolts through me.

Hanging the towel on a hook, I pad over to him, exhaustion begging me to rest. Sleep has never sounded so alluring. But the bandage and healing tinctures next to him signal that I must wait a little longer.

I sit beside him on the bed with my legs underneath me, and without a word, he brushes my hair aside and pulls the loose neckline of my shirt over my shoulder to apply the tincture. His touch is deft and precise, and before I know it, he's covered the wound with a bandage and pulled the neckline back into place. Next, he attends to the cut on my forearm, pulling my arm forward to rest on his thigh. While he's working, I consider his finer details. The freckle on his bottom lip. The shadows beneath his cheekbones accentuated by soft candlelight. His long, straight lashes. Once he's finished, he leans back to inspect his work, wearing a divot between his brows as he concentrates. Disappointment twinges in my chest. I don't want him to stop touching me. For this to be over.

"Liam?"

His gaze flicks to mine. "Yes?"

And perhaps it's the safety I feel with him that causes the sudden surge of bravery, or just exhaust-induced delirium. Either way, I don't think either of us expects it when I cup his face with my hands and press my lips to his stubble-rough cheek. I linger there, for perhaps a moment too long, but he certainly doesn't complain. His head whips to mine, his pupils blown wide. And for once, I witness him lose the war for control.

My breath catches in my throat as he pulls me by my hips onto his lap, and I watch his eyes snag on my mouth. His tongue darts out to lick his bottom lip as one hand moves to frame my face, his other sliding to my ribs. If he leans forward just a little bit more, our mouths will meet. My skin sizzles at the thought, and butterflies flutter in my stomach. I want this. I've wanted this, I think, for a while. Ever since Roarke.

Perhaps before then. And then he frowns.

"You're hot," he murmurs, feeling my other cheek. He makes a noise at that, too, and curses. "Too hot."

"That's strange. I don't feel hot," I shiver again, for emphasis. I thought it was that I wasn't wearing pants. Or perhaps simple exhaustion.

For a moment, he seems puzzled, and then he groans with realization. "Tell me. Do you recall reading about poison withdrawal fever?"

It takes a considerable amount of effort to sift through my mind for an answer. "Ermmm, with certain kinds of poison, if it is removed from the body too quickly, it can cause fever, fatigue, and in severe cases, respiratory depression." I sigh as realization hits. "Oh."

The butterflies in my stomach all drop to the floor.

He nods slowly. "Your skin is scorching, and you can barely hold your head up."

"I've been busy. You were there."

"Right. You can sleep soon. But I'll need to keep an eye on you tonight, to make sure you don't wake up dead tomorrow."

My eyebrows raise to my hairline. "You're asking me to sleep here? With you?"

One edge of his mouth lifts. "I'll gladly sleep on the floor if the idea of sharing a bed revolts you so. But I was hoping that perhaps you don't despise me as much as before." For emphasis, his hands lower to my hips and squeeze.

The feeling of him there induces a tingly sort of heat that I can do nothing with at the moment except grit my teeth against.

It's strange. As of last night, I thought we were back to keeping each other at arm's length after the things I said. I thought I'd run him off for the last time. But no. Liam is nothing if not tenacious, it seems. But I do owe him an apology for it.

My eyes dip to his chest. "Liam, about the other night. I want you to know that I didn't mean it. What I said in the library. My shadow was behind you and it . . ." I falter. I still shudder when I think of what I saw. And yet, I don't think it would purposely hurt Liam. Quite the opposite. But the fact remains that I don't fully understand its capabilities, and until I do, I can never fully let my guard down. Especially when Liam incites this reaction from *both* of us.

". . . it did something that scared me. And I did the only thing I know. But I don't think that of you. I never have. You had every right to be angry."

He swallows, and I'm momentarily preoccupied with the notion of scraping my teeth across his throat.

His voice drags me back. "You have every right to say no. At any time."

"It wasn't a no. I—" I suck in a deep breath. "You didn't know about the markings. And I still don't fully understand them. It felt like I was tricking you."

"Oh, I'm fully aware of what I've gotten myself into, curse or no curse," he counters.

"And what's that?"

His thumbs push the underside of my jaw up and he leans in, brushing the tip of his nose against the skin of my throat, sending incandescent bursts of nothing good careening through me. "Nothing I can't handle."

Desire coils low in my belly, but as quickly as it happened, he releases me and pulls away, breaking the spell. "Make your choice. Am I sleeping on the ground tonight or not, Strider?"

I purse my lips, pretending to think. After a few more moments, I finally relent. "Alright, then."

He tilts his head, a challenge gleaming in his eyes. "Alright, *what*?"

I laugh tiredly. "Must you?"

Pressing me close, his gaze lingers on my mouth before meeting my eyes. "I want to hear you say it."

For perhaps the first time, I give him what he wants without a fight. "Stay with me, Liam."

An unscrupulous grin spreads across his face. Twisting, he deposits me gently on the left side of the bed and tugs the blankets up over me. They're soft, and smell like him, too. Rising to his feet, he touches the one and only orb giving off light, above his bedside table, and plunges us into darkness. I hear him reach the other side of the bed, then feel it sag beneath his weight as he slips in beside me. We're close enough that I can feel the heat emanating from his skin.

Rolling onto my side to face him, I can just make out his features in the dark. The dark fringe of his lashes, the bow of his top lip, his thick, arched brows. His hand is a welcome warmth on my forehead, and I close my eyes as it traces down the side of my face, along my jaw, down my neck, across my collar bones, to where it finally stills on my chest. For a long while, it rests there as he monitors my breathing.

"I'm alright," I whisper.

It takes him a while to respond. "I was afraid you wouldn't be."

"You're not afraid of anything."

"That's not true. I was very afraid tonight. That you were suffering because of me."

"I wasn't. And even if I was, I can take it."

He makes a noise. "That's worse."

A few moments go by.

"Liam?"

"Love?"

"I know we're bound together by blood. But thank you. For coming back for me."

His hand moves from my chest to wrap around the side of my neck, just brushing the underside of my jaw. It's a tender movement, and it whisks my breath away. "I will come back for you every time."

My lips lift into a secret grin. This time, the warmth in my chest has nothing to do with his touch.

"Tell me about when you got The Wraith."

A flash of teeth as he smiles. "You want a bedtime story?"

"Mhm."

But the truth is, I just like the sound of his voice.

As he ponders, his finger idly traces the shell of my ear. I don't think he knows he's doing it. "Well, it all started with a broken compass, a witch who only spoke in riddles, and a boy who wanted to touch the horizon."

As he speaks, his fingers move to wind through my hair, twisting strands here and there, brushing them from my face. It seems to bring him comfort to touch me, as if at any given moment, I might disappear. I let my eyes flutter shut, the deep lull of his voice as rain drums above us impossible to resist any longer. And I have the fleeting thought that if ever I find peace, I imagine it would feel something like this.

48
HOLLAND AND ARTIE

T oday has been absolutely exhausting.

I rose with the suns to get a start on the day's work and have not stopped moving since. With preparations for the hibernal solstice taking place tomorrow in full swing, there is much to be done. Today, in addition to my usual tasks, I have swept the eaves, laundered the clothes, hung the clothes to dry, helped the kitchen prepare the vegetables and marinades for all fifteen main courses, aided the gardeners in casting a rather strong de-weeding charm for the front gardens, and even ventured into the town plaza for more cinnamon sticks.

Of course, no one had cinnamon sticks because everyone wants cinnamon sticks right now, so I had to wheedle my way into some very overpriced ones, but at least I have them.

By the time I return to the castle grounds, I decide I've earned a few moments of respite. Just a few. There's a bench beneath a massive, sprawling oak tree, with, in my opinion, the best view in Celosia. From here, one can see the sea and the twinkling city lights clustered throughout the trees. Even in hiberna, the trees never lose their leaves. Yet another reminder of how ripe this land is with magic. In Savastane, our seasons are not so pronounced. In the cold months, everything dies. Sometimes, on my darkest days, I wonder how that is fair.

It is here that, with a long-suffering sigh, I take my first rest of the day. Cold bites at my nose and cheeks, and I thank the king's generosity in providing me a charmed hibernal coat, spelled against harsh weather. The fur is warm and soft against my neck, and I wrap it tighter around myself as I gaze out at the majestic view.

"Mind if I join you?"

My entire body jolts at the voice, and I leap to my feet immediately. "I was just going," I say automatically, ashamed someone caught me slacking off. But . . . I know that voice. Even so, I can't believe it.

Holland emerges through the trees, his skin damp with sweat. The smile he offers me is tired, but earnest, as he replies, "Please, Artie. I could use the company. Stay?"

Indecision threatens to rip me in half. If I were caught loitering when I should be working, even if it is with Prince Holland, I could bring shame on Savastane. On Vesper. But . . .

He seems to read my mind. "What if I ordered you to keep me company?"

I can't help but chuckle. "Then I suppose I'd have to comply, wouldn't I?"

He motions to the bench, and I sit back down, trying in vain to stifle a disbelieving grin, and the flush that creeps up my neck every time he's near. Holland takes a seat next to me, and he's so close, I can smell him. Sweat, but something crisp and inviting, too. His soap, perhaps.

I expect him to launch into conversation, ever the charismatic and charming prince, but he's surprisingly quiet for a while, his blue eyes trained on the striped horizon. Where it touches the ocean, it is ablaze in orange with a gray, wispy ceiling. Above that, stormy gray and deepest blue, topped with more pillars of stony clouds. We sit there admiring it like old companions, as if we'd read each other cover to cover so many times, we know every line. Every word.

But that's not true. We don't know each other at all. My imagination is always getting the best of me.

"This is my favorite view in all of Celosia," he says after a while, when the suns are almost set and the sky is soft and glorious.

I turn to him. "Mine too."

"You look surprised," he muses, and his dimple shows.

"I—" A laugh bubbles out of me. "I would have thought there would be somewhere better, just for princes and kings and queens. But that's silly, I suppose."

"Even if there was, this would still be my favorite," he replies, gesturing beyond us. "I come here quite often, on the way back from the mines."

Prince Holland is well known for disappearing for days on end to train in the old, abandoned mines. At the young age of twenty-three, he's undoubtedly the best swordsman in the realm, and it's no secret why. He works tirelessly at it, and when he's not practicing, he's off on campaigns, specially appointed by his father. Already, he's feared by many. But it's hard to reconcile that part of him with the beautiful boy that's sitting beside me now.

"Is that where you were, just now?" I hope my question isn't too bold.

He turns to me, and I wonder if I'm sitting too close to him. If I could get in trouble for this.

"You caught me. On busy days like today, I try to get out of the way. Wouldn't want to slow anyone down."

"You could never be in my way," I say, then blush and look away.

From the corner of my eye, I feel him studying me. "How are you liking it here, Artie?"

"In Celosia?"

"In Celosia. With . . . us."

For some reason, my cheeks start to burn anew. Perhaps it's the cold. "I like it very much. Your family has bestowed upon us a great honor to be here and represent Savastane, and we are forever in your–"

A wave of his hand stops me. "No, no. Don't do that. I didn't ask on behalf of my father, and I have no interest in an answer on behalf of Savastane. Do you, Artemisia, like it here?"

I look at him. Really look at him. Take in his sky-blue eyes, the ends of his blond hair curling slightly from his earlier exertion, the beginnings of stubble on the edge of his jaw. "I love it here. It's beautiful, and everyone has been kind to us. I–" I exhale, wondering if I'm about to make a mistake. Well, we will most likely never have a moment like this again, so what does it matter? "Sometimes I wonder if it's fair. How the magic chooses certain people and certain places. Savastane has some magic, but not as much as Celosia, and in the hibernal season, unless we are very diligent and careful with our rations, we could very well starve. But here, we are preparing a banquet. Here, there is such excess."

"Well, the land of the Crown will always be the most blessed to sustain its ruler," Holland replies carefully. I get the impression he's all but had that statement branded into his skin.

"I know, but what of places farther away? What of places that have almost lost magic entirely? What of Weavers, Holland? There is an imbalance. And I thought magic was always supposed to have balance."

He considers for a moment, and I fear I've overstepped, but then he says, "I think about this quite often. I thought I was alone in that. Everyone else always seems so happy."

"I am happy. But that doesn't mean everything is perfect. In other areas of this realm, people do suffer."

He sighs, scrubbing a hand over his jaw as he contemplates. "We are content here, you're right. My father is a powerful man, but he is also afraid. He's afraid of what it means that some people are born with magic within them. He doesn't care about the places without magic, because to him, it simply means they're not a threat. But it's the opposite. Wars grow from seeds of imbalance."

I wait for him to elaborate, and he does.

"If it were me, I'd want to make sure magic was everywhere. Even if I must give my own, I'd do it. Does a ruler truly love his people if he's not willing to give himself to his realm?"

He looks to me expectantly, and I huff a breath.

"I'd do the opposite. We can do just as well without any of it."

His mouth falls open. "Without magic? You'd want to take it away?"

A breath of a laugh escapes me at the foolishness of it. It sounds absurd spoken aloud like that. "I suppose that would be impossible, wouldn't it? Magic comes from the five crowns of the realms, and those can't be destroyed. But if you think about it, magic is the one thing ultimately causing the imbalances, so why not take it away and place everyone on equal footing?"

Holland has still not recovered. "But magic is how our animals stay healthy, how our plants grow. Without it, we would be lost."

"There was a time before the First Sovereigns, before the land bestowed upon them the crowns. There was a time before magic. We would learn how to live without it."

A thoughtful silence ensues my declaration, but when our gazes meet, we both can't help but laugh at the silliness of the conversation. Of course, neither of us is capable of the impossible. Yes, one day, Holland will be king. But I am nothing more than a lady-in-waiting to a rambunctious and spirited girl, and magic will reside in this land forever.

"Perhaps you are right," he says as the last of the sunslight disappears and orblights spark to life in the woods. "My father treats Weavers like butterflies, trapping them in glass jars instead of letting them fly away for fear they might one day become poisonous. Perhaps I am too eager to compensate for his sins."

"That is not a bad thing."

"I'm glad you think so," Holland says, a wistful expression on his face that almost breaks my heart. "Sometimes I feel awful for it. But if everyone were the same . . ."

"You're not awful," I assure him. "Not at all."

"I like your honesty, Artie. No one is ever honest with me. You're perceptive."

I give him a small, grateful smile. "It felt good to speak my mind. No one cares for the thoughts of a . . . well . . ."

The sincerity of his gaze is disarming as he says, "Don't. Don't belittle yourself. Not when you're so lovely."

I have to look away, lest he see the shock on my face. The flush staining my cheeks. The love in my eyes. For a fleeting second, I wonder what would happen if I confessed to being a Curse Speaker. If he would spurn me, or, or . . .

But then he stands, and it breaks the spell. A wave of sadness washes over me, as if I have just woken from the most wonderful dream and will never recapture it ever again. But then he extends a hand, and hope flutters in my chest.

"Please let me escort you back to the castle. It's the least I can offer after you've so graciously suffered my ramblings."

I hesitate. "But if we're seen—"

He grabs my hand, and a thrill goes through me. "Believe me, it's my honor to be seen with you, Artemisia."

49
PATHS

When I jerk awake, I can tell by the suns filtering through the window that it's late afternoon. Maybe early evening. I've slept all day.

The strange dream from last night clings to me like wet clothing. Groaning, I turn over, then sit up abruptly.

This is not my bed. Nor is this my clothing. I am incredibly sore.

What did I—oh, now I remember. Thank the Proctor it wasn't *that*. For a little while, I simply lay here, paging through the memories of last night. At some point, my fingers try to close into a fist but crunch over something instead. Lifting my hand to my face, I see that it's a small piece of rolled parchment. Hastily, I unfurl it and devour the message, written in small, but elegant script.

Sleep as much as you need, sweetheart. When you're ready, there's something I'd like to discuss. I sent the ring off this morning, by the way. Two of three tasks done.

P.S. Who is Artie? You dream of her.

He didn't sign it. He didn't have to. I sigh, wondering if I am ready to face Liam after what transpired between us last night. He knows. He knows about the shadow, the curse, and it didn't change a thing. If I close my eyes, I can still recall the path his fingers took in my hair. And the things he said to me . . .

His mouth on my skin . . .

Heat that has nothing to do with poison climbs up my neck and inflames my cheeks. After last night, things are different. But I won't know exactly what that means until I see him again. I refuse to dwell on it in the meantime.

It's a few more long, dithering moments before I eventually drag myself from Liam's decadent bed and into the bathing room. A quick glance in the mirror reveals that I look a *horror*. Purple crescents bruise the skin beneath my eyes, and my face is a sea of nicks and slices. My lips are colorless, my cheeks wan.

The poison really did almost kill me.

I shuffle back into Liam's room and glance around. Ah. He's left me a pile of clean clothes from my room. He must have retrieved them this morning. A fresh pair of tight, taupe trousers, with an olive-colored sleeveless top. Its stiff fabric juts up to cover my neck, then comes down in a V that doesn't close until it reaches my sternum. The rest of the top ends just below my ribs, the edges embroidered in fine cream thread.

Once I have my boots and knives back on, I feel a little more like myself.

And as I run some cleaning paste around my teeth, I decide that before I try to scrounge up some food, there's somewhere I need to go first.

Someone I need to see.

Standing outside Matteo's room, I raise my hand to knock, but stop myself when I hear voices emanating from inside. One, naturally, is Matteo. The other, surprisingly, is Basi. And he sounds uncharacteristically incensed, his halting accent more pronounced than usual.

"The answer is no, Matteo. The same as it always is."

"But why? Captain Blackwater won't let me fight until you agree to train me. You're holding me back."

"Doesn't seem like it stopped you from disobeying orders last night."

"I want to *fight*, Basi. Why am I not worthy of your time?" Matteo shouts, and I shrink back from the emotion in his voice. The hurt, the loneliness, the frustration.

"It has never been about worthiness, so stop putting yourself in danger. You could have been *killed*," Basi roars.

Silence is a gulf until he speaks again.

"I will say this one last time. I do not teach to fight. I teach to *kill*. It is all I know how to do–"

"But you teach Iona," Matteo interjects. "Why her, and not me?" There's no jealousy in his question. Only desperation.

"Because she is a killer," Basi snaps. "She has killed long before me and will do so long after I am gone. I am merely guiding the knife that she was already holding. I just hope that she never turns that knife on us. Gods help us, if she does."

Silently, I turn so that my back is against the wall and slide down until I meet the floor. I place my chin in my hands and breathe through the truth of his words. It feels like a punch straight to the gut, though I know Basi doesn't mean it to be hurtful.

It's just a fact, which is worse.

Floorboards creak from inside the room, and it sounds like Basi is moving closer to Matteo and further from the door.

"Look at me. Look at my scars. Understand the marks that killing has left on me and know that you do not see the worst of it. There are men who break things apart, like me. And there are men who put things back together. You must decide which path is yours."

A shaky breath.

"I don't have a path," the boy says softly. "I am the child of a disgraced baron, who can't go home, or my uncle will have me killed on sight. So, I joined a pirate ship, only to be told I'm no pirate, either. I don't know what I'm supposed to do, Basi. I just–" He struggles for words. "I want to help."

"Could you kill a man, Matteo? Truly? Look him in the eyes as his soul leaves his body forever, by your hand? Look at me and tell me you could. Tell me you can live with blood on your hands you can never wash off."

Silence.

His voice softens. "Listen to me. Put your head down, follow orders, and keep watching."

"For what?"

"Your path, boy. You'll know when you see it." Basi makes a low noise in his throat. "By the skies, you're only nineteen. You should be chasing girls and sneaking mead, not seeking your purpose."

"Captain Blackwater was already captain of The Wraith when he was my age," Matteo argues in a tone that sounds very much nineteen.

"Yes, well, he always knew what he was willing to sacrifice. Remember that." Heavy footsteps approach the door, and I stand. When the door opens and we make eye contact, all I can manage is a tight-lipped grimace. Basi's gaze dips down to the object in my hand, and he sighs.

"You're going to give that to him, aren't you?"

I shrug.

His gaze rises to mine. "Even after what I just said."

I nod.

His only response before he stomps away is, "No one ever listens to old Basi."

I wait a few moments to collect my thoughts before I enter Matteo's room. I find him sitting on his cot, his knees drawn up to his chest. His right arm hangs in a sling, and his usually bright, brown eyes look tired. His hair is mussed, and I get the impression he hasn't slept much, if at all.

When he sees me, a look of surprise flits across his face, especially when he sees what I've brought with me.

"Hello, shithead," I say, closing the door behind me.

He sputters out an awkward laugh. "This is . . . erm, hello, Iona."

"Well, I saw you get your ass kicked last night," I mutter, sitting down cross-legged in front of him. "Figured I needed to come see about you."

"I'm alright," he says sheepishly, rubbing his left hand down the back of his neck. "Broke my arm, though. Lirael is going to be very unhappy with me."

"I didn't know you weren't supposed to fight," I admit.

He looks away. "Captain Blackwater doesn't want me to get hurt. He knows I don't come from a place where it was really taught to me. At least, not at this level."

And yet, Liam took pity on the boy and took him on as a crew member, anyway.

"Erm, I'm glad you visited, actually," Matteo continues, red splotches spreading up his neck. "I should thank you for saving my life last night. And I'm glad you're alright. We were all worried about you."

Now we're both flummoxed.

"It's—" I take a deep breath. "I suppose we're even. You didn't have to come after me, but you did."

He looks at me strangely, his nose scrunched up and his eyes narrowed. "You're our crew member. Of course, we'd come after you. The entire crew was *furious*."

I stare at him as I process what he said. Not just Liam, but the entire crew.

I look away, nodding.

"Anyway," I say, my voice thick, "I saw what happened to your sword, too. So, I thought you could use this instead."

I hand him Cursekiller.

His eyes flare, his mouth popping open in a perfect O. After a few double-takes to make sure I'm not fucking with him, he says in a breathy voice, "This is the sword you got in Roarke."

I nod. He pays attention. "It is. But it's too heavy for me, so there's no point in hoarding a perfectly good sword."

He makes a few rudimentary motions with it, and even I can tell it's perfect for him. And for a moment, the joy on his face lights up the entire room. But then his expression falls, and he looks back at me.

"I can't take this from you. I don't know how to use it properly."

"Then figure it out," I retort. "It's yours. Besides, I was told it was a hero's sword. And if there's one thing I'm not, it's that."

His brows furrow. "Neither am I. I can't do . . . anything."

But I've said what I wanted to say, and my stomach is growling. I stand, stretching my arms up over my head and yawning. "Like I said, figure it out. Find your path, or whatever Basi said. Or cut your own way through. Whatever it takes. You can do that." My voice softens. "You will find your way, Eames."

He stares down at the sword, looking lost and overwhelmed. I put my hands on my hips. "Are you coming to dinner?"

"I'm not hungry," he says. "But thank you for coming by." He glances up, and I can see a little bit of life come back in his eyes. "This means a lot. I won't let you down."

"I know."

Odd as it is, I mean it.

It's later than I thought it was, and by the time I reach the mess hall, it's deserted. Well, except for one person. A lone, bearded fellow sits at a long table talking to himself. He's got a chessboard in front of him, and as I approach, I realize he's playing himself. Well, he's only managed to move one pawn so far, but still.

"Teller," I say, by way of greeting.

He turns around, eyes wide with surprise. "Good ev'nin' to ya, lass. Ye caught me."

I slide into the bench across from him, resting my chin onto laced fingers as I wait for my stew to cool. "You were right about the storm."

In fact, it's still storming. Not nearly as bad as last night, but the sky is still nothing but dark, soupy clouds; the ocean a cantankerous mess.

The old man smiles. "I'm always right about th' storms."

"Are you, now?" When he offers nothing, I prod. "Did you cause this, Teller?"

His laugh is a gravelly thing. "No one can cause storms. They're too damn big. But—" he brings his hand to the side of his mouth like he's telling a secret, "I can pull and push the clouds. Make 'em move a bit faster. Makes 'em angry when I do it, though. They prefer their own pace. Slow bastards."

I follow his train of thought. "You had the storm start early, so the Reds wouldn't see The Wraith coming. So Liam could ambush them."

His mischievous grin is answer enough, and right this moment, I see him as a little boy. Huge, blue eyes, and a penchant for telling the sky what to do.

"And now it's dawdlin' over our heads, givin' us a lashin' for hurryin' it along," he remarks.

Yet another Weaver on board.

"Are you waiting for someone?" I ask, motioning to the chessboard.

His grin grows wider. "Ye offerin'?"

"I'm no good at chess. Never properly learned."

"Bah. I'm no master, neither."

"Could've fooled me, playing against yourself."

He blinks, then a slow, knowing smile creeps across his face. "I never played by myself, not once. It's funny, I sit here with the board in front o' me, an' every time someone ends up plunkin' their ass down and playin' with me."

Figures. We haven't started playing, and he's already outsmarted me.

After my ass is whooped well and soundly five times in a row—the wily old man lied about being bad at the game—I beg my leave, but not before promising to play again tomorrow. I know of someone else who might enjoy the game as well, and make a mental note to drag Matteo out of hiding tomorrow to come play with us.

Instead of heading to the library, I trudge up the stairs to the deck. Outside, the sky is still leaking rain now and then, but I don't mind. It's warm, and I'm still a little enchanted by it. I pass by a few crewmembers—Rin, Eryk, and Cuin—but it soon becomes apparent that Liam is not here. I turn in a circle, my eyes scouring the deck for his long, familiar shape. He's usually out here around this time, so where–

"Strider, up here."

My head snaps back as my eyes lift to the sky. He's in the crow's nest.

"Are you coming down?" I call up to him.

"Are you coming *up*?"

With a breathy chuckle, I grab hold of the rope ladder and begin my careful ascent. It's higher than it looks, but I've never been afraid of heights. Once I've reached the nest, Liam appears over the railing and extends a hand. I take it, and he pulls me easily up and over. It's barely big enough for one person, let alone two, and we have to sit with our backs against the pole jutting out from the middle of the basket-shaped area. Our arms and thighs are flush against each other, and I almost ask why he forced me up here in this tiny space, but the view has the question dying on my lips.

An orange sunsset stains the sky, setting the gray shelf of clouds above it on fire.

Beneath, the sea glistens and roils on forever, in shades of black and startling blue, depending on the light. It's so magnificent, I almost forget to breathe. It's moments like this that I understand why Liam would rather die than ever give this up. I am getting perilously close to the same sentiment.

"Oh, Liam." The words leave my lips as barely a wisp.

"I know."

I don't know exactly how long it is that we watch the suns go down, a warm wind combing our hair back from our faces. But eventually, Liam speaks.

"There are some things you should know, Strider."

I turn to him and can't help but notice how the setting suns warm his skin and lights silver sparks in his eyes.

He belongs nowhere but here.

"But first," his thumb brushes beneath my jaw, then falls to the curve of my neck. I could swear his voice lowers slightly. "How are you feeling?"

"Tired," I admit. "But alive. Thanks to you."

One side of his mouth slants up. "We'll get to that."

"Mmm," I say, appraising him carefully. "You know, I overheard Basi and Matteo today. I didn't know you had forbidden Matteo from fighting."

I can tell the subject surprises him, and his eyes go to the skies, as if hoping to find his response embedded in the clouds. "Matteo is . . . he's just so young. And I know it's hypocritical of me to say that, when I was . . ." He stops himself. "He's already lost his parents, and it seems his uncle has wasted no time in seizing control of Koska after the shipwreck. I imagine if he ever returned, he'd be killed. And now he'll never get answers as to why his father—who, from what I gather, was always a good Baron—allowed their own people to be picked apart by De'Havelin's men. It seems to me someone was twisting his arm, but you can't get answers from a dead man. And he has to live with that. I couldn't turn him away. But I also won't watch him get slaughtered because he has nowhere else to go."

"Basi won't train him."

Liam scrubs a hand over his face. "I know. It's . . . a problem for me."

"He has a point, though. There are," I smile bleakly, "enough of us." I gesture to him and myself.

"People who kill things easily?"

Snorting, I nod. "What did you wish to discuss?"

He turns fully to face me.

"You bared your secrets to me yesterday and trusted me to keep them. Now, it's my turn."

50

A PROPER THANK YOU

"I suppose I should start from the beginning."

The last of the suns dips beneath the waves as Liam starts his story.

"I've mentioned my upbringing in Talis. I wasn't born there. I am originally from a land called Inverness, beyond the borders of this realm. Both my brother Collin and I were born there, four years apart. But we didn't stay for long. My real father is a shade of a man driven solely by ambition and power. Not long after I was born, a rival of his tried to murder my mother, and she barely survived it. Afraid they would come for one of her sons next, she fled Inverness and never returned. My father stayed, unable to give up his desire for power. To this day, I've never met him. I wouldn't know what he looks like. But it seems he got what he wanted. I hear Viktor Braythwaite is a powerful man indeed. Though he lost everything to get there."

"Braythwaite? Not Blackwater?" I ask.

He smiles bitterly. "Whatever name I make for myself shall be mine alone. I want nothing to do with that narcissist."

"Has he ever tried to contact you or Collin?"

His demeanor turns to ice. "We have both received many letters from him. They have all made for wonderful kindling. So, not too long after she landed in Talis, my mother married my stepfather, a man who had dedicated his life to serving the king in his navy. He was strict. Harsh. Unforgiving. I suppose for my mother, it made sense to run from one man ruled by his own ambition to another governed only by his own need for structure. Collin was less affected by it than I. He was four years older and knew to shut up and do as he was told the first time.

"I, on the other hand, couldn't fathom being anyone's subordinate when I was older. So, while Collin trained to follow in our stepfather's footsteps and join the king's fleet when he turned eighteen, I found an internship with a fairly large Talisian merchant ship. All the while, my stepfather trained us both in swordsmanship. For all his faults, the man was damn good with a sword. Real damn good. Even if his methods could border on brutality."

I narrow my eyes. "How so?"

Liam gives a hollow laugh. "The man had such unrequited rage, though he'd never admit it. The realm was utter chaos, and he wanted to feel some semblance of control. He loved that about my mother: her free spirit. How unburdened and curious she was. But devils below, he hated it in me. He tried to beat it out of me every day of my life. It only made me practice that much harder. All I wanted in the entire realm was to best him. And I did, eventually. Though my right knee will never be the same."

My brows scrunch together as ire for a man I've never met uncoils within me. "I've never noticed an issue with your knee."

His gaze slides to mine. "I can't exactly make it obvious I have a weakness. Besides, it's healed for the most part. I just have to be careful. Anyway, when Collin turned eighteen, it was time for him to leave for Celosia. By that time, my mother's health had become fraught with episodes of frailty—in part, from the attempted assassination. And, I think it almost killed her to watch Collin leave. Her firstborn. The rock of our family.

"I panicked on the day he was due to leave. So much so, I challenged him to a duel. The deal was, if I won, he would stay, and when I was of age, I would go in his place. He agreed. We made a blood oath upon it. And then he beat the ever-loving shit out of me. I didn't have a chance. And to this day, I despise myself for losing.

"He promised to write when he could. At first, he did. I received letters from him at least twice a month. But then, twice became once, and once became not at all. A year passed in which I heard not a single word from him, and all we could do was hope. Until one day, a Gray showed up to tell us that Collin had been killed in battle. Gone, just like that. The first thought I had was that perhaps if I'd gone with him, he'd still be alive. Perhaps if I hadn't been such a deviant, he wouldn't have felt that he had to pacify our stepfather and enlist. If I hadn't lost, he'd still be here. I'd failed him."

The strain in his voice strikes a chord in me that reverberates throughout my entire body.

The night that The Vice's men tried to kill me, I'd told him he'd failed me. No, I'd screamed it. And his reaction, the way he'd flinched . . . Between that and watching an entire ship of crewmates die at Balor's hands, I cannot fathom the weight of it. There are many things I'd give anything to change, the hateful words I'd flung at Liam that night being one of them. I'd been so angry. So quick to blame. Never in a million years would I have thought that he, too, was holding himself in such contempt. Now I see why he's so insistent that Matteo not partake in raids or battles. He views him as yet another way to fail. If Matteo were to be killed, it would gut Liam more than he'd ever admit.

It seems guilt is a monster we both see when we close our eyes. I grab his hand. "Liam. That's not fair."

He fixes me with a flat stare. "It's what happened. If I'd been less selfish, less focused on my own desires, better at dueling, none of this would have happened. I'd still have a brother."

I squeeze—hard. "You were fourteen."

"Old enough that I should have known better than to fall for a feint, trust me." He laughs darkly. "Save the sympathy, Strider. No one will ever best me again."

I let go of his hand to slap the back of his head. He reels back to gawk at me. "What was that for?"

"Come off it," I say. "Have you ever thought about how absurd it is that Collin agreed to duel with you in the first place, knowing he was four years older? Did you even have a chance at beating him? Why give you the hope? That was . . ." I trail off, scoffing.

He frowns. "Go on then. Out with it."

"Your brother was cruel for not just fucking leaving. And now you have a reason to blame yourself for what happened." I shake my head resolutely. "Not your fault, Liam. Neither is having dreams of your own. Dreams are one of the only things that are truly ours."

He stares at me for a moment longer before clearing his throat and looking away.

"Well. That was when I decided I couldn't wait around anymore. I would make my own way; everyone else be damned. The day my father retired from duty was the day I left, vowing to myself I wouldn't return until I had my own damn ship. And a cure for my mother's ailment. A year and a half later, after quite a bit of unspeakable debauchery—" he shoots me a salacious grin, "—I claimed The Wraith as my own, commanded my first crew, and pillaged more than enough money to keep my mother comfortable until she passed."

"Did you find a cure?"

Something hard glints in his eyes. "Almost. But I'll tell you the story of my first encounter with Balor some other time."

I'm so incredibly glad that fucker is dead. "Which brings me to the letters."

A soft drizzle of rain spatters our faces, enough to slick some strands of Liam's hair to his brows. It must have done something similar to me, for Liam brushes a thick bunch of hair behind my ear. My gaze lifts to his, and I feel a small smile spreading across my lips.

"Oh, you think that because I was sweet to you last night, you can touch me any time you want?"

He rolls his eyes good-naturedly. "Please. You didn't stop me, now did you?" He makes a tsk-ing sound. "And here I was, so thrilled with our progress. By the way," he leans close, his eyes dipping to my mouth. "Speaking of last night. When you're ready to give me a proper thank you for saving your ass, I'll be waiting. Aye?"

I snort. "You'll accept what I give and be glad of it."

His smile broadens, displaying his perfect white teeth. "Sweetheart, I'm used to the taking of things. You'll do well to remember that."

I cross my arms, smirking. "Finish your story, Liam."

With an exaggerated sigh, he sits back and plants a boot on the railing in front of him. "Ah, yes. The letters. A few years after I established myself as a pirate captain, I started receiving the strangest letters. Unsigned, from an undisclosed location. Whoever was sending them was specifically interested in me because I held no alliances, no obligations. They were simple. Whoever was writing them had information about the royal fleet. Not just that, but certain ships. Where they'd be and when. My job? To sink them and leave no trace."

The missing ships Balor mentioned. "It was you? This whole time?"

His grin turns savage. "How do you think I'm so disgustingly wealthy?"

"You get to keep whatever riches they had onboard," I surmise.

"Indeed." He chuckles. "You look skeptical. What would you have done?"

My answer is immediate. "I'd have burned the letters. Sounds like a setup."

He cocks his head, and approval glints in his eyes. "That was my first inclination, too. But whoever sent the letters seemed to anticipate that, so they sent a sweetener." He pauses for dramatic effect, and I move to slap his head again, but he catches my wrist midair. With a sultry laugh, he pulls my hand down against his chest, where he laces our fingers together, tucking his arm over mine.

"For safe keeping," he says to me with a saccharine smile. With his other, he pulls out a haggard-looking sheet of parchment and hands it to me. Leaning over it to shield it from any wayward raindrops, I scan its contents, biting the inside of my cheek. It's a list of names and what seem to be corresponding locations—one of which I know intimately. Marrin. Koska is listed, too. But the most interesting part is the description next to each location: the number of Grays, and diagrams of the base. Entrances, guard routes, and schedules.

I scan the page again, committing as much of it to memory as I can.

"It's a list of villages, towns, and ports the Grays planned to infiltrate. It only took a few look-sees to verify the accuracy of the information. The names, I believe, are what they call each base."

He carefully folds it and puts it back in his pocket, safe from the rain.

"So, whoever is sending you these letters is some sort of rat in Celosia? This information would be highly difficult to come by."

"Something like that. So, curiosity got the best of me, and I set out to find these ships in need of a good sink. Come to find out, every single one of them was a ship full of Grays. No cargo, no guests, only an empty ship. Well, mostly empty. Except for the unoccupied cages."

My whole body tenses, and my lips flatten when it comes together.

"The person writing the letters was having you sink ships meant to kidnap Weavers. Creatures. But—" my mind races. "What about the Reds? Is everyone in on it?"

"My theory is that different soldiers have different roles. I tortured countless Grays to get information on the Pits, or wherever the Weavers get taken. None of them knew—trust me. I think the Grays are the ones who take Weavers, but at some point, they are passed off to the Reds. If they're smart, there are many stops on the way to the destination, so only very few actually know where the captured Weavers end up. Unfortunately, I was merely stopping the Grays before they could take any Weavers in the first place."

I stare at him, completely shocked. "And no one has sought vengeance on you for all the trouble you've caused?"

"Oh, sweetheart, you know I leave no survivors. For all the ways I hated him, Balor taught me a very good lesson. If you're going to start a fight, make certain you end it, too. No one forgets a black eye. Because we were able to take them by surprise last night, I doubt anything will come of that, either."

My mind combs over all this new information. And I try hard to ignore the thrum of blood in my ears, and the warmth pooling low in my belly at the revelation. He is perhaps not the aimless vagabond I, along with the entire kingdom, thought he was. This is what he meant, when he said he and the crew had practice.

There is much to be done when the kingdom isn't looking. And who's worried about one little pickpocket and a greedy, self-serving pirate?

He was right. Look at all the trouble we've caused.

But there's something I've been wondering for quite some time now. "Does the king know? About the trafficking?"

He leans his head back against the pole to look at me fully. "It wouldn't surprise me either way. Fewer Weavers roaming around means less for him to worry about. But I don't know for certain. And I don't think The Pits is the only place they're being taken. There are simply too many going missing."

I take a moment to digest everything before another question bubbles up. "Is that why you were in Marrin?"

He smirks. "I sank a ship headed your way and thought I'd come and see the state of the place for myself. And that's when I received the impetus for this whole debacle. Whoever is writing these letters wants to meet. At the ball."

I go very still.

"Normally, I'd decline. Though I have no reason to doubt this person's motivations, I prefer to stay solitary. However . . ." He pauses, rubbing his bottom lip. The movement, though small and inconsequential, sends ripples through me. *Concentrate.* "They mentioned that if I meet them, they have information on Collin. What happened to him."

My mouth pops open. "What happened to him? Was he not killed in battle?"

Liam's face is inscrutable as he replies, "That's what we were told. But apparently, that's not what happened. Collin, according to this person, is still alive."

The ramifications of this buzz around in my head. All sorts of outcomes, possibilities, and traps. If Collin is still alive, why wouldn't he have contacted Liam?

"What if they're lying? What if it's a trap?"

Liam shrugs. "They have no idea who I've told about this. Who I've shown the list to. It could be just as much a trap for them as it is for me. If Collin is alive, I have to know."

"What does this person want?" The more I think about it, the more unsettled I become.

"It seems they want to strike some type of partnership. Whoever this is does not have the means to undercut the king. I do." He raises his chin, and his eyes glint a dangerous shade of green. "And it will be my deepest pleasure."

My brows crease in thought. "You think they'd know what Balor was talking about? This other entity Balor served?"

He shrugs. "It would be convenient, but I've no idea."

Another pause. Then, "That night, when we agreed to the terms of all this, and I asked what you wanted from it all. You said—"

"Power," we say together.

He nods, a nostalgic smile spreading across his face. "I suppose I was being a bit difficult that night. However, in a way, it was the truth. What is more powerful than slowly crippling the most feared man in the realm, without making a single concession?"

"Yet," I say softly, and his expression darkens.

"Yet," he concedes.

I exhale slowly. "Where are we to meet this person?"

His eyes narrow. "We?"

"I'm coming to the ball too, remember? And you're certainly not meeting this person alone. What if they plan to kill you, to dispose of loose ends?"

One end of his mouth flicks up. "They can try."

"And if you're wrong, I'll be there to save your cocky ass."

"If you must. We are to meet in the hedge maze at twelve bells."

Thunder growls in the distance, and a spark of lightning crackles through the air. We share an apprehensive glance, and Liam motions toward the ladder. The conversation, for now, is over.

"Ladies first."

By the time we make it to the deck, it's raining again. Not as hard as the night before, but enough to quickly soak my clothes through.

But the droplets are warm and soft, and I hardly pay them any mind as I watch Liam climb nimbly down the ladder, then drop the rest of the way to the deck with a heavy thud. He closes the short distance to the helm, steadying it with both hands as the sea starts to thrash. Although The Wraith is typically fairly intuitive when it comes to a sense of direction, I've noticed that, particularly when it storms, Liam likes to give her a guiding hand. I wonder if the rain makes it more difficult for her to see, somehow.

I follow him there, arms crossed over my chest, still deep in thought. He's nothing like the man I accused him of being. He's saved countless Weavers from a fate in the Pits. He's ruthless and tender and conniving and astonishing, and I am still learning how to reconcile all those things with the striking man in front of me.

"Who were you planning to take to the ball? Before me?" I inquire, after watching him wrangle the helm into stillness for a few moments.

There's laughter in his eyes when they find mine. "A beautiful, empty-headed idiot who would never think of stealing from me, and certainly never cause me this much trouble. Who would dance the night away while I dealt with the business at hand and give me a good romp afterwards for all the fun."

I throw my head back and have a good cackle. "I am, undoubtedly, the worst thing that's ever happened to you."

There's a funny little grin on his face. "I thought that, at first." His hand shoots out to snatch my wrist. "About that proper thank you."

I have no resistance left in me. Not after last night. Not after I've been thinking about that mouth all damn day. "Will it shut you up?"

His eyes alight like green fire. He jerks me forward until I'm lodged between him and the helm. Leaving less than a breath between us.

"Don't pretend you don't want this, too," he croons.

"Fine, then." Grabbing a fistful of his vest, I yank him to me and pull his mouth to mine. There's a moment—half a heartbeat—in which terror seizes me, and I wonder if I've made a grave mistake. It feels like the undertow pulling at my legs, and I have only this moment left to swim away. Or let it take me.

But Liam's arm clamps around my waist, crushing me to his chest. His other hand slides beneath my jaw, and I realize I've been drowning for a long time, and this is my very first taste of air.

I cannot get enough.

And yet, there is nothing frantic about the way Liam kisses me. He takes his time, as if memorizing the shape of my mouth with his own. Every sensuous press of his lips is an exploration, and it's not long before he deepens the kiss, his hand moving to claw the nape of my neck. An elated gasp escapes me as he takes my bottom lip in his teeth, then swipes his tongue over it as it enters my mouth. My palms scrape down his rough jaw and over his neck as every ounce of control over my body I've meticulously honed over the years is undone by him.

This will not satiate me. Now that I've had a taste of him, all I want is a bigger bite.

Rain plasters our clothes to our skin as I run my tongue over those perfect teeth of his. He makes a low, velvety noise in his throat, and it almost sends me over an edge I didn't know existed. I think of last night, of all the indecent thoughts I was having about his mouth, and it only makes me kiss him harder. Deeper.

But it is Liam who is doing the claiming. His tongue is unrelenting, making slow, languid sweeps of my mouth, and if he wasn't holding me to him, I might melt between the floorboards. His teeth scrape my lips, reminding me over and over of how cruel he can be. His hand fists in my hair, and I have the thought that he could ask anything of me right now, and I would allow it.

Given the way my body is reacting to his touch, there is much I wish to demand of him, too. I am reminded of what it felt like to see Liam Blackwater for the first time back in Marrin: how I was both terrified and enthralled by him. Even then, he called to me on some carnal level. And while I knew enough to run from him then, it seems we both enjoyed the chase too much. Some things never change.

Lightning flashes, and another round of thunder tumbles nearby. My eyes flutter open to find Liam's gaze roving over me hungrily, his lips rosy from my teeth. Both of our chests are heaving, noses still close enough to touch. Our breath mingles, and his thumbs push my jaw up further, exposing the column of my neck to him.

Lowering his eyes to my mouth, he dips his head, bringing his lips close enough to brush mine on the way down.

"Next time, I won't be so gentle."

He presses a wet, hungry kiss to the base of my throat, and my lips part in a silent groan. His teeth scrape against the sensitive skin there, liquefying my entire body. "What makes you think this happens again?"

"Oh, sweetheart." His right hand slides from my jaw to the base of the back of my neck, where his grip tightens, giving every nerve ending I own the impression that I've been struck by lightning. "I'm not finished with you."

Another kiss, our tongues rolling lazily over each other.

I laugh softly against his mouth. "Do you always get what you want?"

"Always, Strider."

Thousands of fireflies flare to life inside my chest. All the heartache, all the lonely nights, and every drop of blood was worth it for this moment.

My fingers thread one last time through his thick hair. "Goodnight, you fiend."

His eyes are molten green as he leaves one last lingering kiss on the hinge of my jaw. "Sweet dreams, my love."

It takes every remaining ounce of pride I have to turn on my heel, walk away, and stay away from him tonight.

51

A NIGHT OFF

Three days later, I rise before the suns to head to training early and begin my stretches and core strengthening exercises. Basi has been teaching me blocks and defense, which requires a substantial amount of core strength and balance. It's been difficult, and I've collected a menagerie of bruises and cuts from his punishing attacks. But better a bruise from Basi than a disembowelment in battle.

I'm passing the stairs when I hear a series of thumps coming from the deck above that sound suspiciously like a body. I freeze, wondering how stupid someone would have to be to raid The Wraith. I slide The Twins from my hip, grateful that someone had nabbed them from Balor's ship, and flick it once to extend only one end into a curved blade. Soundlessly, I climb the stairs, then press my ear to the door. From the other side, I can hear the low rumblings of voices, but can't make out what they're saying.

Well, I suppose I'll have to find out.

I shove open the door, blade at the ready, only to find Liam and Matteo sparring in the emerging sunlight. Matteo, who was already retreating, whips his head to face me, and just as an enormous grin splits his face, Liam knocks him on his ass.

The pirate captain sighs, wiping sweat from his brow with his forearm as he glances in my direction. His eyes seem to momentarily stick on me before he turns back to Matteo, extending a hand.

"Focus," he chides. "Battle is chaotic. You cannot get distracted. Even for a spectacular woman."

Matteo makes a gagging sound, and Liam throws me a lopsided smile.

"That goes for you, too," the younger boy mutters, getting to his feet.

"What was that?" Liam barks.

Matteo scrapes a hand down his face. "Nothing, nothing."

Chuckling to myself, I leave them to it.

By the end of the week, I'm exhausted. Every night after supper, instead of my usual ventures in the library, I've been playing chess with Teller and a reluctant Matteo. At first, he insisted on watching, his eyes devouring every move, every morsel of advice Teller gives us. But after the second night, he starts whispering suggestions in my ear.

Keep the pawns united. Get the knight out early.

Behind his earnest face lies a sharp intellect, and he is quick to learn from his mistakes. It's not long before I realize he's much better than I, and I hand him the reins gladly. Between the two of us, we actually manage to beat Teller a few times, which feels like a feat, given how whip-smart the old man is. A wily trickster.

Tonight, I rest my chin on laced fingers, only half paying attention to the game. Matteo moves our rook across the board into position to eventually strike the queen, but if Teller is worried about that, he doesn't show it.

He moves his bishop.

Matteo moves the queen out of the way.

And Teller wins again with a pawn neither of us thought would ever be any trouble. Matteo groans, leaning back against the wall and putting his face in his hands, and Teller's gravelly laugh echoes in the cavernous mess hall. I cover my face, laughing in disbelief. "Never forget about th' pawns," he says, shrugging. "Again?"

"I'm done," I declare, getting up from the bench slowly. My legs are killing me from sparring today. I glance over to Matteo, but he's busy studying the board, his chin in his palm.

"One more time," he says slowly.

Teller's eyes shine with glee, and I leave them resetting the board. I've no doubt they'll play late into the night.

On the way to my room, I catch sight of Luhan rounding a corner. I've barely seen him since the Balor incident. Between healing broken bones from the fight and corralling the crew back into normalcy, he's been busy, and I've missed him. I turn on my heel and jog until I've caught up to him as he plants a foot on the bottom rung of the stairs leading to the deck.

"Lu," I call after him. "Wait."

He turns, and a smile warms his face. He looks weary, and it plants an ache in my chest. "Iona." He extends a hand, and I close the distance between us to wrap my arms around his slim waist. His arm comes around my shoulder and squeezes. "You're up late."

"I've been playing chess with Teller and Matteo," I tell him, tilting my head back to look at him. "It's become a bit addictive."

He nods in understanding. "He lets you win just enough to keep you coming back, doesn't he?"

My mouth pops open. "He's been letting us win?"

Luhan has the decency to look contrite but ends up laughing anyway. "I figured you'd have known."

I let out a forlorn groan as I scrub a hand through my hair. I'm not entirely surprised, but still. Matteo can never know. My gaze drops to the object in Luhan's other hand, the one he didn't use to hug me.

"Oh? What's this?" I point to the bottle of rum and feel the edges of my lips curl into something devious.

Luhan follows my gaze and shrugs. "It's been a shit week, and I have the night off. The Reds so generously had an entire stash of it. Care to join?"

I've never been much of a drinker, but I've missed Lu, and at the very least, I can accompany him as he partakes as much as he pleases.

"Lead the way," I say.

And he does. Right to Liam's quarters.

Liam is hovering over his bookcase, reading a splayed book when we enter. Lu enters first, holding up the rum as if it's a boon of war. Liam's smile is wide and disarming as Lu slides through the double doors, but when he registers me, it changes into something feline. He straightens and snaps the book shut.

A quick glance at the cover reveals it's a book on—my breath catches. He was reading a book on curses.

"Iona found me in the stairwell," Lu explains as he perches on Liam's desk and busies himself by digging the cork out with a dagger. "I figured you wouldn't mind if she came along."

"I believe we can be cordial," Liam replies, flashing me a sharp grin. It's a significant struggle not to jump his bones and kiss him until we're both incoherent.

Luhan snorts, darting a knowing look between us. Nothing escapes his notice. Nothing. Putting myself back together, I saunter past Liam, putting perhaps a tiny bit of extra sway in my hips as I do so. It does not go unnoticed, and I feel quite smug as I fold my legs beneath me and sit on the floor, facing Lu. Liam follows suit, crossing his ankles and leaning back on his hands. The cork comes off, and Lu joins us. We pass the bottle around our little triangle, not bothering with glasses. I decide immediately that rum is disgusting.

"It tastes like rancid coconut water," I say, making a face. I hold up the bottle, frowning at the brown liquid inside. "It even looks rancid."

Luhan tries to take it from me, but I hold it out of reach. "Give it to me, then. You're wasting it."

"I never said I wouldn't drink it," I argue. "I've drunk worse."

"I believe you," Lu grumbles, finally wrapping his fingers around the bottle and snatching it from me.

The conversation flows easily, and soon, they're regaling me with tales of their early adventures.

"Luhan has been with me since the beginning. When all I had to my name was a ship that could barely float," Liam tells me. They share a knowing grin.

"I was also there, Iona, when Liam got The Wraith. Only sixteen, and already a captain." There's an unmistakable note of pride in his voice. "You simply cannot imagine the trouble we got into."

"I couldn't find a first mate to save my life," Liam complains. "They all kept dying."

"You kept sailing into blatant danger," Luhan retorts. "Trying to prove yourself. Moons, it's a marvel you didn't lose an arm or fuck up that face of yours."

"That would have been a real shame. It's all I have going for me."

Luhan snorts, side-eyeing me. "If I told you his arrogance used to be worse, would you believe it?"

"No, I wouldn't," I wince, then turn to Liam. "How could anyone stomach you?"

He flashes me a smug grin. "Don't cry for me, Strider. I did just fine."

"Apparently, you did very fine, crotch lice."

Luhan dissolves into laughter, and though Liam cuffs the back of my head, he can't hide the mirth in his eyes.

"There was one instance," Luhan says, brightening at the memory, "when Liam thought it'd be a good idea to sail straight into the worst sea storm you can imagine. Waves the size of mountains, winds that could blow a dragon off course. And crimson lighting."

My eyebrows draw together. "I heard crimson lightning is a foretelling of death—that anyone . . ."

"Anyone who sees it is going to die soon," Luhan finishes. "Well, it's a lie. I saw it too, and I'm still here. Anyway, after that, Liam got a compass that actually fucking works."

Liam clarifies, "Around the time I got The Wraith, I'd also been gifted a very peculiar compass for helping an old woman find something she'd lost. She told me it was charmed to always point true."

"She said, 'always point through, '" Luhan corrects.

"That makes no sense, and you know it," Liam mutters. He digs around in his pocket for a moment, then takes out a silver compass I'd never seen him use before, and soon, I see why. There are no directions on it whatsoever, only a singular dot at the top. Currently, the arrow is spinning clockwise, stopping periodically to spin counterclockwise.

Pursing my lips, I ask, "What, exactly, is it pointing to?"

Liam's grin is immediate. "That's the question, isn't it?"

I squint. "It's got to be pointing toward something."

Beside me, Luhan groans. "Not you, too. It's defective, idiots. Broken. You may as well throw it into the sea."

Liam's eyes flick up, and I get the impression this is an old, but fond, argument of theirs. "Never. One day, I'll figure it out."

"Look, it's alright. Just admit you were conned by that old woman."

"I was not conned," he protests. "Its use hasn't announced itself yet. That's all."

"You're going to be an old man, still carrying that thing around," Luhan sighs, shaking his head. "Oliver was right. You get something in your head, and it sticks there forever."

Oliver.

At the mention of the name, the mirth drains from the room as if someone pulled the stopper. My eyes snap to Liam, but he's watching Lu intently. There's a softness in his gaze.

Lu sighs heavily, drawing his knees to his chest. For a few moments, he loses himself in a memory, his eyes glazed with it. When he blinks out of it, his dark gaze settles on Liam.

"I never really talk about him, do I?"

Liam shakes his head gently. "You don't have to."

"Moons, he was so much fun, though."

One corner of Liam's mouth lifts. "Aye. He was."

Luhan looks to me. "Want to hear how I became the First Mate, Iona?"

"Only if you want to tell it." If ever I sound kind, I hope it is now. I'm greeted with the saddest smile I've ever seen.

"It's my favorite story."

52

OLIVER

Luhan says, "I am Prince Luhan Kat'tai of the Whisperwood, the Flesh Mender, the first son of the crowned king of Iridisia. My sister, Gwyneira, who is two years older than I, was born with an old soul but a militant mind. Our childhoods were stern but never cruel. My mother and father loved the kingdom and nurtured us well enough so that we would not harbor any great wickedness when eventually we sat on the throne.

"My childhood memories are of poring over Iridisian history, sitting in on military strategics, learning which foot moves first when an Iridisian waltz plays. If I close my eyes, I can still hear the drone of my tutors, the whisper of a page being turned. Iridisian ways are different from here, you see. The crown doesn't pass only upon the death of its previous owner, but instead, once the previous ruler either confers it of their own free will, or they rule for two centuries, whichever comes first. It must pass through blood, though the exact relation is not specified. It was always to be me, though. My parents never wavered on that.

"And neither did I. It was all I'd ever known, after all. There had never been a day the prospect of ruling had not stood like a monolith in my horizon. I didn't dread it. In fact, I thought I'd be fairly good at it.

It's just how it was. It was also the only life I'd ever considered for myself. It was easy to embody the expectations they had of me when I'd never considered otherwise.

"On the day I turned sixteen, I met my betrothed.

"Sara had been promised to me since the day she'd been born, as is Iridisian custom. She came from a powerful family. She herself could touch the soil and grow a honeyfruit tree, right then and there. She could have grown an entire orchard of them if she so pleased. And moons, was she beautiful, kind, and clever. I thought, perhaps this won't be so bad. Perhaps this will work.

"And then, a few days later, I met her brother Oliver. He'd arrived later due to a bad bout of health, and I had been advised to keep away from him. He's a poorly lad, I'd been told.

"Unfortunate disposition. Thin-blooded. I'd pictured some sad, sallow-looking creature with skin dripping off his bones, maybe a tuft of hair here and there. But Oliver just looked like a boy. Bright, cunning blue eyes, skin a little waxy, but there was a splotch of color to his cheeks, and he was so quick to smile. It was never a kind smile, though. Always a bit naughty, because he was always in the midst of getting away with something. You see, Oliver had learned from a young age that no one ever suspected the sick boy of wrongdoing, not when he's always so tired, bedridden, or just now recovering. He always had some trick up his sleeve or squirreled away somewhere else. He was quite capable, as long as he was able to rest in between.

"We became inseparable. We'd climb to the highest point of the castle and watch the sea, and he'd tell me about how one day, he'd sail away. Then, inevitably, we'd bicker about his health, but he'd always insist that he'd feel better out there, where he'd never be shut in a musty, dark room ever again. We'd go to the docks, he and I, and watch the ships come and go. He never got tired of it. And he had it in his mind that every ship that left the port was destined for some high adventure. He longed for one of his own.

"I loved him immediately. It felt like I always had. We spent almost every day together, and every night when we could. Sara didn't care—she acquired the throne no matter who shared her bed. And she didn't show much proclivity for relations either way besides what was required to bear a child. I'd marry Sara and create an heir with her, but neither of us harbored any notions of being more than companions.

"The issue, Iona, arose when my mother and father found out.

"You see, the Kat'tai name had ruled Iridisia for generations. We have a longer lifespan than most due to the crown, so when I say generations, I mean centuries of first sons bearing more sons. It meant a great deal to my parents to carry on our legacy, whatever the cost. They feared that, if I became preoccupied with Oliver, I might forget my duty, or forego it entirely, and our great tradition would end with me.

"One night, Gwyn came to my room. She told me that it had been decided to send Oliver away across the sea, where I could never find him, so that I could focus on my duties here without distraction. Somewhere he'd receive better care, they claimed. I'm sure they told him it was best for me, and that bastard probably acquiesced without a word.

"For the first time, I had to choose between a life of easy certainty, of complacency, or the unknown with a boy who made me feel alive. It was easy."

"I found him at the pier, one foot on the plank, ready to board a mysterious ship. At first, he was horrified, furious, aghast at what I'd done. But as we bickered about it, I came to understand that a pirate captain was there, hunting for a first mate. A young, ambitious pirate captain who wanted nothing more than to sail the realm and make a name for himself.

"I told this captain that he was getting two for the price of one, and I'd forego a salary in exchange for his discretion when it came to me, and a bit of understanding when it came to Oliver. We set sail that morning.

"We did more in the ensuing decade than some men accomplish throughout their entire lives. Every day we risked our necks, and yet I've never known such peace. Oliver was right. He barely had spells. He was hardly sick anymore. I may not have been able to heal him, but the sea could. The open skies did. Not a day went by that he wasn't raising some sort of ruckus or pulling off some elaborate prank. Moons, he was brimming with life. I could barely keep up.

"And then, one day, for whatever reason, he had a spell again. And again, a few days later. He started sleeping more. Eating less. It started to feel as if every day, there was a little less of him. But he didn't want to dock. He was adamant about that."

He stops, his eyes going glassy. I dread his next words.

"Before it got too bad, he said to me, 'They call it spending time with someone. But no moment I ever had with you felt spent. It felt like a gift. And for me, it was an entire lifetime. I'm going one way or another, quicker than I'd like. I always have been. But don't be too sad. I will wait for you to catch up.'"

Luhan stops, breathes deeply, and gathers himself. His eyes are hard and shiny. So are mine—and Liam's.

"Everyone, at some point, will experience what it feels like to lose someone. But I am a bloody healer, and I still couldn't save the one person who—"

He doesn't finish it. Clears his throat.

"It's been two years, and I still hear his laugh sometimes. I still make my oatmeal the same way he did and use the same ratty blanket he liked because somehow it still smells like him. I still have his clothes. It's very difficult to reconcile that to you, this is just a story, but to me, he was my entire world. Though it's been a long time now, I still can't believe he's not here."

Silence settles over us for a little while, until, after a polite amount of time, Liam raises his mug. "To Oliver. And how much we miss that troublesome fuck."

To my immense relief, Lu laughs. "To Oliver."

Liam's voice softens. "He was like a brother to me, you know."

"I know," Luhan says, shoving Liam's shoulder. "I know. He loved you so much."

For the next little while, Luhan delights me with tales of their exploits from seasons past. His stories, and the very particular manner in which he tells them, convey an unbridled sense of joy that I'm glad to be part of, even from afar.

"What of your mother and father, though?" I ask. "Did they ever send for you?"

"Of course they did, once," Luhan waves a dismissive hand. "I declined, and shortly after that, the realms were sealed off. But I have a feeling that they assume I'll grow tired of this romp and return one day. When you live as long as Iridisians do, even the worst slights and mishaps smooth themselves out eventually. Besides, Gwynnie will make a much better ruler than I. It turns out, my flights of fancy are rather compelling."

He moves to take a swig from the rum bottle only to find it empty. Lu makes a face and pouts. "Gone too soon." He stands. "I shall get more."

I share a look with Liam, whom I can immediately tell is resigned to weathering this out with his friend until the very end. Perhaps it's best I leave them to it. We share a small smile before I return my attention to Luhan. "I'll accompany you."

He flashes a red-cheeked, uninhibited grin, and I wish I could fold it away for rainy days. Lu and I head to the doors as he chatters blithely on. And though I told myself not to, at the last moment, I look back to Liam.

He's simply leaning against his desk, a fond little expression on his face as he watches after us. I fold that away, too.

53

BRAVERY

At first, we maintain a constant stream of chatter on the way to the mess hall to collect more rum. I can't tell whether Lu is truly drunk, adores telling me stories of Oliver, or both. Nothing about his gait or diction reveals even a hint of overindulgence, but then again, I wouldn't be surprised if that had been wrung out of him long ago.

Luhan is a prince.

It makes so much sense. His haughty demeanor, his penchant for bossiness, his refined mannerisms. And now he's stuck here, in Alvion—

No, not stuck. There are still ways to get through for those who know how to look, he'd told me. If Lu ever did return to Iridisia, how would he be received? Would his parents be furious, or shun him, or was he telling the truth, and they'd shrug it off? What of Sara and Gwyn? All these questions spin around my mind, and I'm so absorbed in them I fail to realize Lu's stopped talking until we've been steeped in silence for longer than a few moments. We're right outside the mess hall.

"Lu?"

He looks . . . stricken. And his eyes are somewhere else—another time. Gently, I touch his arm. His eyes snap to mine, and he sucks in a shuddering breath. Without a second thought, I crush his body to mine in a tight embrace.

"I've never known you to be so touchy," he says with forced disdain, though his arms tighten. "Moons, you've really filled out."

A fond smile tugs at my lips. "You've taken good care of me."

He chuckles softly. "I have."

We part, the tension broken, and head inside to where the stash of alcohol is kept, in a small pantry beyond the kitchen. I hop onto a counter while Lu fishes it out. "Do you want to talk about it?"

He pauses. "No." A moment passes. "Yes." His nose wrinkles, his eyes dark. "Sometimes I wonder if I could have saved him. If I could have tried harder."

I process that carefully, recalling what he's told me about the limits of his healing capabilities. "You're a Bone Weaver. Was the sickness in his bones?"

"No," Luhan admits, averting his gaze. "But—"

When his upturned eyes meet mine, they're bottomless, dark pits. "Haven't you wondered what the Weaving takes from me, Iona?"

Before I respond, my gaze sweeps over the mess hall to ensure we're alone. Not because I'm afraid of someone hearing us discuss Weaving, but because I think Lu is about to tell me a secret. And I'll kill to protect it. And him.

"When I say I am a Bone Weaver, I am speaking the truth. However, that is not the end of my ability. I can heal all of it. Flesh, muscle, and skin. But only physical injuries."

"Not illness," I reiterate.

To that, he says nothing, and my stomach drops. For a few moments, he stares off into the corner, gone somewhere I cannot follow.

"When I was a little boy, Gwyn and I were playing in the gardens when she decided to climb a tree. She was trying to climb all the way to the top, despite my protests, and sure enough, she fell. Broke her tiny little shoulder. I remember kneeling over her, looking at the way it jutted out, and feeling like I could simply push it back in. Imagine my shock when I did just that. My parents were elated that I was a healer.

"A few years later, I broke my finger in a practice duel. Thinking nothing of it, I tried to heal it myself and found that I couldn't. Nothing happened, no matter how I tried. I had to have it set and splinted, like anyone else. Imagine my existential horror that my esteemed abilities had suddenly fled. But I wondered about it. So, that night, I crept outside and caught a bird. I broke its wing, then immediately healed it. It flew off, cursing my name.

"Something else occurred to me, then. I took one of my daggers and sliced a line down my palm, then healed it instantly."

One word comes to mind.

Balance.

"And that's when I realized what the magic takes from me. I can heal myself any way I like until I heal someone else. If I heal someone's bone fracture, I can no longer heal my own breaks. I can heal someone's cut, but if I were to be stabbed one day in battle, I'd bleed out like anyone else. So, yes, call me selfish, call me a liar for that. But Iridisians can live for a very long time, and I'll be damned if I give that up. But . . . I would have. For him."

"Lu," I murmur. "You did everything you could for Oliver."

He recoils from me. "What if I didn't? What if there's some despicable, self-preserving part of me that held my magic back for myself?"

I roll my eyes. "You are haughty and judgmental, but you wouldn't have let him die if you could have saved him."

"You can't know that about me," he says miserably.

"But I believe it all the same," I insist, gripping his wiry forearm. "I'm sorry, Lu. You shouldn't have to bear that burden alone."

"I don't." His eyes lift to mine, a curious expression in them. "Liam almost drove himself mad, looking for a cure while Oliver was alive. We both were . . . desperate."

A memory comes to me, then. All those books in Liam's library of cures for ailments and diseases. With every passing day, it gets harder to overlook his devotion to his crew. To the people he cares about. My stomach does a funny little dip.

"You don't have to explain yourself to me," I say, sweeping that information away for later. "It's your magic."

"I know that," he retorts, then softens. "I had a feeling you'd understand."

"Does Liam know?"

"No. No one else knows."

"Why'd you tell me, then?"

He laughs. "You're the worst person I know."

"I feel the same about you."

Now we're both grinning like idiots as we head for the doors again. "So then, how old are you?"

He yawns. "Oh, don't worry. I've lived twenty-six years. Liam and I are the same age, in fact. I am but an infant."

"How long might you live?"

He shoots me my favorite mischievous look. "Oh, a few centuries."

We converse for a few moments more before I tell him I won't be accompanying him back to Liam's quarters. I need some time to think about the past few days. He pouts, but quickly gets over it, shutting the doors to the mess hall behind us.

"Suit yourself," he sniffs. "I know why you're leaving, anyway."

"Because I'm exhausted?"

He hits me with a heavy-lidded stare. "I preferred it when you and Liam hated each other. This off-putting, nervous energy that's been exuding from you both as of late is exhausting. Just fuck already."

I gasp and shove him in the arm. He shoves me back. Harder. I swat his hand away, and he grabs my wrist and pulls me off balance. By the time we finish wrestling, we're both chortling.

"I'm serious, Iona," he insists, giving me a wide berth after I land a playful elbow jab in his ribs.

"Serious about fucking?" I straighten, hands on my hips.

He makes a noise in his throat. "Did you not listen to anything I said earlier?"

I frown. "Of course I did."

He flicks my nose. "Good things don't stand there waiting for you." He turns on his heel, the bottle of rum swinging at his thigh. Before he turns the corner, he calls after me, "At some point, you have to be brave enough to chase after them for yourself."

54

DEATH OF A GHOST

Several nights later, I wake from another nightmare with a start. That one was . . . awful. I can still feel the claw of little fingers pulling at me. Hear my own screams as they drag me down.

A lone candle sputters on my bedside table, casting long shadows that loom over me. I move to sit up but find that I can't. I try to kick the blanket off, but my body remains frozen. My fingers refuse to move. The skin on my back starts to burn as the shadows on the wall grow impossibly tall and darken, as if they're not shadows at all but voids. Dark space. Slowly, one shadow takes the shape of an arched doorway, so depthless I'm convinced that if I were to put my hand there, it would not meet the wall at all but simply proceed on through.

Out steps my shadow, and if I could scream, I would. Instead, I watch in silent terror. It says nothing. Only cocks its head to the side. I know it sees me. It crooks a finger, motioning me to follow, and silently as it appeared, it glides back into the arch and disappears.

I gasp, the spell broken. I'm clammy with sweat. My pulse is a racket in my ears, my hands clenched so tightly, it hurts to unfurl them. I sit up and fling my blankets to the floor. But when I look at the wall, my shadow has suddenly reappeared. It does nothing out of the ordinary.

"What are you doing?" I implore it. "What do you want?"

Naturally, it doesn't respond.

With a noise of frustration, I pull my boots on with shaky hands and throw my door open. I need some air.

There isn't enough room for the two of us in here.

The moment I push the doors open and stalk onto the deck, I start to feel better. Sucking in a deep breath of salty air, I make my way to the bow. An endless expanse of stars greets me, and a slightly chilly breeze brushes the hair away from my face. It smells like rain—and rosemary soap.

"You don't have night duty tonight," I say into the dark.

Liam comes to stand beside me, leaning easily on the railing. "I gave the rest of the crew the night off. Couldn't sleep."

I huff a brittle laugh as I wrap my arms around myself, turning to face the deck. "Me neither."

Liam's finger, light as a feather, touches my chin and guides my face toward his. "You look as if you've seen a ghost."

"Seven of them, actually. All the time."

"More nightmares?"

I nod. "My shadow, too. Any time I'm afraid, it seems to take advantage of that, and I'm worried one day I won't be able to make it stop."

Liam's quiet for a while, and the only noise is the peaceful slap of the waves on the hull far below. And so, I'm surprised when his arm slings around my waist to pull me into his side. Something in me relaxes at the solid heat of him. His hand rests behind me on the railing, our hips and thighs flush.

"Collin had nightmares, too. Bad ones, when he was young." He takes a deep breath, but I don't want him to stop. I've grown so fond of his voice. His lilting, dignified accent.

"He did?"

He nods. "He was a Weaver. I don't think I told you that. His magic started manifesting when he was young. Too young. He could blink out of sight and reappear somewhere else like Balor. But he could travel much farther. Places he'd never visited before. Balor only seemed to be able to travel a few paces at a time.

"At first, when he didn't have good control over it, it was terrifying. He was afraid that he'd blink away one day and end up in the middle of the ocean, or the Grimwood, and wouldn't be able to find his way back. I know our parents lived in constant fear of that, but it never happened.

"That's what his nightmares were about. I remember waking up to his screams, only to find my mother holding him. She'd spend hours getting him to breathe normally again, rocking him back to sleep sometimes for hours on end. It made for some long nights, and at the time, I didn't understand why she did it that way. Looking back, it's so obvious. She was giving him a tether. Something to ground him. And it did help. I catch myself doing it too, still—using touch when I feel like I'm losing myself, or someone else."

His words sound guarded. Heavy, as if he's kept them hidden for a long time, and this is the first time he's dragged them out to the light. I recall all the times, too, when he'd grabbed my arm, or my face, when I was hurting or scared or angry. I'd thought it was meant to be intimidating, but now I realize it's how he stabilizes himself. It's how he keeps me from going somewhere he cannot follow, even if it's only in my mind. Or his.

Every time I gain insight into him, it feels like I'm giving away another piece of my heart.

Something occurs to me. "When you were fighting Balor, I saw you doing something with your hand when he would disappear. It looked like you were feeling for him."

Liam's head bobs. "It was a gamble. Whenever Collin would reappear, if I were standing close enough, I would feel it. It felt like crackling, almost. Like . . . pure, condensed magic."

"It felt like that for Balor, too, then."

"Yes. That's the only way I guessed where he appeared. Otherwise, he would have killed me." I flinch. The thought is as impossible as it is abhorrent. By now, my pulse has slowed, and the pressure in my chest has eased to a bearable weight. It's time to tell him about the demons that plague me. After all, he told me about his. But it's more than that. It's the last door I have closed to him. My last reason to keep my distance. I want him to know me. All of me.

"Liam," I say softly. "I have to tell you something."

I feel his eyes come to rest on me, but I can't meet them.

"I told you in Roarke about the other children who taught me to steal. We were a pack, running around Marrin. Five of us, in all. We protected each other. Made sure everyone had something to eat. They were all I had.

"About five or six years ago, we were chased by some Grays. I was separated from the rest, and by the time I found the others, they were cornered in the woods by three Grays." My breath comes sharply at the memory, and Liam's grip tightens around my waist. He presses a kiss to my temple, and it reverberates throughout my entire body. It gives me strength.

"You don't have to, Strider," he says into my hair.

"Yes, I do." I steel myself, my lips pressed together tightly, my gaze trained on the floor. "One of the Grays had already broken Mizra's arm. I remember seeing it hanging there, limp. Wren jumped in front of her, but she was just a tiny thing, and—and he clubbed her hard in the head. I think she died right there. Right then.

"That's when I . . . I saw the shadow for the first time. My shadow —but wrong. I remember seeing it slithering on the ground toward them, and my shoulder blades started burning so badly, I thought my skin was scorched off."

My breaths come in great shudders, and Liam pulls me closer to his chest, as if he could protect me from my own memories. And the funny thing is, sometimes, I believe he could.

"That's the last thing I remember before I lost consciousness. The pain was too much. That was my first dark spot—when the shadow misbehaves like that. When I came to, I . . . I was standing there, holding a dagger, and everyone else was dead. Everyone." My voice fades to barely a whisper. "I don't think it meant to . . . hurt them. I don't know why it would have. But it doesn't matter, does it? They're still dead."

A wave of nausea almost doubles me over as I recall the tiny, bloody bodies lying on the ground. Eyes staring up at a dusty sky. Gone.

My hand covers my mouth, but I have to get it out. "All these years, I thought it was bound to me by a curse, this shadow, but now I know. It was mine, all along. I did that. I killed them. That's why these episodes, these dark spots, disturb me so badly. They're a reminder that at any moment, I could lose control." I pause. "No, they're a reminder I never had it."

My next words come out in halting increments. "I see them all the time. There is no place in the realm that I could run, and they wouldn't follow. And I deserve it."

"Are you so certain?" Tenderly, Liam's fingers hook beneath my jaw, tilting my face up to meet his. "Of the time that I've known you, this is what I've seen. You honored your word to Matteo about Lirael, though what they're doing is naive and dangerous. In Roarke, you broke a twelve-year-old curse. Those children on Balor's ship are no longer condemned to a life of killing. They have a chance at a good life because of you. These were your choices. You didn't choose what happened in Marrin, though it was a terrible, horrible accident. And I am so sorry, Strider."

My chin wobbles with shame. "It doesn't matter what we call it. They died because of me."

His expression grows pained. "You didn't ask for any of this. I know what happened was horrible, so horrible, but you cannot continue to hold yourself accountable. You lost control over something you still don't understand all these years later. And not for lack of trying. You were a child."

"So were you." But that doesn't stop you from blaming yourself for your mother's death and Collin's departure, I want to say.

Liam's hand slides down my neck to rest heavily on my shoulder. "Perhaps we could both benefit from blaming ourselves a little less. It won't detract from the grief or the mourning, but you don't have to do that alone."

"What if I lose control and hurt someone else?" I whisper. I'm not willing to accept this. "I'd never forgive myself."

"You already don't forgive yourself. You—" he runs a hand over his mouth, choosing his words carefully, "—you spend all your time either training with Basi or poring over books on how to extricate yourself from this thing. At some point, you will have to trust yourself. And if it's me you're worried about, you're wasting your time."

My eyes meet his, and suddenly the longing I feel for him, for a realm in which there are no malignant shadows that cling to me, takes the breath from my lungs. Tears fill my eyes, and I huff a wobbly, embarrassed laugh. "I'm sorry."

He doesn't smile. "I'm sorry you had to spend so much time alone, while all this guilt was eating you alive."

"I wanted to. I wanted to become a ghost. I wanted to be despised. I didn't deserve to leave Marrin. I deserved to rot there with what I'd done."

His eyes flash as a note of warning creeps into his voice. "You're wrong. And you've self-flagellated long enough."

I inhale shakily. "I don't know how to let them go. It doesn't feel fair."

He shrugs. "We'll do it one finger at a time."

I feel hollow, like all my innards have been scraped out. For a moment, I feel them all surrounding me, accusing me, blaming me. My friends who never grew up. But when I lift my eyes to face them, they're not there. Of course they're not. I buried them, one by one, a very long time ago. My breaths come in rough spurts, but they do come. For a little while, we pass the time in companionable silence as I mentally recover from the confession. Idly, his fingers blaze a trail up and down my spine. Neither of us has moved away from the other.

Finally, it is Liam who breaks the silence. "Tired, Strider?" I shake my head in a sort of numb daze. I am wide awake. A devious smile spreads across his face. "I have an idea."

Warmth spills into my bloodstream, but abruptly, he steps out of reach. "I'll be right back," he says, a mischievous glint in his eye. He doesn't bother waiting for a response before he turns on his heel and disappears through the door leading below.

He reappears quickly enough, carrying a large object in his hands. The closer he comes, I begin to realize it's . . . a book. A magnificent tome. He grunts as he sets it on a nearby barrel, and I follow him, curiously peering over his shoulder. He thumbs through the table of contents, trails a finger down the page, then turns to a spot about halfway through the book. He holds his place with a finger, closing the book, then turns to me.

"What's this about?" I gesture to the enormous book, one eyebrow arched.

With a flourish, he opens it up to the page he'd found. For a moment, I'm certain I'm hallucinating.

No, I'm not. That's . . . music coming out of that book. Elegant strings and piano. Waltzing music. My muscles lock up, and my eyes go wide as he extends a hand.

"Did you think I'd forgotten that sooner or later, you'd have to learn to dance? We're going to a ball, after all."

I swat his hand away. "Now?"

"Now."

"Is this punishment? Are you punishing me?"

His laughter booms around us. "No."

"I already know how to dance."

"Mhm. Liar."

I am now beginning to panic. "We don't have to dance, even if it is a ball."

Sighing, he cocks his head. "We do if we want to appear somewhat cultured. Which I am."

"In theory." I cross my arms, glaring defiantly, but he ignores me and pulls me by my wrist to the middle of the deck anyway. In the background, the music ebbs and flows, and under another circumstance, I would have thought it quite lovely. Right now, however, it is terrifying.

"It's the middle of the night, you nutter."

"Hush," he commands, placing his right hand on my lower back, while the left takes my right hand in his. He places my left hand behind his neck, and it takes quite a bit of effort not to thread my fingers in his silky hair. "Dance with me, coward."

I expel a shaky breath. Tonight has really gotten away from me. "I'd rather fight Balor again than learn some useless dance."

His eyes gleam. "Good thing I plan to teach you seven."

He walks me through the basic principles of a waltz—the one, two, three of it all. Which seems simple enough, until we actually try it, and I realize I have to let him lead.

"Strider," Liam says patiently, after the fourth time we've bumped into each other. "You have to trust me."

"I'm not good at this," I balk. This demands something softer of me that I'm not certain I can produce. Something patient, and graceful, and elegant. I have never known myself to be any of those things. The music ends, and a new song begins. A lone violin, its notes spiking up and down in a lively tune.

"We'll practice," he promises. "Every night, if we must. Chin up, now. Straighten your spine. Good."

He leads me into a spin, and though it feels silly, a little part of me, one I hadn't met yet, thrills. It is sort of romantic, this midnight waltz. The stars are a spectacular canopy above our heads, and Liam knows exactly what he's doing. He dances like he fights, every move smooth and easy.

"Either you're the realm's most talented dancer, or you've heard these songs before," I muse, noting the way he anticipates every swell and dip of the melody.

"This was my mother's book of classical waltzes. She played these a lot, growing up, and insisted we learn when we were little." He spins me out, only for me to stumble back into his waiting arms. "We visited court every few years, and I think she took great pride in raising two chivalrous sons." His mouth twists into a wicked grin when he says the word 'chivalrous'.

"Mm, and what would she say if she could see you now?"

"She'd be proud that I am able to explore the world and be

whomever I wish. Both a scoundrel and a gentleman, whenever it suits me."

"Every mother's dream for her son."

This time when he leads me into a twirl, I return without misstep, and my pulse thrums with triumph. We glide around the deck, and before I know it, we've danced through several songs. Liam is a wonderful partner, and the truth is, I trust him. When he tells me I'm safe, I believe him.

As the edges of the sky begin to pale with morning's arrival, Liam lifts me by my waist in a graceful arc. He takes his sweet time bringing me back down, our bodies flush, eyes locked as the music cascades into a finale. When he sets me back on my feet, I still feel like I'm floating. And I can't tear my eyes away from his face. He leans in, stopping just shy of my mouth. His breath feathers against my lips, and my heart stutters. My hands don't move from his chest, nor his from around my ribs.

"Was that so bad?" He asks softly.

I shake my head, and a reluctant smile gets through. "You know that it wasn't."

He looks incredibly pleased. Perhaps even a little smug that he's won me over. "We only have a few weeks left before the ball. We will need to practice."

"Can we do more lifting bits?"

He pretends to think about it. "You drive a hard bargain. Consider it done."

Easiest deal I've ever made.

55

THIS IS WHAT IT FEELS LIKE

The following week, Luhan and I are enjoying breakfast when Liam plunks himself across from us, looking enormously pleased with himself.

"Not only am I incredibly handsome, but I also possess the mind of a scholar, and I have figured out how to complete the last task."

Luhan, very patiently, sets down his fork, having clearly been through this many times.

Liam leans forward, a bright, mischievous spark in his eye. It appears that for the past several days, he has been scheming. This morning, he has finally decided to let us in on his machinations. "The third task can be completed in Celosia. I can't believe I didn't think of it before."

Luhan glances at me. "What's the last one, again?"

"A piece of the sky," I answer, my chin resting in my hand.

His frown deepens as he lapses into silence, lost in thought. Eventually, he gives up. "I've no idea what you're planning. And your ego is getting out of hand."

"I've always thought so," I say. "What perilous adventure is to befall us this time?"

Liam merely shrugs and gets to his feet. "I suppose you'll just have to trust me." He throws his arms out wide. "Prepare yourselves for land, ye miscreant bastards. We reach Celosia in one week's time."

How Liam plans to complete the last task, I haven't a clue. No matter how many times I've asked today, he refuses to tell me. Even that night when we're practicing a new dance, he refuses.

"You'll see soon enough," he insists with a wry grin, twirling me out. When I come back in, I'm glowering.

"I hate surprises."

"After all we've been through, you still don't trust me?" I recognize the trap and carefully sidestep it.

"I want to know what you're planning," I counter, turning sharply with him as we sweep across the deck. The music slows to a sensual swoon of cello, and it occurs to me that perhaps a change in tactics will persuade him. I slide the fingers of my left hand up the back of his neck, all the way into his hair. From the way his grip suddenly tightens on my back, it's clear that he notices. That, and the way his eyes flash.

He spins me around but holds me that way, my back to his chest, my right arm pinned between us. His left hand slides beneath my collar bones as his mouth comes dangerously close to where my jaw meets my neck. I whip my head around to face him and nip at the tip of his nose, flashing a sultry smile.

His laugh is barely a rasp, hot against my skin. "What do you think you're doing, sweetheart?"

Somehow, we're still swaying, though my only concern has become where our skin is and is not touching.

"Give me a hint." The words drip like honey out of my mouth, and I feel him tense behind me.

"Say please."

"Hell no."

He whirls me around to face him, our bodies crushed together. His eyes dip down as his right hand directs mine to join my other behind his neck. With his now free hand, the other still supporting the small of my back, he skims it down my waist, over the swell of my hip, to my thigh, and even lower, to my knee. He grabs hold and hoists it up to his hip, and before I can catch my breath, he dips me low. A wispy breath escapes my lips, and when our eyes meet, my blood becomes liquid fire, bubbling beneath my skin.

"It's just one little word, Strider."

My entire world becomes this man's mouth, and how badly I want to taste it again. His hands, and how I ache for them to run over my body without constraint. And yet . . . I don't want the game to end.

"But then I would lose." My voice is smoke.

"I'd make it up to you," he croons, hitching my leg higher and running a finger along my thigh.

My eyes flutter closed as he brings us back up, ever so slowly. I barely hear the music anymore as we come face to face, and my leg slides back down to the ground. Tilting my head, I drag my right hand down his neck and let my fingers trail down his chest, where they come to rest right beneath his sternum. He watches the movement intently, his eyes shining with something I have half a mind to back away from. The other half wonders what would happen if I were brave enough to go even further.

"Perhaps a sample, so I know what's at stake, then," I say.

His gaze flicks to mine with an intensity reminiscent of when we first met. When all we wanted to do was break each other. Perhaps what we feel now isn't as different from that as we would like; he still looks at me like prey.

His hand clamps around my throat. Not to cut off air, but to claim. One side of his mouth lifts when my eyes flare. "I'm afraid that's not possible. I have no intention of curbing my appetite once I set upon you."

This isn't about the last task anymore. I swallow thickly, then take a deep, clarifying breath and snatch my hands away. With more than a little reluctance, he releases me.

"Then I'll wish you goodnight, Captain."

He shakes his head, his grin fading to a distant smirk as he steps back and releases me. "You play a cruel game, darling."

I throw him an annoyed look over my shoulder. "Don't forget. We made the rules together."

There is a pocket of night nestled in the secret early hours before sunrise in which time doesn't exist. I've spent countless moments wrapped in its mystique.

Reading. Hunting. Wondering. Dreaming.

There's a specific sort of isolation in these underbelly hours, but an intimacy, too. A softness that undercuts the hard edges of loneliness, a tenderness to the dark reserved only for me. It's been a while since I've been up at this sacred time, but old habits are hard to kill, so I head to the sparring room to make use of this dark little eternity.

After a round of stretches, I begin with the sequences Basi taught me. At this point, I've done them so many times, my body moves of its own volition. The routine of it comforts me.

Hook, hook, breathe, feint, roll, breathe.

My bare feet make no noise as I dodge and kick at invisible enemies, grunting with the effort. I tuck into a roll and twist to flick a knife at a spot by the door frame behind me—

And almost fall on my ass when I see who's leaning against the wall, watching. Liam doesn't blink as the knife thuds into the wall, not two inches from his ear. I was so absorbed in what I was doing, I didn't hear him enter. I've no inkling how long he's been there, since I've been facing the other way.

Eyebrows raised, the pirate rips the dagger free and flips it in an easy arc, catching it by the hilt every time. Planting my hands on my hips, I swipe a forearm over my face, shoving loose tendrils of hair back from my damp skin.

"How long have you been there?"

"Long enough."

He peels himself from the wall and saunters toward me, and my heart starts thudding even faster.

With the way things ended a few hours ago, tension still feels taut as a bow between us. I need more time to cool off from him.

"Matteo begged off training today. I ran him ragged yesterday, poor lad. So, I thought I'd brush up on some things, myself." His eyes rake down my body, then back up to meet my gaze. "Seems you had a similar idea."

I cross my arms. "Couldn't sleep."

"Me neither," he murmurs, his right eyebrow arching. "Seems as good a time as any to see what you've got, Strider."

"You want to spar? With me? Now?"

His expression remains infuriatingly neutral. "Why not?"

"You know why not," I mutter, crossing my arms. It's as close as I dare come to the truth. I don't trust either of us where any kind of touching is involved. Not anymore.

"I'm afraid I don't. Care to elaborate?"

My glare is nothing short of scathing. But suddenly he's shrugging off his vest, and I must force myself not to gawk at his bare chest, or the panels of muscle lining his stomach, or his corded arms. Smug satisfaction glints in his eyes as he sees me wrangling my gaze anywhere else.

Wait a moment.

He's doing that on purpose.

My tongue skates across my bottom lip. Well then. To hell with it.

Not dropping eye contact for even a moment, I mirror his movements and shrug out of my shirt to reveal a tight dark band of fabric beneath. A flicker of something flashes across Liam's face before he forces his expression back to normalcy: confident boredom. My mouth curls into a sharp smile as I roll my neck. We step onto the platform and begin to slowly circle each other.

"Any weapons?" I ask.

A short laugh. "Neither of us needs one." He's right.

He lunges first, a predatory gleam in his eye as he feints right but grabs for me.

Knocking his arm away, I go for a quick jab to his ribs that connects, but he twists out of the way before I can do any significant damage. I'm eager to try again, get in a genuine hit, but he's so damn fast. I lunge for him three times in a row, each attack becoming increasingly aggressive.

And every time I've almost got him, he leaps away, just out of my reach.

"So intent to ensnare me," he taunts.

"You started this, if you'll recall," I reply, watching his every move carefully.

"Ah, but I've made it no secret I want my hands on you."

To demonstrate, he tries to grab me, but I send him backward with a sharp jab of my elbow.

For a while, it's a game of cat and mouse. Circling, only to lunge for each other in a flurry of hand-to-hand combat, never inflicting any real damage. It doesn't take long for a flush to creep into his face and sweat to glisten down his neck, his obliques. He grabs my ankle when I try to kick his feet out from under him and pulls me off balance, and of all things, I'm laughing.

Cackling.

At one point, I feint successfully, and in an effort to catch up with me, he throws his momentum so hard in the opposite direction that he slips on the floor, barely catching himself. His full-bodied belly laughs fill every hollow inside of me.

After what must be about half a bell, we come together again, but he catches my wrist when I throw a punch to his jaw, wrenching my arm so hard that I have no choice but to follow its trajectory and turn with it. Our bodies are flush, my back to his chest. I feel his breath on my neck as he leans down, his grip on my wrist unyielding.

"This won't do, Strider." Though he chides me, neither of us seems entirely displeased with the circumstances. "This is a highly vulnerable position for you. Let's see, I could drag my blade across your neck—" he demonstrates by dragging a finger across my throat, garnering a snort from me, ". . . or spill your guts on the floor," his hand trails painfully slow down my sternum, to my stomach, where there is no fabric to shield me from the heat of his touch. My laugh evaporates, and suddenly, I'm paying very close attention to what he has to say, ". . . or more unsavory behavior, if I so choose."

"You wouldn't take advantage of me like that," I say slowly, trying to school my breath from turning into pants.

"Oh, but I would." He undoes all my progress by sliding his tongue up my neck as his fingers slide beneath my waistband.

My mouth falls open, and my body ignites with delicious lust. But he can't have me that easily.

I wrap my leg behind his and throw all my weight backward, sending us both crashing to the floor. I twist midair to land on top, my forearm perpendicular to his throat, an imagined knife pointed at his ribs.

"Dead," I pronounce.

Liam arches an eyebrow, and I follow his pointed gaze to where he holds an invisible blade to my side.

"Draw?"

"Never." I shove my arm even harder into his throat, for emphasis.

He sighs. Then, abruptly, he flips us so that I'm underneath him, pinned by his muscular thighs. On instinct, my arms go straight for his face, but he grabs them both by the wrist and pins them above my head. Now, it's my turn to be grabbed by the throat. Again. His fingers dig into my skin, not to leave a bruise, but with enough pressure to set my blood to churning.

"Should have left it at a draw," he muses, digging his thumb into my jugular just hard enough to elicit a gasp.

"Should have told me what we're doing in Celosia," I manage, squirming beneath him. Liam seems temporarily distracted by it, his eyes glazing over.

"Don't do that."

I blink. "Do what?"

And then, my mouth spreads into a grin when I realize what he meant.

I writhe beneath him again, studying every minute change in his expression as he watches me, transfixed. The devious shine of his eyes, the way he slowly licks his lips as he lowers himself to say against my mouth, "Do you know, Strider, how many nights I've pictured you writhing beneath me, just like that?"

Something primal comes over me. "What else have you been dreaming of, Blackwater?"

His lips lift into a salacious smile, and I know I've stepped into a trap. "I'll show you if you say 'please.'"

"I'll let you do whatever you wish, if you tell me what I want to know."

His gaze rakes hungrily up and down my body, prone beneath his own. Our flushed skin glistens with sweat, but neither of us seems to care in the least.

"Give me a few moments, and you'll forget all about Celosia. You'll forget your own name."

"Prove it."

Tension sizzles as his body lowers to meet mine, and our hips grind together to music only we hear.

"You started this, and I'm going to make sure you finish," he says into my ear, and I feel a shiver scrape all the way down my spine as he licks along the edge of my jaw. My lips part as I suck in small, surprised breaths.

"Close your eyes."

Proctor save me, but I do it.

I fight another shiver as his right hand, ever so slowly, travels down my chest to wander over my breasts, where it lingers long enough to tweak my nipple through the thin fabric. A half-startled, half-pleased breathy sound escapes my lips as he does it again, harder. And then his mouth. My body jolts when he takes the tight bud in his teeth, then sucks. Then the other side. All the while, his hand drifts down to my stomach, and finally, lower. He reaches the waistband of my pants, then stops, and I think I might come apart. His fingers dip beneath, his calluses scraping the sensitive skin there.

"This is what it feels like when you tease me," he admonishes, and

I feel his teeth against my jaw, and then his lips. "But suddenly, I'm feeling generous."

His fingers venture lower to graze my underwear.

"Do you trust me?"

"Yes," I breathe.

I feel his smile on my skin, and then my entire world becomes his fingers as they finally reach exactly where I've been needing them. I could sigh in relief, but I'm too wound up with anticipation. I don't realize I'm biting my lower lip until he speaks again. "Don't worry, love. I'm going to take good care of you."

He slides a finger up and down and makes a deep noise of approval in his throat. "Just the way I want you," he murmurs.

He makes slow, tantalizing circles on my bed of nerves, sending waves of pleasure up my body. My hands fight for freedom, desperate for something to cling to, but he doesn't release them. And somewhere between his mouth leaving hot kisses on my throat and his pace quickening, I start to lose myself. I am a slave to those fingers, moving in steady, practiced strokes now. I am insatiable. I only ever want more from him.

"Liam." It is both a plea and a command. He hears.

His mouth crashes into mine the same moment his finger plunges inside of me. My legs splay out, and I feel just as much as hear his approval. Our mouths meet in a frenzy of teeth and tongue, sucking and tasting and biting each other with an urgency I cannot stave. I didn't know how badly I'd wanted him—needed him.

There is no restraint, like the first time we kissed in the rain. We are ravenous.

Finally, he releases my wrists, and my hands immediately tangle in the unruly strands of his hair, roam down to his jaw, then lower, to his bare chest. I want to feel every inch of him. A thrill goes through me that, at least in these secret moments, he's mine. To touch. To have. His tongue slides across my bottom lip, then meets my own, swirling around my mouth, and I moan softly when his finger, pulsing relentlessly inside of me, crooks to stimulate something exceedingly sensitive.

"Do that again," I say into his mouth, and when he obliges, my hips buck in response. "I'm—" I gasp when one finger becomes two, my head falling back and bones going soft.

His teeth tug at my bottom lip, and I bite him back, my hand daring to venture past his stomach. Lower, still. I'm hazy with lust. Reckless with it. And when I've finally found what I'm looking for, he presses his hardness into me, his kisses becoming more demanding. Deeper. He grinds into me, and I palm him hungrily.

But I want to feel him the way he's feeling me. I undo the laces of his pants and slip my hand inside to pull him out, gasping when I feel the smooth, hot skin there.

I match his strokes, and he presses into me greedily.

"Harder," he rasps against my mouth. "That's it."

My stomach muscles tighten, my hands clenching as something builds higher and higher within me. A low, guttural sound escapes my parted lips, but he swallows the noise.

"Don't stop," I pant, completely at the mercy of what he's doing between my legs. I'd do anything for him. I'd even say please, but luckily, I don't have to. My stomach muscles tighten, and suddenly, I feel like I'm about to break wonderfully apart.

"I'm— I'm about to—"

"No," he commands in my ear. At the same moment, he takes my hand off of him. "I'm not finished yet."

Before I can respond, he jerks my britches down my hips to expose my underwear beneath, sitting high on my hips and low beneath my stomach.

My pulse stutters in delight as I kick my pants off entirely. "Are you going to fuck me, Liam?"

There is a dangerous intent on his face, not dissimilar to the bloodlust I've seen him endure. As if no one, not even the Proctor himself, could rip him away from what he's about to do to me. "No," he grinds out as he crawls over me. "Not like this. But I still want to feel you."

His mouth crushes mine before I can parse his meaning, but I'm so hyper aware of his every touch, I shiver with anticipation as he spreads me apart with his thighs. I watch him take himself in one hand, pump twice, and position his crown at my entrance. Just the pressure from him there alone, the sight of his need beading there, is almost enough to undo me. With a languid, sensuous roll of his hips, he rubs himself along my entire seam, lingering where I'm most sensitive. He does it again, and we both watch, entranced. My legs are starting to quiver.

"You feel . . ." His words taper off in a low sigh as he palms my breast. He plants hot, open-mouthed kisses on my chest and neck, and this time I don't even bother to stifle my moans. He knows how to touch me. He always has.

His tongue sweeps my mouth. As his thrusts slowly gain speed, the pleasant tingle between my legs intensifies, demanding more friction. Soon, my legs wrap around his waist as our hips grind together. Gone is the controlled, fluid motion he started with. We're rutting. His fingers knot in my hair as a coarse groan escapes his lips. We're losing ourselves to each other.

If being physical with him feels like this, and he's not even inside of me, I will not survive Liam Blackwater. As he set out to do, he will devastate me. At least I'm taking him down with me.

Our breaths become serrated, and soon, I'm clawing into his shoulders as my teeth scrape down the column of his neck. My hips move of their own volition, slave to the colossal pleasure building there. My core contracts tighter and tighter as the elation mounts, when Liam growls headily into my throat, "You're fucking mine."

My eyes roll up in my head, and I see the heavens as euphoria breaks over me in unrelenting waves. Liam breathes my name once, and then I feel his body spasm as warmth spills onto my stomach. My legs tremble with ecstasy, my body useless and spent. I'm left in a giddy, luscious haze, feeling lighter than feathers. Liam rests his forehead on my shoulder, consumed by his own lingering paradise, his breaths short and ragged.

I've never felt anything like that. No fuck I've ever had has been even close. And he didn't even fuck me.

My eyes flutter open as I inhale a shaky, satisfied breath.

Liam surprises me by dipping his head to kiss me again. It's less rabid this time. As if, now that his appetite has been sated, he wants to take some time to taste. His hands weave through my hair as he tilts my face to meet his, and the kiss deepens, threatening to take my breath away all over again. Our eyes open at the same time, and perhaps it's the sweet remnants of the orgasm, or the after-sparring high, but I am seized with the thought that I've missed him my entire life. That somehow, every day, I was expecting his arrival.

Reluctantly, he pulls away to grab his discarded shirt and wipe it gently across my stomach, cleaning away all traces of himself. Once that's done, I shimmy back into the pants I hastily kicked off while we were otherwise engaged.

"I think it's time," he says evenly, as he politely turns to lace his pants back up, "for us both to take a cold shower."

"But—" I try to argue, but he stops me with a finger.

"I will see you this evening, love."

My brows furrow deeply. "Why stop now?"

"Because soon, Basi will be here, and I have no wish to endure a scolding from a man with that many battle scars. And, when I fuck you, Strider, it won't be in a sweaty sparring room."

Well, he may as well have put his hands down my pants again with the way his words make me feel.

He stands, then extends a hand to help me up. I sigh. "Still no hint?"

I don't miss the smugness when he replies, "You don't need one. You trust me, remember?"

But this went well beyond making a bleeding point, and we both know it.

ACT III
THE GIRL AND HER PAST

56

SICKLES AND SHADOW

There are no trumpets announcing our grand arrival on the day we reach Celosia. In fact, I can barely see past my own nose for the heavy shawl of mist enveloping the ship. I'd read about it, but it is one thing to read of something, and another entirely to feel its damp, cloying weight on my skin. They say it acts as a defense, probing ships for curses and rooting out evil before it can dock. It feels sentient, the mist. I have the strangest feeling that if I could peer into the deepest part of it, something would peer right back.

My blood thrums with anticipation and a steady dose of impatience. We have made it just in time; the night of the Dead Moons is imminent. Today, we complete the final task.

Tomorrow, the ball.

Liam has assured me he has something in the shape of a dress arranged for me, and all I have to do is meet the dressmaker tomorrow and allow for any tweaks.

Teller comes to stand beside me, squinting. "Nev'r liked this part. Feels pryin'," he comments.

"I've never seen anything like it."

He grunts. "You'll be saying that 'bout all of Celosia. In fact—" he screws up his face, then breaks into a smile. "Look there."

I follow where he's pointing, and at first, I see nothing but the colorless, infinite cloud surrounding us. But then, very slowly, a figure emerges.

An enormous figure bearing a sword.

My heart flies into my throat, but in the span of another moment, I realize it's not moving. It's a statue, its hands raised in attack for all eternity, jutting out of the sea. A stone beard billows in invisible wind, a silent scream tearing from his mouth. As we pass beneath his reach, I admire the intricacies of his armor. It must be spelled to resist the erosion of the waves, for every detail stands out in impossible clarity. A crown of razor-sharp leaves rests upon his head.

In all the excitement, I forgot about them—the First Sovereigns.

"The first Celosian king," Teller confirms. "King Moravik."

As the fog begins to lift, more statues appear, all braced for attack.

A breathtaking Avian queen, her great feathered wings spread wide as she braces to take to the skies, a battle axe gripped tightly in both hands. Her crown, a ring of slender spikes, sits atop her head, a weapon unto itself.

Queen Celeste.

We pass a snarling sea king, deadly barbs ridging his spine and forearms, and needle-like teeth bared to match. His crown drips pearls and shards of aquamarine, and we sail beneath his extended spear, lancing the water as if once long ago, here had lain his greatest nemesis.

King Caspian.

Next, the tall, waifish figure of the Iridisian Queen. Her jewel-encrusted crown sits daintily on her head, hair long and straight. Her heart-shaped face is stoic as she faces an invisible foe, the hilt of her great longsword clasped between her hands and pointing down into the water.

Queen Aine. Luhan's distant relative.

The final statue we pass is the most menacing of all. She stands straight-backed, staring into the horizon, although her owlish, pupil-less eyes seem to track our movement as we sail past her.

Her hair blows wildly around her face in a maelstrom, and I can practically hear her cloak snapping around her legs. Her arm is crooked, her fingers clawed upwards. Atop her head, a crown of bones. On her face, a nightmare grin, and much too wide.

Insidia. The first witch queen.

Teller grabs my arm. "This is yer first time seeing Celosia, aye? Climb up to the crow's nest so ye can see it right. Go on now. The mist'll be clearin' any moment now."

I take his advice and clamber nimbly up the netting that serves as a ladder. I can't even see the top because of the mist. Once I reach it, I haul myself one leg at a time over the railing. As Teller predicted, it's not long before the final wisps of the mist clear to reveal a city unlike any other. At the sight of Celosia, a deluge of emotion seizes me, and I blink away a burning in my eyes.

Roarke was enchanting as gardens are, tenderly cared for and maintained. Small, but loved.

Celosia is opulence and splendor. I can feel it all the way from here, like static against my skin. Tall, domed buildings gleam with gold beneath towering trees, and canals of pale blue wind throughout the city. In the very distance, the castle sprawls high, high above all the rest.

Something in my gut twists unpleasantly at the splendor of it all, knowing that while I was eating rats in Marrin, Celosians have been luxuriating in paradise. Even so, I cannot deny how breathtaking it is.

The piers teem with high spirits and lively chatter, and the whole crew is practically vibrating with anticipation by the time we're cleared to disembark.

Today, I selected rich brown trousers and a close-fitting top with fabric attached to a silver ring around my neck. As I gathered the top bit of my hair to pull back into a knot this morning, I realized that this is the first time my hair has ever been long enough to tie back. I'm still not used to the way it tickles the back of my neck, or gets in my eyes when I'm sparring, but I can't bring myself to cut it again. I like the dark, twisty mass of it. And I haven't felt a compulsion to cut it in quite some time.

I head through town first. I like getting a lay of the land. Absorbing the sights and smells of a new place. It's a feeling I've grown to relish deeply. The market is already in full swing by the time I stroll into it. I stop at a stall for breakfast, purchasing a steaming, yeasty pastry that smells of orange and sugar. At another stall, I buy a spiced honey tea to complement it.

The pastry is so decadent that upon devouring it, I go back for another.

With a full belly, I peruse the vendors at my leisure, stopping here and there to study the various trinkets and goods for sale. One woman claims to sell a watch that marks the owner's time of death; another sells miniature wood carvings that move and prowl exactly like their animal likenesses. The food on display is like nothing I've ever seen: vegetables and fruits of all colors, shapes, and sizes, and the pelts and hides of animals I've never even heard of.

Until now, beauty like this has only existed in my mind. In books. I'm so enchanted by everything I encounter, I have to stifle the urge to reach out and touch every stone, every item, just to reaffirm to myself this is real. I'm glad I'm alone so no one can see my wide-eyed wonder, my awestruck breaths. I feel like a child, struck mute with all the colors and sounds. I wish ardently that the entire realm could experience this.

My boot shifts and crunches something unexpected. I glance down, lifting my foot to reveal a leaf, but instead of its normal verdant green, it's begun to fade into a brilliant yellow. Its ends have curled and browned, hence the crunch. The leaves never turned like this in Marrin, but I know what it means all the same.

Autumna is coming.

Once I've had my fill of the market, I head to The Chapel, by far the most popular place in the entire port. All the surrounding activity seems to eventually point here, to this raucous, dirty tavern. Drunken voices pour out of its open windows, as well as a jaunty little sea shanty played by a piano. The plan was for Liam to arrange rooms for us all, so I imagine he must still be inside. I loiter for a few moments, bracing myself for the swell of bodies inside. I hate crowds. Always have. And my pockets are already full of loot from the market, so it can't even be put to use.

"What're you waiting for, Iona?"

"Scared of a good time?"

I glance over to Arjun, Ishaan, Luhan, and a few others, who must be coming from the ship. A few had to stay behind to dock it properly and set the wards. Arjun and Ishaan are both stifling chuckles, but Luhan wisely keeps it at a cocked eyebrow.

"Careful, she brought The Twins today," he remarks, looking pointedly at the weapon sheathed at my hip.

"And Basi's been teaching me to use it," I add dryly. "Want to see?"

"Give it a rest," Arjun waves a hand at me as they brush past, eager to begin their day of debauchery. Luhan sidles up next to me, casting a look of distaste in The Chapel's general direction.

"Go on, then. Morning ale waits for no one." I gesture with my chin.

"It's good fun, don't get me wrong. But I need some quiet, and we need some more non-perishables and soap."

I smirk. "Everyone seems to be treating this like a respite except for you."

"Trust me. It is a gift indeed to steal away for a few hours and enjoy the pleasure of my own company. In addition, I do plan on spending an exorbitant amount of gold on something pretty and entirely unnecessary."

I have half a mind to abandon the task today and accompany Luhan instead. Spending time with Liam has become too complicated. Spending time with Luhan is easy. Always has been. We snipe and grouse and bicker, and I never wonder about where we stand. "I'll come find you when we return, and we can look together. We won't be gone for too long."

His gaze is much too insightful. "Oh, enough of that. Be gone for too long. Galavant all over this place, for all I care. No one is stopping you, least of all me." With that, he saunters off without looking back. "Good luck. You'll need it."

Something tells me he isn't talking about the last task, and I'm cursing him silently for being so damned observant.

"Oh, wait. Luhan?" An impulse just seized me. He pauses and twists around, raising one eyebrow.

"Get me some kohl? Maybe some lip stain? For my face."

The corner of his mouth twitches, but I know he's been waiting for this day since he met me. "I'll peruse."

Well.

Might as well see what all the fuss is about. I push open the swinging double doors and am immediately greeted with a bouquet of scents: ale, sweat, and cooking meat. My nose wrinkles, but I plunge into the crowd anyway, scanning the room for a head of black hair above the rest.

No luck.

I'm almost to the bar when a girlish squeal cuts through the cacophony, and my eyes slide toward the sound. The crowd parts, and my breath hitches.

Now I see what's taking so long.

Liam's leaning against the bar, and he's not alone. No, I watch with growing horror as a curvy, honey-haired beauty rushes toward him, slings her arms around his neck, and kisses him on the cheek. Her face is flushed, her smile charming.

She is sunslight and sugar; I, sickles and shadow. And something like acid burns a hole in my gut.

My surroundings become a distant hum, my neck prickling with sudden heat. My hands fist at my sides. I've got to get a grip.

Alas, someone else accomplishes that first.

A hand wraps around my wrist, and I whirl around, a dagger in my hand and at the person's throat in one breath. It's a man with shoulder-length, dark-blond hair and a rugged beard. And he's smiling at me. He releases me, both hands coming up in a gesture of peace.

"Apologies, miss," he says, taking a step back. "I saw you come in, and, well—" He clears his throat. "I've never seen you here before. I tried to get your attention, but—"

Slowly, I take the knife away from his throat, still simmering. "You make a habit of going around and grabbing women that catch your eye?"

He chuckles, seemingly unperturbed by my demeanor. "Normally, I'm not met with a blade."

"Next time I won't be so kind."

His blue-gray eyes flare. The more aggressively I act toward him, the more he seems to lap it up. Fucking pirates. "What's your name, pretty?"

Revulsion flares as I turn sharply toward the exit, only to almost walk into Liam's chest. I glance up to find him glaring. Not at me, but the man I was just leaving.

"Strider. Is he bothering you?"

"Ugh. I should have known. You're with him?" The man asks from behind me. There's disappointment in his voice, and a tinge of something else. Something like a challenge.

Glancing over my shoulder, I look him up and down, a sneer on my lips, "For you? Doesn't matter."

We both turn to leave, but the man pushes after us.

"Blackwater," the man says conversationally. "You've been due to wash up for quite a while now. Finally fuck your way through every woman in Alvion?"

"Ramsay. You're . . . always here." Liam doesn't address the insult, but I have a feeling the slight wasn't meant for him, anyway.

No, when we turn to leave, the man called Ramsay's eyes are still pinned on me. And he's grinning as though he can see his words stuck in my mind like a fly in a web. I feel a slight pressure as Liam places a hand on the small of my back as we leave the tavern, but the moment we step into the suns, I walk ahead of him, out of his reach. Liam registers my mood immediately.

"Strider? What happened in there? Did he—"

I don't bother turning around, though I take great care to scour any emotion from my voice before speaking. "Nothing happened. Let's go."

His footsteps stop, and sighing, I stop too. Indecision wars within me. Should I tell him I saw him with that woman? And *then* what?

His expression is careful, and for some reason, that pisses me off even more. "Look, what he said—"

"It doesn't matter," I cut him off, then take a breath. My voice softens. "You don't owe me an explanation."

It's true. I am not his, nor he mine, so I don't know why my insides are writhing in jealousy like this. At the thought of that girl with her pretty, open face.

And others. Of course, there have been others.

For a few moments, his mask cracks, and he looks torn. But all he says is, "If you change your mind, let me know."

We leave it at that, and I shove all my festering doubt and jealousy down. We have work to do, and in a rapidly dwindling amount of time, none of this will matter anyway.

57

THE LAGOON

Celosia is a naturally lovely sight. Even in the heart of the town, granules of sand crunch beneath my boots. I see no starving children begging for coins, no spite in anyone's eye. I see hard work rewarded with a decent life here. It feels worlds away from Marrin.

Sparkling, teal water burbles happily beneath sturdy wooden bridges crawling in ivy. It's here that we stop for a moment so Liam can buy us some lemongrass water and a quick meal, and I take advantage of the pause to try and absorb the sights.

"This place is crawling with pirates," I observe, taking a sip of my drink. It tastes like Estiva itself—bright, tangy, and refreshing. The meat and rice bowl is hearty and wonderful. I walk across the bridge, resting my forearms on the railing, overlooking the water.

"Aye, it is," Liam responds, coming to lean on the railing beside me. There's a brightness to his eyes today, and a small, persistent smile he hasn't quite been able to suppress. "This is The Vice's territory. Most pirates you see serve him."

"It doesn't seem half bad here," I remark, brows raised.

"No, not at all. He's out for himself, it's true, but that doesn't mean he desires suffering for everyone else. If it's a side effect of something he wants, then so be it. But not a goal of his, from what I've seen. He's clever enough to understand that if the people who work for you are happy enough, they'll do whatever you want."

"Is he here? The Vice?"

Liam takes another sip and runs his tongue across his bottom lip. The motion is quite distracting. "He could be. No one would know. But I find it hard to imagine he'd stay put, when so many would do unspeakable things to put his head on a platter for a taste of his power."

We take a few moments to soak in the bustling town and finish our meals before we cross the bridge and head toward the beaches. The crowd thins the closer we get to the water, although I can't imagine why. The water is breathtaking. It ripples in gentle waves of turquoise, clear enough for me to see the dappled sandy bottom of the ocean floor all the way out. I bend down to scoop some into my hands, letting it pour through my fingers in sparkling cascades. Brown-flecked seabirds squawk above us, swooping down to the water's surface now and then to nab a minnow.

I didn't know how it would feel to be alone with him after what transpired between us a week ago. It turns out, it feels the same. I feel no embarrassment or regret. It was what we both wanted—needed—at the time. We'd not seen each other much since. Liam was busy with his duties as captain, and I had plenty to do with my time.

I cannot deny that my relationship with Liam has become more than physical. It would be delusional to discredit the tenderness he has shown me and the secrets we have divulged to each other. We have become more than partners, but exactly what I mean to him now, I couldn't begin to guess. And that's the problem. It was easy to get swept up in each other on the ship, even though we both know there is an impending end to our agreement. It's just that the end was always so far away, and now it's here.

Now that the world has opened back up, I can't help but wonder. How many others has he lain claim to in the throes of pleasure?

You're fucking mine.

I still hear it. I still feel his power over me. In that moment, I was his. But he was also mine.

Stop. It doesn't matter.

I keep losing myself to these impossible daydreams, and every time I come hurtling back, I hit the ground harder than before. If I don't stop, I am going to break something.

Have I lost perspective on what this is? Even if we wanted this to continue, I don't know how we'd do it. I have a shadow to kill, and he has a kingdom to hobble. Not to mention whatever he discovers about Collin. Who knows how that might change things? I can't exactly ask him to accompany me, or wait for me, when I am nothing but a grain of sand in comparison to Liam Blackwater's grand plans.

And that is no one's fault. It's the way it is. I will have to accept that. It is my own fault I got carried away in a current I knew to avoid.

But the rush was magnificent.

For a while, we pass the time with easy banter until the sunslight glints off one of his gold rings, forcing me into a squint.

"Why do you wear your rings like that, anyway?"

He looks down. "Like what?"

"Three on your right hand, on the middle three fingers. I saw someone earlier wearing their rings like that, too. A woman. It's very particular."

He raises his hand, admiring their gleam in the afternoon suns. "It is particular, in fact."

I wait expectantly for him to continue, but he takes so long that I expect he's going to leave it there. He doesn't. "Talis, and a few other southern provinces, have a very unique marriage tradition. These three rings represent our lifetimes. Little bands of infinity. When two people decide to marry, in Talis, it's more of a joining. Two souls become intertwined until the end of time. Each person has their three bands already, but after the ceremony, they'd move from this placement you see here—" he gestures to one band on each finger, "—to a stacked formation on the fourth finger of the left hand."

"Why?"

We stop, and a peculiar, gentle expression softens his features.

"Because it's symbolism, that's why. We live life after life. And once we find the one our soul seeks, we become drawn to them. We find them over and over, every time." He roots around in his pocket, makes a noise, and takes out a bit of thread. Gently, he grabs my hand and selects the fourth finger of my left hand. As he speaks, he wraps the thread around my finger, once, twice, three times. "A band for each life in which we find each other. One for the past, one for now, and one for the next. Always. Every time."

I gaze at my finger, lost for a moment. I've never been one to yearn for romance. Love.

It's always seemed frivolous, and meaningless longing can't fill my belly or build me shelter. Love is a luxury I never thought I'd have a care for. But to find the counterpart to your soul in someone else, again and again . . . that is something I'd like to feel.

I dare to lift my eyes to Liam's face only to find his green gaze already trained on me. "Would you?" I start. It's a struggle to speak around the swell of emotion clogging my throat. "Do that with someone? One day?"

His attention dips briefly down to my finger. "Aye. I would." He says it like the answer surprises him, and I smile at him through the ache beneath my ribs.

"Would you?" He asks. I realize he's still got my hand in his, but I don't have the courage to take it away. Not when he's looking at me like that.

"Yes," I tell him. "Some day."

We walk until the town is far behind us and the shore becomes rocky. Massive bits of stone and rock jut out from the waves, some large enough to form islands of their own. I stop, gazing out at the horizon.

"The Celosian grottos," I realize. I've read about these. Thousands of sea caves, formed from erosion and centuries of tides. "People from all over the realm come to explore them."

"That they do. They contain all sorts of little treasures and oddities. Come now, just a little further."

Ducking beneath a canopy of broad-leafed trees, we delve into the trees. The flora isn't dense by any means, but lush and decadent. Patches of unruly wildflowers adorn the greenery, suffusing the air with the scent of nectar and honey along with the ever-present brine of the sea. But the deeper we go, the call of seabirds fades, giving way to the familiar croak of frogs, punctuated by the splash of tiny, skittish creatures when they hear us approaching. There's no trail that I can discern, so Liam must be leading based on memory or instinct alone.

"Almost there," he says, as if sensing the direction of my thoughts.

Here, the brush has become a bit denser, and I can't see beyond the thick leaves directly in front of us. But the distant sound of falling water is unmistakable, so when Liam lifts a branch out of my way, I duck beneath, expecting to find a body of water beyond.

I was right, to an extent.

Indeed, the trees have opened to reveal what appears to be a long-forgotten lagoon. Clear, blue-green water laps at a rocky shore, sloping into bottomless water that winds deep into the forest. And that's not all.

This place was once some sort of castle.

Bits of dark marble floor remain scattered throughout the rock, and old, broken pillars jut up around the perimeter of the lagoon. On the other side, a wooden swing sits motionless beneath a weeping willow, choked out by delicate green vines. Even in ruins, this place is beautiful.

"You're looking at what was once the Siren's castle," Liam says. And then he gestures to the water. "Care for a swim?"

58
LITTLE DEATHS

For a while, we drift along the winding current. The water isn't very deep; it comes just above my head. Sunslight spills brightly through the rustling canopy of trees above us, sparking golden ripples in the gentle waters. Here, the ruins are more intact. Down a little way and to our right, cracked marble steps lead out of the water and into an arched, golden doorway. Ivy drips down the ruined walls of the castle, but whatever spires of roofs there might once have been have either collapsed or have been nudged out of the way by towering trees. Following the bank, it appears the castle, or what is left of it, sprawls on for quite some time. Even in its dilapidated state, it's clear that this was once a sacred, open place where one could simply walk out of their bedroom and into the lagoon. Here, nature and dwelling were one and the same. Idly, I trail my arm through the water, and my eyes widen when I leave a sparkling yellow trail behind me.

"The sirens may be gone, but their magic remains," Liam comments.

My gaze goes to him, and I notice that his eyes look especially verdant right now. "This is so beautiful."

His smile illuminates his whole face. "I thought you'd like it. I found this place around the time when I'd first acquired The Wraith and had nothing better to do than explore. The biggest shame is, I'd almost forgotten about it."

"Does anyone else know of it?"

He shakes his head, a funny little smile playing on his lips. "Just you and me, Strider."

Pure glee sparkles in my chest. Our secret little lagoon.

We swim for a while longer, exploring the remnants of the castle. No part of it is inaccessible through the lagoon, so we never have to leave the water. I'd loathe to do so; the water feels so lovely, and I can't stop admiring the glow that trails us. We pass by an enormous ballroom, surrounded by crumbling columns draped in ivy. Its domed ceiling is cracked and no longer whole, but lavish paintings of merpeople are still visible, although mostly faded. On we drift, until Liam grabs hold of my hand to steer us beneath an arched bridge, where the trees open to the sky above.

"And here we are. The solution to the third task, at last." Finally, I understand what Liam has been getting at.

With no current to disturb it, the lagoon has gone still. So still, that if I look at it just right, it's not water at all, but the sunset streaked with pink and orange. Clouds scud across, their bottoms dark with impending night. It's as if we're swimming in the sky. I scoop up a handful of water, and a cloud passes through it.

And with the specks of swirling magic, there are stars, too.

Indeed, I'm holding a piece of the sky. Lingering magic from the sirens indeed.

Liam glides closer, and I don't realize I'm holding my breath until he reaches toward me. All he does is scoop up some of the water from my hands into a small vial around his neck. Even in the vial, it swirls bluish orange with streaks of pink clouds.

Flipping onto my back, I let my arms float out, and for a little while, I'm swimming in the sky. My eyes drift closed, and I surrender myself completely to the peace of the moment.

"What are you thinking about, Strider?" Eventually, Liam's voice brushes against my skin like the finest silk.

My eyes open to a lavender sky. "I want more of this. More beautiful, quiet places."

I'm not ready for this to be over. With you.

I hear him wade closer to me and right myself in the water. My hair drapes heavily on the back of my neck, swirling around my shoulders. Liam comes to a stop close enough to reach out a hand and touch him, but I notice he does not make an effort beyond that.

"We can go wherever we please, once this is finished."

I sigh, looking away. I've no desire for empty promises. Not from him. "I wish that were true."

He watches me pensively, swirling a hand through the water gently. "How do you mean?"

I shake my head. "We don't have to talk about this now."

He shifts closer, apprehension hunching his shoulders. "Strider, say what you want to say."

My eyes lock onto his as exasperation grabs hold of me. "This whole ordeal is so that you can meet with someone who may or may not enlist you in a secret war against the throne. If they have need of you somewhere, you said you would go."

"Aye, I did."

"So then, depending on what they ask of you, you would not be free to escort me around Alvion anymore."

"That may be true, but I would not be a slave to orders, either. We don't have enough information to speculate, now do we?"

"Liam, I cannot make any promises until I can find a way to rid myself of the shadow. You know that."

His brows cinch together. "I do know that, but it also doesn't mean I'd never see you again. And you don't have to do it alone in the first place."

"Yes, I do." The pitch of my voice starts to lower, and I wrangle it back into place.

It frustrates the hell out of me he refuses to acknowledge the truth. "If I cannot find a Curse Speaker to help me, Willa told me her mother could. But The Spine is deep in the Grimwood. It would take days, perhaps weeks to get there. I cannot ask you to come. You have obligations to your crew. Your brother, perhaps. And every day, the kingdom is taking more Weavers."

"I'll kindly ask you not to decide on my behalf," he retorts. "What do you want, Strider? Tell me."

"So much," I shout, then regret it when my voice echoes through the tranquility.

It feels like a glass ornament shattering on the floor, ruining everything. "You took me from the only life I'd ever known, and now the realm feels too big. I want to help you. I do. But is that what I'm doing when I fight? Helping? There will always be more Grays to kill. More Reds. I could consign myself to their slaughter for the rest of my life and accomplish nothing. Is that all I'm meant for? Is the best part of me the death I bring to faceless men? Who am I, without the shadow? The curse?"

Basi's words ring through my mind.

I just hope that she never turns that knife on us. Gods help us, if she does.

Then Baylor's: *You don't want any part of this abomination.*

"Is all I am a pirate?"

"No. A womanizer, too."

My hand flies to my mouth. It was meant to come out as a joke, but the look on Liam's face is anything but humorous. His eyes narrow, and his expression darkens. If I could stuff the words back into my mouth, I would. Callous. That was so callous and cruel.

That scum pirate's words hit the mark much deeper than I'd realized. "I knew that bothered you. Strider, Ramsay is a cockroach."

"I know." I shake my head tiredly. "I'm sorry. Forget that."

"No, stop," he argues, and closes the gap between us when I try to wade away. "Strider, you're not—"

I stare at him, waiting.

"You're not a conquest to me."

I don't know whether I want to laugh or cry. There's so much I want to say, but I don't know how. I can't ask him what I mean to him, because if he asked me the same question, I wouldn't know how to tell him he's everything I never thought I'd have. And soon, I will have to give him up. Why is he so set on making this so difficult?

The image of him in The Chapel with that woman comes to mind again, and before I can stop myself, I say, "I saw you with her. That girl in the tavern. I saw her kiss you."

Realization hits him hard. "Mirabelle."

I nod slowly. "You have history, don't you?"

His jaw tightens, but he doesn't hesitate. "Yes. When I was younger, I came here often. But it's been years, Strider. And it was never more than sex. There is nothing there."

"Liam. I saw her looking at you. Whatever happened, it wasn't nothing to her," I say quietly.

"You're wrong. Her father passed The Chapel down to her to run, so she stayed here. And I left. Neither of us was under any pretense that it was more than that."

But my mind is racing. She wasn't enough for him, a soft, pretty thing like that. Why would it be different for me when I've given him as much strife as I have? It's as if he can see my very thoughts, for he lays a hand on the dip of my shoulder, where the scar from Balor's poison pearls my skin.

His face lowers to mine, and his expression is so earnest, it flays my heart to see it. "Strider. Don't pull away. Stay with me."

I want him. More than anything, I want him.

Even if he means what he says, there is much about myself I have yet to uncover. There's too much in the way, and though I want him to choose me, I find that right now, it's not fair to ask. Not yet. And I'm realizing that I cannot expect him to wait until I get there. Perhaps one day, we will find each other again.

In the meantime, it will hurt. Badly. "Strider, please."

Every time he says my name, a firefly drops dead in my belly. I feel each and every one of their little deaths. I cannot bring myself to look at him.

Beneath the water, I feel his fingers graze mine. I pull my hand away. "We should go."

The flicker of hurt in his eyes is hard to miss, but he accepts the rebuke without further argument. His expression shutters closed, and he pulls away.

"Come on, then." His voice is gentle, but void of all the warmth I've grown used to.

We've made it about halfway back in stilted silence when Liam stops and turns to me, his expression stormy. "What happened back there?"

"Nothing," I mumble, exasperated. "Forget it. I'm sorry. I should never have said anything."

His scowl deepens. "No. That's exactly what I don't want. If this is going to work between you and me, you have to talk to me. Devils know I can't pull it out of you."

The final thread holding me together snaps. "If what is going to work between you and me? Our bargain is almost finished, isn't it? We're leaving in different directions, are we not?"

He stares at me in disbelief. "You're going to stand there, green with jealousy over a woman I haven't thought about since I met you, and in the same breath refuse to acknowledge that this is well beyond the fucking bargain?"

"Is it?" I practically shout.

He groans, rolling his eyes. "Stop. Stop pretending that you don't know. You know. You're just too much of a fucking coward to admit it because you don't know what to do about it. You pick fights with me and make yourself insufferable because you still, after all this time, can't allow yourself to feel something good. And don't you dare blame this on Mirabelle. My past has nothing to do with you. With us."

The truth sinks its teeth into me and shakes, but I can't stop myself from hitting back. "I don't care about your past," I spread my arms in frustration. "But give me one good reason to pour myself into a man who makes it a point to never sleep in the same location twice."

"I haven't asked you to bind your soul to mine, Strider. Just for some honesty from time to time. I thought I deserved at least that."

"You want honesty?" I jab a finger in his chest. "You're the fucking coward. Always leaving, but no particular destination in mind. What are you looking so hard for, Liam? And why can't you find it? What hollow are you so desperately trying to fill?"

He barks a cold laugh. "That's rich, coming from you. You couldn't even see past your own self-loathing to realize you were dying in that place. I had to buy you to rip you away from a hell of your own making."

That's it. The foul words tear out of me before I can stop them. "Right. You bought me, and I still won't let you have me. I'm the last woman left in Alvion who hasn't, apparently."

"Unbelievable." His eyes have frozen over. "Let's not play more games. With you and me? It's not about sex, Strider. It's not about possession. Never has been. Come and find me when you've come to terms with that."

If we're going to have it out, I might as well kick over every piece of furniture in this gods-forsaken argument. "Maybe not for you, it's not. What was his name? Ramsay?"

His face contorts with disgust.

"Yes," I say. "That was his name. Perhaps I'll find him tonight."

He waves a hand. "As you wish." Then, as an afterthought, he adds with a cruel slant of his mouth, "Run away, now, Little Ghost. It's what you do best."

And that's how I leave him.

By the time I make it back to The Chapel, a foul black mood rampages within me, kicking up debris and roaring in my ears. No matter how fast I ran, I couldn't escape Liam's voice echoing in my mind calling me a coward.

59

RUTHLESS

N ow that I'm alone, I can finally see straight. My teeth practically vibrate with fury, but my thoughts are crisp and clear, sharp as broken pieces of glass. By the time I've gotten my key and prowled up all three flights of steps to my room, I have a list of tasks in my head. Simple, easy steps to keep in motion.

I am calm.

I have never been calmer.

My room is larger than the one on The Wraith and consists of the largest bed I will have ever slept in, a quaint little vanity, and even a bathing room. I rummage through my clothes, searching for a particular set of—

Ah. Here it is.

Setting the new, dry clothes aside, I peel off my shirt and pants, turn the lever in the shower stall, and scrub myself clean of any residual sea salt with soap that smells of lime and mint. It's different, even pleasant, without having to worry about time or someone pounding on the door, demanding their turn. For a long time, I stand beneath the spout, eyes closed and relinquish myself to the warmth of the water. My mind wanders, lost in the eddies of my own turmoil. I press the palms of my hands over my eyes as Liam's cruel words slice into me again.

But worse than his words are my own. I never wanted to hurt him like that. Not Liam. Proctor's teeth, I don't know what happens to me when I'm around him. My emotions shine too brightly to recognize, burn too hot to pick apart. I'm fumbling my way through this and making a huge fucking mess. But I don't understand why he wants to prolong the inevitable. We can have our fun until the ball, but then after that, I can't promise him anything, nor he me. Why is he so convinced otherwise?

I slap the wall in frustration.

I refuse to allow myself to hope for something I cannot withstand if I'm wrong. Why can't he see that?

Shutting the water off, I step out of the stall, wrapped tightly in a soft gray towel, and pad over to put on my clothes. It's as I pull up my left stocking that someone raps once, twice, three times on the door, and my blood steams.

"Fuck off," I holler.

There's a pause, then, a knock I can only describe as defiant. It's too soon. I'm not ready to see him.

I stalk to the door and throw it open. "I will rip you a brand new asshole with my bare han—"

My mouth snaps shut when I find myself face to face with not Liam at all, but Luhan, who is looking mildly alarmed at best.

"Oh, Lu. It's you."

"May I ask why I must fuck off?"

"I thought you were someone else."

Sighing, I step aside for him, and he breezes past, looking quite pleased with himself as he sprawls out on my bed. In his hands, he's holding a small bag, and whatever is in it clatters noisily. I peer from side to side, making sure no one else is around before I close the door behind me and lock it.

I turn on the spot to find Luhan peering at the wall with a strange expression. "What?"

"Your shadow looked at me before you did."

A shiver runs through me, and I follow his gaze only to find the shadow mirroring me perfectly. "Behave," I growl at it, stabbing a finger at it.

It shakes its head, then looks back to Lu and waves.

He smiles and waves back. "She likes me more than you."

"You can have it."

After I'd confessed to Liam about my suspicions about the markings and my shadow, of course, I'd come clean to Lu too. He took it in stride. He'd already seen the markings, anyway.

"So, did you and Liam get into a spat?"

I stiffen, and my stomach flips unpleasantly. The way he looked at me . . . I can't imagine us returning to the way things were after what we said to each other. We went for the throat.

"Why? Did he say something about it?"

He scoffs. "He came in earlier like a maelstrom. He tries to hide it, but I always know when he's pissed. I fear for whoever plays him in Bishops tonight."

"We . . . yes. We had a disagreement." Averting my eyes, I finish tugging up my stocking, and Luhan's eyes trail down my legs, then back up.

"I see."

Straightening, I assess myself in the mirror. I chose a black corseted dress—the first time I've ever worn one, as a matter of fact—with intricate, crisscrossed latticework on the bodice. The loose skirt grazes my mid-thigh, where my sheer black stockings begin. But whatever demureness I might have had going for me is ruined by my boots. Well, and my coat: a long, formidable leather thing the rusted color of dried blood.

It's perfect. I like dresses, come to find out.

Luhan jangles the bag again, and I turn to him. "I believe you'll be wanting this next."

"The face color?"

"Mhm."

I stride to him to take the bag, but quick as a snake, he snatches my left hand, turning it over.

"What's this?" He's looking at the thread woven around my finger.

I yank my hand back uselessly, pleading with my eyes for him to drop it. "Nothing." But if there's one thing Luhan excels at, it's haranguing me over nonsense.

"This doesn't look like nothing, Iona."

Our eyes meet, and I have to look away when mine prick with tears. I blink them away, but not before Lu sighs.

"He was explaining how joining ceremonies work. The three rings, and all. I forgot the string was still there."

"Is that all?"

"We accomplished the third task. Nothing more."

A sound of frustration rumbles in his throat. "You two were gone quite some time for all this nothing to occur."

"Nothing did occur," I insist, taking the bag out of his hands with perhaps more gusto than necessary.

"Hmmm. Perhaps that's the problem." He twists around to where he's lying on his belly, and I take a seat at the vanity where I can see him in the mirror. Emptying the bag onto the surface, I quickly survey Luhan's bounty: crimson lip stain, rouge, a bit of compressed brown powder for my eyes, and kohl.

"This is perfect," I remark, making eye contact with him in the mirror and cobbling together a smile. "What did you get yourself?"

"Oh, some enchanted jewelry, a few books, some potion ingredients I've been looking for. This, that, the other, and so on. What did you and Liam fight about?"

My smile fades, and I busy myself pressing a bit of rouge onto my cheeks. While I don't relish the idea of talking about it, it might be nice to confide in someone who knows Liam so well. I haul in a long breath.

"Liam seems to think we can just go back to how things are now after the ball, and I . . . disagree. I don't think it will be that simple."

I wish it were.

"I don't know what to do, Lu. I want to help all the Weavers who are being taken from their homes. I want to punish the people in power for doing it. And the markings on my back, too... I want to understand what they mean." I trail off, regathering my thoughts. "But I also want to know what it feels like to just . . . live. I barely know myself."

He gives me an encouraging nod. "That's understandable."

"Liam is so certain of himself. What he does and doesn't want. But he comes and he goes like the tide. You know how he is."

He's regarding me with a more serious expression now, his dark eyes thoughtful as he watches me in the mirror. "I do. Better than most. Let me guess, he got frustrated with you because you told him, mmm . . . a quarter of this."

I sigh, deflating into my chair. "It's hard to tell him what I feel when I'm still untangling it myself. All my life, I've had to be so careful of what I felt, so my shadow wouldn't hurt someone. It responds so strongly to emotion. So, I made myself feel nothing. Took myself away." I glance over to the shadow, but it remains still. "But it didn't work."

It's always known how I felt about Liam. It knew before I did.

I continue, "It doesn't matter. We may never see each other again after tomorrow. I will have to find peace with that."

"I think it does matter. Very much," Lu argues. I wince, because it feels like it matters.

Luhan groans, slaps a pillow over his face, kicks his feet a little, then tosses the pillow onto the floor. "Annoying," he murmurs. Then, to me: "Take too long picking things apart, and you'll find yourself out of time."

His words feel like a spear through my flesh. Oliver. Lu knew immediately that he wanted to spend whatever time they had left together, and they did.

I hear Luhan muttering to himself, and then he appears behind me, his hands falling heavily to my shoulders. "Let me tell you something about Liam. And about you. I've noticed the way you look at each other. I've only seen that expression on Liam's face once before. It was when he acquired The Wraith. I was there for it all, you know. Through the blood, the sweat, the idiotic bargains he made. It almost killed him to get that ship. But when Liam decides he wants something," Lu shrugs. "He'll chase it to the ends of the realm. It's how he is. You're right. He has always known what he wants."

I swallow. "He looks at me like that?"

"Every time."

Even though I'm still hurting from our fight, a twinge of hope glimmers somewhere within me.

You pick fights with me and make yourself insufferable because you still, after all this time, can't allow yourself to feel something good.

He's right. Be brave, Iona. Be brave. Try.

"Lu, we're idiots."

"I've always said that. Now look here, you don't know what you're doing."

"And you do?" I close my eyes so he can press powder on my eyelids. His touch is light and certain.

"I only spent years watching my sister do it," he says. "I know a thing or two. Open your eyes."

I do, only to find him studying my face carefully. Humming to himself, he adds a bit of color to my cheekbones with his forefinger, then hands me the lip stain.

"Surely you can do this part," he says, a smile woven throughout the words. "A little in the corners, then spread it out, and add more if you need."

Facing the mirror, I do as he instructed, until I'm satisfied. Standing behind me, he sets his hands on my shoulders and lets out a slow, measured breath.

"Liam may be wayward and ambitious, but he's loyal until death to those he cares for. If you need more time, Iona, he would wait. He wouldn't hurt you."

If I'm being honest with myself, it's not him I'm worried about.

And suddenly, I've no intention of sitting in this room thinking about this a moment longer. "I need a drink."

"I was hoping you'd say that."

"How do I look?"

His eyes dip down my legs, then all the way back up. "Ruthless."

My mouth is a red slash. "Good."

60

MAD BITCH

The Chapel is in full swing by the time we enter the bar.

Tables have been pushed together to allow for as many entrants as possible in the gambling and card games, while others, much too drunk to play, shout over the music at each other. Women of the night, swathed in shadow, writhe over patrons in the corners, while servers weave through the crowd with all the expertise of dancers. Every inch of this place is crammed full of stumbling, pitching, dancing, skulking bodies. A peculiarly unattended piano plunks out loud, lively music, giving the place some unexpected charm.

Unfortunately, I despise it immediately. Far too many people. Although the crowd makes it easy to do what I do best.

"Where did you get that, Iona?" Luhan glances over his shoulder at me as I take another bite of an enormous roasted turkey leg. It was easy to pluck from a nearby table of roaring drunkards—they're more interested in ale than dinner anyway.

"Here and there." I offer him some fried bread, and though he rolls his eyes, he accepts. That's what I thought.

We approach the bar, and at first, no seats remain. That is, until I wrap my arm around and jam a blade beneath the neck of the man sitting at the edge of the bar.

"Move," I whisper in his ear.

Without even looking, he all but falls off his stool and scuttles away. I glance at the portly man in the chair beside him, who sighs, but follows suit, muttering something about feral women.

Smoothly, we take their places, and with a flick of his wrist, Luhan summons some ale for us both. It's dark, sludgy stuff, and upon first swallow, I almost spit it out.

"This is appalling," I tell Luhan, who's knocking it back without breathing.

"But it does the trick," he replies with a shrug, wiping his mouth with the back of his hand.

"The ale we drink on The Wraith is practically water compared to this."

I try another sip, grimacing, but keep it down. It's only through sheer willpower that I drink it down halfway. Now I understand why everyone seems to be belligerent. I've got to be careful with this. We both swivel around to watch the debauchery, elbows propped behind us on the bar, commenting or giggling into our drinks, which become cackles when Lu ends up blowing foam everywhere accidentally.

"Why are you acting like this? Have you forgotten who I am, you stupid girl?"

The laughter dies on my lips. My gaze snaps toward the source of the heated words to find none other than Ramsay, the pirate from earlier. His back is to me, but I recognize him anyway. I can't quite see who's on the receiving end, only that he's hunched over them like a vulture. The smaller person says something to him; his shoulder blades scrunch with disdain.

"What do you mean, no? I wasn't asking. You're lucky I pay you any attention at all. You're nothing. No one."

The other person—a woman—says something else, and he grabs her roughly. Before I can lurch to my feet, she shoves him off and storms away. I catch sight of a splotchy red face and hard eyes as

Mirabelle cuts a path right past me. I intend to follow her when a voice slices through the roar of the crowd and stops me cold.

"Well, well. Hello, again." Ramsay.

I know I threatened Liam with sleeping with him earlier, but I was lying through my teeth. The thought of letting this man lay one grimy finger on me makes me want to shed my skin and grow a new set. After what I've just seen, I've half a mind to castrate him right here and now.

"I was hoping I'd see you again," he says. "It seems Lady Luck smiles on me. And my, my, don't you look inviting."

I silently seethe.

Beside me, Luhan glances toward him with distaste. "Be gone, filthy."

"Luhan. Same condescending lout as always. But you?" His eyes flick up and down my person, and I recoil with disgust. "Shame on Blackwater. He should know better than to leave a pretty thing like you unattended. Who knows who might come steal you away?"

Luhan drawls with a curled lip, "I wouldn't advise it."

The pirate leans against the bar next to me, undeterred. "How about I buy you a drink, and we go somewhere private-like, so I can change your mind."

"No."

He grins, shaking his head. "Playing hard to get. I like that. I like that a lot." He turns toward the bar, splaying his hands on the wood. "Oy, get me another ale, and the lady will have—"

In one move, I've slipped one of my daggers free and planted it into the slice of space between his third and fourth fingers. He leaps back, retracting his hand as if burned.

"What in the blazing hells?"

"Leave this place, or next time, it won't be a finger I take," I say.

For a moment, he looks furious. But then, his lips split into a wide grin as he turns to shout across the tavern.

"Blackwater, is this one always so cold? The least you could have done is warm her up for me."

I stiffen, and, following his gaze, finally find Liam. He's tucked away in the farthest corner of the tavern, lounging at a long table littered with cards belonging to disappointed men. His hair is askew from the wind earlier, but instead of looking unkempt, he looks rakish. He's changed into a loose black shirt, but left it unbuttoned all the way down his sternum, showcasing his tattooed chest. With his chin propped on his fist and kohl lining his lower eyelids, he looks every bit the notorious scoundrel his peers seem to know him as. The Sea Snake, indeed. A serving girl traipses past, making a feast of him with her ravenous gaze. When he flashes her the crook of a smile, she stumbles over her own boots, but his interest has already moved on.

To me.

When our eyes lock, it feels like a jolt of lightning. But if Liam feels anything at all, it's carefully concealed. His attention flicks back to the scum next to me. "Ramsay, I tire of waiting on you. It's your turn. Or are you going to fold again?"

The pirate chuckles as he sets an arm behind me on the bar. "I've found a game I like better."

I clench my jaw, and perhaps it's my imagination, but so does Liam.

"You don't want to play that game. Trust me." The menace in his tone is unmistakable, and nearby tables look up in alarm. Ramsay, it seems, either doesn't notice or doesn't care.

"And if I do? Is she yours or not, mate?"

Fights are like storms. You can smell one coming. Liam glances first to Ramsay, then to me. A question.

The question.

A moment passes wherein all goes silent. The piano stopped; the crowd shushed. It's only him and me, and the string that connects us. That will always connect us, whether we like it or not. Liam simply realized it faster than I did.

I lift my left hand. The one with the black thread still wrapped around my finger. And Liam's face splits into a dastardly grin.

"Oh, she's mine, alright."

Ramsay glowers back. "Come and get her, then, mate."

Liam kicks his chair back, and it crashes loudly to the floor behind him. Ramsay's men rise, drawing their swords.

I, on the other hand, am quite calm as my gaze settles on Ramsay. "I am the last woman you will treat this way."

His smile is wide enough to show all his crooked teeth. "I like a bit of a struggle."

There goes the last strand of self-control to my name.

My elbow connects with his nose with a delicious crunch, and I swivel in my seat to kick him in the chest, sending him stumbling backward. If there hadn't been a table behind him to catch himself on, he'd certainly have fallen to the floor. Cards go flying and curses ring out at the interrupted card game, but the pirate pays no mind. With a red grin, he wipes the trickle of blood leaking from his nose with the back of his hand. I slide from the stool, brandishing my daggers. By now, we've garnered attention, and the crowd has made way for us. Whistles and shouts of encouragement fill the room, while the barkeeps hardly pay any mind—those poor souls.

"Come on, sweet," he protests, shaking his head. "I only wanted a little kiss."

"Oh, you'll get your kiss," I challenge, flipping my dagger up in the air.

His eyes gleam dangerously, and he rushes me.

And I was ready. Goddamn, I was ready for him, but I never get the chance to clock him before Liam steps in front of me and punches him so hard he lurches sideways and into the crowd.

He rounds on me. "What the devil are you doing?"

"Get out of the fucking way," I yell at the same time.

I do my best to shove him away, but he may as well be a mountain that sprouted up in the middle of the damn bar. I slap his arm in annoyance. "Move."

"No."

"Go finish your little card game."

"I can't. That's the buffoon I was about to swindle."

"He started this."

His eyes glitter. "I saw."

He doesn't have time to say anything more before Ramsay, who apparently cannot be deterred, stalks back into the ring, rubbing his jaw.

"Must be a good fuck, if she's worth all this."

Liam's gaze slides to mine. "I'm going to kill him if he says that one more time."

"Hm." My eyes flick to Ramsay, and my lips spread into a wide grin. "What did you say you want to do to me?"

"FU—"

Before he can finish, Liam's fist connects with his mouth, and blood sprays into the crowd. Maybe a few teeth. Hard to say. Someone pushes Ramsay back into the makeshift ring, and he comes hurdling back, fist cocked, but at the last moment, Liam ducks, resulting in an unfortunate bystander getting the ever-loving shit knocked out of them.

That's all it takes for The Chapel to devolve into one giant fistfight. Even the piano gets involved, shifting suddenly into a fast, chaotic tune. Everywhere I look, someone's getting socked in the face or thrown over a table. One poor fellow is getting bashed by a table leg. In the back, I catch sight of Matteo, looking absolutely delighted to be included. He jumps over a low kick delivered by someone from Ramsay's crew, throws ale in his face, and punches him hard enough that he stays down. I can hear his triumphant crow all the way from here. A brawl breaks out on top of the bar, but the bartender doesn't so much as blink before expertly moving a full mug of ale out of the way to avoid a body crashing down in its place. Not a single drop is spilled. Impressive. The bartender hands it to Luhan, who's moved to the far end, and seems engrossed in a conversation with another handsome pirate. They seem completely unbothered by the chaos around them.

At least he's having a good night.

A loud curse draws my attention back to the middle of the room, where Liam and Ramsay face off. Ramsay's mouth is moving, and I strain to hear what he's saying as I wade through the crowd. The closer I get, the better I can hear their exchange.

"What's a matter, Blackwater? Can't share? Afraid she'll forget all about you?" Liam slams his head into a table, but the taunts continue relentlessly.

"Mirabelle certainly did," Ramsay gives a ragged laugh, even as Liam flings him to the floor. "She ran straight to me when you left. I fucked her all better. Never thanked you for that one. The first few times weren't so pretty, but I knew what she needed."

He gets back to his feet, but he's swaying a little. And, though Liam could very easily end the fight, he doesn't. Instead, his gaze shifts behind Ramsay, and he inclines his head.

Ramsay turns around in time for Mirabelle to kick him in the crotch so hard, I doubt he'll be using it any time soon. If ever.

He crumples to the ground, letting out a horrific groan, but still somehow manages to reach for her.

He finds the tip of a sword instead, and flinches at its cold greeting. "You," he inhales a shaky breath. "Fucking bitch."

I raise the point to his neck. A red pearl of blood trickles down his neck and stains the collar of his shirt. "What was that?"

"I said, you're a fucking bitch."

I lurch forward to my knees, our faces close, the blade even closer. "It's funny. All of this. No matter what I do, I'm some sort of bitch. I punch back, and I'm a mad bitch. I say no to your putrid advances, and I'm a cold bitch. Feral bitch. Abominable bitch. But it doesn't bother me. Not anymore. You know why?"

His eyes are two unapologetic pits, and I feel no remorse for what happens next. "I'm the bitch holding the blade now."

With a flick of my wrist, I draw a jagged, crimson smile across his throat, and he falls away to land at Mirabella's feet. She stands motionless, gazing down with a blank look on her face. But then our gazes meet, and she inclines her head.

She turns on her heel and disappears into the crowd.

I stand to find Liam watching me from a few paces away. Behind him, a chair flies across the room and splinters against a wall, but neither of us even flinches. Then, it's as if everything slows to a standstill. Leaving me, and him, and the caustic words we'd hurled at each other.

I thought I was being careful, but I wasn't. If we have only so much time left, I want to spend it all with you. Even if it hurts more when it's over.

I'm sorry. Please don't give up on me.

There is no softness in the set of Liam's mouth as he stalks toward me, no hint of forgiveness. Fury presses his lips thin and imparts a lethal sheen to his eyes. I steel myself for his impending wrath, resigning myself to enduring it. I swallow, hands at my sides. Take a slow breath.

He looks like he's going to kill me this time.

He reaches me in a matter of moments, and without a word, he roughly grasps the back of my neck, pulls me to him, and kisses me. Really kisses me. A burning, demanding sort of kiss that brands my very soul.

My hands fly up to knot themselves in his hair as he presses me to him. All the anger, all the hurt, all the uncertainty come to a head, and I take it out on him. Our teeth clash, and I yank him to me by the fabric of his shirt, but that only makes him kiss me harder. His tongue slips inside my mouth at the same time his fingers slide along my jaw, and I'm thankful for the calamity around us so he can't hear my sigh.

Abruptly, he pulls away, taking my hand. Wordlessly, I follow.

He leads us through the pulsing crowd, shoving a few brutes away who get too close, and up the stairs. We're halfway up the second set when he suddenly stops, pushing me against the wall to run his hands roughly over my bodice, trailing hot, urgent kisses along my neck and jaw.

"You," he murmurs against my shoulder as his hands linger over my breast and squeeze, "will be my undoing. I could have killed him for looking at you. I wanted to rip his spinal cord from his body with my bare hands."

"There are more interesting things you can do with your hands," I say, then bite his earlobe.

He makes a guttural, low noise in his throat before tearing himself away and pulling me up the stairs, until we're back to my room. Kicking the door open, we stumble inside, still entangled in each other. I shrug my coat off while his fingers move feverishly to undo the laces of my corset.

I gasp when he picks me up by my thighs and, crossing the room, throws me onto the bed. In one swift movement, he's ripped the dress off me, and I'm wearing nothing but my underthings, stockings, and boots. He towers over me, his eyes meandering up and down my body. Taking his time.

His chest heaves as if he's just swam the entire Silver Seas, his lips parted as his tongue swipes across his lower lip. His hair falls messily across his forehead, and I realize what I mistook for violent intent earlier was pure lust. They're not so different, I'm coming to realize. Not for us.

"Strider," he rumbles, running a finger reverently up my inner thigh. "You and I need to come to an understanding."

He crawls on top of me, hitching my thighs high around his hips as he moves. "You have always been mine. I am yours. And for months, I've been burning alive with thoughts of how I'd claim you. Where I wanted to touch you so that you'd sigh like this," he runs an expert finger between my legs, pulling the sound he'd just described out of me immediately. "How long I could get away with licking you before you beg me to stop." His teeth skim along my jaw. "And whether you'll let me bend you over and fuck you hard as I can, or perhaps you'll want it slow."

He kisses me slow and deep, his hands roving toward my exposed breasts. He takes them in his palms, pinching and tweaking to the point of pain. It drives me insane, and I squirm beneath its command.

"Say the word, Strider," he says against my lips, and I start to smolder. "You know which one."

"And if I don't?"

"I'll leave you here to nurse my bruised pride, and we'll never speak of it again. I told you a long time ago. I need to know you want this too. All of it."

There is nothing in all the realms I want more than this. More than him. This one time, I'll let him win.

"Please."

He descends upon me, and my thoughts, like sparrows scattering to the wind.

61

MINE

His mouth crushes against mine, but this time, there's a new fervor to him. To both of us.

Months of stored-up hatred, anger, yearning, and desire erupt like meteors.

His tongue swirls around my mouth as I hastily unbutton and rip his vest off so I can scrape my nails down the expanse of his stomach, and even further. After ripping his laces apart and dragging his pants over his hips, I stroke his hardness hungrily. The gravelly noise of pleasure he emits sends an indescribable elation through me.

His fingers trail down my body to the lacy scrap of fabric covering the last bit of me, slipping underneath. My body spasms at his touch, and I feel his crooked grin before I see it. He wastes no time, rubbing me in a way he knows will arch my spine and make my hips buck.

"That's it, love," he murmurs, moving down my body and leaving a trail of kisses as he goes. His stubble scratches pleasantly against increasingly sensitive skin, and he lingers below my belly button, delivering slow, teasing kisses there. Now and then, his eyes flick up to mine, gleaming deviously.

"This," he rumbles, running his hands over the scrap of lace alleging as underwear to ever so slowly peel it down. "I like this, but alas, it must come off."

Easing himself off the bed, he slides my underwear down my legs. I prop myself up on my elbows, breathing hard as he nudges my thighs open and pulls my boots off, leaving just the stockings now.

"Darling, spread your legs for me." He runs his tongue along one inner thigh, and then the other, and my lips part at the sensation. And then his head lowers, and my eyes roll back in my head.

"Oh. *Ohhh.*"

I thought that before, in the sparring room, was the height of pleasure, but I was wrong. Liam's wet, cruel mouth between my legs is ecstasy. He alternates, quite tantalizingly, between sucking and moving his tongue in slow, lazy circles, and I lose all decency. I splay my legs as wide as they can go, wanting more of his mouth on as much of me as possible. He intermittently stops to run his tongue along all of me, and after the third time, I can't stifle the deep moan it draws out of me, like he's got my soul on a string.

My hands clench his hair, desperate for some semblance of control even though I know I surrendered that the moment I said *please*. He's insatiable, licking me like I'm the sweetest nectar, and all too soon, I'm on the precipice of coming apart. I want this every night for the rest of my life. I want to shatter so he can put me back together.

I *want*.

"Liam," I moan, my voice thick as syrup. My hips roll of their own accord with the rhythm of his tongue, completely at the mercy of his mouth. It's when his tongue enters me that I start gasping.

"Liam, oh, *oh*, Liam—"

My entire body tenses, my stomach muscles taut as a bow as my legs quiver, then finally, the wave breaks, sending me into mind-numbing oblivion. I clench the bedding beneath me as my head falls back in complete bliss. He peels the tights off me, leaving me at last completely bare.

"Oh, sweetheart." His tongue continues its work, and my spine arches at the sensitivity. Standing, he steps fully out of his pants and kicks his boots off, and then he's crawling back to me, his eyes glazed with self-indulgence as he takes a nipple in his mouth and sucks.

I inhale sharply, my hands drifting down his body until I find his length again and start to stroke it, slow and teasing.

"Those damn clever hands of yours," he says into my skin, and I exhale softly as I feel him react to my touch.

He brings his mouth back to mine and kisses me even deeper than before, bringing a hand down to guide mine into stroking even harder, even faster. For a moment, we both look down, entranced by the enthusiastic effect we're having on each other. A finger enters me, and my hips writhe when it crooks. I slap my hand over my mouth to smother the moan it elicits, but Liam snatches it away, pinning it to the bed.

"*Never* do that," he hisses. "If I make you scream, then scream."

"Hasn't happened yet," I pant, and in response, he inserts a second finger.

"Patience, Strider. I'll give you what you want."

"I hope you know what you're doing," I grin wickedly, dragging my thumb across his lower lip, exposing his teeth.

"Don't worry, sweetheart," he murmurs, then bites my thumb. "I do. But have you . . . "

"I ate my fill of harkweed in Marrin." A naturally growing plant that prevents ovulation. I ate so much of it, I'd be surprised if I ever bear children in my lifetime.

Appeased, he gathers my knees up on either side of his hips, kissing me like he's worshipping my mouth. He enters me slowly, taking his time, measuring my expression, my every tiny gasp as he descends further. By the time he's fully inside of me, I've buried my hands in the silk of his hair and crushed my mouth to his.

Finally, our bodies move as one.

His thrusts start slow, and while I know it's because he doesn't want to hurt me, I want more. My impatience is much worse than any pain. Eagerly, I move my hips to meet his, and soon, I'm bringing my legs up even higher so he can bury himself in me to the hilt. I've fucked before, yes, but it was always quick and savage, an itch to be scratched. No kissing, no frills. Just instinct.

Never like this.

I've never felt adored and craved and used and revered, all at once. I've never let myself go with no fear of repercussions. Oh, how we've waited for each other. An entire lifetime, it feels like. *Every lifetime.*

His hips roll gracefully, building speed, and with every thrust my breaths come faster and harder. Another release begins to build, my legs trembling when he pulls himself out and flips me over to all fours, nudging my thighs apart with his own. This time, I don't stop the moan that escapes my lips when he enters me again, nor when his fingers begin to stroke tight, unrelenting circles between my legs as he shoves my head into a pillow. The brutality of it all threatens to completely undo me.

This is what he means when he says that I am his.

With every slap of our bodies, my breath becomes shallower, and the pressure inside of me rises until I no longer retain control. The sound that leaves my lips is a gravelly, wild thing that feels as unbridled as I do now, and I grind myself against his hand, against his hips, until finally I find mind-numbing release. I rise onto my knees as he slings a hand across my chest, the other meticulously wringing every last bit of pleasure out of me. His own euphoria finds him soon after, and I feel his hips jerk and stutter with it as he sighs into my hair.

Gently, he pulls out of me, and we collapse onto the bed with exultant grins. I marvel at the man in front of me. There's no part of him that isn't lithe and marvelously defined. I drink up the sight of him, as if I may never again get the chance.

For a while, neither of us utters a word, content to let our breaths slow as we come down from spectacular heights. I close my eyes in rapture, relishing all the places he touched and tasted, and even as I drag my fingers slowly up and down his stomach, I feel myself wanting more already. However, I also know that a rift existed between us until very recently, and what just transpired between us doesn't repair that. In fact, it could very well make it worse.

When I open my eyes, he's staring at me with an expression so tender, it breaks my heart.

His knuckles brush my cheek, my jaw, my neck.

"Do you want to . . ." He trails off, but I know what he meant. I nod, and he starts.

"I'm so sorry, Strider. What I said earlier was foul and unwarranted. I used things you'd told me in confidence against you and I . . . It will never happen again. I swear it."

Tears prick my eyes when I think of the horrible things we said to each other out of complete and total desperation. "I'm sorry too, Liam. I get cruel when I'm afraid."

"I do too, it seems."

That surprises me. "You were afraid?"

He brushes some hair away from my cheek. "I'm afraid that one day, you'll pull so far away, I can't find my way back to you. But if it's time you need, Strider, I will wait for you. I do mean that."

"I know." I exhale slowly, closing my eyes. "I got angry when I saw you with Mirabelle, and it wasn't fair. I wasn't thinking straight."

His hand splays out on my cheek. "I should have warned you."

"I wouldn't have made that easy, either."

One side of his mouth curls up. "That, I believe. But in truth, it was years ago when we . . . well. I'd see her when I came to port, we'd have our fun, and then I'd leave. If it was more serious than that for her, I never knew."

He falters, and his expression turns contrite. It's the closest I've seen him come to real regret. "Or perhaps I was just a foolish boy who didn't care. If you'd met me then, you'd have despised me. I was a vain, self-centered cad."

"I'm having a difficult time seeing it." I crack a smile.

"Oh, I'm sure."

I sit up, pulling the blankets with me to cover my chest. "You were right about me, though. I am a coward." He sits up to speak, but I hold up a finger.

"I am still learning how to accept good things without looking over my shoulder for their repercussions. It's . . . Well. It's hard."

"Am I a good thing?" He asks quietly. Hopefully.

"You are many things to me."

His fingers, like a butterfly's wings, brush along my jaw and down my neck. They trail down my arm, bringing my hand to his mouth. He presses a kiss, delicate and sweet, into my palm. I close my eyes, savoring every moment, using it to bolster my courage.

"Such as?" He asks. I feel the bed creak as he moves behind me— between myself and the headboard, and his hand snakes around to trace my collarbone. My scars. I shiver beneath his touch, so light compared to the rough urgency to which we succumbed moments ago.

"You are my worst enemy."

"I see." In one motion, he pulls me flush against him and presses his lips to my neck. My eyes nearly roll back in my skull as I rest my head on his shoulder, hungry for more of his mouth. His slow kisses sear my skin.

"What else?"

"The bane of my existence."

The sound of his chuckle makes me smile. "But?"

I pretend to ponder, but almost lose my train of thought when his hand slips below the sheets. "But when you're near, my insides light up with fireflies that only glow for you."

He pauses his work. I turn to meet his intoxicating gaze, and for a moment, a great solemnity cuts through the lust. "I know exactly what you mean."

My voice drops to a whisper. "I will come back."

Liquid green eyes caress my face. "I will be waiting."

His mouth returns to my neck as his hand dutifully continues its service down below. It's not long before my legs tremble with a boneless, spectacular pressure. Quiet, breathy moans slip out of me in tandem with his fingers when suddenly, his other hand wraps around my throat and squeezes.

That's all it takes for me to career over the edge.

Liam's mouth on mine swallows any noise I might have made as he eases me onto my back. Now that the storm has passed, we're in no hurry. His kisses are a leisurely sunset against clear, endless skies. Our hands wander anywhere they wish to go, worshipping every sacred piece of each other. Buried in my hair, scraping down his back, clamping down onto my hips. Memorizing each other by feel, by taste. The little noises we make.

I would know every ridge of his spine if life were so kind.

Some time later, we join again. It's different now, though. Now that we've had each other once, gone is the initial fervor, only to be replaced by something far more intimate. His hips roll slowly. Deliberately. Almost all the way out, then back in. It takes a few times before I stop gasping when he does it. But I want *more*. My fingers dig into his rear, but try as I might to get him to go faster, he won't do it.

"Sweetheart," he warns, meeting my gaze.

"Faster." It comes out as a breathless plea, but all I get is a slow, wicked grin as he shakes his head.

I feel my core becoming molten for him as he leans down for an open-mouthed kiss.

Between his tongue sliding around in my mouth and the friction of his wandering hands, another crest starts to build. A languid, sugary heat that threatens to obliterate my senses.

Soon I'm writhing beneath him, whimpering as my body clenches with anticipation.

"You're mine," Liam breathes into my neck, fisting the pillow under my head as his hips grind slowly, punishingly. And then ecstasy spills over me like a sunrise, warm and magnificent. I'm left feeling both depleted and fulfilled. Liam groans as his hips roll with the final spasms of the encounter, and we share one last scorching kiss.

Afterwards, I slip into the most decadent, silky sleep I've ever known. And I do not dream.

62

THE MIDNIGHT PHANTASM

earest revelers,

Well done.

With the three tasks completed in the nick of time, the Crown officially invites thou to King DeHavelin's Midnight Phantasm, a masquerade ball, taking place on the night of the Dead Moons at the Celosian Palace Gardens. Pray, honor this night of wandering spirits by dressing in thine most extravagantly macabre.

At ten bells exact, find a door. One that doesn't already lead somewhere else. Knock three times. And most importantly, arrive separately from thy partner. Indulge us one last game, lovelies.

Fantastically,
  The Crown

63

DELEGATION

We'd set upon each other once more during the night. Though I'd thought I'd be exhausted, it's the opposite. I'm invigorated. My blood feels fizzy, my body buoyant. I bound down the stairs, eager to make one last lap around Celosia before I need to get my dress. Last night, Lu had agreed to go with me.

The tavern is deserted at this early hour, except for the one person I'd hoped to avoid. Mirabelle flits around the empty room, straightening chairs, sweeping up broken glass, and wiping off the counters. I watch her for a moment, leaning in the doorway. To work in a place like this, one's senses must be keen. It's not long at all before she turns to acknowledge me with a warm smile on her face.

When she sees it's me, the smile loses its luster. "Iona. Good morning."

I cock my head to the side. "How do you know my name?"

"Oh, forgive me. Liam told me yesterday. I'm Mirabelle."

"I . . . know," I admit, stepping through the arch. My eyes seek out the spot where Ramsay's body lay bleeding out last night, only to find a meticulously scrubbed expanse of floor instead.

No real trace of the tavern-wide brawl from last night, save for a few dents in the wall and perhaps a wobbly chair or two where the legs were bashed over someone's head.

"Did you do all this?" I gesture to the place in awe.

She blows a strand of gold out of her face. "It didn't take as long as you'd think. Celosia is abundant in magic, so I don't have to do too much myself. I have at least four books in the back on charms to remove stains."

"It's pristine."

She acknowledges the compliment with a slight nod. "My father turned the place over to me many years ago. I've had a lot of practice. Last night was fairly routine, if you can believe it."

Stooping down to scrape some glass into my palm, I ask, "Do you have any help? Seems like quite a bit to leave to only one person."

Her laugh is the tinkle of bells. "Oh, yes. But I'm pretty choosy about what I delegate to others. I don't mind cleaning so that I know it's done right. I keep all the ledgers myself, too. There are other tasks I'm not terribly precious about and prefer for others to do for me, like bartending and pest control."

My gaze flicks to hers, only to find she's watching me, her dark eyes surprisingly shrewd. I find my feet and toss the shards of glass into the nearest bin. "Pest control?"

"Yes. *Pests*. See, now that I practically own the place, I can't very well go around killing my own patrons. Especially the powerful ones. Despicable pirate captains, for example. But occasionally, I get lucky. I can't very well help the brawls that break out when the liquor starts flowing, nor the deaths that come from them, now can I?"

I recall Ramsay shouting at her last night. How conveniently close the interaction was—right within earshot. Did she instigate that on purpose?

Did she mean for me to take him out from the beginning?

"I see," I say, striving to buff the astonishment out of my expression. "And if I'd lost the fight?"

She comes to stand in front of me, and though she's shorter than I am, there's a forthrightness to her stance that feels downright formidable, and there isn't a cloud on her lovely face as she replies, "Who says I was talking about only one pest?"

A moment of stunned silence sits between us, and then a broad smile splits my face. "Touché. But rest assured, you won't see me again."

Her pink lips quirk. "If I do, don't mind the knife in your back. Know that it won't be by my hand then, either."

For the life of me, I cannot tell if she's joking or not. She's smiling, but it seems unattended, like a candle left burning after everyone's already gone to bed.

"Appreciate the warning." I salute a hasty farewell and have almost made it to the swinging double doors when she calls after me.

"And Iona?"

I twist, prepared for one last sugar-coated threat, but all she says is, "I knew you'd win the fight. If you hadn't, Liam would have stepped in before anything happened to you." She inhales deeply, brushing dust from her skirts. "I knew what I was giving up when I took over this place. So, if it must be you, take care of him. If you don't, remember that my reach is long, and I do like to delegate."

"On that, we understand each other."

I scrutinize her one last time. I'd thought her a sweet, simple girl at first, but I was wrong.

There's a cunning lurking in her brown eyes, well hidden behind a mask of placid beauty. I notice for the first time an aquamarine stone hanging from her neck. It looks *expensive*. She sees me looking and tucks it back into her dress with a wry grin.

I couldn't hate her if I tried.

"Goodbye, Mirabelle."

"Goodbye, Iona."

I push through the doors and into a pool of sunlight.

Lu and I spend the day admiring the sights. Shops along the waterfront dazzle with their display windows of lacy, delicate dresses, leather goods, and colorful potions claiming to preserve memories or add five years to a lifespan. I could spend days here. And the people. I haven't looked upon a single face that wasn't beautiful.

I hadn't realized I'd come to a halt until Lu elbows me in the ribs. "Stop dawdling, we're going to be late."

I fight off my protest that he's the one who wants to stop and admire every shop front and follow him further into the city. After a few steps, though, I freeze, my head snapping to the right.

I could have sworn that there, beneath an awning, someone was watching me. I stand completely still for a couple more moments, my instincts howling at me to *move* as my eyes scan the crowd.

But I detect nothing strange, and certainly no one observing me. At least, not anymore.

"You don't know where it is," I accuse after we've circled the same tree three times now. It has sprawling, umbrella-like branches that overlook the sea. They're so thick; someone has fashioned swings from them. Two girls with swishing tails occupy them now, their giggles high-pitched with glee as they swing over the ledge and into open air.

"I know I've seen this place before," Luhan insists, propping his hands on his hips as his gaze sweeps over the area.

I huff, crossing my arms as I scan the shops for the thousandth time. Liam had given me the name of the shop, Aisla's Apparel, with explicit instructions on its location. It had seemed easy enough at the time.

Something brushes against my legs, and I look down in surprise to see a silver-furred cat rubbing against my ankles.

"The hell do you want?" I've never trusted animals as long as I can remember. To be fair, they've never seemed to like me, either. The cat looks up at me with round, lilac eyes and meows importantly, its charcoal ears twitching.

"What do we have here?" Luhan croons, bending down to scratch it beneath its chin.

"We don't have time," I grumble, but Luhan ignores me, talking nonsense to the stupid cat instead.

"Can you take us to Aisla's Apparel? I'll buy you the best fish guts you've ever had." Suddenly, the cat jumps to her feet and scampers through the crowd. We look at each other, mouths agape.

"No," I say immediately. "I'm not following that thing."

"Let's just see where it went," Luhan argues, taking my arm to tug me forward and down the cobblestoned street. "Come on. Have a little fun for once, Iona."

"We're going to feel like such idiots when we follow this fucking cat and all it wanted to show us was a regurgitated mole it found two days ago—"

I stop.

The cat sits, licking a paw, on the steps of an older-looking shop with fuchsia blossoms hanging on either side of its entrance. There's no sign on the front announcing its business, but rather, two words scrawled across its heavy, wooden door.

Aisla's Apparel.

Beneath hangs a small sign.

Open This Time.

Luhan eyes me with a smug, wide smile. "You were saying?"

I open my mouth to tell him exactly what I was about to say when the door opens to reveal a middle-aged woman with startling but kind blue eyes.

"Iona?" She asks.

"Y-yes?"

Luhan elbows me, and I clear my throat. It makes sense that she knew I was coming today if Liam had made previous arrangements, but he couldn't have told her a time.

"Yes. That's me."

"And Luhan?"

Now it's Luhan's turn to sputter. "How did you know—"

Her smile widens, putting creases around her eyes, and I find myself warming to her immediately. "I always know who's coming and going. Now, come inside. You're late."

The cat tries to follow us inside, but I take care to shut the door in its face before it has a chance to slink inside. Hate cats.

64

TEN BELLS EXACT

"As you may have gathered, my name is Aisla," the shop owner says as she leads us to the back of the room, past a wall of clocks. Each one shows a different time. The most prominent clock shows a quarter past nine bells, and I stop, momentarily alarmed.

"Aisla? What time is it?"

Up ahead, she stops, twisting to look at me. "Quarter past nine bells."

I gawk at her. "But—but how? It was much earlier when we arrived."

"I'm sure it was," she says. "This must be your first time in Celosia."

When I stare at her, she continues placidly, "Time, like magic, has thicker and thinner spots. Here, it is thin, fragile. So, it passes by much quicker. Understand?"

"How . . . common is that?" Judging by the look on Luhan's face, this is his first time hearing this, too.

"It's a fairly recent development. I think it has something to do with magic being so spotty as of late. It must congregate somewhere nearby. Now come along, we don't have much longer."

"If we leave the shop, will it go back to the way it was?"

"Afraid not," she says, shaking her head kindly. "One cannot change the past, only the future."

Confusing.

We weave through various mannequins adorned with all sorts of hats, jackets, and dresses. My eyes linger on a few, admiring the delicate threadwork and beading. Some of these must have taken months. What stands out to me the most, though, isn't the mastery, as impressive as it is. It's the styles of clothing, some of which I've never seen before—bizarre metallics and bold asymmetries, while other articles of clothing look quite ancient. The far wall is completely covered in spools of all colors of thread, fabrics, and patterns—so much so that the actual wall isn't visible at all.

We reach the back of the shop, and she pulls back a heavy velvet curtain to reveal a few chairs, some hooks, a privacy screen, and a floor-length mirror rimmed in silver. It has mirrored panels on each side that jut out, allowing one to see different aspects of their attire. This must be where I will try on my dress.

"So," she says warmly as she pulls the curtain back, closing us off from the gallery of mannequins. "Captain Blackwater requested that I make a dress for you for tonight's Midnight Phantasm. Using what he could tell me about you, I've made you something I hope you'll quite like. I'm rather proud myself."

I feel myself grinning. "And what did Liam—er, Captain Blackwater, tell you about me?"

Aisla laces her hands delicately in front of her. "He said you'd ask me that and told me to tell you to 'Fuck off and ask me yourself, you nosy woman.'"

Luhan doubles over and laughs so hard; he wheezes. I cross my arms, nodding to myself.

"Well, let us see what he thinks I'll like, I suppose."

"Let us see," Aisla echoes, and gestures to the privacy screen. "I'll accompany you to help with the stays of the dress, if you don't mind. And—I have all my patrons do this. A little tradition. If you will, close your eyes. I'll tell you when to open them."

It's a strange feeling, I'll admit, to have a total stranger pulling, tugging, and fastening me in while I stand here, helpless. I lift my arms, step up, and straighten my spine when she commands, though not unkindly. Whatever fabric she used feels like water as it brushes across my skin. Cool and light, barely there. Something hard and cold rests against my spine, and I'm eager to see what it could be.

"How did you know my measurements?" I ask to pass the time.

"I didn't. I use enchanted thread, you see, which conforms to the body when it's worn for the first time. Now. Hold your arms out in front of you," she instructs, and I feel her tugging gloves on.

Finally, after a never-ending amount of situating, I hear her breathe something that sounds a lot like approval.

"Are you ready, dear?" Comes Aisla's voice.

"Yes," I breathe, my heartbeat seconding my excitement.

"Take my hand and keep your eyes closed," she instructs, then leads me carefully out from behind the screen, presumably in front of the giant mirrors.

From where he was lounging in the chair, I hear Luhan's sharp inhale and hope it's a good thing.

"Open," Aisla says from off to the side, after she finishes doing something with the skirts. My eyelids snap open, and I let out a gasp of my own.

I stand draped in red. What Aisla has put me in is as breathtaking as it is formidable. My waist is accentuated by a stiff, textured corset embellished with clusters of lace flowers. Though it rises all the way to my neck, there is an extended diamond-shaped cutout that starts below my collarbones and doesn't end until well beneath my sternum. Meticulously beaded rubies gather at my hips and congregate randomly in my skirts, along with more lace accents. The skirts billow out around me, forming a pool of dark crimson at my feet. Matching gloves climb up my arms all the way to my upper bicep. Whatever material they're made of, they glisten in the light as if I dipped my arms into a pool of blood. They feel like a second skin.

When I turn to see the rest of the dress, that's when I understand Aisla's genius. Almost my entire back is bare, except for an anatomically accurate golden spine, complete with all thirty-three vertebrae and ribs that curl horizontally, ending in sharp points. It starts at the base of my neck, sewn into the fabric, and ends where my hips begin—scandalously low.

Leaving my curse on full display.

"Wait," I reel on Aisla, distraught. "The markings on my back. I don't want anyone to see."

If she's upset by my reaction, she doesn't show it. "I disagree. Tonight of all nights is the time to be who you truly are. No one will think anything of it besides how intricate your costuming is. I couldn't have dreamed up something so perfect myself."

I turn my back to the mirror, studying the carvings in my skin against the curvature of the spine. She has a point, I suppose. Paired with the dreadful splendor of the dress, it looks like nothing more than a finishing flourish to complete my macabre ensemble.

I look to Luhan, who nods in agreement. He stands, turning me around to run his finger down the spine of the dress, and lets out a low whistle.

"You look spectacular," he says, and I hear the earnestness in his voice.

Twisting to face him, I quip, "That's the first kind thing you've ever said to me, Lu."

"Well, wear better clothing. Like this," he retorts, spinning me slowly. The beading in my skirts catches the light, and my breath hitches in my chest at how truly marvelous it is.

I meet Aisla's gaze in the mirror, smiling widely. "You've done an incredible job. It's . . . it's—"

"Perfect," she finishes, hiding a little laugh. "I agree. I've outdone myself this time. Now here, you can't go to a masquerade without a mask."

She reaches behind the screen to procure a glittering red mask with sides that twist up and around into spiraling horns. I adore it the moment I see it. When I hold it over my face, my eyes glow like orbs.

"Now," she says, pulling up a chair for me to sit in. "Finish up your hair and your face. It's almost time."

And with a swish of skirts, she leaves us to finish the job.

Somehow, Luhan manages to wrangle my hair back into a twist, shiny and sleek. I'd brought my lip stain and kohl, which I apply with more ease than last time. When I'm finished, my mouth is a red slick, my eyes gold rimmed with black.

Eighty-seven days ago, I was a starved, beaten wisp of a thing on the cusp of an anonymous death. In one pocket, rage; the other, guilt, and a disobedient shadow to grapple with, too. Without a friend in the world besides the imaginary ones in stories. Eighty-seven days isn't a very long time at all, and yet, a lifetime has passed, and a new one begins tonight at ten bells. One in which I rid myself once and for all of this shadow. Once that comes to pass, Liam and I can try again.

So then, I don't know why I'm so sad.

"Oh, Iona." Before I can protest, Luhan envelops me in his arms, hugging me tightly to his chest. My arms wrap around him, too, and leaning my cheek against his shoulder, I let the riptide of my emotions drag me under. But the difference between now and eighty-seven days ago is that this time, I know how to swim.

"You look so lovely," Lu says, resting his chin on the crown of my hair. "Truly. I'm very proud of you, you know."

"For what? Wearing a dress?"

He breathes a laugh. "Well, yes, I suppose that, too. I don't know. I like the person you've become. Now that you've stopped hating everyone."

My eyes sting all over again, and I embrace him even harder. "If it's any consolation, I liked you from the start, Lu."

"Of course you did," he says, and I hear the smile in his voice. "Who wouldn't?"

It's then that we're interrupted by bells. We both stop speaking mid-sentence after six of them come to pass.

Then seven. Eight.

Nine.

Ten.

"Impossible," I say.

At the same time, he exclaims, "How?"

"I told you to mind the time," Aisla chides from around the corner, having left presumably to give us some space. "Better run along now."

We stare at each other. I've had almost three months to prepare for this very moment, but now that it's here, I'm dumbfounded. Terrified. After tonight, everything will be different.

"Lu, I don't want everything to change."

I don't want to leave The Wraith. I'll miss the crew. The chess games with Teller and Matteo. Arguments over history with Ishaan and Arjun. The irreplaceable companionship I've found with Luhan.

And Liam.

Lu's steadfastness grounds me. "You'll always have us. Me. And tonight? You'll drink too much wine and dance until your feet hurt, and you both will have the night of your lives. You'll tell me all about it tomorrow, and Liam will have to remind you that you *did* have fun even though all your stories come across like complaints."

I manage a shaky smile. "You're right. You're right."

Striding to the small table, I sort hurriedly through the mess there until I find what I need: the kohl liner.

At ten bells exact, find a door. One that doesn't already lead somewhere else. Knock three times. Midnight Phantasm awaits.

"Let's go outside."

65

CROWS IN THE WOOD

Only after I've given Aisla my many thanks, and tipped her handsomely since Liam already paid her, Luhan and I depart the little shop and take a sharp left, disappearing down a narrow alleyway. It's dark outside. Almost void-like. Of course it is—the sky is without its moons tonight, and the stars cannot compensate for their absence.

That fucking cat seems to have latched on to Luhan, seeing as it waited outside on the steps for us. The moment I flung the door open, it sprang to its feet, yowling happily at the sight of us.

In the alleyway, I stop once I find a blank expanse of brick and begin to draw using the kohl—two long vertical lines, taller than I, connected by a horizontal line at the top. Once I'm finished, I take a step back, surveying my work.

A door that doesn't already lead somewhere else.

"I see now why you couldn't have made it as an artist," Luhan quips, the cat in his arms purring loudly.

"Hush," I say over the deafening beat of my heart. Here I go.

Stepping close, I knock once, twice, three times with my gloved hand.

Swallowing, I step away and hold my breath. Even the cat's purrs suddenly stop, as if she, too, is interested.

Moments pass, and nothing happens. My teeth worry my lips, and Luhan cocks his head expectantly.

I finally dare to take a breath when suddenly there's a resounding crack, and I watch in disbelief as the brick shudders, but only inside the lines I've drawn. Then, with a sharp *crack*, the bricks inside swing open, revealing swirling, silvery mist behind. A door.

Out steps a black-cloaked figure. The cat leaps out of Lu's arms and dashes out of sight.

Both of us recede a step, shocked at the gruesome creature—what looms before us cannot be human. For one, it's too tall. It had to crouch to come through the doorway, and I drew it well above my head to begin with. Its fingers, clad in black gloves, are long and spindly. Claws, more like.

And the mask. Smooth black feathers, perhaps of a crow or vulture, fan out from the face, covering the entire head. The rest resembles the skull of a bird, picked clean by carrion beasts, evidenced by glittering rubies here and there, resembling bits of residual blood and flesh. Its beak is a wicked, downward curve that ends at about chest level. I cannot see the thing's eyes for the black lace obscuring them.

A feeling of wrongness, of dread, overcomes me. The message on the invitation said *nothing* of an usher. Slowly, the thing unfurls a ringed talon and motions me closer.

"Don't," Luhan blurts. His face is pale.

"I have to," I say, even though my skin crawls. "Liam is there. I can't abandon him."

"We'll find another way," he insists, a note of desperation in his voice as he clutches my arm. "Something feels wrong. This is wrong."

I glance over to the thing, its hand still outstretched. It hasn't moved. Doesn't seem to even breathe.

"It's alright," I say, wringing the fear from my voice. "I'll be alright, Luhan. I must go now."

His grip is so tight, it hurts. "Something is *wrong*."

My eyes flick to the doorway, and I realize the mist is a little darker now, as if the magic keeping it open is fading.

I'm running out of time.

"I'll come back," I promise Luhan, lowering my voice. The fear in his eyes hurts to look at. "It's alright. You need to let go."

Reluctantly, he releases me, but his features remain tight with concern as I approach the bird creature. Only once I'm close enough to feel the magic emanating from the door, a static-y buzz that brushes against my skin, does it move at last.

"Your name?"

I startle at the voice that comes from behind the mask, surprised by how human it sounds.

A high, smooth tenor.

"Iona Strider," I say, forcing myself to stare into its eye holes with a confidence I don't feel.

Its hand goes to the small of my back, ushering me toward the door. This is it, then. I didn't expect to be so afraid.

I look over my shoulder one last time to see Luhan standing there, hands at his sides, watching with a look of utter helplessness on his face. The cat, back again, brushes against his ankles, and I could swear it grins up at me. I open my mouth to say something encouraging to Lu, but suddenly the mist shrouds my vision, and I hear the creak of a closing door.

Fear clenches my guts and *squeezes*, and I press my lips together to stop a whimper.

As suddenly as it appeared, the mist scatters at our feet after a few steps, and we find ourselves in a dark wood. A narrow trail meanders before us, lined with swinging lanterns. Mist pervades the forest beyond the trail, licking at its perimeter as if the lanterns are the only thing holding it at bay. Its tendrils snake around giant trees whose branches serve as arches over our heads. I've no way of telling how tall the trees really are; the mist is so thick. Something niggles at the back of my neck, and it's not long before I realize what's bothering me about the scene.

The forest is dead silent.

Nothing stirs, not the pitter-patter of tiny animal feet rummaging for food, nor the rustling of insects through the brush. Not a single flutter of wings or chirp from above. I may as well be standing in a mausoleum. What if the mist is some sort of poison?

I turn to the crow, shivering. "What is this place? Where have you taken me?"

Of course, it doesn't answer. Instead, the crow glides purposefully ahead, another swinging lantern having appeared in its clutches.

Without another option and feeling strongly that I don't want to find myself lost, I follow. The only sound beside my harried breaths is the scrape of my dress against the ground and my pulse beating wildly in my ears. The crow, on the other hand, makes no noise at all. I can barely make out distant lights through the fog, but it becomes quickly apparent that with each fork in the trail, the crow is not leading me toward them, but away.

I stop where I am, my fear finally coming to a hard, shiny point. The crow stops, too, although it doesn't turn around.

"Who are you?" I demand, hitching my skirts up in case I need to run.

Silence, thick and oppressive, spills into every crack and crevice. And even so, I wait. "An old friend."

This is wrong. All of it. "I don't know you."

A healthy pause. "Not anymore."

Confusion spikes through me. "What does that mean?" No response. I try again. "I need to get to the ball."

"No, you don't." Very slowly, the crow turns around, and a wave of unease washes over me. In a blink, the figure disappears, only to reappear right in front of me, its clawed hand digging into my arm.

"You don't listen. You didn't listen to that boy when he told you not to come here tonight. And you didn't listen to me when I told you never to come back. Now they know, and it's too late." His voice is a spine-rending screech.

"What's too late?" I ask.

"*All of it.*"

"Please," I beg. "Tell me what you mean."

"If you go to the ball, it will all be for nothing."

The words are a nail in my heart. Liam. I must find Liam, and we will leave. Before I know what I'm doing, I lurch into motion and run faster than I ever have, back toward the light. Toward *Liam*.

Laughter, shrill and high, scrambles after me, seemingly coming from the mist itself. "Stay away from me," I scream, nearly tripping over a wayward root.

"*Never stop running*," the crow calls to me, and my hand flies to my mouth even as I scramble down the gloomy, twisted path.

Never stop running. It's the same words I've lived by all my life, finally spoken aloud. I halt, my world crashing to a stop.

"It was you? That came from *you*?" But that makes no sense.

And what did it mean, I can't come back? I've *never* been to Celosia.

I knew those words. What have I forgotten? What lurks in the memories I don't have?

"I'm tired of running," I scream in a shaky voice. "Why can't I stop?"

My voice breaks. "*Why*?"

My words are swallowed whole by the woods and the mist within. Slowly, I turn, realizing I have no idea where I am. The mist has grown so thick I can't see past the length of my own arm. I breathe down gulps of soupy air, realizing that in these woods, I am alone.

I wonder, for a nightmarish second, if this is similar to The Wraith when I first arrived, and if I will be wandering through the mists for all eternity. Did I somehow open the wrong door?

I think of Luhan's face, the way he all but begged me not to go. I should have listened. But Liam is waiting for me. What if something happens to him? Terror crawls up my throat, and I trudge forward. The path, if it can still be called that, becomes uneven and overgrown with spindly branches that claw at my skirts. Kicking at them to no avail, I force my way through anyway, but the mist is so dense now I can barely even see in front of my nose. Suddenly, something brushes against my face, and I rear back, thrusting my arms out in front of me to fend it off, cursing darkly. My mask slips in the process, but I catch it before it falls.

"Watch it."

The mist parts, then evaporates entirely.

I'm standing not in a misty forest, but beneath a silvery willow tree, its branches a shimmering encasement. I am not alone. Peering down at me is a masked man, slight of build and still somehow imposing. A vision of white. Slick white-blond hair, skin, jacket, pants. Even his mask is crusted in pearls, shards of white diamonds, and frosted glass.

And he's looking at me like I've sprouted another head. "Who are you?" I ask tersely, taking a step forward.

His pointy little chin jerks indignantly. "Who are *you*?"

That's when I see that his teeth have been painted black, all black, as if, despite his pristine outer shell, he's rotting inside. And he's very drunk. There's a wine bottle graveyard at his feet.

"I am Iona Strider," I say, hastily smoothing my skirts and patting down my hair.

Something in his imperious countenance changes when I say my name. He becomes very still, or at least as still as he can be, given his slight unsteadiness.

"W*hat did you say*?" He spits the words out as if they're foul. His gloves creak as he makes fists at his side.

I don't know how, but I seem to have done something wrong.

"That's my name. Iona." I repeat, softer this time. "Is this the masquerade?"

Ignoring my question, he stalks over to me, swaying, until he's so close I can see the frost of his pale blue eyes behind the mask. They look sad.

He pinches my chin, tilting my face up to his, but I don't jerk away. I don't get the impression he aims to hurt me.

"Your eyes look just like hers," he murmurs. I'm not sure he meant to say it out loud, nor if this person was someone he loved or despised. Then, "Who put you up to this?"

He releases me with an imperious flick of his fingers, pushing my face to the side. Very slowly, I turn back to face him head-on. I am beginning to lose my patience.

"I have no idea what you're talking about. Is this the masquerade or not?"

But he's in some stupor. "You even sound like her. But she *died*. He killed her."

He, I realize, cannot help me. He seems barely able to help himself, and I'm only making things worse.

"I'm sorry, but I'm not your ghost."

His lip curls. "Leave me."

"Gladly," I retort, waving a gloved arm and turning on my heel. "I hope your night improves, whoever you are."

For some reason, I cast a glance over my shoulder before slipping between the strands of leaves, and feel almost sorry for the pale boy, who, more than anything else, looks lost.

The leaves, like curtains, part. It appears I found the Midnight Phantasm after all.

66

MASQUERADE

I've never seen such splendor.

I have somehow appeared in the middle of what must be the gardens of the De'Havelin castle. Spurts of flowers characterize the lawn, crawling possessively along the many gazebos scattered about the grounds. Twinkling lights hang delicately from the boughs of low-hanging trees, casting an ethereal glow on the guests below. The infamous hedge maze looms on the far end of the garden, and couples stroll in and out, the sounds of their delight wafting on the jasmine-scented breeze.

Wisps of ethereal figures waltz across the gardens, visible only for a moment before they materialize elsewhere. Candelabras flicker, casting undulating shadows of people that aren't there. On a pedestal surrounded by red blooms, a man dressed as a jester plays a haunting tune from his violin as he balances on a ball. Long tables overflowing with food and drink populate the place, and as I stalk past, my eyes can't help but linger on the opulence.

Fountains of shimmering orange wine. Towers of bite-sized pastries drowning in glaze. Platters of roasted duck swimming in honey sauce, with every vegetable known to man scattered about: rainbow carrots, purple potatoes, green leafy vegetables covered in garlic and cream. I've never seen so much food in one place, only to be mostly ignored in favor of the spirits.

All this, and not too long ago, I would have been thrilled to come across dead vermin.

I make my way to the castle, where, judging from the roar of voices and music, the masquerade is in full swing. I pass by a woman wearing a dress of snake scales. Head to toe, it gleams emerald in the light. The man beside her wears an all-white tuxedo, except for his shoulders. They glitter with hundreds of tiny red beads, and the fabric around them is stained red, like blood seeping down his arms. They nod to me as I swish by, the woman's red mouth curling at the ends. I pass another woman wearing lace and cream, but the bottom of her dress is somehow illuminated from within, leaving hands, so many hands, on display, their palms pressed against her skirts as if trapped there. They *move*, too.

As I pass, the woman comments in a lazy voice, "The curse is a nice touch."

"It's real," I respond, and her amused laugh chases me. Smirking, I finally reach the castle doors, propped wide open into the night. If I thought the gardens were decadent, the innards of the castle are beyond my wildest dreams.

Pearly steps descend into a white marble-floored ballroom, and mirrored walls make it look as if the dancing endures for all eternity. Although . . . the more I look, the more convinced I become that there are certain figures in the mirrors that aren't present on the dance floor. In one corner of the massive room, a string quartet plucks away at a bouncy waltz, and the ballroom swirls and sweeps in time. The ceiling has been bewitched to emulate the moonsless night sky, freckled with swirling constellations in a swathe of indigo. More candelabras line the walls, imparting an eerie, atmospheric glow.

Masks of all shapes and colors leer at me—devils and domino masks, ghouls and beasts, monsters and porcelain. The beasts are certainly out tonight.

It all feels so gauzy, so surreal. And then the spell is broken when I see the man responsible for it all.

King De'havelin reclines on his throne on the far end of the ballroom. His crown of golden leaves sparkles, resplendent atop his matching hair. From the trim of his beard to his boots, every bit of him is polished to perfection. Yet, he is alone on his throne. He makes no attempt to join the revelry around him. His fingers tap anxiously on the armrests of his throne as his eyes flit from face to face, though what he's looking for in a sea of masks, I couldn't guess. He manages to somehow seem both bored and paranoid. Mostly, he looks lonely. A room filled with subjects at his own party, and yet he stands apart.

He won't get any sympathy from me.

In fact, it's a feat for me not to jump up on a table and lob a fork at his eyeball. Kick over the wine fountains and set the lavish curtains ablaze. But that would ruin Liam's plans. So, I take a cleansing breath and douse the flames licking at my insides.

Not yet, Iona.

As I cast one final look around the room, I see them.

Five figures on the far side of the room, standing still and straight while everyone else is twirling and merrymaking. Two women, three men.

A jackal, its mouth gaping open in silent cackles.

A fox, elegant but sly.

A stag, antlers curling into majesty.

A cat, silver mask gleaming in the light.

And lastly, the crow from the woods, looming over them all.

Even though their eyes are obscured, I know they're watching me. I feel their gazes poking holes into my body.

My mouth goes dry as my eyes narrow, and suddenly I'm sweeping down the stairs, intent on finding them. The fear I felt earlier has rearranged itself into desperation for answers, and I shove through the crowd.

They know me. How?

"Don't you dare run," I mutter under my breath. "Don't you dare."

Every few moments, I lose sight of them as a couple waltzes into my path, and my heart seizes, only for them to still be there, heads tilted. As if they pity me.

Someone grabs my arm, and I whirl around, teeth bared, to find a young woman wearing a sage green dress. Her decolletage crawls with vicious thorns that match the tiara adorning her head.

"Your dress is beautiful," she says, her speech slurred from overindulgence.

"And yours," I say hurriedly, not bothering with a curtsy as I whip my head around, only to see that they've vanished.

"No," I groan, craning my head this way and that to catch a glimpse of one of them, but it's as if they were nothing but a figment of my imagination. Scattered. Gone. I let out a sound of frustration, feeling suddenly overwhelmed and exhausted, surrounded by all this extravagance and complete *waste*. Cursing to myself, I snatch a glass of wine from a nearby table and take large, vengeful sips as I scan the crowd helplessly.

I despise this. This king, these people, the disparity—all of it.

Setting the glass back onto the table, I set my sights on another flight of stairs leading out of this hell, and begin the slow, arduous process of wading through the sea of masks toward them. I've made it about halfway through, my head swiveling this way and that as I scour the crowd for the animal masks, when suddenly I'm whisked off my feet and into a dance. Dazed, I look up into the pointed snout of a jackal mask. The same one I saw earlier, standing with the crow and others. The hairs on the back of my neck stand at attention, and every instinct I have screams at me to run.

Instead, I say, "A gentleman would have asked before forcing me into a dance."

The man behind the mask chuckles. He's enormous. His suit barely contains him. "I am no gentleman."

My spine goes rigid. "No. You're an animal."

"And you're a bloody nightmare."

I sneer up at him. "You've no idea."

His laughter is rich as he whirls me out. "Oh, but I do."

Then I'm in another's arms, the fox's.

"Who are you?" I demand as we twirl around the room.

He's silent as his cold fingers twine my own, but I feel his stare needling me from behind his mask. I lurch to get away, but his grip is unyielding, caging me. I catch sight of us in the wall-length mirror, my red skirts swirling around me, my face stark against it. White. I watch the fox as he leans down to whisper in my ear.

"You're not asking the most interesting question. What you should be asking is, who are *you*?"

My teeth clamp together as I reach for his lapel, but I find nothing but air. He simply vanished. I collide with another body, swept up into a graceful twirl. I round on the person, fully intending on clubbing whoever it is, but all logic and reason is flung from my mind when I see him.

"There you are," he purrs.

He's dressed in his trademark color. Black. No one wears it like Liam Blackwater.

Everything, from his pants to his suit to his waistcoat, fits him like a glove. Elaborate threading accentuates the collar and buttons of his coat, while dark patterns that curiously resemble his tattoos invite the eye to roam down his vest. I'm used to seeing him in all black attire, but not like this. Not with his hair slicked back from his face, save for a few stubborn strands that refuse their orders. Not with this gold-trimmed collar hugging the back of his neck as if he's some sort of aristocrat. Even his boots have achieved a new level of polish, and they were already always so clean. A skull-like mask covers his eyes and nose, leaving only the lower half of his face on display. His eyes shine through the holes like gems. Eyes I know so very well.

I'd know him anywhere.

Even among the pearls of society, he is by far the most captivating. He's looking at me as if, for once, that mouth of his doesn't quite know what to say. I am so relieved to see him. The past few moments feel like a bad dream, and I've finally woken up.

"I beg your pardon, do I know you?"

His lips twitch. "Apologies. My name is Liam."

"And my name is Iona."

"Iona, I've been looking for you."

Innumerable fiery little stars flare to life inside my chest. "You find me every time."

He lifts me into a twirl, and my dress fans out around us in a cascade of red as my arms wrap around his neck. I breathe in the scent of him, of salty skies and endless suns, and wish it could always be this way. Just me and him.

"You look spectacular," he whispers as he sets me down, his touch trailing down my arms. "Strider, you're beautiful."

I brush my gloved knuckles down his smooth cheek. "So are you."

A new song begins with the plucking of a violin. At first, it's slow, and we sway back and forth, our shadows wavering elegantly on the floor. It's a mournful melody, but achingly lovely.

After a few moments, the rhythm picks up and we glide seamlessly across the floor, neither of us missing a step. The song turns sensual, the violin crooning.

He dips me low. His fingers trace a scorching trail down my exposed chest as his mouth presses against my ear. "I can't decide if I like you better in this dress, or out of it."

"You know," I muse as the harp joins in, a delicate waterfall of notes. He brings me back up, his expression turning carefully neutral as he pulls me in close. "You don't have to choose. We still have tonight."

He inhales, letting it out in a slow whoosh. "One last night. I'd better make it count." He meant it as a joke, but it feels like a gut punch.

"It's not goodbye," I say, though I can't be certain it's the truth. "I don't want it to be goodbye."

There. That's better.

First, his mother. Then, Collin. Oliver. Now, me. Leaving him, one after another. After he tried so hard to stop them. To save them.

He gives me a reassuring look. "I'll not get in your way, Strider. As someone who spent years searching for himself in every nook and cranny of the realm, I understand why you need to go." He lets out a one-note laugh. "I thought three months was enough time to brace myself for letting you go. Turns out it wasn't. It's harder than I anticipated, that's all."

My heart trips over itself. "You always come back for me. Now, it's my turn."

We whirl around, and suddenly I'm pinned against his chest. "You asked me a question yesterday. I have your answer, by the way."

I frown up at him. "I don't recall."

We step in time with the music, almost floating. "You asked me what I've been looking for, all this time."

Shame floods me at the mention of the horrible things I said during our fight. "Liam, I was being an asshole when I said that. I didn't—"

"But it's a genuine question. One I didn't have a good answer for until recently. Eighty-seven days ago, to be exact."

Don't, I want to say.

His hand brushes my cheek. "At first, I wanted to save my mother from her illness. But it wasn't just that. I wanted adventure. To feel alive on the precipice of peril. Then, I wanted notoriety. Wealth. But it was never enough. I never knew what it was to be content; there was always more to seek. Then, you tore into my life. A tenacious little beast of a thing, and I realized that not for one single moment since I met you have I felt unsatisfied. I love the sea because it is ferocious and unpredictable and wild, and I never thought I could give it up, but with you, Strider, with you, I would never have to. I'm not telling you this to make it harder to leave. That, I understand. I'm telling you this so you know you have something to come back to. Whenever you're ready."

The fissure in my heart that Liam put there eighty-seven days ago splits wide open. "Oh, Liam." I trace his jaw, his bottom lip. "Give me time to find the pieces of myself that have been lost. Let me break this curse. Then, I promise. I will find my way back to you."

Instead of responding, Liam hoists me into the air, only to bring me down slowly, so slowly, our bodies crushed together. The music swells into a crescendo, but suddenly everyone seems to fade into the background. There is no castle, no curse, no ticking clock—only us. The moment my feet touch the floor, he rips his mask off, cups my jaw, and kisses me with such unexpected intensity, I almost gasp. The crowd around us titters and squeals, but I pay no mind. If I know one thing, it is this: nothing will stop me from finding him once I have finished what I have come here to do. Nothing.

Chimes ring out, and my eyes snap open. Quarter till twelve bells.

"The maze," I breathe, pulling away. "We should go."

Then, we will leave. Together. Liam's expression hardens. "*I* should go."

My lips part, and I feel a scowl coming on. "You're not going by yourself. I told you that."

"It could be dangerous," he retorts half-heartedly.

"What if it's a trap, and because you insisted on going by yourself, you get ambushed? You have no idea who you're meeting in there. I'm coming. You can't stop me."

"I *could* stop you," he mutters, but there's no bite to it. He stares unhappily at me, working his jaw, and finally relents. "But I won't. I trust you." Liam hesitates for a moment, then grabs my arm. "If things go badly, run. Aye?"

"Aye."

I see it in the set of his mouth, though. We both know I'm done running.

67

THE FOG

We leave the castle and stroll through the gardens, the hedge maze looming in the distance. It's strange to look up to a gaping hole in the sky where the moons are supposed to be. I know this happens every year, but something about it feels deeply unsettling. This whole night feels that way, truth be told.

Though I want to tell Liam of my strange arrival, I don't want to set him off balance before whatever, or whoever, he's about to encounter. He's got enough on him as it is. I know how he thinks. He's barely allowing me to accompany him as it is; if he senses there is the slightest chance I could be in danger, he will abandon meeting the letter-writer to keep me safe.

The alternative is that I leave alone. But if this meeting goes awry, and Liam were to get hurt, I'd never forgive myself.

I will tell him once we're finished. It's the best I can do.

We pass a couple holding hands, murmuring to each other in one of the twinkling gazebos. Her dress is nothing but the most delicate gauze shrouded around her body, as if she walked through a series of spider webs. In fact, once we get a little closer, I realize that hundreds of tiny, glittering spiders are crawling through the fabric. They pay no attention to us as we pass, so I make every effort not to gawk.

The path leading to the maze is lined with crimson spider lilies and lanterns, and though I saw many couples coming in and out when I first arrived, it now seems to be mostly deserted.

Perhaps the late hour? However, shrieks of laughter and animated conversation drift from inside the maze, which comforts me immensely. At least we won't be alone in there. A thin mist spills from the entrance, and Liam and I glance at each other.

"Never liked mazes," he comments.

"Let's get this over with," I say.

And after, let's go home.

We step inside.

It becomes clear almost immediately that, within the maze, things are not as they appear, nor what they should be. We take a right, expecting to find at least three people according to the sounds of giggles coming from that direction. But when we round the corner, we are alone, except for several statues wearing grotesque masks. They leer down at us; their mouths stretched into menacing grins.

"I heard voices," I mutter, confused.

"Aye," Liam responds, glancing up warily at the statues.

We pass them, and I risk a glance behind us, only to see that their heads have swiveled to look after us. Skin crawling, I pick up the pace.

As we walk, I start to notice the majority of the hedge walls are covered with bright, crawling flowers. So, at every corner, I use a dagger to lop off a few blooms so we can tell which direction we chose. Either both of our senses of direction are off, which they're not, or the flowers are growing back, because we have yet to reach an intersection that isn't flourishing with blooms. Not a gap to be seen. It feels as if we've made no progress, and yet, the more we delve, the more silent it becomes. Noiseless like the woods I ran through to get here.

The mist has thickened.

My resolve wavers. Something is wrong. The same *wrong* I encountered in the woods with the crow. I am doing Liam a disservice by not telling him what I experienced earlier. He deserves to know.

"Liam, I need to tell you something."

In low, hushed tones, I tell him everything. Every lurid detail up until he stole me away on the dance floor. By the end of the story, his grip on my hand is hard enough to grind bone.

"Ow," I cry, snatching my hand away and glowering.

His eyes widen, and he takes a few steps back, running a hand over his mouth. His mask still dangles from his left hand.

"I'm sorry. Bloody hell, I'm so sorry, Strider. I . . . *agghh*. We should have left."

"I wasn't going to leave you."

"I would have left *with* you," he argues. His hands go to his hips, and he stares up at the sky as if he has one veritable strand of patience left.

"That's exactly why I didn't want to tell you. We're here, Liam. After all this time. I couldn't let you walk away when you're this close to the impetus for *everything*. What about Collin?"

"Stop deciding things for me," he snaps, pacing. "I do what I think is best, and in hindsight *I think it best* that we *left* the moment I clapped eyes on you in that fucking castle."

"We're doing it again." The softness of my voice jars him worse than if I'd screamed.

He stops dead in his tracks. "Doing what?"

"Fighting when we're scared."

He has nothing to say to that.

"Do what you came here to do, Liam. Take as long as you need. Then we'll leave and never return, and this will all be nothing but a strange memory."

He stares hard at me as he mulls it over. If we leave now, he may never get the chance to learn of Collin's fate. The letter-writer might get spooked and cut ties with him. Finally, he groans. "I'm not finished with you about this."

I throw my hands up in the air. "Do your worst. Later."

We trudge forward, but my guts begin to twist with apprehension.

We haven't come across a single other person in here. And it's so quiet. Too quiet, except for the sound of our footsteps and our breathing. Round we go, right, then left, then left again, but the maze seems to go on forever. I've stopped cutting off flowers, since they seem to regrow the moment we turn our backs.

Then we hear it.

Screams that cut through the silence like a blade. A voice we both know exceedingly well.

Luhan.

We trade wide glances for a split moment, then lurch into a sprint. Ice trickles down my spine. My heart rams against my chest. How the hell did he end up here? It sounds like he's in utter *agony*. I've never heard *anyone* scream like that. Like he's getting turned inside out.

Proctor's teeth. Is this a trick? Perhaps.

What if it isn't?

I push the horrific thoughts away, concentrating on where it seems to be coming from.

With every step, the fog grows denser. We round the corner—

Another scream rips through the air. This time, from my right. Then, the wet sound of something ripping. And someone laughing. A man.

"Luhan!"

I lurch toward the noise, slipping on the damp ground, but the path seems to go on forever.

"How are we supposed to find him?" I whimper to Liam. My nerves are frayed, my hands shaking. If anything happens to Luhan . . .

I realize Liam never answered me.

I turn to him only to find that I'm alone.

My mouth opens to scream, but suddenly, white hot pain explodes in the back of my skull, and I'm gone before I hit the ground.

68

THE LAST MEMORY

A scream rips me out of my sleep and into a waking nightmare.

I lurch out of bed, not even bothering to shrug on my robes. There's no time. In nothing but a nightgown, I fling open my doors toward the sound. Somewhere in the foyer, glass shatters. Objects clatter to the ground.

Something—a table?—makes a horrendous screeching sound like it's being dragged across the marble floor.

I bolt past a window to try and get a sense of the time, but it's as if a black shroud is covering the castle. I can't see anything at all. There are no stars. No moons. Fellow maids and housekeepers peek out into the hallway with wide, scared eyes, but I surge past them.

Fear, true fear, sinks its claws into me.

Whatever is happening, Vesper is in danger. I know that scream. I am too late.

I run faster than I ever have in my life down the hall, toward another blood-curdling scream.

I am almost to the set of doors from which the screams are emanating when suddenly Holland bursts through them, his golden hair sticking up wildly, his eyes haunted and hollow. There are scratch marks on his face, as if something attempted to gouge his eyes out.

Before I can utter a word, he grabs my waist, shaking his head violently as he wrenches me backward.

"Don't go in there." His grip is so tight, it hurts. It's going to leave a bruise. I've never been so scared. "Artie, don't go in there."

"Let go of me," I shriek, squirming and kicking to get loose. I don't care if I get punished.

"Is she in there? Is Vesper in there? What's happening?"

"She's in there, alright," Holland pants through his teeth. He looks exhausted.

I surge forward, my voice high with hysteria. "Is she hurt?"

Of all things, he laughs—a shrill, hysterical sound that is so unlike Holland, I feel momentarily sure that this is a dream. Everyone is losing their mind. Even me.

I'm seeing things on the walls.

"She doesn't need you. She doesn't need anyone," Holland says, clamping his arms around me even tighter. It must be the panic, for there's a maniacal look in his eyes. Like he's not afraid but *exhilarated*.

Silas rounds the corner, uncharacteristically disheveled with sleep. With his white pallor, pale hair, and wild eyes, he looks like a phantom. Another scream emanates from inside the room, and without a moment's hesitation, Silas rushes the doors. He pulls once with his hands, then with his entire body.

The doors quiver but remain shut. However, something spills through the cracks. Something undulating and oily and intangible.

Magic.

"Let me in, Vesper," he shouts, pounding on the door. "NOW."

"Let me go," I plead, my eyes burning with tears as more vases topple loudly to the ground, and nearby castle occupants start to shout. "She needs me."

Holland's eyes are shiny and wide, and his hands shake as he holds me in place. His lips move, but I can barely register what he's saying above the pounding of blood in my ears.

"What?" It's more of a sob than the actual word.

His gaze bores into mine, and the conviction I see there turns my blood to ice. "She's a Weaver."

Three words crack open my entire world.

It's been three years since that horrible night.

The night when everything changed, and Vesper became a Weaver.

It's all still so strange to me. I've never seen a Weaver come into their magic so late. Usually, they're born with it already there, as if preordained. That's how it was for me. But I don't know what else it could be. I've never seen powers like hers. Frightening. Dreadful.

I shouldn't think that.

She's still the same little girl I've always known and loved. She still needs someone to take care of her. Brush her hair, make her bed, and fuss over her vegetable intake. I will always tell her stories when she can't sleep.

Although, since the king ordained her a Rook, I've seen less of her than I ever have. The Rooks, I've learned, are not considered people here. They are the kingdom's most well-guarded secrets—a gilded pit of the realm's most venomous vipers.

The training was nightmarish.

Every night, she'd come home hollow-eyed and tight-lipped, covered in a tapestry of bruises and slices.

"Who is doing this to you?" I'd demand, seething. She's a child. Who could do that to a child? She was only thirteen when she came into her magic.

She never told me, of course. No one knows who the other Rooks are. The only reason Vesper hasn't been relocated herself is that she is still, firstly, a ward of Savastane. I doubt Lord and Lady Osias even know what has transpired. We are still trying to understand ourselves.

"It's necessary," she'd tell me evenly of her injuries, looking at me with eyes I'm still unused to. No longer the dark brown they've always been, but a startling, burning gold. One of many ways in which little pieces of her changed that night.

Sometimes, I catch her shadow watching me. There are corners of her room, late at night, that seem dark enough to fall through and never return.

I've noticed a change between her and Silas, too. On more than one occasion, I've overheard them in an alcove, arguing in hushed, barbed tones. I wonder if it has anything to do with Vesper's extensive training with Holland. I catch Silas watching them. His eyes can be so cold.

I know they're friends, but that boy frightens me sometimes.

The most unsettling change, at least to me, is that despite the exhaustive tutoring, despite the brutality of the training, and even though she will be indentured to the king for the rest of her life, she seems happy.

This year, she is sixteen, making her the youngest Rook ever to be enlisted into the king's service.

Today is Prince Silas's eighteenth birthday.

Naturally, there will be a grand ball thrown in his honor, and I've been bustling around all day to prepare. Now, at nine bells, the celebration is in full swing, and I've just stepped outside to gather more mint for the strawberry pies. I weave through the gardens by orblight, watching my step to avoid trampling the parsley, basil, or rosemary. The mint is in the last row, of course. It's as I bend down to pick a few handfuls that I freeze. There's the romantic string music coming from the grand ballroom, and the chirp of crickets, and the hum of chatter of our guests—

There it is again.

This time, I'm pretty certain it's a scream I'm hearing. It's coming from inside the castle.

Every muscle tenses. I glance around for any sign of danger—an invasion of some sort, perhaps, but the night seems to be otherwise undisrupted.

Vesper. Vesper is in the castle, too. I last saw her with Silas, the King, and the queen. If there is danger, any danger at all, I know without a doubt that Vesper will engage with it. She will try to protect them.

But who is protecting her?

Casting my wicker basket of herbs aside, I take off at a sprint toward the castle. The music hasn't stopped, so it seems whatever has happened hasn't seeped into the ballroom yet. My mind reels through the possibilities when suddenly the ground-level doors burst open, and I find myself face-to-face with the one person I needed to find.

I don't know how to make sense of what I'm looking at.

Vesper's ice blue dress, delicate lace layers on the bodice courtesy of hours of work by me, is covered in blood. Her face . . . the horror etched there . . . the blood spattered over her mouth.

"I didn't mean to," she says in a strange, breathy voice that's so unlike her. Her unsettling, ethereal eyes are glowing, and I fight the urge to take a step back.

"V," I say in a wobbly voice, "what happened?"

A single tear rolls down her face. By the time it reaches her chin, it's stained red. "My shadow—m-m-my shadow—" she starts shaking so badly, I grab her arms to hold her in place, and I feel a terror inside my chest unlike any other. "She h-h-h-hurt the queen. But I didn't tell her to. She's n-n-never done that. Ever."

My fingers dig into her skin, and my breath hitches.

"The queen is d-d-d-dead, Artie. But I didn't . . ." she shakes her head, her hands flying to her mouth as her chest starts to judder. "I didn't m-m-mean to. It felt like I was a puppet, and someone was moving me, but I didn't want to. I fought it. It wanted me to hurt the king, but I resisted and—and—" her eyes are impossibly wide, and she's shaking her head hard enough to rattle her brain. "I loved her, Artie. I would never . . ." Her eyes meet mine, pleading, Desperate. Foreign. "Do you believe me?"

I stare at her face, a face I've known for most of my life. We are only seven years apart.

I don't have to comb through my most fond memories of her or count the ways in which she's good and not evil, or consider her darker tendencies, because it makes no difference. I never had a sister, but Vesper is close enough. I believe her.

"Yes," I say, grabbing her hand. "Come, now. We need to run."

Her eyes widen in shock, and she looks on the verge of sobbing.

"No. No. Artie, I can explain to them. I can explain that I didn't mean to. It was an accident. Surely, they'll understand."

"No, V," I say, in what I hope is a gentle voice. "I'm afraid not."

We plunge into the Grimwood before the whole place explodes into shades of Gray and Red.

All too quickly, I hear the pursuit close behind us, snapping twigs and rustling leaves. When I turn my head to look behind us, I see nothing but dark wood. A chill seeps down my spine. Something is following us.

But Vesper has come to an abrupt stop, and though I urge her forward, she won't move.

It's as if she no longer hears me. "Einar?"

Suddenly, a boy appears in front of us, right in front of us, and I'd have screamed if Vesper hadn't clapped a hand over my mouth.

He—Einar—does not feel compelled to introduce himself to me. Instead, moss-green eyes narrow on Vesper, and he grabs her by the shoulders, shaking hard. "They're summoning all the Rooks. They're saying you murdered Queen Lorelai. Tell me it's not true. Tell me."

There's a beat of silence where I consider tackling this strange boy to the ground if he doesn't release her, but Vesper cuts through the silence with a strangled sob. "My shadow did. But I didn't want to. I didn't tell her to. I think—I think someone else told her to. And she listened."

His face pales. "That's not how Weaving works. No one controls your magic but you."

Her face crumples. "I'm not a Weaver. I'm something else, Einar. I think you were right about me."

They share a long, pointed look, and I have the distinct feeling that there is quite a bit of significant information that Vesper has withheld from me. My stomach drops. She's always told me everything. So much has changed.

A distant rustling sounds, shortly followed by a voice. "Come out, come out, wherever you are."

Holland.

My heart doesn't know whether to soar or plummet. I turn to

Vesper, but her attention is still trained on the boy with unruly copper hair. They seem to share a deep camaraderie, almost like—

Oh. He's a Rook, too. That's why I've never seen him before.

"Holland will try to kill me," Vesper says in the smallest voice I've ever heard.

"He will succeed," Einar says. "I'll make sure of it."

My mouth twists into a snarl, but they share a tight smile as he unsheathes his sword and tosses it to her. I'm utterly confused. Is he helping or not?

"I'm going with you, after," he says quietly, wincing when another twig snaps, much closer now. "I know some merchants, we'll sneak on their boats—"

"No," Vesper snaps. "Einar, no. You must stay here. You can't let this happen again to someone else. It's too horrible. You're the only Rook left that isn't—" she makes a face "—vile."

The freckled boy accepts the refusal with stoic dignity. "You realize you can never stop running after this."

Vesper nods, then looks to me with a shaky smile. "I will have Artie, and we will be alright."

Warmth permeates my chest, and though I've no idea where we are to go, or if we will ever be able to return home, I know she's right. We will take care of each other.

"Take Artie and hide," Vesper commands, and my mouth falls open.

"You don't mean to fight Holland, do you?" I whisper, bewildered. "You cannot hope to best him. He's unbeatable. He will kill you."

"That's the point. Please—trust me. If I don't do this, he'll never stop chasing us," she says, pushing me away. "You and Einar go, before he sees you. Go now!" Her eyes, like golden coals, begin to glow as the dark around us deepens. "No matter what you see, do not come out."

Reluctantly, I let Einar tug me back through the foliage, behind a fallen tree. On our bellies, we crawl along it until we reach its decayed branches and peer through them. Though my view is impeded, I can still make out Vesper's slight form and the way she stiffens when

Holland emerges through the trees. His sword gleams in the moonslight, and I want to cry.

It wasn't supposed to be this way.

I look to the Rook next to me, but he's staring intently at Holland and Vesper, paying me no mind at all. How can making himself invisible help Vesper now? If he's a Rook, why isn't he helping her?

Is it because he intends to stay and spy? I understood so little of their conversation. Once Vesper and I are away from here, I'll have her explain. She owes me at least that.

"Where do you think you're going, you fucking traitor?" Holland snarls.

Vesper says nothing. Simply bends her knees and hoists her sword arm forward in a ready stance. My heart aches to see it. I don't wish to see either of them hurt.

But the queen is dead.

"Nothing to say for yourself?" Holland demands, taking two steps forward. "Did you always plan to kill her? Did your father tell you to do this?"

For a few moments, there is no sound but the wind in the trees. Even the insects and creatures of the forest watch in silence as prince and soldier draw arms against each other. Then Vesper speaks. "You may kill me tonight, but I'll never leave you, Holland. On the darkest nights, you'll see me in its corners. When the shadows grow long, you'll feel my fingers around your neck."

She smiles, and it's so gruesome, I almost turn away. I almost wonder if I've made a mistake. "When you take your last breath, it won't be Death that comes to carry you away. It'll be me. I'll be waiting for you."

The bite of her words chills me. And though Holland carries the confidence of the best swordsman in the kingdom, there is an unmistakable trace of fear that crosses his face.

They lunge at each other, and when their swords meet, it's louder than thunder. It's the worst sound I've ever heard. Each blow seems to reverberate throughout my chest and cut open a different part of me.

Gone are the dreams I harbored of living out the rest of my days in beautiful, wondrous Celosia with the man I loved, even if from afar. I would have hoarded our stolen moments like gems in my pockets, with the sister I never had, even though there are parts of her now that are separate from me. She would have changed, and I would have stayed the same.

Living a quiet but fulfilling life. I would have been so happy.

I blink, and all my dreams drift away on the night breeze.

Beyond, Vesper and Holland duel viciously. Their swords sing through the air and clash against each other repeatedly. They trade blows meant to kill, and very nearly do just that so many times. I had no idea Vesper had become so skilled with a sword. Every time I think Holland's got her, she blocks with strength beyond her years or parries with skill that exceeds my understanding. But Holland is older, larger, and all his time spent training in the mines gives him the upper hand.

He gains ground on her, pushing them both out of the woods and toward the cliff just beyond the tree line. It's a sheer drop off to a watery grave below. My body tenses, and I push up on my elbows to see them, but Einar drags me back down.

"No," he mouths, his solemn eyes boring into mine. "This is the important part."

He tenses suddenly, his fingers clenched into fists. Veins bulge from his temple, but though my gaze swivels between him and Vesper and the fight, I see nothing happening.

And so, I have no hope of reaching Vesper in time when Holland, with a swipe clearly meant to decapitate, slices a gash over Vesper's left ear. She recoils, stepping back.

It was one step too far. Vesper falls over the edge.

My mouth opens in a silent scream as my entire chest caves in. My breaths come in juddering gasps.

But Einar hasn't moved. A cold hand wraps around my wrist; I follow his eyes to where Holland stands, still as a statue. As if he cannot believe what he's done. After a few moments, he wobbles to the edge of the cliff and peers down. Whatever he sees causes him to clap a hand over his mouth and stumble back. Abruptly, he buries his face in his hands and sobs. His whole body shakes with them, and when the screams come, my heart breaks.

I hear them, long after he's gone. Finally, Einar relaxes. Sweat coats his skin.

Dampens his shirt.

"Go," he pants.

I run to the edge of the cliff, my heart in my throat. Before I make it, I see one hand, then another, then Vesper's wonderful, red face pop up beyond the ledge. She grunts with the exertion of pulling herself up, and I eagerly crouch to lend a hand.

"How?"

"Einar . . . played a . . . trick."

"He—he made Holland think you'd fallen somehow?" I surmise, in a bit of a stupor.

"He's an illusionist," she says through clenched teeth. "But he doesn't like to use his power. It—"

Leaves crunch behind us.

Oh, no. Not now.

I whirl around to see an approaching Gray, barely a dot in the woods. My eyes dart to Einar, but he's still hidden behind the tree. Drained.

He cannot help me. Vesper is still halfway off the cliff. We're cornered. I am on my own.

I cannot allow the Gray to interrupt. An idea forms, and I have no choice but to snatch it and run. Getting to my feet, I hurdle through the woods toward him, and only once I'm in his direct line of vision do I burst into tears. He freezes, taken aback by my outburst.

"Help me," I gasp, throwing myself into his arms. "I can't—I can't believe—"

"Where did she go?" The distorted voice asks, and I flail about, screaming.

"I—I don't know." I slide a dagger from its sheath on the Gray's hip as tears streak down my face, and don't give myself a chance to hesitate as I drive it up into his neck; blood spurts.

Before I can disentangle myself from him, the Gray stumbles

forward, and we fall heavily to the ground. But not before he rips the knife out of my hand.

Agony is a band around my thigh, and I gnash my teeth together to keep from screaming. Grunting with the effort, I wriggle out from underneath the dead Gray and roll him over. With short, pained gasps, I get to a sitting position and roll my skirts up to find a gash so deep in my thigh that I see bone.

He got me before he died.

Panic hits me like a wall, and I have no choice but to lie back down as hot tears cascade down my cheek. It is like this that I cry, careful not to make any noise at all. It is a little while before I hear footfalls approaching.

"Oh, Artie," Vesper gasps, appearing over me. The gash above her ear weeps blood, and it covers her neck, her shoulder. It'll leave a scar. When she sees my thigh, her hands fly to her mouth, and I see the realization in her eyes. It's the same one I had.

I cannot go with her. Not like this.

I would only slow her down.

"Here, let's get you up," she says, but when I sit up, the pain becomes unbearable. Blood is a pool beneath me, and I'm starting to feel lightheaded.

"No," I shake my head. "You must go. Now. Without me."

Panic shines in her eyes, but I press on, smoothing the tremor from my voice as much as I can. "Einar said he can get you on a merchant ship, and that is what you must do. You can never return, though. And you must never use the name Vesper Osias again. What is the name you used when you'd play pretend with Silas?"

I see the hurt in her face at the mention of her former best friend's name. He'll despise her for the rest of his life, I'm certain. "Iona Strider."

"That's your new name," I say softly. "Do you have control over your shadows, yes or no?"

Uncertainty clouds her features. "I was still training. I don't know. It's still so strange, and—"

That's all the information I need. I place a hand on her back, between her shoulder blades, and she lowers herself to me, because she thinks I'm embracing her. I am.

I'm also cursing her.

She hisses through her teeth when it starts to burn, pushing at me, but I hold her even tighter until I'm finished. "This will dampen your magic, to make it easier to control, but it will erode over time. I cannot stop that."

I don't tell her that it's a two-fold curse.

"Artie, you can come with me. We can get you healed," she whimpers, tugging at my hand, but I can't bear the thought of standing.

"I'm afraid not." My chest aches. "You'll have to go without me this time."

"But you take care of me," she sobs, throwing her arms around my neck. "You've always taken care of me."

"You'll learn."

"Then I'm staying, too." Oh, my heart.

I shake my head too fast. "If you stay, they'll kill you. All of this will be for nothing."

"I'll come back for you."

"No," I say vehemently. "You will never return here. Understand?" She says nothing, but her eyes shine with defiant, furious tears. "Understand?"

"I love you, Artie."

I steel myself against the despondence I feel. "I love you, Vesper. It's time for you to go. I'll be alright. They won't hurt me."

I nod to Einar, and he pulls Vesper away, who is well and truly keening now. I watch their figures retreat until shadows swallow them up, and my only solace is that they're not Vesper's.

Of course, the Grays find me here and drag me back to the castle. Of course, they interrogate me. When I am unable to answer any questions about the assassination of Queen Lorelai, they turn violent.

It starts with a few strips of flesh—a few beatings.

Then I'm missing entire days, and waking up in a pool of my own blood and vomit. When that doesn't work, they throw me in The Craw, where one end of my cell falls away into an endless ravine.

Everyone breaks after a few days in here.

But I have no reason to break, for I have done nothing wrong.

My sole consolation is that if Vesper can escape Celosia, she will be safe after a few days. And she will never return, for she will not remember me. Not only did I place a dulling curse on her, but I wove in a memory curse, too. It will work slowly, but over the course of the next few weeks, she will forget Celosia and Savastane entirely. Wherever she arrives, her memories will slowly adapt and overwrite themselves to be of that place instead.

If ever I were to see her again, she would not know me. It is as much a comfort as it breaks my heart.

The Grays inform me that the king stole away in the middle of the night with his army to wreak retribution on my homeland for sending their daughter as an assassin to murder the queen.

Savastane is not large. If they were not expecting the attack, it is not difficult to believe that it was a massacre.

They tell me there is nothing left of my homeland, nothing but ash and bones.

There is no one around to hear my wails but the beast in the void below, so I scream and grieve and rage until my voice is nothing but a rattle.

On bad days, I worry they left me down here to rot. On my worst days, I wonder if they simply forgot about me.

I had always heard that the magic in The Craw will eat men alive if they don't jump to their death first. The ends of my hair are starting to pale, so I suppose my choices are becoming clear. It's just that I once knew a prince with gold in his hair. I forget his name. But I have this feeling that one day, he will come for me.

I hope it's soon, for my skin is starting to burn, and the magic has begun whispering horrid things. I don't quite feel like myself anymore.

69

LOOK WHAT THE MAGIC HAS DONE TO US

I gasp, coming out of the dream like I was drowning. No, not a dream at all.

A *memory*. *Her* memories. Artemisia. And the other girl. Vesper.

This whole time, I never considered she was . . . me. Not because I could never properly remember what I saw. I just couldn't see myself in her through Artemisia's perspective. The dark eye color, the long, glossy hair. My entire face and build are so different now from the girl I once seemed to be. In my mind's eye, I have always been scarred, fearful, and wiry. Never one to flounce about a kingdom as if the realm bowed to me. Even now, I look so different.

The dreams—memories—are always blurred around the edges when I wake from them, as if my mind is trying its best to expunge them because it knows they are not mine to begin with.

But.

I was a Rook.

All the times Basi questioned my skill, my instincts, he'd been right. Once, I had known the footwork. My muscles still remembered, even if my mind did not. I was educated. Well-mannered. Prim, even.

In the strange, dark passageway in which I find myself, I cover my face, suddenly overcome with the revelation. If I were sixteen when I fled Celosia, when the queen died, that means it's been seven years since. I am twenty-three years old.

So then, I really did lose control of my shadow that day in Marrin. That memory is real. The realization feels like a knife plunged into my chest, and I lay my head against a cool, moist wall.

If I break the curse, do I get my memories back? Would I want them, if I could?

Would I want to remember my family, even though Savastane is a wasteland? My heart squeezes painfully at the thought. I am the reason for The Sorrows. An entire kingdom was razed to the ground because of me. If I sit with that understanding, I will surely rip myself apart. I push it away for another time.

I cannot imagine, for the life of me, why I would have killed the queen. I was happy, from the memories I saw. Artie was happy. But I've never felt what I described—like someone was trying to maneuver it. Was I lying?

Even when I lose control of my shadow, it does not feel like that. Rather, my grip on something is simply starting to slip. What did I mean, I wasn't a Weaver? While I've always suspected that, what made me sure? What have I forgotten that I need to remember about the night I came into my power?

Einar seemed to know. If I can find that boy, he might know what's wrong with me. My eyes fly open, and I suck in a startled breath.

I think—I think Einar already found *me*.

Didn't the Crow tell me the same thing Einar told me seven years ago? That would mean . . . that would mean those other figures wearing the masks were also Rooks. They saw me. They'll be coming for me if they've realized who I am. If Einar didn't keep his word. Seven years, after all, is a long time, and Einar is still a Rook. Who knows where his loyalties lie now?

Although he did try to tell me to run. And I, like a fucking fool, did not listen.

I plunge back into the memories, combing over them for details I may have missed. They are hazy at best, and I wonder how I have them in the first place. I recall Artie's hand on my back when she laid the curse on me, and realize that when my magic leaks from me—how else can it be described, if not that—that is why the marks *burn* like they do. It is the curse activating, fighting to force my shadow back into obedience. The curse has been growing weaker, which is why my shadow has been growing stronger.

I wonder what I could do, then, if the shackles of my curse were removed. How powerful am I, when there is no leash on *me*?

Taking a deep, shaking breath, I finally stand, surveying my surroundings. I am smothered in a disembodying darkness. So, I stand still, letting it consume me. Fighting the dark, I've learned, is like fighting the sea. The more you struggle, the more viciously it will drag you down. But if you stay still and calm enough, you might just float.

Magic, too much of it, crackles. My tongue is coated with it, and I want to spit it out. Wherever I am, it is wet. Faintly, I register dripping of some kind. When I move my feet, I feel that the ground is uneven but mostly smooth, and when I reach my hand out, I touch stone.

Tentatively, I take a small step forward, and then another. More uneven stone with a wall on the right side. Two more steps, and then I freeze.

Something, somewhere far below, moves. I hear its rough skin, perhaps scales of some sort, scrape against something. Darkness ripples out and away from it, and I feel the disturbance against my skin. Claws screech against stone. Whatever it is, it is gargantuan. A thick, throaty gurgle echoes from somewhere beneath me, and I swallow.

Whatever it was, it appears to be gone, for I feel the disturbance no more, and all is silent again. Suddenly, a torch flares to life not too far in front of me, and then another, and so on, illuminating a narrow, winding path lined with them on both sides. Between each torch, black gates glint eerily from the firelight. Grabbing one of the torches from the wall, I approach a gate and, with no small amount of trepidation, peer inside.

Alas, nobody's home.

On the other side of the gates is a thin stretch of stone, barely large enough for someone to lie down. Abruptly, it drops off into nothing. Nothing at all.

It all clicks into place, then.

They're not gates at all, but cells, for this is a prison. A prison that gives its occupants two choices: stay, and the magic will corrode you until there is nothing left. Or, jump, and if the fall doesn't kill you, whatever lurks below will.

They call it mercy.

We call it The Craw, Celosia's prison.

I almost chuckle to myself at the irony of it all. I always knew one way or another, I'd end up here. I never imagined it would be so quiet.

Carefully, I walk down the line of cells, my footsteps and the crackle of the torch almost deafening in the tomb-like silence. Where are the prisoners?

How do I get out? How did I get here in the first place?

Ahead, movement makes me come to a halting stop, my right hand clutching my blade so tightly my fingers ache. I wish I'd brought The Twins. I wish so many things.

In the very last cell to the left, something stirs within the pool of darkness. Then, one by one, the torches sputter out, all except for the ones nearest that cell.

I know that cell. I just saw it.

A sharp sob bubbles out of my throat, so sudden and violent, I clap both hands over my mouth. No. It's been seven years. She would be dead by now. Something moves out of the corner of my eye, and I flinch away from it. But it is only my shadow, straining toward the cell. Both her arms reach, fingers extended.

Toward something moving there. "Hello, Vesper."

The voice scares me so badly, I back into the wall opposite the cell, my hands still clamped over my mouth. I'm shaking like a leaf; I don't trust myself to speak.

"Don't be afraid," the voice, like many people speaking all at once, says.

"I'm not," I whisper. "I'm just sad."

There is a pause, and then, "Don't be sad. It is so beautiful down here. Do you hear the music? The magic sings to me."

I swallow thickly. "I'm sorry. I don't hear it."

A scratchy sigh, like dead leaves being blown across cobblestones. "That's sad, too."

Gathering up all my courage, I reach the cell, but even with my torch, the darkness that pools there is thick enough to choke on. There is something inside. Something huddled in the corner, nothing more than tatters of shadow. It moves again, and my skin prickles as a chill slices down my spine.

It's watching me. "What is your name?"

"That's a funny question. She had a name once, but I can't remember it. I've been down here so long." There is another long, hair-raising pause, and when the voice comes again, it's much closer. "I don't think she survived, V."

"Artie." Sobs spasm through me at the name, and finally, finally, she steps into a pool of torchlight.

She has colorless eyes and long, colorless hair from where the magic has pulled and yanked and gouged out every scrap of the woman she used to be. Her face, although unlined, holds no youth. It is as if she has been both preserved and hollowed out by time. Where magic left a void, it did not remain empty. That much, I can see from her eyes. They swirl and slosh as if something watches from behind them.

There is nothing left of the kind, dark-haired beauty I knew once. She told the truth.

Artemisia is gone.

Her white, long fingers wrap around the bars. "You remember her."

"I saw her memories. Like dreams."

She considers that. "Symmetry. Your memories for hers."

The realization stuns me. Of course, there would be a payment for taking my memories.

Of course.

"She told me you weren't supposed to come back here."

My chin wobbles, and I hide it with a hand. "Artie. Someone should have come for you. Oh, no. I'm sorry." I can barely speak past the sobs. She's been down here for seven years. *Seven years.* "I'm so sorry. I didn't know."

She regards me with curiosity, as if I'm an animal she finds amusing.

"I—I've got to get you out," I stutter. "You've been here for much too long—"

"I've been here for centuries."

"I've got to get you out—"

"You were never supposed to come back," she screams suddenly, and I recoil, stumbling backward, but a pale, clawed hand reaches out from the cage and grabs hold of my wrist. Her skin is cold as a corpse, and I can't stop the scream that rips from my throat. The torch falls from my hand and rolls away, sputtering out.

She brings me close, sniffing the air.

"I smell her curse on you. It's old. Rancid."

"You did it to protect me." I struggle to escape her grip, but she won't let go. Her strength is supernatural. Impossible. Maybe if I can remind her, she'll remember. And she'll come back.

Maybe—

Her smile is hellish. "Poor thing. Poor thing." It widens, revealing sharp teeth behind pale lips. "No more cages."

"Let me go," I shriek, panicked, but her grip may as well be steel, and I watch in horror as something black spreads grotesquely up my arm, over my shoulder, and to my back.

"What are you doing?"

It burns. Oh, god, it *burns.*

"I brought you here to set us free," she says.

No. Not like this.

The burning flares, and I buckle to my knees on the hard stone, teeth gritted in agony. It feels like my spine is cracking open, vertebrae by vertebrae. My screams echo as I sink to all fours. The very ground beneath me seems to quake, and a darkness pulses from where I stand, staining the stone and the very air around me.

"Artie, make it stop. *Please.*" I crawl to the bars and latch on with what little strength I have left. She crouches to meet me, angling her face. For a moment, the sadness in her eyes looks almost human. She reaches through the bars and grabs hold of my hand.

"Together, we will make things better," she whispers, but I can barely hear her over the roaring in my ears, and my own guttural screams. Then her many voices turn slick. "Look what the magic has done to us."

The last thing I see before the pain overwhelms me entirely is my own flickering shadow on the wall, but unlike me, it does not crumple.

It stands.

70

A MIDNIGHT OF MY OWN MAKING

I blink awake, my mind as foggy as the grounds around me. I'm sprawled on soft grass, dewy with mist. My hair has come out of its pins and hangs messily around my face. I am otherwise unharmed.

I appear to be in a courtyard of some sort. It almost looks like the core of a maze.

A maze.

The memories swarm over me with a force that leaves me gasping for breath, and I double over, my hand over my mouth. The notion occurs to me that perhaps if I make myself small, so small, and stay quiet, the world will pass me by while I come to terms with what I saw.

Artie. Oh, Artie.

I can't comprehend that this place that seems utterly foreign to me used to be my home. I'd lived here for years. I was . . . a Rook—the very thing I despise most in this realm: a puppet of the king. And I assassinated his wife. A woman who, by all accounts, was kind.

What kind of hellish *creature* was Vesper Osias? I am a stranger in my own body.

However . . . there's a thrumming in my blood that wasn't there before. I feel light, as if manacles I never knew I was wearing have fallen off. Like I'm taking my first breath of fresh air in years, and all the cobwebs in my mind have been swept away.

My eyes alight on a skull mask a few paces away. Liam's mask; he must have dropped it.

I go and pick it up. My own mask falls to the ground, where it stays, and I draw a hidden dagger from my thigh. Slowly, my gaze crawls to something that shouldn't be here, but is. My shadow, a darker patch of night. It raises a hand to point, drawing my attention to the torchlight on the far wall of a corridor in the maze, and the shouting of men. Urgent, frantic shouting. A small cadre of Grays rounds the corner, weapons already drawn.

"Stop right there," one of them commands at the same time another shouts, "That's her!"

I still, the mask clutched tightly in my hands.

"Vesper Osias, come with us. You're under arrest."

I can tell by the poorly disguised tremor in his voice that they did not expect to actually find me here or have to contend with bringing me into captivity. I've been thinking: if I were the youngest Rook, I must have been quite fearsome. Rooks are, after all, the most powerful Weavers in Celosia.

I make no move at all.

"Come with us," the leader says in a soothing voice one would use with a child. "Easy now. No need to be afraid."

There's that word. Afraid?

I think of the woman who died in the Marrin prison, beaten to death.

The children who were taken from their homes to be thrust into the Pits. Their families will never know peace or normalcy again. The children will either die young or become harbingers of violence.

Aya, and the stumps of her wings. The trail of blood she left on the wall.

I think of myself, nearly dead in that cell in Marrin, beneath a heap of crimes that didn't belong to me. Oh, I was terrified. I would have died completely alone.

No, it's not fear I feel. It is the opening of a door that has been closed for much too long.

Now, it is time to see what's on the other side.

My fingers splay, and the darkness, all too eager to do my bidding, follows. It's already dark tonight, but what seeps out of me is something more. Something worse. It stains the night a darker, more infinite shade of black and drapes itself over everything like a shroud. One by one, the Gray's torches are snuffed out, casting us in unnatural darkness. They gasp and exclaim in confusion.

I don't stop there.

I urge the wave of shadow beyond, to the castle. It's breathtaking how easy it is to smother it all. It feels so simple, so instinctual, to urge my shadows forward. Screams of shock and fear pierce the night air. I must see how far I can go, so I reach past the castle to the rest of Celosia. I snake my shadows through every alley and street, extinguishing every scrap of light and flame, and plunging the entire city into a midnight of my own making. After all these years of being wadded up inside of me, this power feels infinite. It begs to be released, and I see no reason to deny it. This whole city and all its selfish opulence can burn for all I care.

In the darkness, I slip on the skull mask.

The Grays on the other side of the courtyard curse and shift, but more than I can hear or see them, I *feel* them in the dark. I mark their little hummingbird heartbeats and shuddering breaths, and bite back a chuckle as I slink toward them.

"Back-to-back," one of them commands, and they stumble into each other, weapons drawn and pointing outwards.

It's obvious they cannot see me, especially when I come close enough to smell the acrid sweat beneath their armor. One of them practically looks straight into my eyes, unseeing.

They certainly don't see my shadow when it approaches them, nor when it starts cutting them down. Blood sprays over my dress, my mask, as my shadow slips its blade into each one of them. It knows precisely where the blade goes. It learned from me.

It is a quick killing. A silent killing, until one of them manages to untangle himself from the rest in an attempt to limp away, but with a flick of my wrist, a dagger embeds itself into the back of his neck, and he falls with a shriek.

All this, and my shoulder blades don't burn. I could weep from the relief. I'm free. I'm *free*.

The words repeat as I step over the bodies and sweep into the maze.

I rely on the shadow as I navigate my way around. It tells me when the coast is clear, when to wait, and when to turn around to avoid more Grays. Though I won't hesitate to kill them, I do not seek that. I seek Luhan. And Liam. Then to never see this place again.

Now and then, a faraway scream punctures the night, but otherwise, pervasive silence. That's how I know the king's soldiers must be everywhere—the lack of noise. I picture them hissing at every guest they encounter to evacuate. How do they know I am here? Did one of the Rooks tip them off?

Had to be. They would know me better than anyone.

After a long stretch of careful evasion, a Gray—somehow, by himself—smacks right into me. He half gasps, half shouts at the unexpected collision, but before he can open his mouth to make an even louder noise, I open his throat and guide him to the floor, so his weapons don't clatter and draw more attention. His blood pools quietly at my boots and soaks the hem of my dress.

I round on my shadow. "Why didn't you warn me?"

It seems distracted. It doesn't even acknowledge me as it stares off to the right. Wavering.

Something hisses, and I turn to find another Gray drawing his sword and charging toward me. Whatever I'd done in the courtyard to make myself near invisible, it's wearing off. There is a toll I must pay for unleashing my darkness after all. I jump to my feet, braced to meet him in combat, when a figure slams into him from a perpendicular corridor and sends him sprawling into the hedge. Before the Gray can find his bearings, he's skewered into the bushes. He lets out a bloody cough, then slumps to the ground, and Liam turns to me with wide, dangerous eyes.

Wordlessly, I rip the mask off and throw myself at him. We wrap our arms around each other much too tightly, and still not enough.

"Are you alright?" He asks in my ear, keeping his voice pitched quiet and low. I nod my head, though that might be a lie, too.

"You?" I mouth.

His nod also looks unconvincing. His face is drawn, like he's seen something horrible but doesn't know how to verbalize it.

"Luhan?"

He shakes his head. "After I lost you, the screams stopped. I've been looking for you ever since."

"Was it a trick to separate us, then?"

He looks uncertain. Spooked. "I don't know. It sounded so much like him."

It did.

"We need to go."

"Strider?" He whispers, his brows drawn together. "I heard some Grays giving orders to find someone fitting *your* description, but I don't understand. They called you Vesper Osias."

My stomach plummets. There's no time. "I promise I will tell you everything. We have to go. Now."

He frowns at me, but without further protest, he accepts. My heart breaks a little at the implicit trust. I wonder if, after tonight, that will still be the case. Nevertheless, we must go.

Keeping low to the ground, we navigate our way out, following my shadow since every torch has been doused by . . . me. By the time we scurry out of the maze, we're both sweating and panting and shaky with nerves. My shadow is visibly tired, and so am I.

The gardens are deserted, the revelry ruined. Tables and chairs lie overturned, and string lights hang in disarray or flung out, snapped, on the ground. There are a few completely unrooted trees, as if a great hand simply reached down and yanked them up. Food and broken glass litter the grounds. The willow tree where I met that boy– Silas, I realize, with a jolt—is utterly destroyed. All this, visible by the stars, and nothing else.

"What happened here?" I ask, gawking at the destruction.

Liam turns to me, shocked. "You didn't feel that? The ground *shook*."

But . . . the ground shook when I was in The Craw, too. When Artie —no, that thing that *used* to be Artie—tore the curse off me.

I feel the blood drain from my face. It was me, then. I did this.

A cold dread hits me then, and I grab Liam's hand and break into a sprint toward the edge of the woods, from whence I came. The shelter of the trees is both familiar and a relief, though we must slow to avoid tripping over roots and brambles. Dried leaves crunch beneath our feet, and my skirts whisper and snag against bark and thorns, but we don't stop until we have put the castle well behind us, and even then, we're still too close. I feel excessively fatigued presently, like sediment has formed within me, and I'm having a hard time breathing.

"Strider?" Concern etches deep lines into Liam's face. He knows I have more endurance than this. He knows something is wrong.

"Give me a moment," I pant, leaning against a tree. It's incredibly dark in the woods, and I'm thankful for Liam's excellent night vision from long nights at sea, or I doubt he'd be able to see at all. I can see as clearly as if the suns were out. Better, even.

If I truly wanted to devour the realms with my shadows—simply swallow them whole, I wonder who could stop me.

I gasp at my own malevolence, covering my face in my hands as I hunch over and smother a moan.

Gently, Liam lays a hand on my hunched back, and that's what does it. That's what hurts the most, how tender he is with me when I have never deserved it. I know that now.

"Liam." I cringe out of his reach. "You have no idea. No idea."

He stares at me, his hand hovering in the air. "What?"

"You see all that out there? You see how every light, every flame, is gone? The ground trembling? This darkness? It was *me*. I did this." My lip curls. "I could have done so much more. I had to stop myself."

Slowly, he shakes his head, and I can tell he's completely taken aback, though he tries his best not to show it. "You can't do something like this."

The laugh that scrapes out of my throat is someone else's. Vesper's. "Oh, but I can."

What happened to me after we were separated comes rushing out, then. Every sordid, strange, and unbelievable detail. I'm afraid that if I don't tell him everything, he'll think I'm salvageable. At first, when I woke in the maze, I had hoped I was. I realize now that it's not possible. If I murdered the queen, they'll never stop until I'm truly dead. They won't make that mistake again. Now I understand why the voice always told me to run. I understand why the crow—Einar—had warned me. And if I'm capable of that, Liam needs to be very far away from me.

By the time I finish, I'm even more out of breath, and Liam is gaping at me in complete disbelief. He almost looks . . . angry about it.

"It was all a trick, Strider," he argues vehemently. "Like how we heard Luhan. There's strange magic here. They took your fears and made them into something else, that's all."

"I thought you'd say that," I say, and slowly, as if I'm showing off my dress, I turn so he can see my back. If the curse is gone, so must be the markings.

I can tell by Liam's silence that my suspicions were right. "What does it look like now?"

A finger draws lightly against my shoulder blade. "Scars." My lips flatten into a grim smirk. Of course. More scars.

When I turn back to face him, I can scarcely look at him; I'm so ashamed. "It wasn't the curse that killed them. My friends. The children. The curse was supposed to protect people from me. To prevent my shadow from coming out. But it didn't work all the way. All those times my shadow evaded my will, when the markings burned me, it was me *overpowering* the curse. No wonder Balor tried to kill me."

"He tried to kill you because he's a sadist, and he wanted to punish me." He moves to grab my hand, but I jerk it away, because the reality of it all has finally struck, and I am not strong enough to withstand it.

Balor was right after all.

Liam's voice is deadly low. "What are you doing?"

"Leaving."

He goes very still. "No, you're not, Strider."

I fly at him, shoving him into a tree. "I'm *not* Strider, don't you understand? I'm someone named Vesper Osias, who *murdered* the fucking queen when I was sixteen. I *watched* myself fleeing from it, and Proctor only knows why anyone helped me get away. It turns out, I have no idea who I am, and neither do you."

His teeth flash in the dark. "You're whoever you decide to be, and you know that."

"It doesn't matter. They will never stop hunting me, and by association, *you,* if we're together. Don't you see that?"

"I've killed his men too," Liam says harshly. "Quite a lot, in case you've forgotten."

"Not the fucking *queen*, you haven't. And her son was my *best friend.*"

"I don't care," Liam roars, grabbing my arms so tightly it hurts. "I won't give you up. I will handle this."

"You can't," I almost scream, tears burning my eyes. "You are free, Liam. If I am with you, you'll always have to look over your shoulder. There are already too many people in cages. It can't be you, too."

"I understand the risks."

My heart breaks into too many pieces to find. "You can't save everyone, Liam."

He presses our foreheads together. "Don't do this. If you must run, whatever stands in your way, I will cut it down. And when you tire, I will make you a home. Don't go."

His words are little twisting knives in my belly, and I fold in on myself, sinking to the ground. My hands cover my face, smearing my tears. "You were my home, Liam."

I'd rather die than see you suffer because of me, and I am willing to live with the repercussions of cutting you loose.

Kneeling, he takes me into his arms, and after a moment, he says evenly, "You did not kill the queen."

"It is not up for discussion. I saw it. I saw the blood on my hands in the visions. I heard the screams."

"But did you *see* it?"

My mouth opens, but nothing comes out. He repeats, "Did you see yourself kill her?"

"I saw—"

"You didn't." He takes me by the hair and pulls me back, so that I'm forced to look at him. "You've always been so eager to believe in the worst of yourself, but I am not. I have seen the worst parts of you, and I am undeterred. I do not believe you killed her."

"If you're wrong?"

"Shut up. Just shut up," he snaps. "You can have your shadows, and you can have a past. I loved you before I knew your name, Vesper Osias. You cannot conjure anything about you that I would spurn. I just desperately wish you'd stop trying."

My mouth falls open, and a tear of a different kind streaks down my cheek. "You love me?"

"Yes," he rasps, bringing both hands to cup my jaw. "Every time, in every life, I love you."

I have never been as good with words as Liam is, and especially not in a moment like this, where I want to tell him I love him so much, I'd cleave the world in two for him. I'd follow him to the end, where realms are created and destroyed in a cluster of stars and light. I'd wait for him for as many lifetimes as it took to see his lopsided grin. To hear him call me Strider one more time. I never thought I'd get to love anyone or be loved like this. I can't understand how I'm already out of time.

Words elude me.

So instead, I rise onto my knees and wrap my arms around his neck, burrowing my face there. My fingers thread through his hair as I memorize the way we fit together: my soul and his. And I cry for the life we might have had.

It is Liam who tears himself away. "I know somewhere we can go that would be safe."

I stare at him, my mind racing, chest heaving.

"I know someone who can help us. The king can't follow us there."

Oh. Inverness. He's referring to his father. His father, from whom his mother fled. Whom he despises.

"Liam," I try, but he is determined.

"He owes me sanctuary after all he's done," he says resolutely. "We can hide there until we formulate a plan. We need to return to The Wraith and set sail immediately, before—"

"Oh, you're not going anywhere."

We both freeze, our heads whipping to the side toward a little clearing shrouded in mist.

Out steps the figure wearing the jackal mask from the masquerade. It's what he's dragging behind him that makes my blood go cold, then scorching.

Luhan.

71

THE MAN IN THE MASK

He's holding Luhan by the neck and dragging him. Luhan, whose pristine pale hair is matted with blood. One eye is swollen shut, the other bruised and on its way. Bloody drool dribbles from his lips, and his body hangs limp like a doll. The man wearing the jackal mask drops him unceremoniously to the ground, where he lies motionless. I can't even tell if he's breathing.

It wasn't a trick after all. Luhan, somehow, is here, and this thing has been *torturing* him.

How? How did they even find him? And why?

Beside me, Liam's face has gone white, his eyes two scorching holes in his head. Though my earlier use of power has left me feeling shaky and lethargic, I feel it stirring me now, lashing its tail. My lips tremble with blinding rage, and I feel a dark spot coming on, unlike any I've ever felt before. One that threatens to consume me for good.

"I had hoped to be the one to find you," the man says from behind his mask in a rough, taunting voice. "Lucky me. Him? Not so lucky."

To emphasize, he kicks Luhan hard in the ribs. Blood spurts from his mouth, and I think I hear a soft groan.

He's *alive*.

My hands shake.

"Don't touch him," Liam roars, yanking his sword from its sheath and lurching forward to attack.

He stops in his tracks when the man tuts softly, crouching down to take Luhan's slender neck in his massive hands. I don't dare breathe. One small motion, and Luhan could die right here in front of us.

Liam's entire body seizes, his eyes wider than I've ever seen them.

"Too easy," the man laughs. "Vesper, you're no fun anymore."

My mouth twists at the name, and the darkness in me spreads. "What do you want?"

"You don't remember old Rian, do you?" I hear the smirk in his voice. "We used to be mates, you and I. Real good mates, back in the day. Then you went and offed the queen, and Holland went about crowing that he'd cut you down in the woods for it. Don't know why he woulda lied about that one, but . . ." He gestures to me and shrugs.

He's silent for a moment, tilting his head as if he's studying me to make sure he's really seeing me. A little breath of disbelief escapes. "So then, where've you been?"

I take a step forward, unable to tear my eyes away from Lu. "Let him go. Please. I'll do anything."

He glances down at Luhan's prone body. "Him? He's on his way out, dearie. It's a bit late for that."

"Why? Why him?" I choke out, bile clawing its way up my throat. Beside me, Liam is vibrating with barely contained wrath. The only reason he hasn't already launched himself forward is so I can fish for answers. Any answers, for I have too many questions to count.

The man's laugh is a mean, sharp sound. "Because you've forgotten, Vesper. We can't have friends. We're set apart. And this is what happens when you try to run." He waves a hand. "People get very hurt, love. If you run again, more will get hurt. Now, you'll be coming with me."

We. Meaning Rooks.

"No, she won't," Liam interjects, stepping in front of me. My stomach drops to the dirt.

"Get out of here," I whisper, my eyes welling with tears. "Please, Liam. Please. He's a Rook."

He turns to look at me, outraged, but the jackal, Rian, cuts him off.

"The young Captain Liam Blackwater, is it? No, no. Please stay. I'd love to take a stab at you. Heard good things."

"Likewise with the stabbing," Liam growls through his teeth.

"Alright," Rian says, lazily procuring a staff from his belt. At his touch, it elongates into a nasty-sharp spear that glints in the dim starlight. He rolls his neck, then stops, reaching toward his mask. It covers his whole head, the mask, rendering him completely disguised, although his bulk is hardly ordinary. With a practiced yank, he slips the mask off, and my nearly stomach heaves at the sight of his face.

I would think, if I'd known him once, I'd remember the jagged slash marks going from the ends of his mouth all the way up his cheeks. I would hope that I'd recall his glowing yellow eyes set deep into a hairless head, or the way his fingers elongate into claws.

But no, nothing comes to me.

Not even when his face splits to reveal a long, lolling tongue and needle-like fangs that go all the way up the slits in his face—not slits. Not slash marks. His mouth. It's *all* his mouth. The jackal mask, in a gruesome way, was fitting.

The next few moments pass in a blur.

The Rook seemingly unhinges his jaws and lets out a deafening, ear-piercing shriek, rears back, and leaps.

Liam barely has time to react before the Rook reaches him, blocking what would have been a fatal blow with his sword. He grunts with the sheer force of the Rook's power, gritting his teeth. Suddenly, he twists away, allowing the massive man to stumble. Liam strikes, driving his sword up and in, but Rian dances away at the last second, laughing.

"That was good, very good," he says lightly. "It's true what they say. You're decent enough."

"Choke on your own intestines, you mangy fucking dog."

"I'll ask you to say that again when I've got you skewered against that tree over there," he says, almost conversationally.

"You've done enough," I hiss, joining the fray. Out of my peripheral, I see Liam jolt at my intrusion.

The jackal turns slowly to me as the expanse of his mouth stretches into a gruesome grin. "Do you remember how to use your shadows, Vesper?"

"Why don't we find out?"

His eyes flare, and it's all the warning I get before he rushes me with inhuman speed. It is instinct alone that jerks me backward and to the side, twisting beneath a swipe that would have opened my throat. Planting my right hand on the ground, I kick his knee sideways, then land another kick in his stomach. He reels backward, the breath knocked out of him, but recovers much too quickly. His claws catch me on the shoulder and rake all the way down my arm, leaving five deep grooves of ragged flesh behind. Blood spatters the ground.

"I taught you that," he breathes, his eyes wide.

No, Basi taught me that.

A scream tears out of my throat, and I surge forward, my blade swiftly following. It misses the Rook as he jumps back, but suddenly lurches to the side, narrowly missing getting skewered through the guts from behind. Liam bares his teeth at the near miss.

"Two on one, eh?" Rian's tongue darts out to lick bloodless lips. "Hardly fair."

By myself, I am relentless and sadistic.

Liam, an unparalleled titan of the blade.

As we did in the ballroom, we dance. And no, it's *not* fucking fair.

Slowly, we force him back and away from Luhan. Our attacks are merciless, one right after the other in dizzying succession. We don't allow him the time to strike, lest he lose an arm. But he's impossibly quick. Every blow almost seems to land, but never does. The moment before blade meets skin, he seems to almost blur out of its path. He's not even *attempting* to attack us back. Liam sees it too, the realization evident in the hard line of his mouth. The Rook is wearing us out on purpose. He's toying with us.

And I started this fight tired.

Clenching my jaw, I adjust my counter in the last moment to ram my knife through his forearm when, suddenly, an unexpected open-handed blow to my head knocks me off my feet and sends me rolling in the grass. I see white and wake up on my back to red.

It takes too long for my vision to focus, and I can't hear for shit over the ringing in my ears. My left arm burns like fire, and I can feel it dripping crimson rivulets from the deep grooves carved there. When I touch my fingers to my temple, they come away wet.

"Iona."

My head snaps to the side to see Luhan, an arm's length away. For a moment, my mind stumbles over the distance I covered to have ended up here. Rian is too strong. My stomach sinks. I don't know if we have what it takes to kill him.

"Luhan," I croak, crawling over to where he lies, sprawled. The ground is soggy from blood. My fingers hover hesitantly over his face, too afraid to hurt him more than he already is. Blood has left thin, meandering stains down his chin, and I wipe them away with my thumb. His eyes, normally vibrant amber, are dark. Too dark.

It seems to take great effort for him to speak. "If y-you hold him still, I can . . . kill him. His—his bones are unbreakable."

"No. Rest so you can heal yourself," I urge shakily, eyes burning.

"He's going to win."

"It's alright. We'll handle it." My chest feels caved in. "I'm so sorry, Luhan. I'm so, so sorry."

"Fi-finish this so we can go home," he whispers, his eyes going in and out of focus.

"I will," I promise him, smoothing some matted hair back from his forehead. "I will."

With great effort, I sit up to see Liam arc his great, black sword overhead and slice deeply into the Rook's shoulder. Flesh is torn asunder, and for a moment, I dare to hope he may sever the whole arm.

Not quite, but still. A deadly wound.

An ear-splitting howl of fury pierces the air, and after that, everything happens too quickly. The Rook, faster than my eyes can follow, latches onto Liam's forearm, delivering a kick to Liam's knee that results in a sickening crunch.

Liam's bad knee. My hand claps over my mouth as Liam's face crumples in pain.

"Who are you without your ship, and without your crew?"

The creature grabs hold of Liam's shoulder, lowers his head, and clamps down with that horrific jaw of his so he can ram his spear clean through Liam's side, pinning him to the tree behind him. Liam slumps over and screams through gritted teeth.

The sound of his pain rattles through me like lightning, leaving a blistered, festering trail in its wake. Every rational thought scatters like rabbits as time comes crashing to a halt. Nothing else exists but Liam and the man who dared hurt him.

Rage devours me, and the shadows around me seep out further into the woods, swallowing anything in their path. The sky darkens, and one by one, the stars fade away.

This is a dark spot.

Rian turns to me, his eyes aglow with victory.

"I told him I'd do it," he sneers. "Poor lad should have listened."

Blood roars in my ears and then goes silent. Shadows drip from my fingers. "You're enjoying this."

"It's nothing personal, but orders are orders, love. All you ever cared about was Silas, anyway."

"Prince Silas?"

He growls, low in his throat. He's not paying attention to the slow, agonized movement behind him.

"Thick as thieves, you two were. Never understood it. He never recovered from what you did. I hope you know that. If I don't kill you, he will."

"You won't be killing anyone tonight."

Rian made several mistakes tonight. His first was in thinking that *should be* dead was the same as dead. It isn't. Which leads to Rian's second mistake: turning his back on a should-be-dead Liam Blackwater. For very quietly, Liam has been shimmying himself off the spear, teeth gritted, eyes squeezed closed. The spear, still embedded in the tree, is covered in his blood. The pain, I imagine, must have been breathtaking.

This time, Liam's sword cuts clean through Rian's arm.

The Rook rounds on him too quickly to counter and buries his claws in Liam's chest.

72

HOME

I hear the wet *thunk* of it. Liam's face goes white with pain. Shock.

My world becomes very small. My world, in fact, becomes a memory. A memory of sitting alone in the library, paralyzed with fear as I could do nothing but watch my very own shadow emerge from a shadowy arch on the wall. It occurs to me, in the span of half a heartbeat, that since it was only ever my own power leaking out of me, perhaps all along, it wasn't terrorizing me but desperately trying to tell me something. Helping me remember.

At the same moment, my eyes fall to my shadow. It's straining toward a particularly dark patch between the trees, a few paces to my right. If I can tell the darkness what to do, why can't I mold it too? And if I can mold it, why not make it a tunnel?

The moment the thought forms, I am overcome with an ironclad conviction that I have done this before. It is possible. I reach out a hand into the patch of black, which is not a patch at all but a hole. A door. A door that leads exactly where I tell it to, because it is night and these shadows are all mine. One last surge of adrenaline fuels me as I stand on trembling legs, walk into the darkness, and come out on the other side of the field.

Right behind Rian.

I bury a knife to the hilt in his spine, and then again, and again. I am past the point of screams, of words. I hear Liam thump to the ground.

The Rook rounds on me, face contorted in pain and shock at my sudden appearance, and I drive another blade into his chest. He stumbles back, blood pouring from his wounds, then rushes me, sending us both sprawling to the ground. We're nothing but teeth and blades and claws as we lash out with everything we have, leaving a trail of blood and spittle in our wake. We're animals, he and I. Because Liam wounded him so severely, it's an even fight now.

His claws gouge a trail down my face, and I have to blink blood out of my eyes as I slip my knife up beneath his ribs. Our faces are so close, I can see specks of black in his dog-yellow eyes. I wonder what he sees in mine.

"You can't kill me," he hisses through bloody teeth. "You've tried for years."

"I'm persistent." For emphasis, I twist the knife, and he screeches.

He lunges, sending us off balance, and we tumble down a hill into a large pond. The impact takes the breath out of me, my guts burning. I try to stand but splash back down into the cold muck. My legs are numb.

I try again, but they won't work, and my stomach *hurts*.

I look down to find my own blade, buried to the hilt in my stomach. Blood blooms outward from where I sit in the water.

"Oh," I say.

In a daze, I locate Rian, who's very slowly sloshing toward me, claws dripping with mud. "I was going to let them have you, but they'll understand." His eyes flash in the darkness. "And I always hated Holland for being the one who got to kill you."

My shadow drifts toward him silently, and I watch it wait, like a cat, to pounce. I almost smile when, all too easily, it latches on to him and *pulls*. I feel so sorry for keeping it on such a tight leash all this time.

The Rook lurches to the side, caught off balance. Realization widens his eyes, and the sickening feeling that I've done this to him before hits me. This must be how I fought him before—using my shadow to hold him down. It's the only way to catch him.

He was hoping I'd forgotten. Well, I had, but my shadow hadn't.

Face contorted, he roars, flailing his one remaining arm and gnashing his teeth to try and get away to no avail. My shadow won't let go of him.

"What do you plan to do, Vesper? You're dying. Release me so I can give you a merciful death."

"You first."

His horrible mouth opens to retort when suddenly, his hand clamps down on his chest, clawing at his own skin. A horrid scream erupts from his throat, and he doubles down, folding his arms over himself when a hideous crack and snapping fills the air, and his ribcage bursts violently through his chest. It is as if his ribs were fastened together at the sternum, and someone simply unlatched them. Blood fountains across the pond, sending thousands of tiny ripples across the otherwise smooth surface, and organs plop into the water. With a splash, he falls to his knees, then succumbs to death face-down in the pond.

For a few moments, silence reigns. I just stare, feeling so much that I feel nothing. Then, faintly, I hear shouting. In the distance, torchlight approaches.

They're coming for me.

Blearily, I turn to where Luhan had been, only to find nothing but flattened grass and blood stains.

"Luhan?"

Leaves rustle in the trees, but that's the only response I get. "Luhan?"

Nothing.

I feel strangely light and numb, and with my waning strength, I rise shakily and stumble out of the water to where he was, but he's gone. Good. I hope he's healed himself and runs far, far from here.

Liam lies motionless beneath a tree. His entire front glistens with blood, and I feel a fear I have never known. It consumes me.

Proctor, please do not take him. Please, please. Do not take him from this world. From me.

If he *is* alive, if I love him, there is only one option. And it breaks my heart. I fall heavily to my hands and knees beside him. "Liam. *Liam.*" Panic chokes me.

Liam can't be dead. If he is dead, I will leave nothing left of this realm. Nothing but endless night and corpses.

Liam's eyes flutter open, and I'm greeted with my favorite color. My breath whooshes out of me, and I almost sob in relief.

"Hello, sweetheart." His voice is barely there, and blood sluices from between his teeth.

His expression turns stricken at the sight of me, my bloody, ravaged face. His fingers trace my jaw as his eyes slide in and out of focus. He's dying.

"Strider—you're hurt."

"No. I'm alright. He's dead."

"Oh. Good." The relief in his small smile makes me want to cry.

"I'm so sorry, Liam. This is all my fault. I never meant for you to get hurt."

"What? No. Strider, *no.*"

"I'm so sorry for this." My face crumples. "I'm so sorry. It won't happen again."

His face, already pale, goes bone white, and he struggles to get up.

The shadows, they draw him back.

Black tendrils wrap lovingly around his arms and legs, dragging him backward toward an especially dark patch in the woods. Not a patch; a door. One that I'm throwing all my remaining power toward, to take him far, far away from here. More soldiers are coming, and I can't let them find him. They'd keep him alive to kill his soul. Because of me.

"*Strider,*" he says, and I never knew one word could contain so much pain. It's yet another blade in me. The way he's looking at me is worse. All he wanted to do was protect me, *love* me, and I am forcing him to flee. I am rejecting him, and in his mind, it will be yet another failure. A betrayal, perhaps. I hope one day he understands my choice. But I'll never know.

"You have to live, Liam." My voice cracks. "For me."

"*Don't*," he implores, flailing violently against my dark hold. But it's no use. The effort brings on a wet coughing fit that leaves his lips shining red. "*Please. Let me choose you.*"

"But you did."

His legs disappear into the shadowy arch, and his mouth goes slack as it hits him—I won't let him save me. Not this time. A slew of emotions flicker across his face as he fully registers what this means:

Betrayal, that I am forcing him to live with another loss.

Fury, because he is powerless to stop me.

Denial, for it happened so fast.

Grief, since he knows what will happen to me.

Finally despair, when he realizes that this is the last time we will see each other. He stops fighting me, then. Goes limp. I take in the shape of his nose, the curve of his lips, the faint freckles beneath his eyes, savoring his beautiful symmetry one last time.

The shadows are up to his shoulders now.

Before he goes through the door, I grab his face in my hands, tears in my eyes. "I love you."

His lips part. Blood drips from a corner of his mouth. His eyes hold the very same look from the day we first met.

A pledge: we are not yet finished.

Then my own shadows yank him backward into the black, leaving me staring at the spot where Liam Blackwater used to be. Engulfed in sudden silence, at last, my body fails me, and I crumple into the dirt.

Minutes, maybe hours later, I wake to the sound of leaves crunching and a body collapsing beside me. My eyes snap open to find Luhan, breathing shallowly, arms wrapped around me as if we're sharing an embrace. The blade in my gut is cast aside, coated in my own blood. That barely feels important, now that Luhan is here.

"I couldn't find you. I thought you'd escaped," I manage, and my voice sounds far away.

Everything hurts. Worse.

"I had to be . . . closer, to kill him," he whispers, each word a labor. "I passed out afterwards . . . it took a lot out of me."

"You did it." I even conjure up a weak smile. "You saved us all."

His smile is mostly in his eyes. "Not yet."

Realization cracks over me like a whip. "*No*," I cry out, shoving his hands off me.

There's so much blood on him. *His* blood. He's not healed. *Why isn't he healed?*

"Heal yourself, not me," I shriek, panicked. "If you heal me, you can't heal yourself anymore."

"It's too late," he says softly. "I don't have the . . . strength to heal myself. But you . . . ."

No.

That's why my pain has intensified. He's started the healing process. It's too late. Sobs, deep, gut-wrenching sobs, rack my body, and he wraps me in his arms again. I wrap mine around his slender frame, balling his shirt in my fists.

"No, Lu. No. No."

"I couldn't save him. But I can save *you*."

"They're going to take me," I sob into his neck. "Let me die."

I feel him shake his head. "Someone . . . has to take care of . . . Liam."

"You have to go home. We were going to go home."

"I . . . am . . . going . . . home."

For a while, I sob into his shirt, letting the grief wash over me as my gut, very painfully, begins the process of knitting itself back together. I have the thought that perhaps, if I hold on to him very tightly, he cannot leave me.

"Tell me something good, and something bad," he whispers.

I close my eyes and take a deep, shuddering breath. I wrap my arms around his slender frame as tightly as I dare without hurting him. Prim, lovely, graceful Luhan. The first person on The Wraith who reached out a hand.

The very beginnings of morning have started to streak between the trees. I try to speak, but someone beats me to it. A boy, with lively blue eyes and rambunctious brown hair, squats down beside us. His smile holds all the love in the realm.

"Lu, you've taken ages. I almost gave up waiting on you."

Luhan blinks, clarity burning through the haze in his eyes as he turns over to look at the boy. For a moment, he simply stares. But Luhan has always had a talent for recovering himself quicker than most. The catch in his throat is nearly imperceptible.

"You know, Oliver, I always thought that for a sick person, you were much too impatient."

Grimacing, Luhan sits up with some help, and the moment he's upright, they embrace fiercely. Wordlessly.

The suns climb a little higher, their rays spilling into the brush and between the trees. "I have missed you," Luhan says.

"I've only been right here," Oliver replies with a slight frown. "It's not been very long. Did Liam miss me, too?"

"Terribly so."

The boy smiles, his eyes glittering. "I didn't get to meet your friend."

Luhan looks over to me with honeyed, glassy eyes. "You *just* missed each other."

"Will they make it without you?" Oliver asks.

I nod, and Lu heartens. "They will take care of each other. Besides, we're not going far."

Oliver extends a hand, and together, they get to their feet. Luhan's shirt is spotless and wrinkle-free. He looks just as he did the day I met him, haughty but impeccable. Old eyes in a young face. My very best friend.

"Not far at all. Right over there." Oliver points to a spot in the woods, where a patch of sunslight pours through the trees. "Are you ready, Lu?"

"Oh, I suppose." He looks back at me, one last time. "Don't forget, Iona. I'm not gone. Just elsewhere."

Luhan gets to his feet, and without a backward glance, they make their way through the brush. Luhan's laughter echoes back to me, and I close my eyes to relish the sound until it fades away.

"The only bad thing is," I whisper around the lump in my throat, "you've gone where I cannot follow, and I'm going to miss you so, so much."

Sometime later, the Grays find me.

"Over here! She's hurt badly. Needs a healer."

"Who's the boy? Looks dead."

"That's the kid Rian took as bait. Anya tipped them off early that Vesper was here. Damn Rooks didn't tell us until it was too late."

"Oh, fuck me. Rian's over here in the pond. He's—Oh my gods." Someone retches.

"Leave it for now. We take the girl and leave the corpses for the witches."

"There's so much blood. How did she survive?"

"She looks half in the grave to me."

"She might be faking. Careful."

"Here, in case—"

Pain explodes in the back of my head. Then nothing.

73

AN OLD FRIEND

They have me chained because they know exactly who I am and what I'm capable of. A sliver of doubt makes them careful.

But a *sliver* is not very much, and *careful* is not enough.

The iron around my wrists has burned a raw ring into my skin and rattles with my every movement. My meals consist of watery broth and metallic-tasting water—if one can call that a meal. It's enough to keep me alive, I suppose.

My body is a map of scars and wounds they have inflicted all my life.

The long line in my scalp, where Prince Holland tried to kill me seven years ago. The pearly divot at the dip in my neck, where Balor poisoned me.

The gouges on my face from Rian's claws.

And the slowly healing hole in my belly, from which I should have died. They send someone twice a day to make sure I'm still breathing, but it seems like a waste, doesn't it, since they're going to publicly execute me.

I spend my time pacing my tiny cell, here in The Craw. The magic needles my skin and becomes downright unbearable when I'm still, so

I never am. Sometimes, I hear whatever it is that lurks at the bottom of the void, slithering. Otherwise, I'm all alone in here.

Artie—I don't know what else to call her—is gone, her door bent and twisted in on itself as if a hurricane passed through and wrenched it open with giant hands. It was like that when I first woke, which makes me think she escaped somehow shortly after I was here that night. I remember the ground shaking and the detritus at the ball.

I wonder if the release of power somehow freed her. It makes no difference. She is long gone.

Even my shadow has forsaken me. Whether she finally abandoned me to wreak havoc on the kingdom herself, or the magic down here snuffed her out, I have no way of knowing.

What I do know is that I have never been so alone. At the very least, I always had her.

I don't know how much time has passed down here. My meals are inconsistent—perhaps to disorient me. There is no light save for the flames from the sconces. There wouldn't be, in the belly of the mountain.

And so, I'm unclear how long it took my visitor to muster up the courage to come see me.

I'm prowling, lost in thought, when I hear the sharp click of footsteps coming down the uneven steps. My head twists to face outside, and I see a flickering shadow approach, growing larger on the wall.

A tall, thin figure comes to a stop in front of my cell, all alone. For a moment, we stare at each other, me draped in shadows, the figure unrecognizable in a blue-silver cloak obscuring their face.

"It was always so unsettling to me. How your eyes would glow like that in the dark." Oh. I know that voice.

He steps forward, close enough to wrap his fingers around the bars. With the other hand, he pushes the hood back to reveal the boy I'd met beneath the willow tree, except he's an unfortunate shade of sober now. His pale eyes gleam with accusation in the firelight.

If I hadn't seen him smile in Artie's memories, I wouldn't have thought it possible. He is nothing like the boy he used to be.

"Silas."

"Vesper."

I can see how it jars him to hear me say his name. I understand. He thought I was dead. "I had to see for myself," he says.

I move out of the shadows and into the flickering light. We're quite a pair, he and I. Beneath his cloak, his clothes are pristine white and cream, pressed to perfection. As for me, I'm still wearing my dress from the ball, though it's now less a dress and more a tattered tapestry of dried mud and grass stains. My skin is caked in dirt and grime, my hair matted in both mine and other peoples' blood. The grooves on my face from Rian's claws have scabbed over, but it still hurts to cry.

His face remains stoic, but I don't miss the way his mouth tightens with disdain at the sight of me. I don't blame him.

"We were friends, weren't we?" My voice is coarse from disuse.

"I resent every moment I ever wasted with you."

I flinch.

"What could you possibly want, Vesper?"

Our gazes meet, and I silently implore him to understand. To have mercy on me. I realize he's waiting on me to give him an answer, though I've no idea what I could possibly say to assuage him of all the years he must have spent hating me.

"Nothing."

He studies me with an icy gaze. "Why did you do this?"

"Do what?"

His composure, like a mask, slips. "Come back here. Pretend like you don't remember. Like you did at the ball. You called yourself Iona Strider, as if I wouldn't recognize the name. *Why*? It's sick."

"I *don't* know you, or this place. Artie took all my memories away that night. She made me leave, and I don't remember a thing. Not you, not my family, not my childhood. None of it."

"Don't." There's a tremor in his voice.

"I saw a few of Artie's memories, but they were like dreams, and . . ." My voice trails off. I don't know what to say. How to convince him. It all sounds insane. "I saw us putting salt in Holland's wine—"

"No."

"Playing pretend—"

"I said *stop*."

"I saw Artie save you from that cursed fruit—"

"*Don't call her Artie,*" he shouts. "You don't deserve to call her that."

"I *loved* her. I know that much," I protest.

He looks appalled. "If you loved her so much, you wouldn't have left her here to rot and suffer the punishment of your actions."

"I never meant—"

"Was it the plan all along? To assassinate my parents? Would you have killed my father too, if we hadn't stopped you?"

"I didn't—I don't know—"

He slams his hands on the bars, and I flinch again.

"Stop *lying*. I *watched* you kill my mother, you fucking snake. Right in front of me. Her hot blood spattered on my face. The worst part is, she treated you like a *daughter*." His voice cracks on the word *daughter*. "How could you, Vesper? *Why?* Tell me why."

His words feel like a cannon to my gut. I stumble backward, trip over the tatters of my dress, and fall to the stone. He saw me do it. He was *there*. I stare up at him as my world collapses. He takes in my reaction with cold disinterest.

"Pathetic."

Desperation surges out of me. "If I'm lying about my memory, why would I have ever come back here, Silas? How does that make any sense?"

"Because you're sick. You're *sick*."

"I'm *sorry*, Silas. But I don't remember."

He scoffs. "Spare me. And I believe you mean *Your Royal Highness*, you deplorable creature." He steps back, his face shuttered closed. Brushing his pants, as if merely being in my proximity tainted him, he takes a deep breath, turns to leave, then pauses.

"My mother died screaming in agony in a pool of her own blood. I can only hope you die in the same way."

With that, he leaves me and does not return.

I do my best to keep my mind occupied. I repeat the list of

occupied Gray territories to myself continuously. I tell myself my favorite stories. I list every poison, its effects, and subsequent remedies.

I think of Luhan. How much I loved him. All the times we laughed and bickered and just spent time together. How he preferred for me to clean the deck. The way he showed me how to cut on the bias. I hoard the little moments to myself.

Of all the lists, there is one I return to above all the rest. It is the list of truths and lies.

I spend days refining it. Scolding myself with it. Agonizing over it. Grieving. Raging.

I am not Iona Strider. I did not grow up in Marrin. My shadow was never a curse. My power never came from the marks on my back. I am not powerless. I was never weak. Only young. Fed the same lies as everyone else. Of course, I starved.

My true name is Vesper Osias. I am the last remaining member of House Osias of Savastane. My people and my family were slaughtered for a crime I alone am said to have committed. I come from a land that no longer exists. I spent my childhood in a foreign kingdom that nurtured me if I was docile, but the moment my shadow grew dark, they hammered me into something sharp, something they could use. The marks on my back were cast by someone I loved to protect me. To keep me from coming back here. But fate is a meddlesome creature, and when she tugs her strings, we always come.

They say I murdered the queen. I do not know that to be true. The question is, if it wasn't me, then who?

If it were me, then why?

This is where I end—every single time.

Yet, no matter what I try, I return to Liam. I recount every conversation, every taunt, every touch. I regret every moment I didn't tell him I loved him. I conjure every image of his face I can remember and cradle them lovingly in my mind's eye.

I don't dream often, but one comes to me in the depths of darkness. Liam, safe and healing, somewhere bright. He sleeps soundly, his hair unruly as it brushes his eyes. His jaw is dark with stubble. At some point, his eyes open to find not me, but my shadow on the wall. Their fingertips meet there, but he winces in pain. Though he lies back down, his eyes never leave the wall. Not until sleep claims him again.

I wake to tear tracks down my cheeks.

Yet no matter how far I stay from how it all ended, my mind inevitably summons the last I saw of him. The hurt on his face, the betrayal. The blood.

Proctor above, don't take him. Please. Let him live. Take me instead.

Whenever I bargain, I brush the filthy thread on my finger, still tied in three loops.

Weeks, or what feels like them, have passed.

The guards have informed me that my execution will be public. It will be in seven days.

So, it is with much relief that, as I sit in my own filth, I feel a familiar tingle down my spine. I sit with my back against the wall of stone in a rare display of stillness, staring at nothing. But someone has arrived.

I turn my head to peer through the bars of my cage to the wall directly across from me, swathed in flickering torchlight on either side. Though it hurts, I crack a small grin at what I see standing there.

Taking great care, I get to my feet and slink to the bars, wrapping my fingers around them.

"Where the hell have you been?"

My shadow, of course, says nothing. Merely stands there, hands at her sides. I notice she's holding something in her hand. I hold my fist out toward her, and feel it appear in my hand. I hold the object up to the torchlight to examine it, and when I realize exactly what she's brought me, I do something I didn't think I'd ever do again.

I laugh.

My cackles fill the entire mountain, and when I'm finished, I hide the grotesque thing in my skirts, still chuckling to myself. I've been wondering how I could possibly escape, since I am facing not one, or two, but three layers I'd have to outsmart.

One, these shackles. My hands and feet.

Two, this cell. There is no traditional lock, of course. They use advanced magic to open and close it.

Three, the fucking mountain itself.

And, they took my knives. My lockpicks, too.

Finger bones serve well in a pinch. Especially unbreakable ones. I raise my eyes to my shadow and smile.

They better run.

ACKNOWLEDGMENTS

As I type this, my cat is jostling the computer by rubbing her garbage mouth on the screen so aggressively, I keep making typos. So first and foremost, I would like to acknowledge Mow Mow. In all seriousness, she was present for almost every word typed in this book. One could say she was my most ardent advocate. If anything, she was some really good, steadfast company.

Writing a book is a lonely and, at times, infuriating journey. You fall in love with characters of your own making, and want nothing more than for the world to love them too. If only you could just tell their story right. But here's the lesson I learned: with writing, there's no *right*. There's just the love of telling a story. And I have loved writing this vicious little story. It feels strange to say that, what with all the violence and strife, but I hope that nestled within those bits, there was also humor, tenderness, and hope. And *lots* of ass kicking.

This story is six years of staying up way too late, working over lunch breaks, weekends, and holidays. Overcoming imposter syndrome, dreaming during my commute, and learning to prioritize what gives me joy.

Most importantly, this story is the summation of the love that surrounds me.

Thank you, Dad, for supporting my insatiable love of reading. For reading Harry Potter to me every night before bedtime, and doing the voices for every single character. It is still the most magical thing I can think of. Thank you for helping me pick out library books when I was too young to drive, or navigate AOL. It was because of your keen eye that I read Twilight, The Hunger Games, Eragon, and many more landmark stories. Thank you for sitting at the table with me, wired on rocket fuel coffee, and embarking on flights of fancy with me. Those are my favorite memories.

To Mom—thank you for always letting me be weird and never trying to correct it. This is very important to me. You always fully supported all my hobbies and interests, and made me feel loved and empowered. That's irreplaceable.

To Falan, thank you, and also, I'm sorry for making you read draft 1 of this story. It really was so bad. I hope it's a little better now. You're the best for that.

To my beta readers: thank you all from the bottom of my heart. Just a fraction of your time having been spent on my story means the world to me. Erin, Mallory, Jenna, and Brent: your feedback was monumental in polishing this thing, and I am forever so grateful for you. Erin, you're next!

To cohort 3A at Happily Ever Authors: thank you for listening to my story each week and providing invaluable feedback. It's so cool we get to empower each other like that. I'm so glad to know you guys. And thank you to Tara, who started it all. You created something really special!

To Andrea and Kay, my editors: thank you one million times over for the work you put into Blackwater. I honestly thought everyone was just being nice until your feedback that very first time. You changed the game for me, and it is thanks to your eagle eyes and incisive feedback that it is what it is today. I'm endlessly glad I found you two.

To my husband, Connor: thank you for enduring years of rants about characters you hadn't even met. Your quiet suffering is much appreciated, and I love you. But I'm also not done.